# THE LAYS OF BELERIAND

2

Of Morgoth &
the
Snaring of Gorlim.

Far in the Northern hills of stone
in caverns black there was a throne
by flame encircled; there the smoke
in coiling columns rose to choke
the breath of life, and there in deep
and gasping dungeons lost would creep
to hopeless death all those who strayed
by doom beneath that ghastly shade.
A King there sat, most dark and fell
of all that under heaven dwell.
Than earth or sea, than moon or star
more ancient was he, mightier far
in mind abysmal than the thought
of Eldar or of Men, and wrought
of strength primeval; ere the stone
was hewn to build the world, alone
he walked in darkness, fierce and dire,
burned, as he wielded it, by fire.
He 'twas that laid in ruin black
the Blessed Realm and fled their back
to Middle-earth anew to build
beneath the mountains mansions filled
with misbegotten slaves of hate:
death's shadow brooded at his gate.
His host he armed with spears of steel
and brands of flame, and at their heel
the wolf walked and the serpent crept
with lidless eyes. Now forth they leapt,
his ruinous legions, kindling war
in field and frith and woodland hoar.
Where long the golden elanor
had gleamed amid the grass they bore
their banners black; where finch had sung
and harpers silver harps had wrung
now dark the ravens wheeled and cried
amid the reek, and far and wide
the swords of Morgoth dripped with red
above the hewn and trampled dead.

The opening of Canto 2 in the *Lay of Leithian* recommenced

# THE HISTORY OF MIDDLE-EARTH

### I
## THE BOOK OF LOST TALES, PART ONE

### II
## THE BOOK OF LOST TALES, PART TWO

### III
## THE LAYS OF BELERIAND

### IV
## THE SHAPING OF MIDDLE-EARTH
#### THE QUENTA, THE AMBARKANTA AND THE ANNALS

### V
## THE LOST ROAD AND OTHER WRITINGS

### VI
## THE RETURN OF THE SHADOW
## THE HISTORY OF THE LORD OF THE RINGS,
## PART ONE

# J. R. R. TOLKIEN

# THE
# LAYS
# OF
# BELERIAND

Edited by Christopher Tolkien

BOSTON

HOUGHTON MIFFLIN COMPANY

For information about permission to reproduce selections from
this book, write to Permissions, Houghton Mifflin Company,
2 Park Street, Boston, Massachusetts 02108.

Library of Congress Cataloging in Publication Data

Tolkien, J.R.R. (John Ronald Reuel), 1892–1973.
The lays of Beleriand.

(The History of Middle-earth; 3)
Includes index.
1. Fantastic poetry, English.   I. Tolkien, Christopher.
II. Title.   III. Series: Tolkien, J. R. R. (John Ronald
Reuel), 1892–1973. History of Middle-earth; 3.
PR6039.032L3 1985      821'.912      85-18013
ISBN 0-395-39429-5
ISBN 0-395-48683-1 (pbk.)

Printed in the United States of America

V  12  11  10  9  8  7  6  5  4  3

# CONTENTS

# PREFACE

This third part of 'The History of Middle-earth' contains the two major poems by J. R. R. Tolkien concerned with the legends of the Elder Days: the *Lay of the Children of Húrin* in alliterative verse, and the *Lay of Leithian* in octosyllabic couplets. The alliterative poem was composed while my father held appointments at the University of Leeds (1920–5); he abandoned it for the *Lay of Leithian* at the end of that time, and never turned to it again. I have found no reference to it in any letter or other writing of his that has survived (other than the few words cited on p. 3), and I do not recollect his ever speaking of it. But this poem, which though extending to more than 2000 lines is only a fragment in relation to what he once planned, is the most sustained embodiment of his abiding love of the resonance and richness of sound that might be achieved in the ancient English metre. It marks also an important stage in the evolution of the Matter of the Elder Days, and contains passages that strongly illumine his imagination of Beleriand; it was, for example, in this poem that the great redoubt of Nargothrond arose from the primitive caves of the Rodothlim in the *Lost Tales*, and only in this poem was Nargothrond described. It exists in two versions, the second being a revision and enlargement that proceeds much less far into the story, and both are given in this book.

My father worked on the *Lay of Leithian* for six years, abandoning it in its turn in September 1931. In 1929 it was read so far as it then went by C. S. Lewis, who sent him a most ingenious commentary on a part of it; I acknowledge with thanks the permission of C. S. Lewis PTE Limited to include this.

In 1937 he said in a letter that 'in spite of certain virtuous passages' the *Lay of Leithian* had 'grave defects' (see p. 366). A decade or more later, he received a detailed, and remarkably unconstrained, criticism of the poem from someone who knew and admired his poetry. I do not know for certain who this was. In choosing 'the staple octosyllabic couplet of romance,' he wrote, my father had chosen one of the most difficult of forms 'if one wishes to avoid monotony and sing-song in a very long poem. I am often astonished by your success, but it is by no means consistently maintained.' His strictures on the diction of the Lay included archaisms so archaic that they needed annotation, distorted order, use of emphatic *doth* or *did* where there is no emphasis, and language sometimes flat and conventional (in contrast to passages of 'gorgeous description'). There is no record of what my father thought of this criticism (written when *The Lord of the Rings* was already completed), but it must be associated in some way with the fact that in 1949 or 1950 he returned to the *Lay of Leithian* and began a revision that soon became virtually a new poem; and relatively little though he wrote of it, its advance on the old version in all those respects in which that had been censured is so great as to give it a sad prominence in the long list of his works that might have been. The new Lay is included in this book, and a page from a fine manuscript of it is reproduced as frontispiece.

The sections of both poems are interleaved with commentaries which are primarily concerned to trace the evolution of the legends and the lands they are set in.

The two pages reproduced from the *Lay of the Children of Húrin* (p. 15) are from the original manuscript of the first version, lines 297–317 and 318–33. For differences between the readings of the manuscript and those of the printed text see pp. 4–5. The page from the *Lay of Leithian* in Elvish script (p. 299) comes from the 'A' version of the original Lay (see pp. 150–1), and there are certain differences in the text from the 'B' version which is that printed. These pages from the original manuscripts are reproduced with the permission of the Bodleian Library, Oxford, and I thank the staff of the Department of Western Manuscripts at the Bodleian for their assistance.

The two earlier volumes in this series (the first and second parts of *The Book of Lost Tales*) are referred to as 'I' and 'II'. The fourth volume will contain the 'Sketch of the Mythology' (1926), from which the *Silmarillion* 'tradition' derived; the *Quenta Noldorinwa* or History of the Noldoli (1930); the first map of the North-west of Middle-earth; the *Ambarkanta* ('Shape of the World') by Rúmil, together with the only existing maps of the entire World; the earliest *Annals of Valinor* and *Annals of Beleriand*, by Pengolod the Wise of Gondolin; and the fragments of translations of the *Quenta* and *Annals* from Elvish into Anglo-Saxon by Ælfwine of England.

# I

# THE LAY OF THE
# CHILDREN OF HÚRIN

There exists a substantial manuscript (28 pages long) entitled 'Sketch of the Mythology with especial reference to "The Children of Húrin"'; and this 'Sketch' is the next complete narrative, in the *prose* tradition, after the *Lost Tales* (though a few fragmentary writings are extant from the intervening time). On the envelope containing this manuscript my father wrote at some later time:

> Original 'Silmarillion'. Form orig[inally] composed c. 1926–30 for R. W. Reynolds to explain background of 'alliterative version' of Túrin & the Dragon: then in progress (unfinished) (begun c. 1918).

He seems to have written first '1921' before correcting this to '1918'.

R. W. Reynolds taught my father at King Edward's School, Birmingham (see Humphrey Carpenter, *Biography*, p. 47). In a passage of his diary written in August 1926 he wrote that 'at the end of last year' he had heard again from R. W. Reynolds, that they had corresponded subsequently, and that he had sent Reynolds many of his poems, including *Tinúviel* and *Túrin* ('*Tinúviel* meets with qualified approval, it is too prolix, but how could I ever cut it down, and the specimen I sent of *Túrin* with little or none'). This would date the 'Sketch' as originally written (it was subsequently heavily revised) definitely in 1926, probably fairly early in the year. It must have accompanied the specimen of *Túrin* (the alliterative poem), the background of which it was written to explain, to Anacapri, where Reynolds was then living in retirement.

My father took up his appointment to the Professorship of Anglo-Saxon at Oxford in the winter term (October–December) of 1925, though for that term he had to continue to teach at Leeds also, since the appointments overlapped. There can be no doubt that at any rate the great bulk of the alliterative *Children of Húrin* (or *Túrin*) was completed at Leeds, and I think it virtually certain that he had ceased to work on it before he moved south: in fact there seems nothing to oppose to the natural assumption that he left 'Túrin' for 'Tinúviel' (the *Lay of Leithian*), which he began according to his diary in the summer of 1925 (see p. 159 and footnote).

For the date of its commencement we have only my father's later (and perhaps hesitant) statement that it was 'begun c. 1918'. A *terminus a quo* is provided by a page of the earliest manuscript of the poem, which is written on a slip from the Oxford English Dictionary bearing the printer's stamp *May 1918*. On the other hand the name *Melian* which occurs near the beginning of the earliest manuscript shows it to be later than the typescript version of the *Tale of Tinúviel*, where the Queen's name was *Gwenethlin* and only became *Melian* in the course of its composition (II. 51); and the manuscript version of that Tale which underlies the typescript seems itself to have been one of the last completed elements in the *Lost Tales* (see I. 204).

*The Children of Húrin* exists in two versions, which I shall refer to as I and II, both of them found in manuscript and later typescript (IA, IB; IIA, IIB). I do not think that the second is significantly later than the first; it is indeed possible, and would not be in any way uncharacteristic, that my father began work on II while he was still composing at a later point in I. II is essentially an expansion of I, with many lines, and blocks of lines, left virtually unchanged. Until the second version is reached it will be sufficient to refer simply to 'A' and 'B', the manuscript and typescript of the first version.

The manuscript A consists of two parts: first (a) a bundle of small slips, numbered 1–32. The poem is here in a very rough state with many alternative readings, and in places at least may represent the actual beginnings, the first words written down. This is followed by (b) a set of large sheets of examination paper from the University of Leeds, numbered 33 ff., where the poem is for the most part written out in a more finished form – the second stage of composition; but my father wrote in line-numbers continuously through (a) and (b) – lines 1–528 in (a), lines 528 ff. in (b). We have thus one sole text, not two, without any overlap; and if (a), the slips, ever existed in the form of (b), the examination sheets, that part has disappeared. In part (b) there are many later emendations in pencil.

Based on this manuscript is the typescript B. This introduces changes not found in A or its emendations; and it was itself emended both in ink and pencil, doubtless involving several movements of revision. To take a single line as exemplification: line 8 was written first in A:

> Lo! Thalion in the throng    of thickest battle

The line was emended, in two stages, to

> Lo! Thalion Húrin    in the throng of battle

and this was the form in B as typed; but B was emended, in two stages, to

> Lo! Húrin Thalion    in the hosts of war

It is obvious that to set this and a great many other similar cases out in a textual apparatus would be a huge task and the result impossibly complicated. The text that follows is therefore, so far as purely metrical-stylistic changes are concerned, that of B as *emended*, and apart from a few special cases there is no mention in the notes of earlier readings.

In the matter of names, however, the poem presents great difficulty; for changes were made at quite different times and were not introduced consistently throughout. If the latest form in any particular passage is made the principle of choice, irrespective of any other consideration, then the text will have *Morwin* at lines 105, 129, *Mavwin* 137 etc., *Morwen* 438, 472; *Ulmo* 1469, but *Ylmir* 1529 and subsequently; *Nirnaith Ornoth* 1448, but *Nirnaith Únoth* 1543. If the later *Nirnaith Ornoth* is adopted at 1543, it seems scarcely justifiable to intrude it at lines 13 and 218 (where the final form is *Nínin Unothradin*). I have decided finally to abandon overall consistency, and to treat individual names as seems best in the circumstances; for example, I give *Ylmir* rather than *Ulmo* at line 1469, for consistency with all the other occurrences, and while changing *Únoth* to *Ornoth* at line 1543 I retain *Ornoth* rather than the much later *Arnediad* at line 26 of the second version – similarly I prefer the earlier *Finweg* to *Fingon* (1975, second version 19, 520) and *Bansil, Glingol* to *Belthil, Glingal* (2027–8). All such points are documented in the notes.

A has no title. In B as typed the title was *The Golden Dragon*, but this was emended to *Túrin Son of Húrin & Glórund the Dragon*. The second version of the poem was first titled *Túrin*, but this was changed to *The Children of Húrin*, and I adopt this, the title by which my father referred to the poem in the 1926 'Sketch', as the general title of the work.

The poem in the first version is divided into a short prologue (Húrin and Morgoth) without sub-title and three long sections, of which the first two ('Túrin's Fostering' and 'Beleg') were only introduced later into the typescript; the third ('Failivrin') is marked both in A and in B as typed.

The detail of the typescript is largely preserved in the present text, but I have made the capitalisation rather more consistent, added in occasional accents, and increased the number of breaks in the text. The space between the half-lines is marked in the second part of the A-text and begins at line 543 in B.

I have avoided the use of numbered notes to the text, and all annotation is related to the line-numbers of the poem. This annotation (very largely concerned with variations of names, and comparisons with names in the *Lost Tales*) is found at the end of each of the three major parts, followed by a commentary on the matter of that part.

Throughout, the *Tale* refers to the *Tale of Turambar and the Foalókë* (II. 69 ff.); *Narn* refers to the *Narn i Hîn Húrin*, in *Unfinished Tales* pp. 57 ff.

★

# TÚRIN SON OF HÚRIN
# &
# GLÓRUND THE DRAGON

Lo! the golden dragon     of the God of Hell,
the gloom of the woods     of the world now gone,
the woes of Men,     and weeping of Elves
fading faintly     down forest pathways,
is now to tell,     and the name most tearful          5
of Níniel the sorrowful,     and the name most sad
of Thalion's son Túrin     o'erthrown by fate.

Lo! Húrin Thalion     in the hosts of war
was whelmed, what time     the white-clad armies
of Elfinesse     were all to ruin          10
by the dread hate driven     of Delu-Morgoth.
That field is yet     by the folk naméd
Nínin Unothradin,     Unnumbered Tears.
There the children of Men,     chieftain and warrior,
fled and fought not,     but the folk of the Elves          15
they betrayed with treason,     save that true man only,
Thalion Erithámrod     and his thanes like gods.
There in host on host     the hill-fiend Orcs
overbore him at last     in that battle terrible,
by the bidding of Bauglir     bound him living,          20
and pulled down the proudest     of the princes of Men.
To Bauglir's halls     in the hills builded,
to the Hells of Iron     and the hidden caverns
they haled the hero     of Hithlum's land,
Thalion Erithámrod,     to their thronéd lord,          25
whose breast was burnt     with a bitter hatred,
and wroth he was     that the wrack of war
had not taken Turgon     ten times a king,
even Finweg's heir;     nor Fëanor's children,
makers of the magic     and immortal gems.          30
For Turgon towering     in terrible anger
a pathway clove him     with his pale sword-blade
out of that slaughter –     yea, his swath was plain
through the hosts of Hell     like hay that lieth
all low on the lea     where the long scythe goes.          35
A countless company     that king did lead
through the darkened dales     and drear mountains

out of ken of his foes,    and he comes not more
in the tale; but the triumph    he turned to doubt
of Morgoth the evil,    whom mad wrath took.                    40
Nor spies sped him,    nor spirits of evil,
nor his wealth of wisdom    to win him tidings,
whither the nation    of the Gnomes was gone.
Now a thought of malice,    when Thalion stood,
bound, unbending,    in his black dungeon,                     45
then moved in his mind    that remembered well
how Men were accounted    all mightless and frail
by the Elves and their kindred;    how only treason
could master the magic    whose mazes wrapped
the children of Corthûn,    and cheated his purpose.          50

'Is it dauntless Hurin,'    quoth Delu-Morgoth,
'stout steel-handed,    who stands before me,
a captive living    as a coward might be?
Knowest thou my name,    or need'st be told
what hope he has    who is haled to Angband –                 55
the bale most bitter,    the Balrogs' torment?'

'I know and I hate.    For that knowledge I fought thee
by fear unfettered,    nor fear I now,'
said Thalion there,    and a thane of Morgoth
on the mouth smote him;    but Morgoth smiled:                 60
'Fear when thou feelest,    and the flames lick thee,
and the whips of the Balrogs    thy white flesh brand.
Yet a way canst win,    an thou wishest, still
to lessen thy lot    of lingering woe.
Go question the captives    of the accursed people            65
I have taken, and tell me    where Turgon is hid;
how with fire and death    I may find him soon,
where he lurketh lost    in lands forgot.
Thou must feign thee a friend    faithful in anguish,
and their inmost hearts    thus open and search.              70
Then, if truth thou tellest,    thy triple bonds
I will bid men unbind,    that abroad thou fare
in my service to search    the secret places
following the footsteps    of these foes of the Gods.'

'Build not thy hopes    so high, O Bauglir –                  75
I am no tool    for thy evil treasons;
torment were sweeter    than a traitor's stain.'

'If torment be sweet,    treasure is liever.
The hoards of a hundred    hundred ages,
the gems and jewels    of the jealous Gods,                                    80
are mine, and a meed    shall I mete thee thence,
yea, wealth to glut    the Worm of Greed.'

'Canst not learn of thy lore    when thou look'st on a foe,
O Bauglir unblest?    Bray no longer
of the things thou hast thieved    from the Three Kindreds.       85
In hate I hold thee,    and thy hests in scorn.'

'Boldly thou bravest me.    Be thy boast rewarded,'
in mirth quod Morgoth,    'to me now the deeds,
and thy aid I ask not;    but anger thee nought
if little they like thee.    Yea, look thereon                                   90
helpless to hinder,    or thy hand to raise.'

Then Thalion was thrust    to Thangorodrim,
that mountain that meets    the misty skies
on high o'er the hills    that Hithlum sees
blackly brooding    on the borders of the north.                                95
To a stool of stone    on its steepest peak
they bound him in bonds,    an unbreakable chain,
and the Lord of Woe    there laughing stood,
then cursed him for ever    and his kin and seed
with a doom of dread,    of death and horror.                                  100
There the mighty man    unmovéd sat;
but unveiled was his vision,    that he viewed afar
all earthly things    with eyes enchanted
that fell on his folk –    a fiend's torment.


I

TÚRIN'S FOSTERING

Lo! the lady Morwin    in the Land of Shadows                                  105
waited in the woodland    for her well-beloved;
but he came never    from the combat home.
No tidings told her    whether taken or dead,
or lost in flight    he lingered yet.
Laid waste his lands,    and his lieges slain,                                  110
and men unmindful    of his mighty lordship
dwelt in Dorlómin    and dealt unkindly

with his widowed wife;    and she went with child,
who a son must succour    now sadly orphaned,
Túrin Thaliodrin    of tender years.                                      115
Then in days of blackness    was her daughter born,
and was naméd Nienor,    a name of tears
that in language of eld    is Lamentation.
Then her thoughts turnéd    to Thingol the Elf-king,
and the dancer of Doriath,    his daughter Tinúviel,               120
whom the boldest of the brave,    Beren Ermabwed,
had won to wife.    He once had known
firmest friendship    to his fellow in arms,
Thalion Erithámrod –    so thought she now,
and said to her son,    'My sweetest child,                          125
our friends are few,    and thy father comes not.
Thou must fare afar    to the folk of the wood,
where Thingol is throned    in the Thousand Caves.
If he remember Morwin    and thy mighty sire
he will fain foster thee,    and feats of arms                       130
he will teach thee, the trade    of targe and sword,
and Thalion's son    no thrall shall be –
but remember thy mother    when thy manhood nears.'

Heavy boded the heart    of Húrin's son,
yet he weened her words    were wild with grief,               135
and he denied her not,    for no need him seemed.
Lo! henchmen had Morwin,    Halog and Gumlin,
who were young of yore    ere the youth of Thalion,
who alone of the lieges    of that lord of Men
steadfast in service    staid beside her:                            140
now she bade them brave    the black mountains,
and the woods whose ways    wander to evil;
though Túrin be tender    and to travail unused,
they must gird them and go;    but glad they were not,
and Morwin mourned    when men saw not.                      145

Came a summer day    when sun filtered
warm through the woodland's    waving branches.
Then Morwin stood    her mourning hiding
by the gate of her garth    in a glade of the woods.
At the breast she mothered    her babe unweaned,         150
and the doorpost held    lest she droop for anguish.
There Gumlin guided    her gallant boy,
and a heavy burden    was borne by Halog;

but the heart of Túrin    was heavy as stone
uncomprehending    its coming anguish.                                        155
He sought for comfort,    with courage saying:
'Quickly will I come    from the courts of Thingol;
long ere manhood    I will lead to Morwin
great tale of treasure,    and true comrades' –
for he wist not the weird    woven by Bauglir,                                160
nor the sundering sorrow    that swept between.
The farewells are taken:    their footsteps are turned
to the dark forest:    the dwelling fadeth
in the tangled trees.    Then in Túrin leapt
his awakened heart,    and he wept blindly,                                   165
calling 'I cannot,    I cannot leave thee.
O Morwin, my mother,    why makest me go?
Hateful are the hills    where hope is lost.
O Morwin, my mother,    I am meshed in tears.
Grim are the hills,    and my home is gone.'                                  170
And there came his cries    calling faintly
down the dark alleys    of the dreary trees,
and one who wept    weary on the threshold
heard how the hills said    'my home is gone.'

The ways were weary    and woven with deceit                                 175
o'er the hills of Hithlum    to the hidden kingdom
deep in the darkness    of Doriath's forest;
and never ere now    for need or wonder
had children of Men    chosen that pathway,
and few of the folk    have followed it since.                               180
There Túrin and the twain    knew torment of thirst,
and hunger and fear    and hideous nights,
for wolfriders    and wandering Orcs
and the Things of Morgoth    thronged the woodland.
Magics were about them,    that they missed their ways                       185
and strayed steerless,    and the stars were hid.
Thus they passed the mountains,    but the mazes of Doriath
wildered and wayworn    in wanhope bound them.
They had nor bread nor water,    and bled of strength
their death they deemed it    to die forewandered,                           190
when they heard a horn    that hooted afar,
and baying dogs.    It was Beleg the hunter,
who farthest fared    of his folk abroad
ahunting by hill    and hollow valley,

who cared not for concourse    and commerce of men.    195
He was great of growth    and goodly-limbed,
but lithe of girth,    and lightly on the ground
his footsteps fell    as he fared towards them,
all garbed in grey    and green and brown –
a son of the wilderness    who wist no sire.    200

'Who are ye?' he asked.    'Outlaws, or maybe
hard hunted men    whom hate pursueth?'

'Nay, for famine and thirst    we faint,' saith Halog,
'wayworn and wildered,    and wot not the road.
Or hast not heard    of the hills of slain,    205
or the tear-drenchéd field    where the terror and fire
of Morgoth devoured    both Men and Elves?
There Thalion Erithámrod    and his thanes like gods
vanished from the earth,    and his valiant lady
weeps yet widowed    as she waits in Hithlum.    210
Thou lookest on the last    of the lieges of Morwin
and Thalion's son Túrin,    who to Thingol's court
are wending by the word    of the wife of Húrin.'

Then Beleg bade them    be blithe, and said:
'The Gods have guided you    to good keeping.    215
I have heard of the house    of Húrin the Steadfast –
and who hath not heard    of the hills of slain,
of Nínin Unothradin,    the Unnumbered Tears?
To that war I went not,    but wage a feud
with the Orcs unending,    whom mine arrows bitter    220
oft stab unseen    and strike to death.
I am the huntsman Beleg    of the Hidden People.'
Then he bade them drink,    and drew from his belt
a flask of leather    full filled with wine
that is bruised from the berries    of the burning South –    225
and the Gnome-folk know it,    and the nation of the Elves,
and by long ways lead it    to the lands of the North.
There bakéd flesh    and bread from his wallet
they had to their hearts' joy;    but their heads were mazed
by the wine of Dor-Winion    that went in their veins,    230
and they soundly slept    on the soft needles
of the tall pine-trees    that towered above.
Later they wakened    and were led by ways
devious winding    through the dark wood-realm

by slade and slope    and swampy thicket                            235
through lonely days    and long night-times,
and but for Beleg    had been baffled utterly
by the magic mazes    of Melian the Queen.
To the shadowy shores    he showed the way
where stilly that stream    strikes 'fore the gates               240
of the cavernous court    of the King of Doriath.
O'er the guarded bridge    he gained a passage,
and thrice they thanked him,    and thought in their hearts
'the Gods are good' —    had they guessed maybe
what the future enfolded    they had feared to live.              245

To the throne of Thingol    the three were come,
and their speech sped them;    for he spake them fair,
and held in honour    Húrin the steadfast,
Beren Ermabwed's    brother-in-arms.
Remembering Morwin,    of mortals fairest,                        250
he turned not Túrin    in contempt away;
said: 'O son of Húrin,    here shalt sojourn
in my cavernous court    for thy kindred's sake.
Nor as slave or servant,    but a second king's son
thou shalt dwell in dear love,    till thou deem'st it time       255
to remember thy mother    Morwin's loneliness.
Thou wisdom shalt win    unwist of Men
and weapons shalt wield    as the warrior Elves,
and Thalion's son    no thrall shall be.'

There tarried the twain    that had tended the child,            260
till their limbs were lightened    and they longed to fare
through dread and danger    to their dear lady.
But Gumlin was gone    in greater years
than Halog, and hoped not    to home again.
Then sickness took him,    and he stayed by Túrin,               265
while Halog hardened    his heart to go.
An Elfin escort    to his aid was given
and magics of Melian,    and a meed of gold.
In his mouth a message    to Morwin was set,
words of the king's will,    how her wish was granted;           270
how Thingol called her    to the Thousand Caves
to fare unfearing    with his folk again,
there to sojourn in solace,    till her son be grown;
for Húrin the hero    was held in mind,
and no might had Morgoth    where Melian dwelt.                   275

Of the errand of the Elves    and that other Halog
the tale tells not,    save in time they came
to the threshold of Morwin,    and Thingol's message
was said where she sate    in her solitary hall.
But she dared not do    as was dearly bidden,                    280
for Nienor her nestling    was not yet weaned.
More, the pride of her people,    princes of Men,
had suffered her send    her son to Thingol
when despair sped her,    but to spend her days
as alms-guest of others,    even Elfin kings,                    285
it liked her little;    and there lived e'en now
a hope in her heart    that Húrin would come,
and the dwelling was dear    where he dwelt of old.
At night she would listen    for a knock at the doors,
or a footstep falling    that she fondly knew;                   290
so she fared not forth,    and her fate was woven.
Yet the thanes of Thingol    she thanked nobly,
and her shame she showed not,    how shorn of glory
to reward their wending    she had wealth too scant;
but gave them in gift    her golden things                      295
that last lingered,    and they led away
a helm of Húrin    that was hewn in war
when he battled with Beren    his brother-in-arms
against ogres and Orcs    and evil foemen;
'twas o'erwritten with runes    by wrights of old.              300
She bade Thingol receive it    and think of her.

Thus Halog her henchman    came home, but the Elves,
the thanes of Thingol,    thrust through the woods,
and the message of Morwin    in a month's journey,
so quick their coming,    to the king was said.                 305
Then was Melian    moved to ruth,
and courteously received    the king her gift,
who deeply delved    had dungeons filled
with Elfin armouries    of ancient gear,
but he handled the helm    as his hoard were scant;             310
said: 'High were the head    that upheld this thing
with that token crowned    of the towering dragon
that Thalion Erithámrod    thrice-renownéd
oft bore into battle    with baleful foes.'
Then a thought was thrust    into Thingol's heart,              315
and Túrin he called    and told when come

that Morwin his mother    a mighty thing
had sent to her son,    his sire's heirloom,
a helm that hammers    had hardened of old,
whose makers had mingled    a magic therein                    320
that its worth was a wonder    and its wearer safe,
guarded from glaive    or gleaming axe –
'Lo! Húrin's helm    hoard thou till manhood
bids thee battle;    then bravely don it';
and Túrin touched it,    but took it not,                      325
too weak to wield    that weight as yet,
and his mind mournéd    for Morwin's answer,
and the first of his sorrows    o'erfilled his soul.

Thus came it to pass    in the court of Thingol
that Túrin tarried    for twelve long years                   330
with Gumlin his guardian,    who guided him thither
when but seven summers    their sorrows had laid
on the son of Thalion.    For the seven first
his lot was lightened,    since he learnt at whiles
from faring folk    what befell in Hithlum,                    335
and tidings were told    by trusty Elves,
how Morwin his mother    was more at ease;
and they named Nienor    that now was growing
to the sweet beauty    of a slender maiden.
Thus his heart knew hope,    and his hap was fairer.          340
There he waxed wonderly    and won him praise
in all lands where Thingol    as lord was held
for the strength of his body    and stoutness of heart.
Much lore he learned,    and loved wisdom,
but fortune followed him    in few desires;                    345
oft wrong and awry    what he wrought turnéd;
what he loved he lost,    what he longed for he won not;
and full friendship    he found not easily,
nor was lightly loved    for his looks were sad.
He was gloomy-hearted,    and glad seldom,                     350
for the sundering sorrow    that seared his youth.

On manhood's threshold    he was mighty holden
in the wielding of weapons;    and in weaving song
he had a minstrel's mastery,    but mirth was not in it,
for he mourned the misery    of the Men of Hithlum.           355
Yet greater his grief    grew thereafter,
when from Hithlum's hills    he heard no more,

Two pages from the original manuscript of *The Lay of the Children of Húrin*

and no traveller told him     tidings of Morwin.
For those days were drawing     to the Doom of the Gnomes,
and the power of the Prince     of the People of Hell,                    360
of the grim Glamhoth,     was grown apace,
till the lands of the North     were loud with their noise,
and they fell on the folk     with flame and ruin
who bent not to Bauglir,     or the borders passed
of dark Dorlómin     with its dreary pines                                365
that Hithlum unhappy     is hight by Men.
There Morgoth shut them,     and the Shadowy Mountains
fenced them from Faërie     and the folk of the wood.
Even Beleg fared not     so far abroad
as once was his wont,     and the woods were filled           370
with the armies of Angband     and evil deeds,
while murder walked     on the marches of Doriath;
only mighty magic     of Melian the Queen
yet held their havoc     from the Hidden People.

To assuage his sorrow     and to sate the rage              375
and hate of his heart     for the hurts of his folk
then Húrin's son     took the helm of his sire
and weapons weighty     for the wielding of men,
and went to the woods     with warlike Elves;
and far in the fight     his feet led him,                        380
into black battle     yet a boy in years.
Ere manhood's measure     he met and slew
the Orcs of Angband     and evil things
that roamed and ravened     on the realm's borders.
There hard his life,     and hurts he got him,               385
the wounds of shaft     and warfain sword,
and his prowess was proven     and his praise renowned,
and beyond his years     he was yielded honour;
for by him was holden     the hand of ruin
from Thingol's folk,     and Thû feared him –                 390
Thû who was thronéd     as thane most mighty
neath Morgoth Bauglir;     whom that mighty one bade
'Go ravage the realm     of the robber Thingol,
and mar the magic     of Melian the Queen.'

Only one was there     in war greater,                         395
higher in honour     in the hearts of the Elves,
than Túrin son of Húrin     untamed in war –
even the huntsman Beleg     of the Hidden People,

the son of the wilderness    who wist no sire
(to bend whose bow    of the black yew-tree                    400
had none the might),    unmatched in knowledge
of the wood's secrets    and the weary hills.
He was leader beloved    of the light-armed bands,
the scouts that scoured,    scorning danger,
afar o'er the fells    their foemen's lairs;                    405
and tales and tidings    timely won them
of camps and councils,    of comings and goings –
all the movements of the might    of Morgoth the Terrible.
Thus Túrin, who trusted    to targe and sword,
who was fain of fighting    with foes well seen,               410
and the banded troops    of his brave comrades
were snared seldom    and smote unlooked-for.

Then the fame of the fights    on the far marches
were carried to the court    of the King of Doriath,
and tales of Túrin    were told in his halls,                  415
and how Beleg the ageless    was brother-in-arms
to the black-haired boy    from the beaten people.
Then the king called them    to come before him
ever and anon    when the Orc-raids waned;
to rest them and revel,    and to raise awhile                 420
the secret songs    of the sons of Ing.
On a time was Túrin    at the table of Thingol –
there was laughter long    and the loud clamour
of a countless company    that quaffed the mead,
amid the wine of Dor-Winion    that went ungrudged            425
in their golden goblets;    and goodly meats
there burdened the boards,    neath the blazing torches
set high in those halls    that were hewn of stone.
There mirth fell on many;    there minstrels clear
did sing to them songs    of the city of Tûn                   430
neath Tain-Gwethil,    towering mountain,
where the great gods sit    and gaze on the world
from the guarded shores    of the gulf of Faërie.
Then one sang of the slaying    at the Swanships' Haven
and the curse that had come    on the kindreds since:          435
all silent sat    and soundless harkened,
and waited the words    save one alone –
the Man among Elves    that Morwin bore.
Unheeding he heard    or high feasting

or lay or laughter,   and looked, it seemed,                    440
to a deep distance   in the dark without,
and strained for sounds   in the still spaces,
for voices that vanished   in the veils of night.
He was lithe and lean,   and his locks were wild,
and woodland weeds   he wore of brown                           445
and grey and green,   and gay jewel
or golden trinket   his garb knew not.

An Elf there was – Orgof –   of the ancient race
that was lost in the lands   where the long marches
from the quiet waters   of Cuiviénen                            450
were made in the mirk   of the midworld's gloom,
ere light was lifted   aloft o'er earth;
but blood of the Gnomes   was blent in his veins.       .
He was close akin   to the King of Doriath –
a hardy hunter   and his heart was brave,                       455
but loose his laughter   and light his tongue,
and his pride outran   his prowess in arms.
He was fain before all   of fine raiment
and of gems and jewels,   and jealous of such
as found favour   before himself.                               460
Now costly clad   in colours gleaming
he sat on a seat   that was set on high
near the king and queen   and close to Túrin.
When those twain were at table   he had taunted him oft,
lightly with laughter,   for his loveless ways,                 465
his haggard raiment   and hair unshorn;
but Túrin untroubled   neither turned his head
nor wasted words   on the wit of Orgof.
But this day of the feast   more deep his gloom
than of wont, and his words   men won harder;                   470
for of twelve long years   the tale was full
since on Morwin his mother   through a maze of tears
he looked the last,   and the long shadows
of the forest had fallen   on his fading home;
and he answered few,   and Orgof nought.                        475
Then the fool's mirth   was filled the more,
to a keener edge   was his carping whetted
at the clothes uncouth   and the uncombéd hair
of Túrin newcome   from the tangled forest.
He drew forth daintily   a dear treasure,                       480

a comb of gold   that he kept about him,
and tendered it to Túrin;   but he turned not his eyes,
nor deigned to heed   or harken to Orgof,
who too deep drunken   that disdain should quell him:
'Nay, an thou knowest not   thy need of comb,                    485
nor its use,' quoth he,   'too young thou leftest
thy mother's ministry,   and 'twere meet to go
that she teach thee tame   thy tangled locks –
if the women of Hithlum   be not wild and loveless,
uncouth and unkempt   as their cast-off sons.'                   490

Then a fierce fury,   like a fire blazing,
was born of bitterness   in his bruiséd heart;
his white wrath woke   at the words of scorn
for the women of Hithlum   washed in tears;
and a heavy horn   to his hand lying,                            495
with gold adorned   for good drinking,
of his might unmindful   thus moved in ire
he seized and, swinging,   swiftly flung it
in the face of Orgof.   'Thou fool', he said,
'fill thy mouth therewith,   and to me no further                500
thus witless prate   by wine bemused' –
but his face was broken,   and he fell backward,
and heavy his head   there hit upon the stone
of the floor rock-paved   mid flagons and vessels
of the o'erturned table   that tumbled on him                    505
as clutching he fell;   and carped no more,
in death silent.   There dumb were all
at bench and board;   in blank amaze
they rose around him,   as with ruth of heart
he gazed aghast   on his grievous deed,                          510
on his wine-stained hand,   with wondering eyes
half-comprehending.   On his heel then he turned
into the night striding,   and none stayed him;
but some their swords   half slipped from sheaths
– they were Orgof's kin –   yet for awe of Thingol               515
they dared not draw   while the dazéd king
stonefacéd stared   on his stricken thane
and no sign showed them.   But the slayer weary
his hands laved   in the hidden stream
that strikes 'fore the gates,   nor stayed his tears:            520
'Who has cast,' he cried,   'a curse upon me;

for all I do is ill,    and an outlaw now,
in bitter banishment    and blood-guilty,
of my fosterfather    I must flee the halls,
nor look on the lady    beloved again' –                              525
yea, his heart to Hithlum    had hastened him now,
but that road he dared not,    lest the wrath he draw
of the Elves after him,    and their anger alight
should speed the spears    in despite of Morgoth
o'er the hills of Hithlum    to hunt him down;                        530
lest a doom more dire    than they dreed of old
be meted his mother    and the Maid of Tears.

In the furthest folds    of the Forest of Doriath,
in the darkest dales    on its drear borders,
in haste he hid him,    lest the hunt take him;                       535
and they found not his footsteps    who fared after,
the thanes of Thingol;    who thirty days
sought him sorrowing,    and searched in vain
with no purpose of ill,    but the pardon bearing
of Thingol throned    in the Thousand Caves.                          540
He in council constrained    the kin of Orgof
to forget their grief    and forgiveness show,
in that wilful bitterness    had barbed the words
of Orgof the Elf;    said 'his hour had come
that his soul should seek    the sad pathway                          545
to the deep valley    of the Dead Awaiting,
there a thousand years    thrice to ponder
in the gloom of Gurthrond    his grim jesting,
ere he fare to Faërie    to feast again.'
Yet of his own treasure    he oped the gates,                         550
and gifts ungrudging    of gold and gems
to the sons he gave    of the slain; and his folk
well deemed the deed.    But that doom of the King
Túrin knew not,    and turned against him
the hands of the Elves    he unhappy believed,                        555
wandering the woodland    woeful-hearted;
for his fate would not    that the folk of the caves
should harbour longer    Húrin's offspring.

★

## NOTES

(Throughout the Notes statements such as '*Delimorgoth* A, and B as typed' (line 11) imply that the reading in the printed text (in that case *Delu-Morgoth*) is a later emendation made to B).

8 *Húrin* is *Úrin* in the *Lost Tales* (and still when this poem was begun, see note to line 213), and his name *Thalion* 'Steadfast', found in *The Silmarillion* and the *Narn*, does not occur in them (though he is called 'the Steadfast').

11 *Delimorgoth* A, and B as typed. *Morgoth* occurs once only in the *Lost Tales*, in the typescript version of the *Tale of Tinúviel* (II.44); see note to line 20.

13 *Nínin Udathriol* A, and B as typed; this occurs in the *Tale* (II.84; for explanation of the name see II.346). When changing *Udathriol* to *Unothradin* my father wrote in the margin of B: 'or *Nirnaithos Unothradin*'.

17 Above *Erithámrod* is pencilled in A *Urinthalion*.

20 B as typed had *Belcha*, which was then changed through *Belegor, Melegor*, to *Bauglir*. (A has a different reading here: *as a myriad rats in measureless army / might pull down the proudest . . .*) *Belcha* occurs in the typescript version of the *Tale of Tinúviel* (II.44), where *Belcha Morgoth* are said to be Melko's names among the Gnomes. *Bauglir* is found as a name of Morgoth in *The Silmarillion* and the *Narn*.

22 *Melko's* A; *Belcha's* B as typed, then the line changed to *To the halls* of *Belegor* (> *Melegor*), and finally to the reading given. See note to line 20.

25 Above *Erithámrod* in A is written *UrinThalion* (see note to line 17); *Úrin* > *Húrin*, and a direction to read *Thalion Húrin*.

29 *Finweg's son* A, and B as typed; the emendation is a later one, and at the same time my father wrote in the margin of B 'he was Fingolfin's son', clearly a comment on the change of *son* to *heir*. *Finweg* is *Finwë Nólemë* Lord of the Noldoli, who in the *Lost Tales* was Turgon's father (I.115), not as he afterwards became his grandfather.

50 *Kor* > *Cor* A, *Cor* B as typed. When emending *Cor* to *Corthûn* my father wrote in the margin of B: '*Corthun* or *Tûn*'.

51 *Thalion* A, and B as typed.
   *Delimorgoth* A, and B as typed (as at line 11).

73 In B there is a mark of insertion between lines 72 and 73. This probably refers to a line in A, not taken up into B: *bound by the (> my) spell of bottomless (> unbroken) might.*

75    *Belcha* A, and B as typed; the same chain of emendations in
      B as at lines 20 and 22.
84    *Bauglir*: as at line 75.
105   *Mavwin* A, and B as typed; in B then emended to *Mailwin*,
      and back to *Mavwin*; *Morwin* written later in the margin of
      B. Exactly the same at 129, and at 137 though here without
      *Morwin* in the margin; at 145 *Mavwin* unemended, but
      *Morwin* in the margin. Thereafter *Mavwin* stands un-
      emended and without marginal note, as far as 438 (see note).
      For consistency I read *Morwin* throughout the first version
      of the poem. – *Mavwin* is the form in the *Tale*; *Mailwin* does
      not occur elsewhere.
117   On the variation *Nienóri/Nienor* in the *Tale* see II. 118–19.
120   *Tinúviel* A, *Tinwiel* B unemended but with *Tinūviel* in the
      margin. *Tinwiel* does not occur elsewhere.
121   *Ermabwed* 'One-handed' is Beren's title or nickname in the
      *Lost Tales*.
137   *Gumlin* is named in the *Tale* (II. 74, etc.); the younger of the
      two guardians of Túrin on his journey to Doriath (here called
      *Halog*) is not.
160   *Belcha* A, and B as typed, emended to *Bauglir*. Cf. notes to
      lines 20, 22, 75.
213   *Urin* > *Húrin* A; but *Húrin* A in line 216.
218   *Nínin Udathriol* A, and B as typed; cf. line 13.
226   The distinction between 'Gnomes' and 'Elves' is still made;
      see I. 43–4.
230   *Dorwinion* A.
306   *For Mavwin was Melian    moved to ruth* A, and B as
      typed, with *Then was Melian moved* written in the margin.
      The second half-line has only three syllables unless *moved* is
      read *movéd*, which is not satisfactory. The second version of
      the poem has here *For Morwen Melian    was moved to
      ruth*. Cf. lines 494, 519.
333   *Túrin Thaliodrin* A (cf. line 115), emended to *the son of
      Thalion*.
361   *Glamhoth* appears in *The Fall of Gondolin* (II. 160), with
      the translation 'folk of dreadful hate'.
364   *Belcha* A, and B as typed; then > *Melegor* > *Bauglir* in B.
392   *Bauglir*: as at line 364.
408   *Morgoth Belcha* A, and B as typed.
430   *Kor* > *Cor* A, *Cor* B as typed. Cf. line 50.
431   *Tengwethil* A, and B as typed. In the early Gnomish dic-
      tionary and in the Name-list to *The Fall of Gondolin* the
      Gnomish name of Taniquetil is *Danigwethil* (I. 266,
      II. 337).
438   *Mavwin* A, and B as typed, but *Mavwin* > *Morwen* a later

emendation in B. I read *Morwin* throughout the first version
of the poem (see note to line 105).

450   *Cuinlimfin* A, and B as typed; *Cuiviénen* a later emendation
in B. The form in the *Lost Tales* is *Koivië-Néni*; *Cuinlimfin*
occurs nowhere else.

461–3  These lines bracketed and marked with an X in B.

471   This line marked with an X in B.

472   *Mavwin* > *Morwen* B; see line 438.

494   *all washed in tears* A, *washed in tears* B (half-line of three
syllables), with an X in the margin and an illegible word
written in pencil before *washed*. Cf. lines 306, 519. The
second version of the poem does not reach this point.

514–16  Against these lines my father wrote in the margin of B: 'Make
Orgof's kin set on him and T. fight his way out.'

517   *stonefacéd stared*: the accent on *stonefacéd* was put in
later and the line marked with an X. – In his essay *On
Translating Beowulf* (1940; *The Monsters and the Critics
and Other Essays* (1983) p. 67) my father gave *stared
stonyfaced* as an example of an Old English metrical type.

519   *his hands laved*: the line is marked with an X in B. Cf. lines
306, 494.

528   With the half-line *and their anger alight* the second, more
finished, part of the manuscript A begins; see p. 4.

529   *Belcha* A, *Morgoth* B as typed.

548   *Guthrond* A, and B as typed.

Commentary on the *Prologue*
and *Part I 'Túrin's Fostering'*

The opening section or 'Prologue' of the poem derives from the opening
of the *Tale* (II. 70–1) and in strictly narrative terms there has been little
development. In lines 18–21 (and especially in the rejected line in A, *as a
myriad rats in measureless army / might pull down the proudest*)
is clearly foreshadowed the story in *The Silmarillion* (p. 195):

> . . . they took him at last alive, by the command of Morgoth, for the
> Orcs grappled him with their hands, which clung to him though he
> hewed off their arms; and ever their numbers were renewed, until at
> last he fell buried beneath them.

On the other hand the motive in the later story for capturing him alive
(Morgoth knew that Húrin had been to Gondolin) is necessarily not
present, since Gondolin in the older phases of the legends was not
discovered till Turgon retreated down Sirion after the Battle of Unnumbered Tears (II. 120, 208). That he was taken alive by Morgoth's

command is however already stated in the poem (line 20), though it is not explained why. In the *Tale* Morgoth's interest in Húrin as a tool for the discovery of Turgon arose from his knowledge that

> the Elves of Kôr thought little of Men, holding them in scant fear or suspicion for their blindness and lack of skill

– an idea that is repeated in the poem (46–8); but this idea seems only to have arisen in Morgoth's mind when he came to Húrin in his dungeon (44 ff.).

The place of Húrin's torment (in the *Tale* 'a lofty place of the mountains') is now defined as *a stool of stone* on the steepest peak of Thangorodrim; and this is the first occurrence of that name.

In the change of *son* to *heir* in line 29 is seen the first hint of a development in the kingly house of the Noldoli, with the appearance of a second generation between Finwë (Finweg) and Turgon; but by the time that my father pencilled this change on the text (and noted 'He was Fingolfin's son') the later genealogical structure was already in being, and this is as it were a casual indication of it.

In 'Túrin's Fostering' there is a close relationship between the *Tale* and the poem, extending to many close similarities of wording – especially abundant in the scene in Thingol's hall leading to the death of Orgof; and some phrases had a long life, surviving from the *Tale*, through the poem, and into the *Narn i Hîn Húrin*, as

> rather would she dwell poor among Men than live sweetly as an almsguest among the woodland Elves          (II. 73)

> but to spend her days
> as alms-guest of others,    even Elfin kings,          (284–6)
> it liked her little

> she would not yet humble her pride to be an alms-guest, not even of a king          (*Narn* p. 70)

– though in the *Narn* the 'alms-guest' passage occurs at a different point, before Túrin left Hithlum (Morwen's hope that Húrin would come back is in the *Narn* her reason for not journeying to Doriath with her son, not for refusing the later invitation to her to go).

Of Morwen's situation in Dor-lómin after the Battle of Unnumbered Tears there are a few things to say. In the poem (111–13)

> men unmindful    of his mighty lordship
> dwelt in Dorlómin    and dealt unkindly
> with his widowed wife

– echoing the *Tale*: 'the strange men who dwelt nigh knew not the dignity of the Lady Mavwin', but there is still no indication of who these men were or where they came from (see II. 126). As so often, the narrative

situation was prepared but its explanation had not emerged. The un-
clarity of the *Tale* as to where Úrin dwelt before the great Battle (see
II. 120) is no longer present: *the dwelling was dear where he
dwelt of old* (288). Nienor was born before Túrin left (on the contradiction in the *Tale* on this point see II. 131); and the chronology of Túrin's
childhood is still that of the *Tale* (see II. 142): seven years old when he
left Hithlum (332), seven years in Doriath while tidings still came from
Morwen (333), twelve years since he came to Doriath when he slew
Orgof (471). In the later story the last figure remained unchanged, which
suggests that the X (mark of dissatisfaction) placed against line 471 had
some other reason.

There are several references in the poem to Húrin and Beren having
been friends and fellows-in-arms (122–4, 248–9, 298). In the *Tale* it was
said originally (when Beren was a Man) that Egnor Beren's father was
akin to Mavwin; this was replaced by a different passage (when Beren
had become a Gnome) according to which Egnor was a friend of Úrin
('and Beren Ermabwed son of Egnor he knew'); see II. 71–2, 139. In the
later version of the *Tale of Tinúviel* (II. 44) Úrin is named as the 'brother
in arms' of Egnor; this was emended to make Úrin's relationship with
Beren himself – as in the poem. In *The Silmarillion* (p. 198) Morwen
thought to send Túrin to Thingol 'for Beren son of Barahir was her
father's kinsman, and he had been moreover a friend of Húrin, ere evil
befell'. There is no mention of the fact in the *Narn* (p. 63): Morwen
merely says: 'Am I not now kin of the king [Thingol]? For Beren son
of Barahir was grandson of Bregor, as was my father also.'

That Beren was still an Elf, not a Man, (deducible on other grounds) is
apparent from lines 178–9:

> and never ere now    for need or wonder
> had children of Men    chosen that pathway

– cf. the *Tale* (II. 72): 'and Túrin son of Úrin was the first of Men to
tread that way', changed from the earlier reading 'and Beren Ermabwed
was the first of Men . . .'

In the parting of Túrin from his mother comparison with the *Tale* will
show some subtle differences which need not be spelled out here. The
younger of Túrin's guardians is now named, Halog (and it is said that
Gumlin and Halog were the only 'henchmen' left to Morwen).

Some very curious things are said of Beleg in the poem. He is twice
(200, 399) called 'a (the) son of the wilderness who wist no sire', and at
line 416 he is 'Beleg the ageless'. There seems to be a mystery about him,
an otherness that sets him apart (as he set himself apart, 195) from the
Elves of Thingol's lordship (see further p. 127). It may be that there is
still a trace of this in the 1930 'Silmarillion', where it is said that none
went from Doriath to the Battle of Unnumbered Tears save Mablung,

and Beleg 'who obeyed no man' (in the later text this becomes 'nor any out of Doriath save Mablung and Beleg, who were unwilling to have no part in these great deeds. To them Thingol gave leave to go . . .'; *The Silmarillion* p. 189). In the poem (219) Beleg says expressly that he did not go to the great Battle. – His great bow of black yew-wood (so in *The Silmarillion*, p. 208, where it is named *Belthronding*) now appears (400): in the *Tale* he is not particularly marked out as a bowman (II. 123).

Beleg's *The gods have guided you* (215) and Turin's guardians' thought *the gods are good* (244) accord with references in the *Lost Tales* to the influence of the Valar on Men and Elves in the Great Lands: see II. 141.

The potent wine that Beleg carried and gave to the travellers from his flask (223 ff.) is notable – brought from *the burning South* and *by long ways* carried *to the lands of the North* – as is the name of the land from which it came: *Dor-Winion* (230, 425). The only other places in my father's writings where this name occurs (so far as I know) are in *The Hobbit*, Chapter IX *Barrels out of Bond*: 'the heady vintage of the great gardens of Dorwinion', and 'the wine of Dorwinion brings deep and pleasant dreams'.* See further p. 127.

The curious element in Thingol's message to Morwen in the *Tale*, explaining why he did not go with his people to the Battle of Unnumbered Tears (II. 73), has now been rejected; but with Morwen's response to the messengers out of Doriath there enters the legend the Dragon-helm of Dor-lómin (297 ff.). As yet little is told of it (though more is said in the second version of the poem, see p. 126): Húrin often bore it in battle (in the *Narn* it is denied that he used it, p. 76); it magically protected its wearer (as still in the *Narn*, p. 75); and it was *with that token crowned   of the towering dragon*, and *o'er-written with runes   by wrights of old* (cf. the *Narn*: 'on it were graven runes of victory'). But nothing is here said of how Húrin came by it, beyond the fact that it was his *heirloom*. Very notable is the passage (307 ff.) in which is described Thingol's handling of the helm *as his hoard were scant*, despite his possession of *dungeons filled / with Elfin armouries   of ancient gear*. I have commented previously (see II. 128–9, 245–6) on the early emphasis on the poverty of Tinwelint (Thingol): here we have the first appearance of the idea of his wealth (present also at the beginning of the *Lay of Leithian*). Also notable is the close echoing of the lines of the poem in the words of the *Narn*, p. 76:

---

*\*Dorwinion* is marked on the decorated map by Pauline Baynes, as a region on the North-western shores of the Sea of Rhûn. It must be presumed that this, like other names on that map, was communicated to her by my father (see *Unfinished Tales* p. 261, footnote), but its placing seems surprising.

Yet Thingol handled the Helm of Hador as though his hoard were
scanty, and he spoke courteous words, saying: 'Proud were the head
that bore this helm, which the sires of Húrin bore.'

There is also a clear echo of lines 315–18

> Then a thought was thrust   into Thingol's heart,
> and Túrin he called   and told when come
> that Morwin his mother   a mighty thing
> had sent to her son,   his sire's heirloom

in the prose of the *Narn*:

> Then a thought came to him, and he summoned Túrin, and told him
> that Morwen had sent to her son a mighty thing, the heirloom of his
> fathers.

Compare also the passages that follow in both works, concerning Túrin's
being too young to lift the Helm, and being in any case too unhappy to
heed it on account of his mother's refusal to leave Hithlum. This was *the
first of his sorrows* (328); in the *Narn* (p. 75) the second.

The account of Túrin's character in boyhood (341 ff.) is very close to
that in the *Tale* (II. 74), which as I have noted before (II. 121) survived
into the *Narn* (p. 77): the latter account indeed echoes the poem
('he learned much lore', 'neither did he win friendship easily'). In the
poem it is now added that *in weaving song/he had a minstrel's
mastery,   but mirth was not in it.*

An important new element in the narrative enters with the companion-
ship of Beleg and Túrin (wearing the Dragon-helm, 377) in warfare on
the marches of Doriath:

> how Beleg the ageless   was brother-in-arms
> to the black-haired boy   from the beaten people.   (416–17)

Of this there is no mention in the *Tale* at all (II. 74). Cf. my Commentary, II. 122:

> Túrin's prowess against the Orcs during his sojourn in Artanor is given
> a more central or indeed unique importance in the tale ('he held the
> wrath of Melko from them for many years'), especially as Beleg, his
> companion-in-arms in the later versions, is not here mentioned.

In the poem the importance to Doriath of Túrin's warfare is not dimin-
ished, however:

> for by him was holden   the hand of ruin
> from Thingol's folk,   and Thû feared him   (389–90)

We meet here for the first time Thû, *thane most mighty/neath*

*Morgoth Bauglir*. It is interesting to learn that Thû knew of Túrin and feared him, also that Morgoth ordered Thû to assault Doriath: this story will reappear in the *Lay of Leithian*.

In the story of Túrin and Orgof the verses are very clearly following the prose of the *Tale*, and there are many close likenesses of wording, as already noted. The relation of this scene to the later story has been discussed previously (II. 121–2). Orgof still has Gnome-blood, which may imply the continuance of the story that there were Gnomes among Thingol's people (see II. 43). The occasion of Túrin's return from the forest to the Thousand Caves (a name that first occurs in the poem) becomes, as it seems, a great feast, with songs of Valinor – quite unlike the later story, where the occasion is in no way marked out and Thingol and Melian were not in Menegroth (*Narn* p. 79); and Túrin and Orgof were *set on high / near the king and queen* (i.e. presumably on the dais, at the 'high table'). Whether it was a rejection of this idea that caused my father to bracket lines 461–3 and mark them with an X I cannot say. *The secret songs of the sons of Ing* referred to in this passage (421) are not indeed songs of the sons of Ing of the Ælfwine history (II. 301 ff.); this Ing is the Gnomish form of Ingwë, Lord of the First Kindred of the Elves (earlier Inwë Lord of the Teleri).*

The lines concerning Orgof dead are noteworthy:

> his hour had come
> that his soul should seek    the sad pathway
> to the deep valley    of the Dead Awaiting,
> there a thousand years    thrice to ponder
> in the gloom of Gurthrond    his grim jesting,
> ere he fare to Faërie    to feast again.                    (544–9)

With this compare the tale of *The Coming of the Valar and the Building of Valinor* (I. 76):

> There [in the hall of Vê] Mandos spake their doom, and there they waited in the darkness, dreaming of their past deeds, until such time as he appointed when they might again be born into their children, and go forth to laugh and sing again.

The name *Gurthrond* (< *Guthrond*) occurs nowhere else; the first element is doubtless *gurth* 'death', as in the name of Túrin's sword *Gurtholfin* (II. 342).

---

*That *Ing* is the Gnomish form of *Ingwë* appears from the 1926 'Sketch of the Mythology' and the 1930 'Silmarillion'. *Ing* was replaced by *Inwë* in *The Cottage of Lost Play*, but there the Gnomish name of Inwë is *Inwithiel*, changed from *Gim Githil* (I. 16, 22).

There remain a few particular points concerning names. At line 366
*Hithlum* is explained as the name of Dorlómin among Men:

> of dark Dorlómin     with its dreary pines
> that Hithlum unhappy     is hight by Men.

This is curious. In the *Lost Tales* the name of the land among Men was
*Aryador*; so in the *Tale of Turambar* (II. 70):

> In those days my folk dwelt in a vale of Hisilómë and that land did Men
> name Aryador in the tongues they then used.

In the 1930 'Silmarillion' it is specifically stated that *Hithlum* and
*Dorlómin* were Gnomish names for *Hisilómë*, and there seems every
reason to suppose that this was always the case. The answer to the puzzle
may however lie in the same passage of the *Tale of Turambar*, where it is
said that

> often was the story of Turambar and the Foalókë in their [i.e. Men's]
> mouths – but rather after the fashion of the Gnomes did they say
> Turumart and the Fuithlug.

Perhaps then the meaning of line 366 is that Men called Hisilómë
*Hithlum* because they used the Gnomish name, not that it was the name
in their own tongue.
In the following lines (367–8)

> the Shadowy Mountains
> fenced them from Faërie     and the folk of the wood.

This is the first occurrence of the name *Shadowy Mountains*, and it is
used as it was afterwards (*Ered Wethrin*); in the *Lost Tales* the mountains forming the southern fence of Hithlum are called the Iron Mountains or the Bitter Hills (see II. 61).
The name *Cuinlimfin* of the Waters of Awakening (note to line 450)
seems to have been a passing idea, soon abandoned.
Lastly, at line 50 occurs (by emendation in B from *Côr*) the unique
compound name *Corthûn*, while at 430 *the city of Côr* was emended to
*the city of Tún*; see II. 292.

★

II

BELEG

Long time alone     he lived in the hills
a hunter of beast     and hater of Men,                    560
or Orcs, or Elves,     till outcast folk

there one by one,    wild and reckless
around him rallied;    and roaming far
they were feared by both foe    and friend of old.
For hot with hate    was the heart of Túrin,                    565
nor a friend found him    such folk of Thingol
as he wandering met    in the wood's fastness.

There Beleg the brave    on the borders of Doriath
they found and fought    – and few were with him –
and o'erborne by numbers    they bound him at last,            570
till their captain came    to their camp at eve.
Afar from that fight    his fate that day
had taken Túrin    on the trail of the Orcs,
as they hastened home    to the Hills of Iron
with the loot laden    of the lands of Men.                     575
Then soon was him said    that a servant of Thingol
they had tied to a tree –    and Túrin coming
stared astonied    on the stern visage
of Beleg the brave    his brother in arms,
of whom he learned the lore    of leaping blades,              580
and of bended bow    and barbéd shaft,
and the wild woodland's    wisdom secret,
when they blent in battle    the blood of their wounds.

Then Túrin's heart    was turned from hate,
and he bade unbind    Beleg the huntsman.                       585
'Now fare thou free!    But, of friendship aught
if thy heart yet holds    for Húrin's son,
never tell thou tale    that Túrin thou sawst
an outlaw unloved    from Elves and Men,
whom Thingol's thanes    yet thirst to slay.                    590
Betray not my trust    or thy troth of yore!'
Then Beleg of the bow    embraced him there –
he had not fared to the feast    or the fall of Orgof –
there kissed him kindly    comfort speaking:
'Lo! nought know I    of the news thou tellest;                595
but outlawed or honoured    thou ever shalt be
the brother of Beleg,    come bliss come woe!
Yet little me likes    that thy leaping sword
the life should drink    of the leaguered Elves.
Are the grim Glamhoth    then grown so few,                     600
or the foes of Faërie    feeble-hearted,
that warlike Men    have no work to do?

Shall the foes of Faërie   be friends of Men?
Betrayest thou thy troth   whom we trusted of yore?'

'Nor of arméd Orc,   nor [of] Elf of the wood,                    605
nor of any on earth   have I honour or love,
O Beleg the bowman.   This band alone
I count as comrades,   my kindred in woe
and friendless fate –   our foes the world.'

'Let the bow of Beleg   to your band be joined;                  610
and swearing death   to the sons of darkness
let us suage our sorrow   and the smart of fate!
Our valour is not vanquished,   nor vain the glory
that once we did win   in the woods of old.'

Thus hope in the heart   of Húrin's offspring               615
awoke at those words;   and them well likéd
of that band the boldest,   save Blodrin only –
Blodrin Bor's son,   who for blood and for gold
alone lusted,   and little he recked
whom he robbed of riches   or reft of life,               620
were it Elf or Orc;   but he opened not
the thoughts of his heart.   There throbbed the harp,
where the fires flickered,   and the flaming brands
of pine were piled   in the place of their camp;
where glad men gathered   in good friendship         625
as dusk fell down   on the drear woodland.
Then a song on a sudden   soaring loudly –
and the trees up-looming   towering harkened –
was raised of the Wrack   of the Realm of the Gods;
of the need of the Gnomes   on the Narrow Crossing;          630
of the fight at Fangros,   and Fëanor's sons'
oath unbreakable.   Then up sprang Beleg:
'That our vaunt and our vows   be not vain for ever,
even such as they swore,   those seven chieftains,
an oath let us swear   that is unchanging               635
as Tain-Gwethil's   towering mountain!'
Their blades were bared,   as blood shining
in the flame of the fires   while they flashed and touched.
As with one man's voice   the words were spoken,
and the oath uttered   that must unrecalled          640
abide for ever,   a bond of truth
and friendship in arms,   and faith in peril.

Thus war was waked    in the woods once more
for the foes of Faërie,    and its fame widely,
and the fear of that fellowship,    now fared abroad;          645
when the horn was heard    of the hunting Elves
that shook the shaws    and the sheer valleys.
Blades were naked    and bows twanging,
and shafts from the shadows    shooting wingéd,
and the sons of darkness    slain and conquered;          650
even in Angband    the Orcs trembled.
Then the word wandered    down the ways of the forest
that Túrin Thalion    was returned to war;
and Thingol heard it,    and his thanes were sped
to lead the lost one    in love to his halls –          655
but his fate was fashioned    that they found him not.
Little gold they got    in that grim warfare,
but weary watches    and wounds for guerdon;
nor on robber-raids    now rode they ever,
who fended from Faërie    the fiends of Hell.          660
But Blodrin Bor's son    for booty lusted,
for the loud laughter    of the lawless days,
and meats unmeasured,    and mead-goblets
refilled and filled,    and the flagons of wine
that went as water    in their wild revels.          665
Now tales have told    that trapped as a child
he was dragged by the Dwarves    to their deep mansions,
and in Nogrod nurtured,    and in nought was like,
spite blood and birth,    to the blissful Elves.
His heart hated    Húrin's offspring          670
and the bowman Beleg;    so biding his while
he fled their fellowship    and forest hidings
to the merciless Orcs,    whose moon-pallid
cruel-curvéd blades    to kill spare not;
than whose greed for gold    none greater burns          675
save in hungry hearts    of the hell-dragons.
He betrayed his troth;    traitor made him
and the forest fastness    of his fellows in arms
he opened to the Orcs,    nor his oath heeded.
There they fought and fell    by foes outnumbered,          680
by treachery trapped    at a time of night
when their fires faded    and few were waking –
some wakened never,    not for wild noises,
nor cries nor curses,    nor clashing steel,

swept as they slumbered    to the slades of death.          685
But Túrin they took,    though towering mighty
at the Huntsman's hand    he hewed his foemen,
as a bear at bay    mid bellowing hounds,
unheeding his hurts;    at the hest of Morgoth
yet living they lapped him,    his limbs entwining,          690
with hairy hands    and hideous arms.
Then Beleg was buried    in the bodies of the fallen,
as sorely wounded    he swooned away;
and all was over,    and the Orcs triumphed.
The dawn over Doriath    dimly kindled          695
saw Blodrin Bor's son    by a beech standing
with throat thirléd    by a thrusting arrow,
whose shaven shaft,    shod with poison,
and feather-wingéd,    was fast in the tree.
He bargained the blood    of his brothers for gold:          700
thus his meed was meted –    in the mirk at random
by an orc-arrow    his oath came home.

From the magic mazes    of Melian the Queen
they haled unhappy    Húrin's offspring,
lest he flee his fate;    but they fared slowly          705
and the leagues were long    of their laboured way
over hill and hollow    to the high places,
where the peaks and pinnacles    of pitiless stone
looming up lofty    are lapped in cloud,
and veiled in vapours    vast and sable;          710
where Eiglir Engrin,    the Iron Hills, lie
o'er the hopeless halls    of Hell upreared
wrought at the roots    of the roaring cliffs
of Thangorodrim's    thunderous mountain.
Thither led they laden    with loot and evil;          715
but Beleg yet breathed    in blood drenchéd
aswoon, till the sun    to the South hastened,
and the eye of day    was opened wide.
Then he woke and wondered,    and weeping took him,
and to Túrin Thalion    his thoughts were turned,          720
that o'erborne in battle    and bound he had seen.
Then he crawled from the corpses    that had covered him over,
weary, wounded,    too weak to stand.
So Thingol's thanes    athirst and bleeding
in the forest found him:    his fate willed not          725

that he should drink the draught     of death from foes.
Thus they bore him back     in bitter torment
his tidings to tell     in the torchlit halls
of Thingol the king;     in the Thousand Caves
to be healéd whole     by the hands enchanted                    730
of Melian Mablui,     the moonlit queen.

Ere a week was outworn     his wounds were cured,
but his heart's heaviness     those hands of snow
nor soothed nor softened,     and sorrow-laden
he fared to the forest.     No fellows sought he              735
in his hopeless hazard,     but in haste alone
he followed the feet     of the foes of Elfland,
the dread daring,     and the dire anguish,
that held the hearts     of Hithlum's men
and Doriath's doughtiest     in a dream of fear.             740
Unmatched among Men,     or magic-wielding
Elves, or hunters     of the Orc-kindred,
or beasts of prey     for blood pining,
was his craft and cunning,     that cold and dead
an unseen slot     could scent o'er stone,                   745
foot-prints could find     on forest pathways
that lightly on the leaves     were laid in moons
long waned, and washed     by windy rains.
The grim Glamhoth's     goblin armies
go cunning-footed,     but his craft failed not             750
to tread their trail,     till the lands were darkened,
and the light was lost     in lands unknown.
Never-dawning night     was netted clinging
in the black branches     of the beetling trees;
oppressed by pungent     pinewood's odours,                  755
and drowsed with dreams     as the darkness thickened,
he strayed steerless.     The stars were hid,
and the moon mantled.     There magic foundered
in the gathering glooms,     there goblins even
(whose deep eyes drill     the darkest shadows)              760
bewildered wandered,     who the way forsook
to grope in the glades,     there greyly loomed
of girth unguessed     in growth of ages
the topless trunks     of trees enchanted.
That fathomless fold     by folk of Elfland                  765
is Taur-na-Fuin,     the Trackless Forest
of Deadly Nightshade,     dreadly naméd.

Abandoned, beaten,    there Beleg lying
to the wind harkened    winding, moaning
in bending boughs;    to branches creaking                    770
up high over head,    where huge pinions
of the pluméd pine-trees    complained darkly
in black foreboding.    There bowed hopeless,
in wit wildered,    and wooing death,
he saw on a sudden    a slender sheen                         775
shine a-shimmering    in the shades afar,
like a glow-worm's lamp    a-gleaming dim.
He marvelled what it might be    as he moved softly;
for he knew not the Gnomes    of need delving
in the deep dungeons    of dark Morgoth.                      780
Unmatched their magic    in metal-working,
who jewels and gems    that rejoiced the Gods
aforetime fashioned,    when they freedom held,
now swinking slaves    of ceaseless labour
in Angband's smithies,    nor ever were suffered              785
to wander away,    warded always.
But little lanterns    of lucent crystal
and silver cold    with subtlest cunning
they strangely fashioned,    and steadfast a flame
burnt unblinking    there blue and pale,                      790
unquenched for ever.    The craft that lit them
was the jewel-makers'    most jealous secret.
Not Morgoth's might,    nor meed nor torment
them vowed, availed    to reveal that lore;
yet lights and lamps    of living radiance,                   795
many and magical,    they made for him.
No dark could dim them    the deeps wandering;
whose lode they lit    was lost seldom
in groundless grot,    or gulfs far under.

'Twas a Gnome he beheld    on the heaped needles              800
of a pine-tree pillowed,    when peering wary
he crept closer.    The covering pelt
was loosed from the lamp    of living radiance
by his side shining.    Slumber-shrouded
his fear-worn face    was fallen in shade.                    805
Lest in webs woven    of unwaking sleep,
spun round by spells    in those spaces dark,
he lie forlorn    and lost for ever,
the Hunter hailed him    in the hushed forest –

to the drowsy deeps    of his dream profound          810
fear ever-following    came falling loud;
as the lancing lightning    he leapt to his feet
full deeming that dread    and death were upon him,
Flinding go-Fuilin    fleeing in anguish
from the mines of Morgoth.    Marvelling he heard    815
the ancient tongue    of the Elves of Tûn;
and Beleg the Bowman    embraced him there,
and learnt his lineage    and luckless fate,
how thrust to thraldom    in a throng of captives,
from the kindred carried    and the cavernous halls    820
of the Gnomes renowned    of Nargothrond,
long years he laboured    under lashes and flails
of the baleful Balrogs,    abiding his time.
A tale he unfolded    of terrible flight
o'er flaming fell    and fuming hollow,    825
o'er the parchéd dunes    of the Plains of Drouth,
till his heart took hope    and his heed was less.
'Then Taur-na-Fuin    entangled my feet
in its mazes enmeshed;    and madness took me
that I wandered witless,    unwary stumbling    830
and beating the boles    of the brooding pines
in idle anger –    and the Orcs heard me.
They were camped in a clearing,    that close at hand
by mercy I missed.    Their marching road
is beaten broad    through the black shadows    835
by wizardry warded    from wandering Elves;
but dread they know    of the Deadly Nightshade,
and in haste only    do they hie that way.
Now cruel cries    and clamorous voices
awoke in the wood,    and winged arrows    840
from horny bows    hummed about me;
and following feet,    fleet and stealthy,
were padding and pattering    on the pine-needles;
and hairy hands    and hungry fingers
in the glooms groping,    as I grovelled fainting    845
till they cowering found me.    Fast they clutched me
beaten and bleeding,    and broken in spirit
they laughing led me,    my lagging footsteps
with their spears speeding.    Their spoils were piled,
and countless captives    in that camp were chained,    850
and Elfin maids    their anguish mourning.

But one they watched,    warded sleepless,
was stern-visaged, strong,    and in stature tall
as are Hithlum's men    of the misty hills.
Full length he lay    and lashed to pickets                    855
in baleful bonds,    yet bold-hearted
his mouth no mercy    of Morgoth sued,
but defied his foes.    Foully they smote him.
Then he called, as clear    as cry of hunter
that hails his hounds    in hollow places,                     860
on the name renowned    of that noblest king –
but men unmindful    remember him little –
Húrin Thalion,    who Erithámrod hight,
the Unbending,    for Orc and Balrog
and Morgoth's might    on the mountain yet                     865
he defies fearless,    on a fangéd peak
of thunder-riven    Thangorodrim.'

In eager anger    then up sprang Beleg,
crying and calling,    careless of Flinding:
'O Túrin, Túrin,    my troth-brother,                          870
to the brazen bonds    shall I abandon thee,
and the darkling doors    of the Deeps of Hell?'

'Thou wilt join his journey    to the jaws of sorrow,
O bowman crazéd,    if thy bellowing cry
to the Orcs should come;    their ears than cats'              875
are keener whetted,    and though the camp from here
be a day distant    where those deeds I saw,
who knows if the Gnome    they now pursue
that crept from their clutches,    as a crawling worm
on belly cowering,    whom they bleeding cast                  880
in deathly swoon    on the dung and slough
of their loathsome lair.    O Light of Valinor!
and ye glorious Gods!    How gleam their eyes,
and their tongues are red!'    'Yet I Túrin will wrest
from their hungry hands,    or to Hell be dragged,             885
or sleep with the slain    in the slades of Death.
Thy lamp shall lead us,    and my lore rekindle
and wise wood-craft!'    'O witless hunter,
thy words are wild –    wolves unsleeping
and wizardry ward    their woeful captives;                    890
unerring their arrows;    the icy steel
of their curvéd blades    cleaves unblunted

the meshes of mail;   the mirk to pierce
those eyes are able;   their awful laughter
the flesh freezes!   I fare not thither,                           895
for fear fetters me    in the Forest of Night:
better die in the dark    dazed, forwandered,
than wilfully woo    that woe and anguish!
I know not the way.'   'Are the knees then weak
of Flinding go-Fuilin?   Shall free-born Gnome          900
thus show himself    a shrinking slave,
who twice entrapped    has twice escaped?
Remember the might    and the mirth of yore,
the renown of the Gnomes    of Nargothrond!'

Thus Beleg the bowman    quoth bold-hearted,           905
but Flinding fought    the fear of his heart,
and loosed the light    of his lamp of blue,
now brighter burning.    In the black mazes
enwound they wandered,    weary searching;
by the tall tree-boles    towering silent                        910
oft barred and baffled;    blindly stumbling
over rock-fast roots    writhing coiléd;
and drowsed with dreams    by the dark odours,
till hope was hidden.    'Hark thee, Flinding;
viewless voices    vague and distant,                            915
a muffled murmur    of marching feet
that are shod with stealth    shakes the stillness.'

'No noise I hear',    the Gnome answered,
'thy hope cheats thee.'   'I hear the chains
clinking, creaking,    the cords straining,                      920
and wolves padding    on worn pathways.
I smell the blood    that is smeared on blades
that are cruel and crooked;    the croaking laughter –
now, listen! louder    and louder comes,'
the hunter said.    'I hear no sound',                           925
quoth Flinding fearful.    'Then follow after!'
with bended bow    then Beleg answered,
'my cunning rekindles,    my craft needs not
thy lamp's leading.'    Leaping swiftly
he shrank in the shadows;    with shrouded lantern        930
Flinding followed him,    and the forest-darkness
and drowsy dimness    drifted slowly
unfolding from them    in fleeing shadows,

and its magic was minished,    till they marvelling saw
they were brought to its borders.    There black-gaping          935
an archway opened.    By ancient trunks
it was framed darkly,    that in far-off days
the lightning felled,    now leaning gaunt
their lichen-leprous    limbs uprooted.
There shadowy bats    that shrilled thinly                       940
flew in and flew out    the air brushing
as they swerved soundless.    A swooning light
faint filtered in,    for facing North
they looked o'er the leagues    of the lands of mourning,
o'er the bleak boulders,    o'er the blistered dunes             945
and dusty drouth    of Dor-na-Fauglith;
o'er that Thirsty Plain,    to the threatening peaks,
now glimpséd grey    through the grim archway,
of the marching might    of the Mountains of Iron,
and faint and far    in the flickering dusk                      950
the thunderous towers    of Thangorodrim.
But backward broad    through the black shadows
from that darkling door    dimly wandered
the ancient Orc-road;    and even as they gazed
the silence suddenly    with sounds of dread                     955
was shaken behind them,    and shivering echoes
from afar came fleeting.    Feet were tramping;
trappings tinkling;    and the troublous murmur
of viewless voices    in the vaulted gloom
came near and nearer.    'Ah! now I hear',                       960
said Flinding fearful;    'flee we swiftly
from hate and horror    and hideous faces,
from fiery eyes    and feet relentless!
Ah! woe that I wandered    thus witless hither!'

Then beat in his breast,    foreboding evil,                     965
with dread unwonted    the dauntless heart
of Beleg the brave.    With blanchéd cheeks
in faded fern    and the feathery leaves
of brown bracken    they buried them deep,
where dank and dark    a ditch was cloven                        970
on the wood's borders    by waters oozing,
dripping down to die    in the drouth below.
Yet hardly were they hid    when a host to view
round a dark turning    in the dusky shadows

came swinging sudden     with a swift thudding                          975
of feet after feet     on fallen leaves.
In rank on rank     of ruthless spears
that war-host went;     weary stumbling
countless captives,     cruelly laden
with bloodstained booty,     in bonds of iron                          980
they haled behind them,     and held in ward
by the wolf-riders     and the wolves of Hell.
Their road of ruin     was a-reek with tears:
many a hall and homestead,     many a hidden refuge
of Gnomish lords     by night beleaguered                             985
their o'ermastering might     of mirth bereft,
and fair things fouled,     and fields curdled
with the bravest blood     of the beaten people.

To an army of war     was the Orc-band waxen
that Blodrin Bor's son     to his bane guided                         990
to the wood-marches,     by the welded hosts
homeward hurrying     to the halls of mourning
swiftly swollen     to a sweeping plague.
Like a throbbing thunder     in the threatening deeps
of cavernous clouds     o'ercast with gloom                           995
now swelled on a sudden     a song most dire,
and their hellward hymn     their home greeted;
flung from the foremost     of the fierce spearmen,
who viewed mid vapours     vast and sable
the threefold peaks     of Thangorodrim,                             1000
it rolled rearward,     rumbling darkly,
like drums in distant     dungeons empty.
Then a werewolf howled;     a word was shouted
like steel on stone;     and stiffly raised
their spears and swords     sprang up thickly                        1005
as the wild wheatfields     of the wargod's realm
with points that palely     pricked the twilight.
As by wind wafted     then waved they all,
and bowed, as the bands     with beating measured
moved on mirthless     from the mirky woods,                         1010
from the topless trunks     of Taur-na-Fuin,
neath the leprous limbs     of the leaning gate.

Then Beleg the bowman     in bracken cowering,
on the loathly legions     through the leaves peering,
saw Túrin the tall     as he tottered forward                        1015

neath the whips of the Orcs    as they whistled o'er him;
and rage arose    in his wrathful heart,
and piercing pity    outpoured his tears.
The hymn was hushed;    the host vanished
down the hellward slopes    of the hill beyond;                    1020
and silence sank    slow and gloomy
round the trunks of the trees    of Taur-na-Fuin,
and nethermost night    drew near outside.

'Follow me, Flinding,    from the forest curséd!
Let us haste to his help,    to Hell if need be                    1025
or to death by the darts    of the dread Glamhoth!':
and Beleg bounded    from the bracken madly,
like a deer driven    by dogs baying
from his hiding in the hills    and hollow places;
and Flinding followed    fearful after him                    1030
neath the yawning gate,    through yew-thickets,
through bogs and bents    and bushes shrunken,
till they reached the rocks    and the riven moorlands
and friendless fells    falling darkly
to the dusty dunes    of Dor-na-Fauglith.                    1035
In a cup outcarven    on the cold hillside,
whose broken brink    was bleakly fringed
with bended bushes    bowed in anguish
from the North-wind's knife,    beneath them far
the feasting camp    of their foes was laid;                    1040
the fiery flare    of fuming torches,
and black bodies    in the blaze they saw
crossing countlessly,    and cries they heard
and the hollow howling    of hungry wolves.

Then a moon mounted    o'er the mists riding,                    1045
and the keen radiance    of the cold moonshine
the shadows sharpened    in the sheer hollows,
and slashed the slopes    with slanting blackness;
in wreaths uprising    the reek of fires
was touched to tremulous    trails of silver.                    1050
Then the fires faded,    and their foemen slumbered
in a sleep of surfeit.    No sentinel watched,
nor guards them girdled –    what good were it
to watch wakeful    in those withered regions
neath Eiglir Engrin,    whence the eyes of Bauglir                    1055
gazed unclosing    from the gates of Hell?

Did not werewolves' eyes    unwinking gleam
in the wan moonlight –    the wolves that sleep not,
that sit in circles    with slavering tongues
round camp or clearing    of the cruel Glamhoth?          1060
Then was Beleg a-shudder,    and the unblinking eyes
nigh chilled his marrow    and chained his flesh
in fear unfathomed,    as flat to earth
by a boulder he lay.    Lo! black cloud-drifts
surged up like smoke    from the sable North,          1065
and the sheen was shrouded    of the shivering moon;
the wind came wailing    from the woeful mountains,
and the heath unhappy    hissed and whispered;
and the moans came faint    of men in torment
in the camp accursed.    His quiver rattled          1070
as he found his feet    and felt his bow,
hard horn-pointed,    by hands of cunning
of black yew wrought;    with bears' sinews
it was stoutly strung;    strength to bend it
had nor Man nor Elf    save the magic helped him          1075
that Beleg the bowman    now bore alone.
No arrows of the Orcs    so unerring wingéd
as his shaven shafts    that could shoot to a mark
that was seen but in glance    ere gloom seized it.
Then Dailir he drew,    his dart beloved;          1080
howso far fared it,    or fell unnoted,
unsought he found it    with sound feathers
and barbs unbroken    (till it broke at last);
and fleet bade he fly    that feather-pinioned
snaketonguéd shaft,    as he snicked the string          1085
in the notch nimbly,    and with naked arm
to his ear drew it.    The air whistled,
and the tingling string    twanged behind it,
soundless a sentinel    sank before it –
there was one of the wolves    that awaked no more.          1090
Now arrows after    he aimed swiftly
that missed not their mark    and meted silent
death in the darkness    dreadly stinging,
till three of the wolves    with throats piercéd,
and four had fallen    with fleet-wingéd          1095
arrows a-quivering    in their quenchéd eyes.
Then great was the gap    in the guard opened,
and Beleg his bow    unbent, and said:

'Wilt come to the camp,     comrade Flinding,
or await me watchful?     If woe betide                    1100
thou might win with word     through the woods homeward
to Thingol the king     how throve my quest,
how Túrin the tall     was trapped by fate,
how Beleg the bowman     to his bane hasted.'
Then Flinding fiercely,     though fear shook him:        1105
'I have followed thee far,     O forest-walker,
nor will leave thee now     our league denying!'
Then both bow and sword     Beleg left there
with his belt unbound     in the bushes tangled
of a dark thicket     in a dell nigh them,                 1110
and Flinding there laid     his flickering lamp
and his nailéd shoes,     and his knife only
he kept, that uncumbered     he might creep silent.

Thus those brave in dread     down the bare hillside
towards the camp clambered     creeping wary,             1115
and dared that deed     in days long past
whose glory has gone     through the gates of earth,
and songs have sung     unceasing ringing
wherever the Elves     in ancient places
had light or laughter     in the later world.             1120
With breath bated     on the brink of the dale
they stood and stared     through stealthy shadows,
till they saw where the circle     of sleepless eyes
was broken; with hearts     beating dully
they passed the places     where pierced and bleeding     1125
the wolves weltered     by wingéd death
unseen smitten;     as smoke noiseless
they slipped silent     through the slumbering throngs
as shadowy wraiths     shifting vaguely
from gloom to gloom,     till the Gods brought them        1130
and the craft and cunning     of the keen huntsman
to Túrin the tall     where he tumbled lay
with face downward     in the filthy mire,
and his feet were fettered,     and fast in bonds
anguish enchained     his arms behind him.                 1135
There he slept or swooned,     as sunk in oblivion
by drugs of darkness     deadly blended;
he heard not their whispers;     no hope stirred him
nor the deep despair     of his dreams fathomed;

to awake his wit    no words availed.                          1140
No blade would bite    on the bonds he wore,
though Flinding felt    for the forgéd knife
of dwarfen steel,    his dagger prizéd,
that at waist he wore    awake or sleeping,
whose edge would eat    through iron noiseless              1145
as a clod of clay    is cleft by the share.
It was wrought by wrights    in the realms of the East,
in black Belegost,    by the bearded Dwarves
of troth unmindful;    it betrayed him now
from its sheath slipping    as o'er shaggy slades          1150
and roughhewn rocks    their road they wended.

'We must bear him back    as best we may,'
said Beleg, bending    his broad shoulders.
Then the head he lifted    of Húrin's offspring,
and Flinding go-Fuilin    the feet claspéd;               1155
and doughty that deed,    for in days long gone
though Men were of mould    less mighty builded
ere the earth's goodness    from the Elves they drew,
though the Elfin kindreds    ere old was the sun
were of might unminished,    nor the moon haunted         1160
faintly fading    as formed of shadows
in places unpeopled,    yet peers they were not
in bone and flesh    and body's fashioning,
and Túrin was tallest    of the ten races
that in Hithlum's hills    their homes builded.          1165
Like a log they lifted    his limbs mighty,
and straining staggered    with stealth and fear,
with bodies bending    and bones aching,
from the cruel dreaming    of the camp of dread,
where spearmen drowsed    sprawling drunken              1170
by their moon-blades keen    with murder whetted
mid their shaven shafts    in sheaves piléd.

Now Beleg the brave    backward led them,
but his foot fumbled    and he fell thudding
with Túrin atop of him,    and trembling stumbled         1175
Flinding forward;    there frozen lying
long while they listened    for alarm stirring,
for hue and cry,    and their hearts cowered;
but unbroken the breathing    of the bands sleeping,
as darkness deepened    to dead midnight,                 1180

and the lifeless hour    when the loosened soul
oft sheds the shackles    of the shivering flesh.
Then dared their dread    to draw its breath,
and they found their feet    in the fouléd earth,
and bent they both    their backs once more                        1185
to their task of toil,    for Túrin woke not.
There the huntsman's hand    was hurt deeply,
as he groped on the ground,    by a gleaming point –
'twas Dailir his dart    dearly prizéd
he had found by his foot    in fragments twain,                     1190
and with barbs bended:    it broke at last
neath his body falling.    It boded ill.

As in dim dreaming,    and dazed with horror,
they won their way    with weary slowness,
foot by footstep,    till fate them granted                        1195
the leaguer at last    of those lairs to pass,
and their burden laid they,    breathless gasping,
on bare-bosméd earth,    and abode a while,
ere by winding ways    they won their path
up the slanting slopes    with silent labour,                      1200
with spended strength    sprawling to cast them
in the darkling dell    neath the deep thicket.
Then sought his sword,    and songs of magic
o'er its eager edge    with Elfin voice
there Beleg murmured,    while bluely glimmered                     1205
the lamp of Flinding    neath the lacéd thorns.
There wondrous wove he    words of sharpness,
and the names of knives    and Gnomish blades
he uttered o'er it:    even Ogbar's spear
and the glaive of Gaurin    whose gleaming stroke                   1210
did rive the rocks    of Rodrim's hall;
the sword of Saithnar,    and the silver blades
of the enchanted children    of chains forgéd
in their deep dungeon;    the dirk of Nargil,
the knife of the North    in Nogrod smithied;                      1215
the sweeping sickle    of the slashing tempest,
the lambent lightning's    leaping falchion
even Celeg Aithorn    that shall cleave the world.

Then whistling whirled he    the whetted sword-blade
and three times three    it threshed the gloom,                    1220
till flame was kindled    flickering strangely

like licking firelight    in the lamp's glimmer
blue and baleful    at the blade's edges.
Lo! a leering laugh    lone and dreadful
by the wind wafted    wavered nigh them;                    1225
their limbs were loosened    in listening horror;
they fancied the feet    of foes approaching,
for the horns hearkening    of the hunt afoot
in the rustling murmur    of roving breezes.
Then quickly curtained    with its covering pelt           1230
was the lantern's light,    and leaping Beleg
with his sword severed    the searing bonds
on wrist and arm    like ropes of hemp
so strong that whetting;    in stupor lying
entangled still    lay Túrin moveless.                     1235
For the feet's fetters    then feeling in the dark
Beleg blundering    with his blade's keenness
unwary wounded    the weary flesh
of wayworn foot,    and welling blood
bedewed his hand –    too dark his magic:                  1240
that sleep profound    was sudden fathomed;
in fear woke Túrin,    and a form he guessed
o'er his body bending    with blade naked.
His death or torment    he deemed was come,
for oft had the Orcs    for evil pastime                   1245
him goaded gleeful    and gashed with knives
that they cast with cunning,    with cruel spears.
Lo! the bonds were burst    that had bound his hands:
his cry of battle    calling hoarsely
he flung him fiercely    on the foe he dreamed,            1250
and Beleg falling    breathless earthward
was crushed beneath him.    Crazed with anguish
then seized that sword    the son of Húrin,
to his hand lying    by the help of doom;
at the throat he thrust;    through he pierced it,         1255
that the blood was buried    in the blood-wet mould;
ere Flinding knew    what fared that night,
all was over.    With oath and curse
he bade the goblins    now guard them well,
or sup on his sword:    'Lo! the son of Húrin              1260
is freed from his fetters.'    His fancy wandered
in the camps and clearings    of the cruel Glamhoth.
Flight he sought not    at Flinding leaping

with his last laughter,    his life to sell
amid foes imagined;    but Fuilin's son                              1265
there stricken with amaze,    starting backward,
cried: 'Magic of Morgoth!    A! madness damned!
with friends thou fightest!' –    then falling suddenly
the lamp o'erturned    in the leaves shrouded
that its light released    illumined pale                             1270
with its flickering flame    the face of Beleg.
Then the boles of the trees    more breathless rooted
stone-faced he stood    staring frozen
on that dreadful death,    and his deed knowing
wildeyed he gazed    with waking horror,                             1275
as in endless anguish    an image carven.
So fearful his face    that Flinding crouched
and watched him, wondering    what webs of doom
dark, remorseless,    dreadly meshed him
by the might of Morgoth;    and he mourned for him,                   1280
and for Beleg, who bow    should bend no more,
his black yew-wood    in battle twanging –
his life had winged    to its long waiting
in the halls of the Moon    o'er the hills of the sea.

Hark! he heard the horns    hooting loudly,                           1285
no ghostly laughter    of grim phantom,
no wraithlike feet    rustling dimly –
the Orcs were up;    their ears had hearkened
the cries of Túrin;    their camp was tumult,
their lust was alight    ere the last shadows                         1290
of night were lifted.    Then numb with fear
in hoarse whisper    to unhearing ears
he told his terror;    for Túrin now
with limbs loosened    leaden-eyed was bent
crouching crumpled    by the corse moveless;                         1295
nor sight nor sound    his senses knew,
and wavering words    he witless murmured,
'A! Beleg,' he whispered,    'my brother-in-arms.'
Though Flinding shook him,    he felt it not:
had he comprehended    he had cared little.                          1300
Then winds were wakened    in wild dungeons
where thrumming thunders    throbbed and rumbled;
storm came striding    with streaming banners
from the four corners    of the fainting world;

then the clouds were cloven    with a crash of lightning,          1305
and slung like stones    from slings uncounted
the hurtling hail    came hissing earthward,
with a deluge dark    of driving rain.
Now wafted high,    now wavering far,
the cries of the Glamhoth    called and hooted,               1310
and the howl of wolves    in the heavens' roaring
was mingled mournful:    they missed their paths,
for swollen swept there    swirling torrents
down the blackening slopes,    and the slot was blind,
so that blundering back    up the beaten road             1315
to the gates of gloom    many goblins wildered
were drowned or drawn    in Deadly Nightshade
to die in the dark;    while dawn came not,
while the storm-riders    strove and thundered
all the sunless day,    and soaked and drenched            1320
Flinding go-Fuilin    with fear speechless
there crouched aquake;    cold and lifeless
lay Beleg the bowman;    brooding dumbly
Túrin Thalion    neath the tangled thorns
sat unseeing    without sound or movement.              1325

The dusty dunes    of Dor-na-Fauglith
hissed and spouted.    Huge rose the spires
of smoking vapour    swathed and reeking,
thick-billowing clouds    from thirst unquenched,
and dawn was kindled    dimly lurid               1330
when a day and night    had dragged away.
The Orcs had gone,    their anger baffled,
o'er the weltering ways    weary faring
to their hopeless halls    in Hell's kingdom;
no thrall took they    Túrin Thalion –               1335
a burden bore he    than their bonds heavier,
in despair fettered    with spirit empty
in mourning hopeless    he remained behind.

★

## NOTES

617    *Blodrin*: *Bauglir* A, and B as typed. See line 618.
618    *Bauglir Ban's son* A, and B as typed (*Bauglir* > *Blodrin*

carefully-made early change, *Ban* > *Bor* hasty and later).
See lines 661, 696, 990.

631   *Fangair* A, *Fangros* B as typed.

636   *Tengwethiel* [*sic*] A, *Tain-Gwethil* B as typed. Cf. line 431.

653   *Túrin Thaliodrin* A, and B as typed. Cf. lines 115, 333, 720.

661, 696   As at line 618.

711   *Aiglir-angrin* A, *Aiglir Angrin* B as typed, emended
roughly in pencil to *Eiglir Engrin*; cf. line 1055. In the *Tale
of Turambar* occurs *Angorodin* (the Iron Mountains),
II.77.

711–14   These lines read in A (and as typed in B, with *of Hell is
reared* for *of the Hells of Iron*):

> where Aiglir-angrin   the Iron Hills lie
> and Thangorodrim's   thunderous mountain
> o'er the hopeless halls   of the Hells of iron
> wrought at the roots   of the ruthless hills.

718   Cf. Bilbo's second riddle to Gollum.

720   As at line 653.

780   *Delimorgoth* A, *Delu-Morgoth* B as typed, *dark Morgoth* a late pencilled emendation. At lines 11 and 51 *Delu-Morgoth* is an emendation of *Delimorgoth* in B.

816   *Tûn* also in A; see lines 50, 430.

818–20   Against these lines my father wrote in the margin of B:
'Captured in battle at gates of Angband.'

826   *o'er the black boulders  of the Blasted Plain* A (marked
with query).

834   *mercy: magic* A, and B as typed; *mercy* in pencil and not
quite certain.

946   *Daideloth* A emended at time of writing to *Dor-na-
Maiglos*, *Dor-na-Fauglith* B as typed. In margin of A is
written: 'a plateau from *Dai* "high", *Deloth* "plain"'; contrast II. 337, entry *Dor-na-Dhaideloth*.

990   *Blodrin Ban's son* A, and B as typed; *Ban's* > *Bor's* later
in B. At lines 617–18, 661, 696 A, and B as typed, had
*Bauglir*, changed to *Blodrin* in B.

1055   *Aiglir Angrin* A, and B as typed; see line 711.
*Bauglir* A and B.

1098   This line is emended in B, but the reading is uncertain:
apparently *Then his bow unbending  Beleg asked him:*

1137   In the margin of B is written *r?*, i.e. *dreadly* for *deadly*.

1147   *East: South* A, and B as typed.

1198   *bosméd* (bosomed) written thus in both A and B.

1214   *Nargil: Loruin* A, with *Nargil* added as an alternative.

1324   *Túrin Thaliodrin* A, and B as typed; see lines 653, 720.

1335   *Thalion-Túrin* A, and B as typed.

## Commentary on *Part II 'Beleg'*

In this part of the poem there are some narrative developments of much
interest. The poem follows the *Tale* (II. 76) in making Beleg become one
of Túrin's band on the marches of Doriath not long after Túrin's departure from the Thousand Caves, and with no intervening event – in *The
Silmarillion* (p. 200) Beleg came to Menegroth, and after speaking to
Thingol set out to seek Túrin, while in the *Narn* (pp. 82–5) there is the
'trial of Túrin', and the intervention of Beleg bringing Nellas as witness,
before he set out on Túrin's trail. In the poem it is explicit that Beleg was
not searching for him, and indeed knew nothing whatever of what had
passed in the Thousand Caves (595). But Túrin's band are no longer the
'wild spirits' of the *Tale*; they are hostile to all comers, whether Orcs or
Men or Elves, including the Elves of Doriath (560–1, 566), as in *The
Silmarillion*, and in far greater detail in the *Narn*, where the band is
called *Gaurwaith*, the Wolf-men, 'to be feared as wolves'.

The element of Beleg's capture and maltreatment by the band now
appears, and also that of Túrin's absence from the camp at the time.
Several features of the story in the *Narn* are indeed already present in the
poem, though absent from the more condensed account in *The Silmarillion*: as Beleg's being tied to a tree by the outlaws (577, *Narn* pp. 92–3),
and the occasion of Túrin's absence – he was

> on the trail of the Orcs,
> as they hastened home    to the Hills of Iron
> with the loot laden    of the lands of Men

just as in the *Narn* (pp. 91–2), where however the story is part of a
complex set of movements among the Woodmen of Brethil, Beleg, the
Gaurwaith, and the Orcs.

Whereas in the *Tale* it was only now that Beleg and Túrin became
companions-in-arms, we have already seen that the poem has the later
story whereby they had fought together on the marches of Doriath before
Túrin's flight from the Thousand Caves (p. 27); and we now have also
the development that Túrin's altered mood at the sight of Beleg tied to
the tree (*Then Túrin's heart    was turned from hate*, 584), and Beleg's
own reproaches (*Shall the foes of Faërie    be friends of Men?* 603),
led to the band's turning their arms henceforth only against *the foes of
Faërie* (644). Of the great oath sworn by the members of the band,
explicitly echoing that of the Sons of Fëanor (634) – and showing
incidentally that in that oath the holy mountain of Taniquetil (Tain-
Gwethil) was taken in witness (636), there is no trace in *The Silmarillion*
or the *Narn*: in the latter, indeed, the outlaws are not conceived in such a
way as to make such an oath-taking at all probable.

Lines 643 ff., describing the prowess of the fellowship in the forest, are
the ultimate origin of the never finally achieved story of the Land of
Dor-Cúarthol (*The Silmarillion* p. 205, *Narn* pp. 152–4); lines 651–4

even in Angband    the Orcs trembled.
Then the word wandered    down the ways of the forest
that Túrin Thalion    was returned to war;
and Thingol heard it . . .

lead in the end to

In Menegroth, and in the deep halls of Nargothrond, and even in the
hidden realm of Gondolin, the fame of the deeds of the Two Captains
was heard; and in Angband also they were known.

But in the later story Túrin was hidden under the name Gorthol, the
Dread Helm, and it was his wearing of the Dragon-helm that revealed
him to Morgoth. There is no suggestion of this in the earlier phase of the
legend; the Dragon-helm makes no further appearance here in the poem.
    A table may serve to clarify the development:

| Tale | Lay | Silmarillion and Narn |
|---|---|---|
| Túrin's prowess on the marches of Doriath (Beleg not mentioned). | Túrin and Beleg companions-in-arms on the marches of Doriath; Túrin wears the Dragon-helm. | As in the poem. |
| Death of Orgof. | Death of Orgof. | Death of Saeros. |
| Túrin leaves Doriath; a band forms round him which includes Beleg. | Túrin leaves Doriath; a band of outlaws forms round him which attacks all comers. | Túrin leaves Doriath and joins a band of desperate outlaws. |
| | The band captures Beleg (who knows nothing of Túrin's leaving Doriath) and ties him to a tree. | The band captures Beleg (who is searching for Túrin bearing Thingol's pardon) (and ties him to a tree, Narn). |
| | Túrin has him set free; suffers a change of heart; Beleg joins the band; all swear an oath. | Túrin has him set free; suffers a change of heart; but Beleg will not join the band and departs. (No mention of oath.) |
| Great prowess of the band. | Great prowess of the band against the Orcs. | (Later Beleg returns and joins the band:) Land of Dor-Cúarthol. |

Before leaving this part of the story, it may be suggested that lines
605 ff., in which Túrin declares to Beleg that *This band alone / I count*

*as comrades*, contain the germ of Túrin's words to him in the *Narn*, p. 94:

> The grace of Thingol will not stretch to receive these companions of my fall, I think; but I will not part with them now, if they do not wish to part with me, &c.

The traitor, who betrayed the band to the Orcs, now first appears. At first he is called *Bauglir* both in A and in B as originally typed; and it might be thought that the name had much too obviously an evil significance. The explanation is quite clearly, however, that *Bauglir* became *Blodrin* at the same time as *Bauglir* replaced *Belcha* as a name of Morgoth. (By the time my father reached line 990 *Blodrin* is the name as first written in both A and B; while similarly at line 1055 *Bauglir* is Morgoth's name, not *Belcha*, both in A and B as first written.) The change of *Ban* (father of Blodrin) to *Bor* was passing; he is *Ban* in the 1926 'Sketch of the Mythology', and so remained until, much later, he disappeared.

Blodrin's origin is interesting:

>                 trapped as a child
> he was dragged by the Dwarves    to their deep mansions,
> and in Nogrod nurtured,    and in nought was like,
> spite blood and birth,    to the blissful Elves.         (666–9)

Thus Blodrin's evil nature is explicitly ascribed to the influence of *the bearded Dwarves / of troth unmindful* (1148–9); and Blodrin follows Ufedhin of the *Tale of the Nauglafring* as an example of the sinister effect of Elvish association with Dwarves – not altogether absent in the tale of Eöl and Maeglin as it appears in *The Silmarillion*. Though the nature – and name – of the traitor in Túrin's band went through Protean mutations afterwards, it is not inconceivable that recollection of the Dwarvish element in Blodrin's history played some part in the emergence of Mîm in this rôle. On the early hostile view of the Dwarves see II. 247. The words of the poem just cited arise from the 'betrayal' of Flinding by his dwarvish knife, which slipped from its sheath; so later, in the *Lay of Leithian*, when Beren attempted to cut a second Silmaril from the Iron Crown (lines 4160–2)

> The dwarvish steel of cunning blade
> by treacherous smiths of Nogrod made
> snapped . . .

The idea expressed in the *Tale* (II. 76) that Túrin was taken alive by Morgoth's command 'lest he cheat the doom that was devised for him' reappears in the poem: *lest he flee his fate* (705).

The rest of the story as told in the poem differs only in detail from that in the *Tale*. The survival of Beleg in the attack by Orcs and his swift recovery from his grievous wounds (II. 77), present in much changed circumstances in *The Silmarillion* (p. 206), is here made perhaps more comprehensible, in that Elves from Doriath, who were searching for Túrin (654–5), found Beleg and took him back to be healed by Melian in the Thousand Caves (727–31). In the account of Beleg's meeting with Flinding in Taur-na-Fuin, led to him by his blue lamp, the poem is following the *Tale* very closely.* My father's painting of the scene (*Pictures by J. R. R. Tolkien* no. 37) was almost certainly made a few years later, when the Elf lying under the tree was still called Flinding son of Fuilin (in the *Tale bo-Dhuilin*, earlier *go-Dhuilin*, son of Duilin; the patronymic prefix has in the poem (814, 900) reverted to the earlier form *go-*, see II. 119).

In the *Tale* it is only said (II. 81) that Flinding was of the people of the Rodothlim 'before the Orcs captured him'; from the poem (819–21) it seems that he was carried off, with many others, from Nargothrond, but this can scarcely be the meaning, since *nought yet knew they* [the Orcs] *of Nargothrond* (1578). The marginal note in B against these lines 'Captured in battle at gates of Angband' refers to the later story, first appearing in the 1930 'Silmarillion'.

The poem follows the *Tale* in the detail of Flinding's story to Beleg, except that in the poem he was recaptured by the Orcs in Taur-na-Fuin (846 ff.) and escaped again (*crept from their clutches   as a crawling worm*, 879), whereas in the *Tale* he was not recaptured but 'fled heedlessly' (II. 79). The notable point in the *Tale* that Flinding 'was overjoyed to have speech with a free Noldo' reappears in the poem: *Marvelling he heard / the ancient tongue   of the Elves of Tûn*. The detail of their encountering of the Orc-host is slightly different: in the *Tale* the Orcs had changed their path, in the poem it seems that Beleg and Flinding merely came more quickly than did the Orcs to the point where the Orc-road emerged from the edge of the forest. In the *Tale* it seems indeed that the Orcs had not left the forest when they encamped for the night: the eyes of the wolves 'shone like points of red light among the trees', and Beleg and Flinding laid Túrin down after his rescue 'in the woods at no great distance from the camp'. The *cup outcarven   on the cold hillside* of the poem (1036), where the Orcs made their bivouac, is the 'bare dell' of *The Silmarillion*.

In contrast to the *Tale* (see p. 26) Beleg is now frequently called *Beleg the bowman*, his great bow (not yet named) is fully described, and his unmatched skill as an archer (1071 ff.). There is also in the poem the feature of the arrow Dailir, unfailingly found and always unharmed (1080 ff.), until it broke when Beleg fell upon it while carrying Túrin (1189–92): of this there is never a mention later. The element of Beleg's

---

*The element of the blue lamp is lacking from the account in *The Silmarillion*; see *Unfinished Tales* p. 51 note 2.

archery either arose from, or itself caused, the change in the story of the entry of Beleg and Flinding into the Orc-camp that now appears: in the *Tale* they merely 'crept between the wolves at a point where there was a great gap between them', whereas in the poem Beleg performed the feat of shooting seven wolves in the darkness, and only so was 'a great gap opened' (1097). But the words of the *Tale*, 'as the luck of the Valar had it Túrin was lying nigh', are echoed in

> till the Gods brought them
> and the craft and cunning    of the keen huntsman
> to Túrin the tall    where he tumbled lay          (1130–2)

The lifting and carrying of Túrin by the two Elves, referred to in the *Tale* as 'a great feat', 'seeing that he was a Man and of greater stature than they' (II. 80), is expanded in the poem (1156 ff.) into a comment on the stature of Men and Elves in the ancient time, which agrees with earlier statements on this topic (see I. 235, II. 142, 220). The notable lines

> though Men were of mould    less mighty builded
> ere the earth's goodness    from the Elves they drew  (1157–8)

are to be related to the statements cited in II. 326: 'As Men's stature grows [the Elves'] diminishes', and 'ever as Men wax more powerful and numerous so the fairies fade and grow small and tenuous, filmy and transparent, but Men larger and more dense and gross'. The mention here (1164) of *the ten races* of Hithlum occurs nowhere else, and it is not clear whether it refers to all the peoples of Men and Elves who in one place or another in the *Lost Tales* are set in Hithlum, which as I have remarked 'seems to have been in danger of having too many inhabitants' (see II. 249, 251).

The *Tale* has it that it was Beleg's knife that had slipped from him as he crept into the camp; in the poem it is Flinding's (1142 ff.). In the *Tale* Beleg returned to fetch his sword from the place where he had left it, since they could carry Túrin no further; in the poem they carried Túrin all the way up to the *dark thicket in a dell* whence they had set out (1110, 1202). The 'whetting spell' of Beleg over his (still unnamed) sword is an entirely new element (and without trace later); it arises in association with line 1141, *No blade would bite    on the bonds he wore*. In style it is reminiscent of Lúthien's 'lengthening spell' in Canto V of the *Lay of Leithian*; but of the names in the spell, of *Ogbar*, *Gaurin*, *Rodrim*, *Saithnar*, *Nargil*, *Celeg Aithorn*, there seems to be now no other trace.

There now occurs in the poem the mysterious *leering laugh* (1224), to which it seems that the *ghostly laughter    of grim phantom* in line 1286 refers, and which is mentioned again in the next part of the poem (1488–90). The narrative purpose of this is evidently to cause the covering of the lamp and to cause Beleg to work too quickly in the darkness at the cutting of the bonds. It may be also that the wounding of

Beleg's hand when he put it on the point of Dailir his arrow (1187) accounts for his clumsiness; for every aspect of this powerful scene had been pondered and refined.

In the poem the great storm is introduced: first presaged in lines 1064 ff., when Beleg and Flinding were at the edge of the dell (as it is in *The Silmarillion*):

> Lo! black cloud-drifts
> surged up like smoke    from the sable North,
> and the sheen was shrouded    of the shivering moon;
> the wind came wailing    from the woeful mountains,
> and the heath unhappy    hissed and whispered

and bursting at last after Beleg's death (1301 ff.), to last all through the following day, during which Túrin and Flinding crouched on the hillside (1320, 1330–1). On account of the storm the Orcs were unable to find Túrin, and departed, as in *The Silmarillion*; in the *Tale* Flinding roused Túrin to flee as soon as the shouts of discovery were heard from the Orc-camp, and nothing more is said of the matter. But in the poem it is still, as in the *Tale*, the sudden uncovering of Flinding's lamp as he fell back from Túrin's assault that illumined Beleg's face; in the last account that my father wrote of this episode he was undecided whether it was the cover falling off the lamp or a great flash of lightning that gave the light, and in the published work I chose the latter.

There remain a few isolated points, mostly concerning names. In this part of the poem we meet for the first time:

*Nargothrond* 821, 904;

*Taur-na-Fuin* (for *Taur Fuin* of the *Lost Tales*) 766, 828; called also *Deadly Nightshade* 767, 837, 1317, and *Forest of Night* 896;

*Dor-na-Fauglith* 946, 1035, 1326, called also *the Plains of Drouth* 826, *the Thirsty Plain* 947 (and in A, note to 826, *the Blasted Plain*). The name *Dor-na-Fauglith* arose during the composition of the poem (see note to 946). By this time the story of the blasting of the great northern plain, so that it became a dusty desert, in the battle that ended the Siege of Angband, must have been conceived, though it does not appear in writing for several years.

Here also is the first reference to the triple peaks of Thangorodrim (1000), called *the thunderous towers* (951), though in the 'Prologue' to the poem it is said that Húrin was set *on its steepest peak* (96); and from lines 713–14 (as rewritten in the B-text) we learn that Angband was *wrought at the roots* of the great mountain.

The name *Fangros* (631; *Fangair* A) occurs once elsewhere, in a very obscure note, where it is apparently connected with the burning of the ships of the Noldoli.

Melian's name *Mablui* – *by the hands enchanted of Melian*

*Mablui*, 731 – clearly contains *mab* 'hand', as in *Mablung*, *Ermabwed* (see II. 339).

That the Dwarves were said in A and originally in B to dwell in the South (1147, emended in B to *East*) is perhaps to be related to the statement in the *Tale of the Nauglafring* that Nogrod lay '*a very long journey southward* beyond the wide forest on the borders of those great heaths nigh Umboth-muilin the Pools of Twilight' (II. 225).

I cannot explain the reference in line 1006 to *the wild wheatfields of the wargod's realm*; nor that in the lines concerning Beleg's fate after death to the long waiting of the dead *in the halls of the Moon* (1284).

# III

## FAILIVRIN

Flinding go-Fuilin    faithful-hearted
the brand of Beleg    with blood stainéd                    1340
lifted with loathing    from the leafy mould,
and hid it in the hollow    of a huge thorn-tree;
then he turned to Túrin    yet tranced brooding,
and softly said he:    'O son of Húrin,
unhappy-hearted,    what helpeth it                          1345
to sit thus in sorrow's    silent torment
without hope or counsel?'    But Húrin's son,
by those words wakened,    wildly answered:
'I abide by Beleg;    nor bid me leave him,
thou voice unfaithful.    Vain are all things.              1350
O Death dark-handed,    draw thou near me;
if remorse may move thee,    from mourning loosed
crush me conquered    to his cold bosom!'
Flinding answered,    and fear left him
for wrath and pity:    'Arouse thy pride!                    1355
Not thus unthinking    on Thangorodrim's
heights enchainéd    did Húrin speak.'
'Curse thy comfort!    Less cold were steel.
If Death comes not    to the death-craving,
I will seek him by the sword.    The sword – where lies it?  1360
O cold and cruel,    where cowerest now,
murderer of thy master?    Amends shalt work,
and slay me swift,    O sleep-giver.'
'Look not, luckless,    thy life to steal,

nor sully anew    his sword unhappy                                    1365
in the flesh of the friend    whose freedom seeking
he fell by fate,    by foes unwounded.
Yea, think that amends    are thine to make,
his wrongéd blade    with wrath appeasing,
its thirst cooling    in the thrice-abhorred                           1370
blood of Bauglir's    baleful legions.
Is the feud achieved    thy father's chains
on thee laid, or lessened    by this last evil?
Dream not that Morgoth    will mourn thy death,
or thy dirges chant    the dread Glamhoth –                            1375
less would like them    thy living hatred
and vows of vengeance;    nor vain is courage,
though victory seldom    be valour's ending.'

Then fiercely Túrin    to his feet leaping
cried new-crazéd:  'Ye coward Orcs,                                    1380
why turn ye tail?    Why tarry ye now,
when the son of Húrin    and the sword of Beleg
in wrath await you?    For wrong and woe
here is vengeance ready.    If ye venture it not,
I will follow your feet    to the four corners                        1385
of the angry earth.    Have after you!'
Fainting Flinding    there fought with him,
and words of wisdom    to his witless ears
he breathless spake:  'Abide, O Túrin,
for need hast thou now    to nurse thy hurt,                          1390
and strength to gather    and strong counsel.
Who flees to fight    wears not fear's token,
and vengeance delayed    its vow achieves.'
The madness passed;    amazed pondering
neath the tangled trees    sat Túrin wordless                         1395
brooding blackly    on bitter vengeance,
till the dusk deepened    on his day of waking,
and the early stars    were opened pale.

Then Beleg's burial    in those bleak regions
did Flinding fashion;    where he fell sadly                          1400
he left him lying,    and lightly o'er him
with long labour    the leaves he poured.
But Túrin tearless    turning suddenly
on the corse cast him,    and kissed the mouth
cold and open,    and closed the eyes.                                1405

His bow laid he    black beside him,
and words of parting    wove about him:
'Now fare well, Beleg,    to feasting long
neath Tengwethil    in the timeless halls
where drink the Gods,    neath domes golden          1410
o'er the sea shining.'    His song was shaken,
but the tears were dried    in his tortured eyes
by the flames of anguish    that filled his soul.
His mind once more    was meshed in darkness
as heaped they high    o'er the head beloved          1415
a mound of mould    and mingled leaves.
Light lay the earth    on the lonely dead;
heavy lay the woe    on the heart that lived.
That grief was graven    with grim token
on his face and form,    nor faded ever:          1420
and this was the third    of the throes of Túrin.

Thence he wandered witless    without wish or purpose;
but for Flinding the faithful    he had fared to death,
or been lost in the lands    of lurking evil.
Renewed in that Gnome    of Nargothrond          1425
was heart and valour    by hatred wakened,
that he guarded and guided    his grim comrade;
with the light of his lamp    he lit their ways,
and they hid by day    to hasten by night,
by darkness shrouded    or dim vapours.          1430

The tale tells not    of their travel weary,
how roamed their road    by the rim of the forest,
whose beetling branches,    black o'erhanging,
did greedy grope    with gloomy malice
to ensnare their souls    in silent darkness.          1435
Yet west they wandered    by ways of thirst
and haggard hunger,    hunted often,
and hiding in holes    and hollow caverns,
by their fate defended.    At the furthest end
of Dor-na-Fauglith's    dusty spaces          1440
to a mighty mound    in the moon looming
they came at midnight:    it was crowned with mist,
bedewed as by drops    of drooping tears.
'A! green that hill    with grass fadeless,
where sleep the swords    of seven kindreds,          1445
where the folk of Faërie    once fell uncounted.

There was fought the field    by folk naméd
Nirnaith Ornoth,    Unnumbered Tears.
'Twas built with the blood    of the beaten people;
neath moon nor sun    is it mounted ever                     1450
by Man nor Elf;    not Morgoth's host
ever dare for dread    to delve therein.'
Thus Flinding faltered,    faintly stirring
Túrin's heaviness,    that he turned his hand
toward Thangorodrim,    and thrice he cursed              1455
the maker of mourning,    Morgoth Bauglir.

Thence later led them    their lagging footsteps
o'er the slender stream    of Sirion's youth;
not long had he leapt    a lace of silver
from his shining well    in those shrouded hills,          1460
the Shadowy Mountains    whose sheer summits
there bend humbled    towards the brooding heights
in mist mantled,    the mountains of the North.
Here the Orcs might pass him;    they else dared not
o'er Sirion swim,    whose swelling water                    1465
through moor and marsh,    mead and woodland,
through caverns carven    in the cold bosom
of Earth far under,    through empty lands
and leagues untrodden,    beloved of Ylmir,
fleeting floweth,    with fame undying                       1470
in the songs of the Gnomes,    to the sea at last.
Thus reached they the roots    and the ruinous feet
of those hoary hills    that Hithlum girdle,
the shaggy pinewoods    of the Shadowy Mountains.
There the twain enfolded    phantom twilight               1475
and dim mazes    dark, unholy,
in Nan Dungorthin    where nameless gods
have shrouded shrines    in shadows secret,
more old than Morgoth    or the ancient lords
the golden Gods    of the guarded West.                     1480
But the ghostly dwellers    of that grey valley
hindered nor hurt them,    and they held their course
with creeping flesh    and quaking limb.
Yet laughter at whiles    with lingering echo,
as distant mockery    of demon voices                        1485
there harsh and hollow    in the hushed twilight
Flinding fancied,    fell, unwholesome

as that leering laughter    lost and dreadful
that rang in the rocks    in the ruthless hour
of Beleg's slaughter.    'Tis Bauglir's voice          1490
that dogs us darkly    with deadly scorn'
he shuddering thought;    but the shreds of fear
and black foreboding    were banished utterly
when they clomb the cliffs    and crumbling rocks
that walled that vale    of watchful evil,          1495
and southward saw    the slopes of Hithlum
more warm and friendly.    That way they fared
during the daylight    o'er dale and ghyll,
o'er mountain pasture,    moor and boulder,
over fell and fall    of flashing waters          1500
that slipped down to Sirion,    to swell his tide
in his eastward basin    onward sweeping
to the South, to the sea,    to his sandy delta.

After seven journeys    lo! sleep took them
on a night of stars    when they nigh had stridden          1505
to those lands beloved    that long had known
Flinding aforetime.    At first morning
the white arrows    of the wheeling sun
gazed down gladly    on green hollows
and smiling slopes    that swept before them.          1510
There builded boles    of beeches ancient
marched in majesty    in myriad leaves
of golden russet    greyly rooted,
in leaves translucent    lightly robéd;
their boughs up-bending    blown at morning          1515
by the wings of winds    that wandered down
o'er blossomy bent    breathing odours
to the wavering water's    winking margin.
There rush and reed    their rustling plumes
and leaves like lances    louted trembling          1520
green with sunlight.    Then glad the soul
of Flinding the fugitive;    in his face the morning
there glimmered golden,    his gleaming hair
was washed with sunlight.    'Awake from sadness,
Túrion Thalion,    and troublous thoughts!          1525
On Ivrin's lake    is endless laughter.
Lo! cool and clear    by crystal fountains
she is fed unfailing,    from defilement warded

by Ylmir the old,   who in ancient days,
wielder of waters,   here worked her beauty.                    1530
From outmost Ocean   yet often comes
his message hither   his magic bearing,
the healing of hearts   and hope and valour
for foes of Bauglir.   Friend is Ylmir
who alone remembers   in the Lands of Mirth               1535
the need of the Gnomes.   Here Narog's waters
(that in tongue of the Gnomes   is 'torrent' naméd)
are born, and blithely   boulders leaping
o'er the bents bounding   with broken foam
swirl down southward   to the secret halls                1540
of Nargothrond   by the Gnomes builded
that death and thraldom   in the dreadful throes
of Nirnaith Ornoth,   a number scanty,
escaped unscathed.   Thence skirting wild
the Hills of the Hunters,   the home of Beren              1545
and the Dancer of Doriath   daughter of Thingol,
it winds and wanders   ere the willowy meads,
Nan-Tathrin's land,   for nineteen leagues
it journeys joyful   to join its flood
with Sirion in the South.   To the salt marshes           1550
where snipe and seamew   and the sea-breezes
first pipe and play   they press together
sweeping soundless   to the seats of Ylmir,
where the waters of Sirion   and the waves of the sea
murmurous mingle.   A marge of sand                        1555
there lies, all lit   by the long sunshine;
there all day rustles   wrinkled Ocean,
and the sea-birds call   in solemn conclave,
whitewingéd hosts   whistling sadly,
uncounted voices   crying endlessly.                      1560
There a shining shingle   on that shore lieth,
whose pebbles as pearl   or pale marble
by spray and spindrift   splashed at evening
in the moon do gleam,   or moan and grind
when the Dweller in the Deep   drives in fury             1565
the waters white   to the walls of the land;
when the long-haired riders   on their lathered horses
with bit and bridle   of blowing foam,
in wrack wreathéd   and ropes of seaweed,
to the thunder gallop   of the thudding of the surf.'     1570

Thus Flinding spake    the spell feeling
of Ylmir the old    and unforgetful,
which hale and holy    haunted Ivrin
and foaming Narog,    so that fared there never
Orc of Morgoth,    and that eager stream                    1575
no plunderer passed.    If their purpose held
to reach the realms    that roamed beyond
(nought yet knew they    of Nargothrond)
they harried o'er Hithlum    the heights scaling
that lay behind    the lake's hollow,                       1580
the Shadowy Mountains    in the sheen mirrored
of the pools of Ivrin.    Pale and eager
Túrin hearkened    to the tale of Flinding:
the washing of waters    in his words sounded,
an echo as of Ylmir's    awful conches                      1585
in the abyss blowing.    There born anew
was hope in his heart    as they hastened down
to the lake of laughter.    A long and narrow
arm it reaches    that ancient rocks
o'ergrown with green    girdle strongly,                    1590
at whose outer end    there open sudden
a gap, a gateway    in the grey boulders;
whence thrusteth thin    in threadlike jets
newborn Narog,    nineteen fathoms
o'er a flickering force    falls in wonder,                 1595
and a glimmering goblet    with glass-lucent
fountains fills he    by his freshets carven
in the cool bosom    of the crystal stones.

There deeply drank    ere day was fallen
Túrin the toilworn    and his true comrade;                 1600
hurt's ease found he,    heart's refreshment,
from the meshes of misery    his mind was loosed,
as they sat on the sward    by the sound of water,
and watched in wonder    the westering sun
o'er the wall wading    of the wild mountains,              1605
whose peaks empurpled    pricked the evening.
Then it dropped to the dark    and deep shadows
up the cliffs creeping    quenched in twilight
the last beacons    leashed with crimson.
To the stars upstanding    stony-mantled                    1610
the mountains waited    till the moon arose

o'er the endless East,    and Ivrin's pools
dreaming deeply    dim reflected
their pallid faces.    In pondering fast
woven, wordless,    they waked no sound,                    1615
till cold breezes    keenly breathing
clear and fragrant    curled about them;
then sought they for sleep    a sand-pavéd
cove outcarven;    there kindled fire,
that brightly blossomed    the beechen faggots              1620
in flowers of flame;    floated upward
a slender smoke,    when sudden Túrin
on the firelit face    of Flinding gazed,
and wondering words    he wavering spake:
'O Gnome, I know not    thy name or purpose                 1625
or father's blood –    what fate binds thee
to a witless wayworn    wanderer's footsteps,
the bane of Beleg,    his brother-in-arms?'

Then Flinding fearful    lest fresh madness
should seize for sorrow    on the soul of Túrin,            1630
retold the tale    of his toil and wandering;
how the trackless folds    of Taur-na-Fuin,
Deadly Nightshade,    dreadly meshed him;
of Beleg the bowman    bold, undaunted,
and that deed they dared    on the dim hillside,            1635
that song has since    unceasing wakened;
of the fate that fell,    he faltering spake,
in the tangled thicket    neath the twining thorns
when Morgoth's might    was moved abroad.
Then his voice vanished    veiled in mourning,              1640
and lo! tears trickled    on Túrin's face
till loosed at last    were the leashed torrents
of his whelming woe.    Long while he wept
soundless, shaken,    the sand clutching
with griping fingers    in grief unfathomed.                1645
But Flinding the faithful    feared no longer;
no comfort cold    he kindly found,
for sleep swept him    into slumber dead.
There a singing voice    sweetly vexed him
and he woke and wondered:    the watchfire faded;           1650
the night was aging,    nought was moving
but a song upsoaring    in the soundless dark

went strong and stern    to the starlit heaven.
'Twas Túrin that towering    on the tarn's margin,
up high o'er the head    of the hushed water                   1655
now falling faintly,    let flare and echo
a song of sorrow    and sad splendour,
the dirge of Beleg's    deathless glory.
There wondrous wove he    words enchanted,
that woods and water    waked and answered,               1660
the rocks were wrung    with ruth for Beleg.
That song he sang    is since remembered,
by Gnomes renewed    in Nargothrond
it widely has wakened    warfain armies
to battle with Bauglir –    'The Bowman's Friendship'.    1665

'Tis told that Túrin    then turned him back
and fared to Flinding,    and flung him down
to sleep soundless    till the sun mounted
to the high heavens    and hasted westward.
A vision he viewed    in the vast spaces                      1670
of slumber roving:    it seemed he roamed
up the bleak boulders    of a bare hillside
to a cup outcarven    in a cruel hollow,
whose broken brink    bushes limb-wracked
by the North-wind's knife    in knotted anguish          1675
did fringe forbidding.    There black unfriendly
was a dark thicket,    a dell of thorn-trees
with yews mingled    that the years had fretted.
The leafless limbs    they lifted hopeless
were blotched and blackened,    barkless, naked,        1680
a lifeless remnant    of the levin's flame,
charred chill fingers    changeless pointing
to the cold twilight.    There called he longing:
'O Beleg, my brother,    O Beleg, tell me
where is buried thy body    in these bitter regions?' –   1685
and the echoes always    him answered 'Beleg';
yet a veiléd voice    vague and distant
he caught that called    like a cry at night
o'er the sea's silence:    'Seek no longer.
My bow is rotten    in the barrow ruinous;                  1690
my grove is burned    by grim lightning;
here dread dwelleth,    none dare profane
this angry earth,    Orc nor goblin;

none gain the gate    of the gloomy forest
by this perilous path;    pass they may not,                    1695
yet my life has winged    to the long waiting
in the halls of the Moon    o'er the hills of the sea.
Courage be thy comfort,    comrade lonely!'

Then he woke in wonder;    his wit was healed,
courage him comforted,    and he called aloud              1700
Flinding go-Fuilin,    to his feet striding.
There the sun slanted    its silver arrows
through the wild tresses    of the waters tumbling
roofed with a radiant    rainbow trembling.
'Whither, O Flinding,    our feet now turn we,              1705
or dwell we for ever    by the dancing water,
by the lake of laughter,    alone, untroubled?'
'To Nargothrond    of the Gnomes, methinks,'
said Flinding, 'my feet    would fain wander,
that Celegorm and Curufin,    the crafty sons              1710
of Fëanor founded    when they fled southward;
there built a bulwark    against Bauglir's hate,
who live now lurking    in league secret
with those five others    in the forests of the East,
fell unflinching    foes of Morgoth.                       1715
Maidros whom Morgoth    maimed and tortured
is lord and leader,    his left wieldeth
his sweeping sword;    there is swift Maglor,
there Damrod and Díriel    and dark Cranthir,
the seven seekers    of their sire's treasure.            1720
Now Orodreth rules    the realms and caverns,
the numbered hosts    of Nargothrond.
There to woman's stature    will be waxen full
frail Finduilas    the fleet maiden
his daughter dear,    in his darkling halls               1725
a light, a laughter,    that I loved of yore,
and yet love in longing,    and love calls me.'

Where Narog's torrent    gnashed and spouted
down his stream bestrewn    with stone and boulder,
swiftly southward    they sought their paths,              1730
and summer smiling    smoothed their journey
through day on day,    down dale and wood
where birds blithely    with brimming music
thrilled and trembled    in thronging trees.

No eyes them watched    onward wending                    1735
till they gained the gorge    where Ginglith turns
all glad and golden    to greet the Narog.
There her gentler torrent    joins his tumult,
and they glide together    on the guarded plain
to the Hunters' Hills    that high to southward          1740
uprear their rocks    robed in verdure.
There watchful waited    the Wards of Narog,
lest the need of the Gnomes    from the North should come,
for the sea in the South    them safe guarded,
and eager Narog    the East defended.                    1745
Their treegirt towers    on the tall hilltops
no light betrayed    in the trees lurking,
no horns hooted    in the hills ringing
in loud alarm;    a leaguer silent
unseen, stealthy,    beset the stranger,                 1750
as of wild things wary    that watch moveless,
then follow fleetly    with feet of velvet
their heedless prey    with padding hatred.
In this fashion fought they,    phantom hunters
that wandering Orc    and wild foeman                    1755
unheard harried,    hemmed in ambush.
The slain are silent,    and silent were the shafts
of the nimble Gnomes    of Nargothrond,
who word or whisper    warded sleepless
from their homes deep-hidden,    that hearsay never      1760
was to Bauglir brought.    Bright hope knew they,
and east over Narog    to open battle
no cause or counsel    had called them yet,
though of shield and shaft    and sheathéd swords,
of warriors wieldy    now waxed their host              1765
to power and prowess,    and paths afar
their scouts and woodmen    scoured in hunting.

Thus the twain were tracked    till the trees thickened
and the river went rushing    neath a rising bank,
in foam hastened    o'er the feet of the hills.          1770
In a gloom of green    there they groped forward;
there his fate defended    from flying death
Túrin Thalion –    a twisted thong
of writhing roots    enwrapped his foot;
as he fell there flashed,    fleet, whitewingéd,         1775

a shrill-shafted arrow     that shore his hair,
and trembled sudden     in a tree behind.
Then Flinding o'er the fallen     fiercely shouted:
'Who shoots unsure     his shafts at friends?
Flinding go-Fuilin     of the folk of Narog                          1780
and the son of Húrin     his sworn comrade
here flee to freedom     from the foes of the North.'

His words in the woods     awoke no echo;
no leaf there lisped,     nor loosened twig
there cracked, no creak     of crawling movement          1785
stirred the silence.     Still and soundless
in the glades about     were the green shadows.
Thus fared they on,     and felt that eyes
unseen saw them,     and swift footsteps
unheard hastened     behind them ever,                          1790
till each shaken bush     or shadowy thicket
they fled furtive     in fear needless,
for thereafter was aimed     no arrow wingéd,
and they came to a country     kindly tended;
through flowery frith     and fair acres                          1795
they fared, and found     of folk empty
the leas and leasows     and the lawns of Narog,
the teeming tilth     by trees enfolded
twixt hills and river.     The hoes unrecked
in the fields were flung,     and fallen ladders          1800
in the long grass lay     of the lush orchards;
every tree there turned     its tangled head
and eyed them secretly,     and the ears listened
of the nodding grasses;     though noontide glowed
on land and leaf,     their limbs were chilled.          1805
Never hall or homestead     its high gables
in the light uplifting     in that land saw they,
but a pathway plain     by passing feet
was broadly beaten.     Thither bent their steps
Flinding go-Fuilin,     whose feet remembered          1810
that white roadway.     In a while they reached
to the acres' end,     that ever narrowing
twixt wall and water     did wane at last
to blossomy banks     by the borders of the way.
A spuming torrent,     in spate tumbling                          1815
from the highest hill     of the Hunters' Wold

clove and crossed it;    there of carven stone
with slim and shapely     slender archway
a bridge was builded,    a bow gleaming
in the froth and flashing    foam of Ingwil,                    1820
that headlong hurried    and hissed beneath.
Where it found the flood,    far-journeyed Narog,
there steeply stood    the strong shoulders
of the hills, o'erhanging    the hurrying water;
there shrouded in trees    a sheer terrace,                    1825
wide and winding,    worn to smoothness,
was fashioned in the face    of the falling slope.
Doors there darkly    dim gigantic
were hewn in the hillside;    huge their timbers,
and their posts and lintels    of ponderous stone.             1830

They were shut unshakeable.    Then shrilled a trumpet
as a phantom fanfare    faintly winding
in the hill from hollow    halls far under;
a creaking portal    with clangour backward
was flung, and forth    there flashed a throng,                1835
leaping lightly,    lances wielding,
and swift encircling    seized bewildered
the wanderers wayworn,    wordless haled them
through the gaping gateway    to the glooms beyond.
Ground and grumbled    on its great hinges                     1840
the door gigantic;    with din ponderous
it clanged and closed    like clap of thunder,
and echoes awful    in empty corridors
there ran and rumbled    under roofs unseen;
the light was lost.    Then led them on                        1845
down long and winding    lanes of darkness
their guards guiding    their groping feet,
till the faint flicker    of fiery torches
flared before them;    fitful murmur
as of many voices    in meeting thronged                       1850
they heard as they hastened.    High sprang the roof.
Round a sudden turning    they swung amazed,
and saw a solemn    silent conclave,
where hundreds hushed    in huge twilight
neath distant domes    darkly vaulted                          1855
them wordless waited.    There waters flowed
with washing echoes    winding swiftly

amid the multitude,    and mounting pale
for fifty fathoms    a fountain sprang,
and wavering wan,    with winking redness                    1860
flushed and flickering    in the fiery lights,
it fell at the feet    in the far shadows
of a king with crown    and carven throne.

A voice they heard    neath the vault rolling,
and the king them called:    'Who come ye here                1865
from the North unloved    to Nargothrond,
a Gnome of bondage    and a nameless Man?
No welcome finds here    wandering outlaw;
save his wish be death    he wins it not,
for those that have looked    on our last refuge             1870
it boots not to beg    other boon of me.'
Then Flinding go-Fuilin    freely answered:
'Has the watch then waned    in the woods of Narog,
since Orodreth ruled    this realm and folk?
Or how have the hunted    thus hither wandered,              1875
if the warders willed it not    thy word obeying;
or how hast not heard    that thy hidden archer,
who shot his shaft    in the shades of the forest,
there learned our lineage,    O Lord of Narog,
and knowing our names    his notched arrows                  1880
loosed no longer?'    Then low and hushed
a murmur moved    in the multitude,
and some were who said:    ''Tis the same in truth:
the long looked-for,    the lost is found,
the narrow path he knew    to Nargothrond                    1885
who was born and bred here    from babe to youth';
and some were who said:    'The son of Fuilin
was lost and looked for    long years agone.
What sign or token    that the same returns
have we heard or seen?    Is this haggard fugitive           1890
with back bended    the bold leader,
the scout who scoured,    scorning danger,
most far afield    of the folk of Narog?'
'That tale was told us,'    returned answer
the Lord Orodreth,    'but belief were rash.                 1895
That alone of the lost,    whom leagues afar
the Orcs of Angband    in evil bonds
have dragged to the deeps,    thou darest home,

by grace or valour,    from grim thraldom,
what proof dost thou proffer?    What plea dost show          1900
that a Man, a mortal,    on our mansions hidden
should look and live,    our league sharing?'

Thus the curse on the kindred    for the cruel slaughter
at the Swans' Haven    there swayed his heart,
but Flinding go-Fuilin    fiercely answered:          1905
'Is the son of Húrin,    who sits on high
in a deathless doom    dreadly chainéd,
unknown, nameless,    in need of plea
to fend from him the fate    of foe and spy?
Flinding the faithful,    the far wanderer,          1910
though form and face    fires of anguish
and bitter bondage,    Balrogs' torment,
have seared and twisted,    for a song of welcome
had hoped in his heart    at that home-coming
that he dreamed of long    in dark labour.          1915
Are these deep places    to dungeons turned,
a lesser Angband    in the land of the Gnomes?'

Thereat was wrath aroused    in Orodreth's heart,
and the muttering waxed    to many voices,
and this and that    the throng shouted;          1920
when sweet and sudden    a song awoke,
a voice of music    o'er that vast murmur
mounted in melody    to the misty domes;
with clear echoes    the caverned arches
it filled, and trembled    frail and slender,          1925
those words weaving    of welcome home
that the wayweary    had wooed from care
since the Gnomes first knew    need and wandering.
Then hushed was the host;    no head was turned,
for long known and loved    was that lifted voice,          1930
and Flinding knew it    at the feet of the king
like stone graven    standing silent
with heart laden;    but Húrin's son
was waked to wonder    and to wistful thought,
and searching the shadows    that the seat shrouded,          1935
the kingly throne,    there caught he thrice
a gleam, a glimmer,    as of garments white.
'Twas frail Finduilas,    fleet and slender,
to woman's stature,    wondrous beauty,

now grown in glory,    that glad welcome                1940
there raised in ruth,    and wrath was stilled.
Locked fast the love    had lain in her heart
that in laughter grew    long years agone
when in the meads merrily    a maiden played
with fleet-footed    Fuilin's youngling.                1945
No searing scars    of sundering years
could blind those eyes    bright with welcome,
and wet with tears    wistful trembling
at the grief there graven    in grim furrows
on the face of Flinding.    'Father,' said she,         1950
'what dream of doubt    dreadly binds thee?
'Tis Flinding go-Fuilin,    whose faith of yore
none dared to doubt.    This dark, lonely,
mournful-fated    Man beside him
if his oath avows    the very offspring                 1955
of Húrin Thalion,    what heart in this throng
shall lack belief    or love refuse?
But are none yet nigh us    that knew of yore
that mighty of Men,    mark of kinship
to seek and see    in these sorrow-laden               1960
form and features?    The friends of Morgoth
not thus, methinks,    through thirst and hunger
come without comrades,    nor have countenance
thus grave and guileless,    glance unflinching.'

Then did Túrin's heart    tremble wondering            1965
at the sweet pity    soft and gentle
of that tender voice    touched with wisdom
that years of yearning    had yielded slow;
and Orodreth, whose heart    knew ruth seldom,
yet loved deeply    that lady dear,                     1970
gave ear and answer    to her eager words,
and his doubt and dread    of dire treachery,
and his quick anger,    he quelled within him.
No few were there found    who had fought of old
where Finweg fell    in flame of swords,                1975
and Húrin Thalion    had hewn the throngs,
the dark Glamhoth's    demon legions,
and who called there looked    and cried aloud:
"'Tis the face of the father    new found on earth,
and his strong stature    and stalwart arms;            1980

though such care and sorrow    never claimed his sire,
whose laughing eyes    were lighted clear
at board or battle,    in bliss or in woe.'
Nor could lack belief    for long the words
and faith of Flinding    when friend and kin                    1985
and his father hastening    that face beheld.
Lo! sire and son    did sweet embrace
neath trees entwining    tangled branches
at the dark doorways    of those deep mansions
that Fuilin's folk    afar builded,                             1990
and dwelt in the deep    of the dark woodland
to the West on the slopes    of the Wold of Hunters.
Of the four kindreds    that followed the king,
the watchtowers' lords,    the wold's keepers
and the guards of the bridge,    the gleaming bow              1995
that was flung o'er the foaming    froth of Ingwil,
from Fuilin's children    were first chosen,
most noble of name,    renowed in valour.

In those halls in the hills    at that homecoming
mirth was mingled    with melting tears                        2000
for the unyielding years    whose yoke of pain
the form and face    of Fuilin's son
had changed and burdened,    chilled the laughter
that leapt once lightly    to his lips and eyes.
Now in kindly love    was care lessened,                       2005
with song assuaged    sadness of hearts;
the lights were lit    and lamps kindled
o'er the burdened board;    there bade they feast
Túrin Thalion    with his true comrade
at the long tables'    laden plenty,                           2010
where dish and goblet    on the dark-gleaming
wood well-waxéd,    where the wine-flagons
engraven glistened    gold and silver.
Then Fuilin filled    with flowing mead,
dear-hoarded drink    dark and potent                          2015
a carven cup    with curious brim,
by ancient art    of olden smiths
fairly fashioned,    filled with marvels;
there gleamed and lived    in grey silver
the folk of Faërie    in the first noontide                    2020
of the Blissful Realms;    with their brows wreathéd

in garlands golden    with their gleaming hair
in the wind flying    and their wayward feet
fitful flickering,    on unfading lawns
the ancient Elves    there everlasting                              2025
danced undying    in the deep pasture
of the gardens of the Gods;    there Glingol shone
and Bansil bloomed    with beams shimmering,
mothwhite moonlight    from its misty flowers;
the hilltops of Tûn    there high and green                        2030
were crowned by Côr,    climbing, winding,
town white-walléd    where the tower of Ing
with pale pinnacle    pierced the twilight,
and its crystal lamp    illumined clear
with slender shaft    the Shadowy Seas.                            2035
Through wrack and ruin,    the wrath of the Gods,
through weary wandering,    waste and exile,
had come that cup,    carved in gladness,
in woe hoarded,    in waning hope
when little was left    of the lore of old.                        2040
Now Fuilin at feast    filled it seldom
save in pledge of love    to proven friend;
blithely bade he    of that beaker drink
for the sake of his son    that sate nigh him
Túrin Thalion    in token sure                                     2045
of a league of love    long enduring.
'O Húrin's child    chief of Hithlum,
with mourning marred,    may the mead of the Elves
thy heart uplift    with hope lightened;
nor fare thou from us    the feast ended,                          2050
here deign to dwell;    if this deep mansion
thus dark-dolven    dimly vaulted
displease thee not,    a place awaits thee.'
There deeply drank    a draught of sweetness
Túrin Thalion    and returned his thanks                           2055
in eager earnest,    while all the folk
with loud laughter    and long feasting,
with mournful lay    or music wild
of magic minstrels    that mighty songs
did weave with wonder,    there wooed their hearts                 2060
from black foreboding;    there bed's repose
their guest was granted,    when in gloom silent
the light and laughter    and the living voices

were quenched in slumber.    Now cold and slim
the sickle of the Moon     was silver tilted                    2065
o'er the wan waters    that washed unsleeping,
nightshadowed Narog,    the Gnome-river.
In tall treetops    of the tangled wood
there hooted hollow    the hunting owls.

Thus fate it fashioned    that in Fuilin's house             2070
the dark destiny    now dwelt awhile
of Túrin the tall.    There he toiled and fought
with the folk of Fuilin    for Flinding's love;
lore long forgotten    learned among them,
for light yet lingered    in those leaguered places,          2075
and wisdom yet lived    in that wild people,
whose minds yet remembered    the Mountains of the West
and the faces of the Gods,    yet filled with glory
more clear and keen    than kindreds of the dark
or Men unwitting    of the mirth of old.                      2080

Thus Fuilin and Flinding    friendship showed him,
and their halls were his home,    while high summer
waned to autumn    and the western gales
the leaves loosened    from the labouring boughs;
the feet of the forest    in fading gold                      2085
and burnished brown    were buried deeply;
a restless rustle    down the roofless aisles
sighed and whispered.    Lo! the Silver Wherry,
the sailing Moon    with slender mast,
was filled with fires    as of furnace golden                 2090
whose hold had hoarded    the heats of summer,
whose shrouds were shaped    of shining flame
uprising ruddy    o'er the rim of Evening
by the misty wharves    on the margin of the world.
Thus the months fleeted    and mightily he fared              2095
in the forest with Flinding,    and his fate waited
slumbering a season,    while he sought for joy
the lore learning    and the league sharing
of the Gnomes renowned    of Nargothrond.

The ways of the woods    he wandered far,                     2100
and the land's secrets    he learned swiftly
by winter unhindered    to weathers hardened,
whether snow or sleet    or slanting rain

from glowering heavens    grey and sunless
cold and cruel    was cast to earth,                                         2105
till the floods were loosed    and the fallow waters
of sweeping Narog,    swollen, angry,
were filled with flotsam    and foaming turbid
passed in tumult;    or twinkling pale
ice-hung evening    was opened wide,                                  2110
a dome of crystal    o'er the deep silence
of the windless wastes    and the woods standing
like frozen phantoms    under flickering stars.
By day or night    danger needless
he dared and sought for,    his dread vengeance                2115
ever seeking unsated    on the sons of Angband;
yet as winter waxed    wild and pathless,
and biting blizzards    the bare faces
lashed and tortured    of the lonely tors
and haggard hilltops,    in the halls more often             2120
was he found in fellowship    with the folk of Narog,
and cunning there added    in the crafts of hand,
and in subtle mastery    of song and music
and peerless poesy,    to his proven lore
and wise woodcraft;    there wondrous tales                       2125
were told to Túrin    in tongues of gold
in those mansions deep,    there many a day
to the hearth and halls    of the haughty king
did those friends now fare    to feast and game,
for frail Finduilas    her father urged                                2130
to his board and favour    to bid those twain,
and it grudging her granted    that grimhearted
king deep-counselled –    cold his anger,
his ruth unready,    his wrath enduring;
yet fierce and fell    by the fires of hate                         2135
his breast was burned    for the broods of Hell
(his son had they slain,    the swift-footed
Halmir the hunter    of hart and boar),
and kinship therein    the king ere long
in his heart discovered    for Húrin's son,                        2140
dark and silent,    as in dreams walking
of anguish and regret    and evergrowing
feud unsated.    Thus favour soon
by the king accorded    of the company of his board
he was member made,    and in many a deed                       2145

and wild venture    to West and North
he achieved renown    among the chosen warriors
and fearless bowmen;    in far battles
in secret ambush    and sudden onslaught,
where fell-tonguéd flew    the flying serpents,                    2150
their shafts envenomed,    in valleys shrouded
he played his part,    but it pleased him little,
who trusted to targe    and tempered sword,
whose hand was hungry    for the hilts it missed
but dared never a blade    since the doom of Beleg            2155
to draw or handle.    Dear-holden was he,
though he wished nor willed it,    and his works were praised.
When tales were told    of times gone by,
of valour they had known,    of vanished triumph,
glory half-forgot,    grief remembered,                          2160
then they bade and begged him    be blithe and sing
of deeds in Doriath    in the dark forest
by the shadowy shores    that shunned the light
where Esgalduin    the Elf-river
by root-fencéd pools    roofed with silence,                   2165
by deep eddies    darkly gurgling,
flowed fleetly on    past the frowning portals
of the Thousand Caves.    Thus his thought recalled
the woodland ways    where once of yore
Beleg the bowman    had a boy guided                           2170
by slade and slope    and swampy thicket
neath trees enchanted;    then his tongue faltered
and his tale was stilled.

                              At Túrin's sorrow
one marvelled and was moved,    a maiden fair
the frail Finduilas    that Failivrin,                          2175
the glimmering sheen    on the glassy pools
of Ivrin's lake    the Elves in love
had named anew.    By night she pondered
and by day wondered    what depth of woe
lay locked in his heart    his life marring;                   2180
for the doom of dread    and death that had fallen
on Beleg the bowman    in unbroken silence
Túrin warded,    nor might tale be won
of Flinding the faithful    of their fare and deeds
in the waste together.    Now waned her love            2185

for the form and face    furrowed with anguish,
for the bended back    and broken strength,
the wistful eyes    and the withered laughter
of Flinding the faithful,    though filled was her heart
with deepwelling pity    and dear friendship.                    2190
Grown old betimes    and grey-frosted,
he was wise and kindly    with wit and counsel,
with sight and foresight,    but slow to wrath
nor fiercely valiant,    yet if fight he must
his share he shirked not,    though the shreds of fear          2195
in his heart yet hung;    he hated no man,
but he seldom smiled,    save suddenly a light
in his grave face glimmered    and his glance was fired:
Finduilas maybe    faring lightly
on the sward he saw    or swinging pale,                        2200
a sheen of silver    down some shadowy hall.*
Yet to Túrin was turned    her troublous heart
against will and wisdom    and waking thought:
in dreams she sought him,    his dark sorrow
with love lightening,    so that laughter shone               2205
in eyes new-kindled,    and her Elfin name
he eager spake,    as in endless spring
they fared free-hearted    through flowers enchanted
with hand in hand    o'er the happy pastures
of that land that is lit    by no light of Earth,              2210
by no moon nor sun,    down mazy ways
to the black abysmal    brink of waking.

From woe unhealed    the wounded heart
of Túrin the tall    was turned to her.
Amazed and moved,    his mind's secret                          2215
half-guessed, half-guarded,    in gloomy hour
of night's watches,    when down narrow winding
paths of pondering    he paced wearily,
he would lonely unlock,    then loyal-hearted
shut fast and shun,    or shroud his grief                      2220
in dreamless sleep,    deep oblivion
where no echo entered    of the endless war
of waking worlds,    woe nor friendship,
flower nor firelight    nor the foam of seas,

*Here the B-typescript ends, and the remainder of the text is manuscript. See the Note
on the Texts, p. 81.

a land illumined    by no light at all.                                           2225

'O! hands unholy,    O! heart of sorrow,
O! outlaw whose evil    is yet unatonéd,
wilt thou, troth-breaker,    a treason new
to thy burden bind;    thy brother-in-arms,
Flinding go-Fuilin    thus foully betray,                              2230
who thy madness tended    in mortal perils,
to thy waters of healing    thy wandering feet
did lead at the last    to lands of peace,
where his life is rooted    and his love dwelleth?
O! stainéd hands    his hope steal not!'                             2235

Thus love was fettered    in loyal fastness
and coldly clad    in courteous word;
yet he would look and long    for her loveliness,
in her gentle words    his joy finding,
her face watching    when he feared no eye                     2240
might mark his mood.    One marked it all –
Failivrin's face,    the fleeting gleams,
like sun through clouds    sailing hurriedly
over faded fields,    that flickered and went out
as Túrin passed;    the tremulous smiles,                        2245
his grave glances    out of guarded shade,
his sighs in secret –    one saw them all,
Flinding go-Fuilin,    who had found his home
and lost his love    to the lying years,
he watched and wondered,    no word speaking,            2250
and his heart grew dark    'twixt hate and pity,
bewildered, weary,    in the webs of fate.
Then Finduilas,    more frail and wan
twixt olden love    now overthrown
and new refused,    did nightly weep;                            2255
and folk wondered    at the fair pallor
of the hands upon her harp,    her hair of gold
on slender shoulders    slipped in tumult,
the glory of her eyes    that gleamed with fires
of secret thought    in silent deeps.                                2260

Many bosoms burdened    with foreboding vague
their glooms disowned    neath glad laughter.
In song and silence,    snow and tempest,
winter wore away;    to the world there came

a year once more    in youth unstained,                          2265
nor were leaves less green,    light less golden,
the flowers less fair,    though in faded hearts
no spring was born,    though speeding nigh
danger and dread    and doom's footsteps
to their halls hasted.    Of the host of iron                     2270
came tale and tidings    ever treading nearer;
Orcs unnumbered    to the East of Narog
roamed and ravened    on the realm's borders,
the might of Morgoth    was moved abroad.
No ambush stayed them;    the archers yielded                     2275
each vale by vale,    though venomed arrows

Here both A and B end abruptly, and I think it is certain that no more of
the poem was ever written.

## NOTES

1409   *Tengwethil* B, *Taingwethil* A. This is the reverse of the
       previous occurrences; see lines 431, 636.

1417–18   These lines are bracketed in B, and line 1418 struck through;
          in the margin is a mark of deletion, but with a query
          beside it.

1448   *Nirnaith Únoth* A, and B as typed; emended in pencil in
       B to *Nirnaith Ornoth*. Earlier in the poem (lines 13, 218)
       the forms were *Nínin Udathriol* emended in B to *Nínin
       Unothradin* (also *Nirnaithos Unothradin* at line 13). Cf.
       line 1543.

1469   *Ulmo* A, and B as typed; in B *Ulmo* struck through in pencil
       and replaced by *Ylmir*, but this also struck through. I read
       *Ylmir*; see note to line 1529.

1525   *Túrin Thalion* A, and B as typed (not *Túrin Thaliodrin*, see
       note to line 1324).

1529   *Ylmir*: so already in A and B as typed; so also at lines 1534,
       1553, 1572, 1585. See note to line 1469.

1537   This line was struck through in pencil in B.

1542–3   These lines were bracketed in pencil in B, and *Not so* written
         in margin. Though *Únoth* was not here emended I read
         *Ornoth* (see note to line 1448).

1558   *the sea-birds call    in solemn conclave*: cf. the tale of *The
       Coming of the Elves and the Making of Kôr*, I. 124.

1673–6   Cf. lines 1036–9.

1696–7    Cf. lines 1283–4.
1710–11    Line 1710 is wholly and 1711 partly crossed out in B, with
marginal additions to make 1711 read:

> [by] Felagund founded    flying southward

Also written in the margin is: '*before* Nirnaith Únoth'. At
line 1711 A has *found* for *founded*, but as the manuscript
was written very rapidly this may not be significant.
1713–20    These lines are bracketed in B, as if needing revision, and two
lines are written in the margin for insertion after 1715:

> that home came never    to their halls of old
> since the field of tears    was fought and lost.

I have not included these lines (written, it seems, at the same
time as the other marginal comments in this passage) in the
text in view of the complexity of the 'historical background' at
this point; see the Commentary, pp. 84–5.
Against this passage is written in the margin:

> but Nargothrond was founded by *Felagund* Finrod's son
> (whose brothers were Angrod Egnor & Orodreth). Curufin
> and Celegorm dwelt at Nargothrond.

1719    *Cranthor* A, *Cranthir* B as typed.
1724    *Finduilas*: *Failivrin* A, and B as typed; *Finduilas* written in
pencil in the margin of B; so also at line 1938. See lines 2130,
2175, 2199.
1938    *Finduilas*: as at line 1724.
1945    The word *youngling* is struck out in B and *Flinding* written
against it, but the resulting *Fuilin's Flinding* (with alliter-
ation in the second half-line) cannot possibly have been
intended. Subsequently another word was written in the
margin, but this is illegible.
1974–5    *Not so* written in the margin of B.
1975    *Finweg* A, and B as typed; late emendation to *Fingon* in B.
I retain *Finweg* since that is still the name in the 1930
'Silmarillion'.
1993–8    In A and in B as typed these lines were differently ordered:

> Of the four kindreds    that followed the king,
> most noble of name,    renowned in valour,
> the watchtowers' lords,    the wold's keepers
> from Fuilin's children    were first chosen,
> and the guards of the bridge,    the gleaming bow
> that was flung o'er the foaming    froth of Ingwil.

2027    *Glingol* A, and B as typed; late emendation to *Glingal* in B. I
retain *Glingol*, the form in the *Lost Tales* and still in the 1930

'Silmarillion'; in the published work *Glingal* is the name of the golden tree of Gondolin.

2028   *Bansil* A, and B as typed; late emendation to *Belthil* in B. I retain *Bansil* for the same reason as *Glingol* in line 2027.

2030   *there high and green     the hill of Tûn* A, and B as typed; emended in pencil in B to the reading given; *was* 2031 not corrected to *were*, but that *hilltops* (plural) was intended is shown by the text C, see p. 82.

2130   I give *Finduilas*, though *Failivrin* was not so emended here in B, as it was at lines 1724, 1938. See notes to lines 2175, 2199.

2164   *Esgaduin* A, and B as typed; emended in pencil to *Esgalduin* in B.

2175   *the frail Finduilas     that Failivrin* as typed B; *the frail Failivrin* changed at the time of writing in A to *Findóriel* (sc. *the frail Findóriel     that Failivrin* &c.).

2199   *Finduilas* A and B; *Failivrin* written in the margin of A. At the subsequent occurrences (*Failivrin* 2242, *Finduilas* 2253) the names both in A and in B are as in the printed text.

*Note on the texts of the section 'Failivrin'*

B comes to an end as a typescript at line 2201, but continues as a well-written manuscript for a further 75 lines. This last part is written on the paper of good quality that my father used for many years in all his writing (University lectures, *The Silmarillion*, *The Lord of the Rings*, etc.) in ink or pencil (i.e. when not typing): this plain paper was supplied to him by the Examination Schools at Oxford University, being the unused pages of the booklets of paper provided for examination candidates. The change in paper does not show however that he had moved from Leeds to Oxford (cf. p. 3), since he acted as an external examiner at Oxford in 1924 and 1925; but it does suggest that the final work on the Lay (before *Leithian* was begun) dates from the latter part of the one year or the earlier part of the next. The conclusion of A is also written on this paper.

There is a further short text to be considered here, a well-written manuscript that extends from line 2005 to line 2225, which I will call 'C'. Textual details show clearly that C followed B – not, I think, at any long interval. Some emendations made to B were made to C also. I give here a list of the more important differences of C from B (small changes of punctuation and sentence-connection are not noticed).

C bears the title *Túrin in the House of Fuilin and his son Flinding*. It is not clear whether this was to be the title of a fourth section of the poem, but it seems unlikely, if the third section was to remain 'Failivrin'.

2005   *Now was care lessened     in kindly love* C

2020   *noontide*] *summer* pencil emendation in C

2027–8  *Glingol > Glingal* and *Bansil > Belthil* pencil emend-
        ations in C as in B

2029    The original reading of B and C was *like magic moon-
        light from its mothwhite flowers*; this was differ-
        ently emended in C, to *like moths of pearl in moon-
        lit flowers*.

2030–2  C as written was exactly as the text of B after emendation
        (with *were* for *was* 2031); these lines were then crossed
        out and the following substituted:

> there high and green    that hill by the sea
> was crowned by Tûn,    climbing, winding
> in tall walls of white,    where the tower of Ing

2036–53  are omitted in C (with *Thence* for *There* 2054).

2069    After *hunting owls* C has lines of omission dots, and the
        text takes up again at line 2081.

2083    *waned to autumn*] *waned towards winter* pencil
        emendations in C

2090    *as of furnace golden*] *as a furnace of gold* C

2114–16  are omitted in C.

2123–8  C omits 2124, 2125b–7, and reads:

> and in subtle mastery    of song and music
> to his wise woodcraft    and wielding of arms.
> To the hearth and halls    of the haughty king

2135–8  C omits these lines (referring to Orodreth's son Halmir,
        slain by Orcs) and reads:

> his ruth unready,    his wrath enduring.
> But kinship of mood    the king ere long

2142b–2143a  C omits these lines, and reads:

> of anguish and regret.    Thus was honour granted
> by the king to Túrin;    of the company of his board

2158    *were told*] *men told* emendation in C.

2164    *Esgalduin* C as written; see note to this line above.

## Commentary on *Part III 'Failivrin'*

In this very remarkable section of the poem a great development has
taken place in the story since the *Tale of Turambar* (if there was an
intervening stage there is now no trace of it); while concurrently the
history of the exiled Noldoli was being deepened and extended from its
representation in the outlines for *Gilfanon's Tale* – a factor that compli-

cates the presentation of the poems, since statements about that history were often superseded during the long process of composition.

Most notable of all in this part of the poem is the description of Nargothrond, unique in the Lay. In all the later rewritings and restructurings of the Túrin saga this part was never touched, apart from the development of the relations between Túrin, Gwindor, and Finduilas which I have given in *Unfinished Tales*, pp. 155–9. In this there is a parallel to Gondolin, very fully described in the tale of *The Fall of Gondolin*, but never again. As I said in the introduction to *Unfinished Tales* (p. 5):

> It is thus the remarkable fact that the only full account that my father ever wrote of the story of Tuor's sojourn in Gondolin, his union with Idril Celebrindal, the birth of Eärendil, the treachery of Maeglin, the sack of the city, and the escape of the fugitives – a story that was a central element in his imagination of the First Age – was the narrative composed in his youth.

Gondolin and Nargothrond were each made once, and not remade. They remained powerful sources and images – the more powerful, perhaps, because never remade, and never remade, perhaps, because so powerful. Both *Tuor* and *Túrin* were indeed to receive written form outside the condensed *Silmarillion* as long prose narratives, and what my father achieved of this intention I have given in the first two sections of *Unfinished Tales*; but though he set out to remake Gondolin he never reached the city again: after climbing the endless slope of the Orfalch Echor and passing through the long line of heraldic gates he paused with Tuor at the vision of Gondolin amid the plain, and never recrossed Tumladen. The remaking of *Túrin* went much further, but here too he skirted the imaginative focus of Nargothrond.

### The founding of Nargothrond

I shall discuss first the 'background' history, which centres on the complex question of the founding of Nargothrond. In the *Tale* (II. 81–2) Nargothrond is not named, and is represented by the Caves of the Rodothlim; as in the poem, Orodreth was the chief of these Gnomes, but he was then an isolated figure, and not yet associated in kinship with other princes. Nothing is said there of the origin of the redoubt, but that it was imagined to have arisen (like Gondolin) after the Battle of Unnumbered Tears is, I think, certain, since in the earliest phase of the legends, as I remarked in commenting on *Gilfanon's Tale* (I. 242),

> the entire later history of the long years of the Siege of Angband, ending with the Battle of Sudden Flame (Dagor Bragollach), of the passage of Men over the Mountains into Beleriand and their taking service with the Noldorin Kings, had yet to emerge; indeed these outlines give the effect of only a brief time elapsing between the

coming of the Noldoli from Kôr and their great defeat [in the Battle of Unnumbered Tears].

In the poem, this idea is still clearly present in lines 1542–4:

> the secret halls
> of Nargothrond    by the Gnomes builded
> that death and thraldom    in the dreadful throes
> of Nirnaith Ornoth,    a number scanty,
> escaped unscathed.

Against this passage my father wrote 'Not so'; and this comment obviously means 'Nargothrond was *not* founded after the Battle of Unnumbered Tears', as is further shown by his note to lines 1710–11:

> (to Nargothrond)
> that Celegorm and Curufin,    the crafty sons
> of Fëanor founded    when they fled southward

against which he wrote: *'before* Nirnaith Únoth'. When, then, was it founded? The 'Sketch of the Mythology', certainly later than the poem (the background of which it was written to explain), already in its earliest form knows of the Leaguer of Angband and of Morgoth's breaking of the Leaguer – though described in the barest possible way, without any reference to the battle that ended it; and it is said there that at that time 'Gnomes and Ilkorins and Men are scattered . . . Celegorm and Curufin found the realm of Nargothrond on the banks of Narog in the south of the Northern lands.' The 'Sketch' (again, in its earliest, unrevised, form) also states that Celegorm and Curufin despatched a host from Nargothrond to the Battle of Unnumbered Tears, that this host joined with that of Maidros and Maglor, but 'arrived too late for the main battle'. 'They are beaten back and driven into the South-east, where they long time dwelt, and did not go back to Nargothrond. There Orodreth ruled the remnant.'

The problem is to explain how it comes about in the earlier story, as found in the poem (Nargothrond founded by Celegorm and Curufin *after* the Battle of Unnumbered Tears), that Celegorm and Curufin are no longer there when Túrin comes, and Orodreth is king. Why do they *live now lurking . . . in the forests of the East* with their five brothers (1713–14)?

The only explanation that I can put forward is as follows. When my father wrote lines 1542–4 his view was that Nargothrond was founded after the Battle of Unnumbered Tears (this is quite explicit). But when he wrote lines 1710–15

> (to Nargothrond)
> that Celegorm and Curufin,    the crafty sons          1710
> of Fëanor founded    when they fled southward;
> there built a bulwark    against Bauglir's hate,

who live now lurking    in league secret
with those five others    in the forests of the East
fell unflinching    foes of Morgoth                                          1715

the later story was already present. (There would be nothing uncharacteristic about this; in the *Lay of Leithian* the story changes from one
Canto to the next.) Thus *when they fled southward* refers to the flight
of Celegorm and Curufin from the battle that ended the Leaguer of
Angband; *they live now lurking . . . in the forests of the East* refers to
the period after the Battle of Unnumbered Tears, when 'they did not go
back to Nargothrond' and 'Orodreth ruled the remnant', as stated in the
'Sketch'.* On this view, my father's note against lines 1710–11 (*'before
Nirnaith Únoth'*) was mistaken – he took the lines to refer to the old story
(as 1542–4 certainly do), whereas in fact they refer to the later. This
explanation may seem far-fetched, but it is less so than the demonstrably
correct solutions to other puzzles in the history of 'The Silmarillion', and
I see no other way out of the difficulty. – The two additional lines to
follow 1715:

that home came never    to their halls of old
since the field of tears    was fought and lost

refer (I think) to Celegorm and Curufin, and reinforce the reference to
the later story (i.e. that after the Battle of Unnumbered Tears they did
not return to Nargothrond).
     The change of lines 1710–11 to make the passage read

(to Nargothrond)
by Felagund founded    flying southward

and the marginal note against 1713–20 'but Nargothrond was founded by
*Felagund* Finrod's son' etc., reflect of course a further stage, though a
stage that came in soon after the 'Sketch' was first written. The essential
shifts in the history of Nargothrond to this point are certainly thus:

(1)    Orodreth ruled the Rodothlim in their caves, first inhabited after
       the Battle of Unnumbered Tears.

(2)    Celegorm and Curufin founded Nargothrond after the Battle of
       Unnumbered Tears.

(3)    Celegorm and Curufin founded Nargothrond after the breaking of
       the Leaguer of Angband; they went with a host to the Battle of
       Unnumbered Tears and did not return, but remained in the East;
       Orodreth ruled the remnant of the Gnomes of Nargothrond.

(4)    Felagund son of Finrod and his brothers Angrod, Egnor, and

----

*Cf. lines 1873–4:
       Has the watch then waned    in the woods of Narog
       *since Orodreth ruled    this realm and folk?*

Orodreth founded Nargothrond after the breaking of the Leaguer of Angband; Celegorm and Curufin dwelt there.

Another sign of development in the history and genealogy of the Gnomish princes is the mention of *Finweg*, later emended in the B-text to *Fingon*, who *fell in flame of swords* at the Battle of Unnumbered Tears (1975). *Finweg* has appeared early in the poem (line 29), but there as a spelling or form of Finwë (Nólemë), founder of the line; this *Finweg* appears in the 'Sketch', as originally written, as the son of Fingolfin.

The Sons of Fëanor have previously all been named only in the *Tale of the Nauglafring* (II. 241); now (1716 ff.), with *Cranthir* (emended from *Cranthor* in B), and *Díriel* for earlier *Dinithel* (*?Durithel*), they reach the forms they long retained. Characteristic epithets appear: Maglor is 'swift', Cranthir 'dark', and Curufin's 'craftiness', already appearing in the *Tale of the Nauglafring*, extends here to Celegorm. Maidros' wielding his sword with his left hand is mentioned, which clearly implies that the story that Morgoth had him hung from a cliff by his right hand, and that Finweg (> Fingon) rescued him, was already present, as it is in the 'Sketch'. His torment and maiming was mentioned in the outlines for *Gilfanon's Tale* (I. 238, 240), but not described.

To turn now to the foreground narrative of this part of the poem. The poem advances on the *Tale* by mentioning the disposal of Beleg's sword, not mentioned in the *Tale*; but here Flinding hides it in the hollow of a tree (1342), and it plays no further part in the story. If the poem had gone further Túrin would have received his black sword in Nargothrond in gift from Orodreth, as happens in the *Tale* (II. 83). In the *Tale* it is said that Túrin 'had not wielded a sword since the slaying of Beleg, but rather had he been contented with a mighty club'; in the poem this reappears with the implication made explicit (2155–6):

> dared never a blade    since the doom of Beleg
> to draw or handle.

The burial of Beleg now appears, with his great bow beside him (1399 ff.), and Túrin's kiss survives from the *Tale*; that the mark of his grief over the death of Beleg (called the third of his sorrows, 1421) never left his face was an enduring feature of the legend.

*Geography*

In the *Tale* (II. 80–1) very little is made of the journey of Flinding and Túrin from the place of Beleg's death to Nargothrond: by the light of Flinding's lamp they 'fared by night and hid by day and were lost in the hills, and the Orcs found them not'. In the poem, on the other hand, the journey is quite fully described, and contains some noteworthy features; moreover there is nothing in the description that contradicts the earliest

'Silmarillion' map (to be given in the next volume), which dates from this period and may have been made originally in association with this poem. The wanderers pass at midnight by the Mound of Slain, looming up under the moon *at the furthest end / of Dor-na-Fauglith's dusty spaces* (1439–40); this feature does not recur again in the story of Túrin. The only previous reference to the great burial-mound is in the outlines for *Gilfanon's Tale*, where it is called the Hill of Death, and was raised by the Sons of Feanor (I. 241). It is said in the poem that Túrin despite his heavy listlessness *turned his hand / toward Thangorodrim* at Flinding's words concerning the Mound, and cursed Morgoth thrice – as did Fëanor in the hour of his death after the Battle-under-Stars (*The Silmarillion* p. 107); the one was doubtless the precursor of the other. The inviolability of the Mound now appears (1450–2).

Túrin and Flinding now crossed Sirion not far from his source in the Shadowy Mountains, where the river was fordable (1457 ff.); this is the first reference to Sirion's Well. Sirion's great journey to the Sea is described, with references to his passage underground (1467; cf. II. 195, 217) and through lands *beloved of Ylmir* (Ulmo). The travellers then find themselves in Nan Dungorthin, which was mentioned in the *Tale of Tinúviel* (see II. 35, 62–3): Huan found Beren and Tinúviel after their escape from Angband in 'that northward region of Artanor that was called afterward Nan Dumgorthin, the land of the dark idols', 'even then a dark land and gloomy and foreboding, and dread wandered beneath its lowering trees'. My father hesitated long about the placing of this land: in the Gnomish dictionary it was east of Artanor (II. 62), in the *Tale of Tinúviel* a 'northward region of Artanor', while here it is west of Sirion, in a valley of the southern slopes of the Shadowy Mountains. In the earliest 'Silmarillion' map Nan Dungorthin was first likewise placed west of Sirion (west of the Isle of Werewolves), before being returned once more to the region north of Doriath, where it remained.

It is said that when Túrin and Flinding climbed out of the vale of Nan Dungorthin they *southward saw the slopes of Hithlum / more warm and friendly* (1496–7). At first sight this seems difficult to understand, but I think that the meaning is: they were indeed on *the slopes of Hithlum* at the time (i.e. below the southern faces of the Shadowy Mountains that fenced Hithlum), but looking southward (actually southwestward) they saw more agreeable regions further along the foothills, towards Ivrin. This is the first appearance of Ivrin, source of the Narog, and it is seen very clearly. The line (1537) giving the meaning of *Narog* (Gnomish, 'torrent') was struck out, but this (I think) was because my father felt that it was intrusive, not that the etymology was rejected. In this connection it may be mentioned that in a list of Old English equivalents of Elvish names, composed some years after the time of the present poem and associated with Ælfwine's translations of Elvish texts into his own language, occur *Narog: Hlýda* and *Nargothrond: Hlýdingaburg*. Hlýda was the name in Old English of March ('the noisy month of wind'; cf. the Quenya name *Súlimë* and the Sindarin name *Gwaeron*); related words are *hlúd* (Modern English *loud*), *hlýd* 'sound', *hlýdan* 'make a sound'. The meaning is here undoubtedly 'the loud one'; it lies behind the English stream-name *Lydbrook*.

Following the course of the Narog southward from Ivrin, the travellers

> gained the gorge     where Ginglith turns
> all glad and golden     to greet the Narog.
> There her gentler torrent     joins his tumult,
> and they glide together     on the guarded plain
> to the Hunters' Hills     that high to southward
> uprear their rocks     robed in verdure.          (1736–41)

A little earlier Flinding has described to Túrin how Narog, passing Nargothrond, 'thence skirted wild the Hills of the Hunters, the home of Beren and the Dancer of Doriath' (1544–6). In these verses are the first appearances of the river Ginglith, the Guarded Plain, and the Hills of the Hunters (all shown on the earliest map), though the hills themselves are described without being named in the *Tale*, II. 96. On the map Nargothrond is shown near the northern extremity of the Hills of the Hunters, which extend far to the southward, falling down to the coast of the Sea west of Sirion's mouths. Various things are said of these hills. In the *Tale* they are 'high and tree-grown'; in the poem they *uprear their rocks     robed in verdure*; in *The Silmarillion* (p. 122), where they are called *Taur-en-Faroth* or *the High Faroth*, they are 'great wooded highlands'; in the *Narn* (p. 116) they are 'brown and bare'. In the poem they are also called *the Hunters' Wold* (1816), *the Wold of Hunters* (1992), where the word is probably used in the old sense of 'forest, wooded uplands'. If we judge by my father's unfinished watercolour of the Doors of Nargothrond, painted in all probability in 1928 (see *Pictures by J. R. R. Tolkien* no. 33), he saw the hills as great rocky heights standing up from thick forest on their lower slopes. At line 1746 the Wards of Narog look out from *their treegirt towers     on the tall hilltops*; these watchtowers were in the north of the Hills of the Hunters and looking northwards (1743–5), and it may not be casual therefore that on the earliest map the northern end (only) of the hills is shown as heavily forested.

As Túrin and Flinding came south down the west bank of Narog the river *hastened o'er the feet of the hills* (1770), and the fields and orchards through which they passed

> ever narrowing
> twixt wall and water     did wane at last
> to blossomy banks     by the borders of the way     (1812–14)

The map likewise shows the Narog drawing steadily closer to the northeastern edge of the Hills of the Hunters. Here the travellers crossed the foaming Ingwil, falling down from the hills, by a slender bridge; this is the first appearance of this stream (cf. *The Silmarillion* p. 122: 'the short and foaming stream Ringwil tumbled headlong into Narog from the High Faroth'), and the bridge over it is mentioned nowhere else. The Land of the Dead that Live (Beren and Tinúviel after their return) is now placed in the Hills of the Hunters (1545–6), where it was originally placed also on the map. This land was moved even more often than was Nan Dungorthin. In the *Tale of the Nauglafring* it was in Hisilómë (but with a note on the manuscript saying that it must be placed in 'Doriath beyond Sirion', II. 249); in the *Tale of Tinúviel* Beren and Tinúviel 'became mighty fairies in the lands about the north of Sirion' (II. 41). From the Hills of the Hunters it would subsequently be moved several times more.

Before leaving the Narog, we meet here for the first time in narrative writing the name *Nan-Tathrin* (1548), in the *Lost Tales* always called by its name in Eldarissa, *Tasarinan* (but *Nantathrin* occurs in the Gnomish dictionary, I. 265, entry *Sirion* and *Dor-tathrin* in the Name-list to *The Fall of Gondolin*, II. 346).

Far fuller than in any later account is the story in the poem of the sojourn of Túrin and his companion at Ivrin, and much that lies behind the passage in *The Silmarillion* (p. 209) is here revealed. In *The Silmarillion* Túrin drank from the water of Ivrin and was at last able to weep, and his madness passed; then he made a song for Beleg (*Laer Cú Beleg*, the Song of the Great Bow), 'singing it aloud heedless of peril'; and then he asked Gwindor who he was. In the Lay all these features of the story are present, somewhat differently ordered. Flinding describes to Túrin the courses of Narog and Sirion and the protection of Ulmo, and Túrin feels some return of hope (1586–7); they hasten down to the lake and drink (1599–1600); and *from the meshes of misery his mind was loosed* (1602). In the early night, as they sat beside their fire by the pools of Ivrin, Túrin asked Flinding his name and fate, and it was Flinding's reply that led Túrin at last to weep. Flinding fell asleep, but woke towards the end of the night to hear Túrin singing the dirge of Beleg by the edge of the lake (and here the song is called 'the Bowman's Friendship'). Túrin then himself fell asleep, and in his sleep he returned to the terrible place on the edge of Taur-na-Fuin where he slew Beleg, seeking the place of his burial and the lightning-blackened trees, and heard the voice of Beleg far off telling him to seek no longer but to take comfort in courage.

> Then he woke in wonder;   his wit was healed,
> courage him comforted,    and he called aloud
> Flinding go-Fuilin,   to his feet striding.      (1699–1701)

The structure of the episode in the Lay is firm and clear, the images strong and enduring. I said in the introduction to *Unfinished Tales* that it was grievous that my father went no further, in the later Tale of Tuor, than the coming of Tuor and Voronwë to the last gate and Tuor's sight of Gondolin across the plain. It is no less grievous that he never retold, in his later prose, the story of Túrin and Gwindor at the Lake of Ivrin. The passage in *The Silmarillion* is no substitute; and it is only from this poem that we can fully grasp the extremity of the disaster for Túrin, that he had killed his friend.

The description in the poem of the stealth and secrecy of the defenders of Nargothrond is derived, in concept, from the *Tale* (II. 81). In the *Tale*

the spies and watchers of the Rodothlim . . . gave warning of their approach, and the folk withdrew before them, such as were abroad from their dwelling. Then they closed their doors and hoped that the strangers might not discover their caves . . .

When Flinding and Túrin came to the mouths of the caves,

the Rodothlim sallied and made them prisoners and drew them within their rocky halls, and they were led before the chief, Orodreth.

All this is taken up into the poem and greatly elaborated; there is also the incident of Túrin's stumbling on a root and thus being missed by the arrow aimed at him, and Flinding's cry of reproach to the unseen archers, after which they were not further molested. It is perhaps not so clear in the poem as in the *Tale* that the farmlands and orchards of Nargothrond were deserted lest the travellers should find the entrance to the caves, especially since a *pathway plain     by passing feet/was broadly beaten* (1808–9) – though it is said that the throng in the great hall of Nargothrond was waiting for them (1856). Moreover, in the *Tale* they were not attacked. As the story is told in the poem, one might wonder why the hidden archers in the woods, if they believed Flinding's cry sufficiently to withhold their arrows, did not emerge at that point and conduct them as prisoners to the caves. The new element of the arrow shot in the woods has not, I think, been altogether assimilated to the old account of the timorous withdrawal of the Rodothlim in the hope that Túrin and Flinding would not find the entrance. But the passage describing the 'home-fields' of Nargothrond is of great interest in itself, for rarely are there references to the agriculture of the peoples of Middle-earth in the Elder Days.

The great Doors of Nargothrond are here first described – the triple doors of timber as my father imagined them are seen in his drawing of the entrance made in Dorset in the summer of 1928, and (in a different conception) *their posts and lintels     of ponderous stone* (1830) in the watercolour of the same period referred to above (*Pictures* nos 33, 34).

In the *Tale* the fear and suspicion among the Rodothlim of Noldoli who had been slaves is attributed to 'the evil deeds of the Gnomes at Cópas Alqalunten', and this element reappears in the poem (1903–4).

Nevertheless, there is no suggestion in the *Tale* of any serious question-
ing of the identity and goodwill of Flinding, greatly changed in aspect
though he was, so that 'few knew him again'.

In the poem, on the other
hand, Orodreth emerges as hostile and formidable, and his character is
carefully outlined: he is quick to anger (1973) but his wrath is cold and
long-enduring (2133–4), he is seldom moved to pity (1969, 2134),
grim-hearted and deep-counselled (2132–3), but capable of deep love
(1970) as also of fierce hate (2135). Afterwards, as the legends developed, Orodreth underwent a steady decline into weakness and insignifi-
cance, which is very curious. Many years later, when meditating the
development of the Túrin saga, my father noted that Orodreth was
'rather a weak character'; cf. the *Narn*, p. 160: 'he turned as he ever did
to Túrin for counsel'. Ultimately he was to be displaced as the second
King of Nargothrond (*Unfinished Tales* p. 255, note 20). But all this is a
far cry from the hard and grim king in his underground hall depicted in
the poem; Felagund had not yet emerged, nor the rebellious power of
Celegorm and Curufin in Nargothrond (see further p. 246).

The killing of Orodreth's son Halmir the hunter by Orcs (2137–8;
omitted in the C-text, p. 82) is a new element, which will reappear,
though not found in *The Silmarillion*, where the name *Halmir* is borne
by a ruler of the People of Haleth.

In the *Tale*, as I noticed in my commentary (II. 124),

Failivrin is already present, and her unrequited love for Túrin, but the
complication of her former relation with Gwindor is quite absent, and
she is not the daughter of Orodreth the King but of one Galweg (who
was to disappear utterly).

In the poem Galweg has already disappeared, and Failivrin has become
Orodreth's daughter, loved by Flinding and returning his love before his
captivity; and it is her plea to her father before the assembled multitude
that sways the king and leads to the admission of Flinding and Túrin to
Nargothrond. Of this intervention there is probably a trace in the very
condensed account in *The Silmarillion* (p. 209):

At first his own people did not know Gwindor, who went out young
and strong, and returned now seeming as one of the aged among
mortal Men, because of his torments and his labours; but Finduilas
daughter of Orodreth the King knew him and welcomed him, for she
had loved him before the Nirnaeth, and so greatly did Gwindor love
her beauty that he named her Faelivrin, which is the gleam of the sun
on the pools of Ivrin.

In the poem she is called *Failivrin* in A and B as written, emended or
not in B to *Finduilas* (1724, 1938, 2130), but the name *Finduilas*
emerges towards the end in the texts as first written (2175, 2199), and
*Failivrin (the glimmering sheen on the glassy pools / of Ivrin's
lake)* is the name by which the Elves renamed *Finduilas*.

In the Lay as in the *Tale* there is no hiding of Túrin's identity, as there is in *The Silmarillion*, where he checked Gwindor, when Gwindor would declare his name, saying that he was Agarwaen, the Bloodstained, son of Úmarth, Ill-fate (p. 210). Finduilas (Failivrin) asks:

> But are none yet nigh us    that knew of yore
> that mighty of Men [Húrin],    mark of kinship
> to seek and see    in these sorrow-laden
> form and features?                                    (1958–61)

and then

> No few were there found    who had fought of old
> where Finweg fell    in flame of swords
> and Húrin Thalion    had hewn the throngs,
> the dark Glamhoth's    demon legions          (1974–7)

and they declared that Turin's face was *the face of the father    new found on earth*. Against the second of these passages my father wrote in the margin: 'Not so.' This is a comment on the idea that there were many Gnomes in Nargothrond who had fought in the Battle of Unnumbered Tears (see pp. 84–5); according to the later story scarcely any went from Nargothrond, and of the small company that did none came back, save Flinding/Gwindor himself. – In *The Silmarillion* (p. 210) Túrin is not said to be the image of his father; on the contrary,

> he was in truth the son of Morwen Eledhwen to look upon: dark-haired and pale-skinned, with grey eyes.

Cf. also the *Narn*, p. 161, where Túrin said to Arminas:

> But if my head be dark and not golden, of that I am not ashamed. For I am not the first of sons in the likeness of his mother.

Húrin himself was

> shorter in stature than other men of his kin; in this he took after his mother's people, but in all else he was like Hador his grandfather, fair of face and golden-haired, strong in body and fiery of mood (*Narn* p. 57).

But Túrin was already conceived to be dark-haired in the Lay:

> the black-haired boy    from the beaten people          (417)

and in the second version of the poem Húrin also has *dark tresses* (p. 97, line 88).

At the feast of welcome in the house of Fuilin Flinding's father, deep in the woods on the slopes of the Hunters' Wold (1989–92), Fuilin filled with mead a great ancient silver cup that had come from Valinor:

                         carved in gladness,
             in woe hoarded,    in waning hope
             when little was left    of the lore of old.        (2038–40)

It was of such things as that cup, carved with images of *the folk of Faërie in the first noontide / of the Blissful Realms*, of the Two Trees, and of the tower of Ing on the hill of Côr, that my father was thinking when he wrote of the treasures that Finrod Felagund brought out of Tirion (*The Silmarillion* p. 114); 'a solace and a burden on the road' (*ibid.* p. 85). – This is the first reference to the tower of Ing (Ingwë, see p. 28) in the Elvish city, whose

                 pale pinnacle    pierced the twilight,
             and its crystal lamp    illumined clear
             with slender shaft    the Shadowy Seas        (2033–5)

as afterwards the silver lamp of the Mindon Eldaliéva 'shone far out into the mists of the sea' (*The Silmarillion* p. 59).

According to the readings of the A and B texts at lines 2030–2 the hill on which the Elvish city was built, figured on Fuilin's cup, is *Tûn*, crowned by the white-walled city of Côr; and this is anomalous, since the name *Tûn* certainly arose as the name of the city (see II. 292), and in the 'Sketch of the Mythology' and the 1930 'Silmarillion' Kôr is the hill and Tûn the city. In the C-text of the poem, however, these lines were changed, and the city is named Tûn (p. 82).

The elaboration at the end of the relationship of Túrin and Finduilas is an indication of the large scale on which this work was planned: seeing how much in bare narrative terms is yet to come (the fall of Nargothrond, the Dragon, the loss of Finduilas, Túrin's journey to Dor-lómin, Morwen and Nienor in Doriath and the journey to Nargothrond, the enspelling of Nienor, Túrin and Nienor among the Woodmen, the coming and death of the Dragon, and the deaths of Nienor and Túrin) it must have run to many more thousands of lines.

There remain a few isolated matters. The name *Esgalduin* now first appears, but the form in A and B as typed (2164), *Esgaduin*, is the original name. The C-text has *Esgalduin* (p. 82).

The Moon is seen in lines 2088–94 as a ship, the Silver Wherry, with mast, hold, and shrouds, sailing from wharves on the margin of the world; but the imagery has no real point of contact with the Ship of the Moon in the *Tale of the Sun and Moon* (I. 192–3).

Ulmo is now called *Ylmir* (first appearing by emendation in B at line 1469, but thereafter in both A and B as first written); in the 'Sketch' he first appears as *Ulmo (Ylmir)*, thereafter as *Ylmir*, suggesting that at this time *Ylmir* was the Gnomish form of his name (in the Gnomish dictionary it was *Gulma*, I. 270). He is also called *the Dweller in the Deep* at line

1565, as he is in the later *Tuor* (*Unfinished Tales* pp. 22, 28). Flinding mentions messages from Ulmo that are heard at Ivrin, and says that Ulmo *alone remembers   in the Lands of Mirth/the need of the Gnomes* (1531 ff.); cf. the *Tale*, II. 77.

Lastly may be noticed Túrin's words of parting to Beleg at his burial (1408–11), in which he foresees for him an afterlife in Valinor, in the halls of the Gods, and does not speak of a time of 'waiting'; cf. lines 1283–4, 1696–7.

————

# THE SECOND VERSION
# OF
# THE CHILDREN OF HÚRIN

This version of the poem (II) is extant in a bundle of very rough manuscript notes (IIA), which do not constitute a complete text, and a typescript (IIB) – the twin of the typescript (IB) of the first version, done with the same distinctive purple ribbon – based on IIA. That II is a later work than I is obvious from a casual scrutiny – to give a single example, the name *Morwen* appears thus both in IIA and IIB. As I have said (p. 4), I do not think that II is significantly later than I, and may indeed have been composed before my father ceased work on I.* Towards the end of II the amount of expansion and change from I becomes very much less, but it seems best to give II in full.

The text of the opening of the second version is complicated by the existence of two further texts, both extending from lines II. 1–94. The earlier of these is another typescript (IIC), which takes up emendations made to IIB and is itself emended: the second is a manuscript (IID) written on 'Oxford' paper (see p. 81), which takes up the changes made to IIC and introduces yet further changes. At the beginning of the poem, therefore, we have lines that exhibit a continuous development through six different texts, as for example line 18 in the first version, which is line 34 in the second:

IA   Yet in host upon host   the hillfiends, the orcs *emended in the manuscript to*:

Yet in host upon host   the hillfiend orcs

IB   There in host on host   the hill-fiend Orcs

*The only external evidence for date (other than the physical nature of the texts, which were clearly made at Leeds, not at Oxford) is the fact that a page of IIA is written on the back of a formal letter from *The Microcosm* (a Leeds literary quarterly, in which my father published the poem *The City of the Gods* in the Spring 1923 issue, see I. 136) acknowledging receipt of a subscription for 1922; the letter was evidently written in 1923.

IIA but in host on host   from the hills of darkness (*with* from the hills swarming *as an alternative*)

IIB but in host on host   from the hills swarming

IIC *as IIB but emended on the typescript to*:

and in host on host   from the hills swarming

IID In host upon host   from the hills swarming

The majority of the changes throughout the successive texts of the poem were made for metrical reasons – in the later revisions, especially for the removal of 'little words', to achieve an effect nearer to that of Old English lines, and to get rid of metrical aids such as -*éd* pronounced as a separate syllable; and as I have said, the provision of a full apparatus would be exceedingly lengthy and complex (and in places scarcely possible, for the actual texts are often more obscure than appears in print). For the second version of the poem, therefore, I give the text of IID (the last one) to its end at line 94 (since the changes from IIB though pervasive are extremely minor), and continue thereafter with IIB (the major typescript of the second version); and as before purely verbal/metrical alterations that have no bearing on the story or on names are not cited in the notes.

IIA has no title; in IIB it was TÚRIN, then THE CHILDREN OF HÚRIN, which is also the title in IIC and IID.

The 'Prologue', greatly expanded in the second version, is still given no subheading, except that in IIC it is marked 'I'; in IIB *Túrin's Fostering* is a section-heading, to which my father afterwards added 'II'.

# THE CHILDREN OF HÚRIN

## I

Ye Gods who girt   your guarded realms
with moveless pinnacles,   mountains pathless,
o'er shrouded shores   sheer uprising
of the Bay of Faëry   on the borders of the World!
Ye Men unmindful   of the mirth of yore,     5
wars and weeping   in the worlds of old,
of Morgoth's might   remembering nought!
Lo! hear what Elves   with ancient harps,
lingering forlorn   in lands untrodden,
fading faintly   down forest pathways,     10
in shadowy isles   on the Shadowy Seas,

sing still in sorrow    of the son of Húrin,
how his webs of doom    were woven dark
with Níniel's sorrow:    names most mournful.

A! Húrin Thalion    in the hosts of battle                          15
was whelmed in war,    when the white banners
of the ruined king    were rent with spears,
in blood beaten;    when the blazing helm
of Finweg fell    in flame of swords,
and his gleaming armies'    gold and silver                         20
shields were shaken,    shining emblems
in darkling tide    of dire hatred,
the cruel Glamhoth's    countless legions,
were lost and foundered –    their light was quenched!
That field yet now    the folk name it                              25
Nirnaith Ornoth,    Unnumbered Tears:
the seven chieftains    of the sons of Men
fled there and fought not,    the folk of the Elves
betrayed with treason.    Their troth alone
unmoved remembered    in the mouths of Hell                         30
Thalion Erithámrod    and his thanes renowned.
Torn and trampled    the triple standard
of the house of Hithlum    was heaped with slain.
In host upon host    from the hills swarming
with hideous arms    the hungry Orcs                                35
enmeshed his might,    and marred with wounds
pulled down the proud    Prince of Mithrim.
At Bauglir's bidding    they bound him living;
to the halls of Hell    neath the hills builded,
to the Mountains of Iron,    mournful, gloomy,                      40
they led the lord    of the Lands of Mist,
Húrin Thalion,    to the throne of hate
in halls upheld    with huge pillars
of black basalt.    There bats wandered,
worms and serpents    enwound the columns;                         45
there Bauglir's breast    was burned within
with blazing rage,    baulked of purpose:
from his trap had broken    Turgon the mighty,
Fingolfin's son;    Fëanor's children,
the makers of the magic and immortal gems.                         50
For Húrin standing    storm unheeding,
unbent in battle,    with bitter laughter

his axe wielded –   as eagle's wings
the sound of its sweep,   swinging deadly;
as livid lightning   it leaped and fell,                            55
as toppling trunks   of trees riven
his foes had fallen.   Thus fought he on,
where blades were blunted   and in blood foundered
the Men of Mithrim;   thus a moment stemmed
with sad remnant   the raging surge                              60
of ruthless Orcs,   and the rear guarded,
that Turgon the terrible   towering in anger
a pathway clove   with pale falchion
from swirling slaughter.   Yea! his swath was plain
through the hosts of Hell,   as hay that is laid              65
on the lea in lines,   where long and keen
goes sweeping scythe.   Thus seven kindreds,
a countless company,   that king guided
through darkened dales   and drear mountains
out of ken of his foes –   he comes no more                   70
in the tale of Túrin.   Triumph of Morgoth
thus to doubt was turned,   dreams of vengeance,
thus his mind was moved   with malice fathomless,
thoughts of darkness,   when the Thalion stood
bound, unbending,   in his black dungeon.                       75

Said the dread Lord of Hell:   'Dauntless Húrin,
stout steel-handed,   stands before me
yet quick a captive,   as a coward might be!
Then knows he my name,   or needs be told
what hope he has   in the halls of iron?                          80
The bale most bitter,   Balrogs' torment!'

Then Húrin answered,   Hithlum's chieftain –
his shining eyes   with sheen of fire
in wrath were reddened:   'O ruinous one,
by fear unfettered   I have fought thee long,                   85
nor dread thee now,   nor thy demon slaves,
fiends and phantoms,   thou foe of Gods!'
His dark tresses,   drenched and tangled,
that fell o'er his face   he flung backward,
in the eye he looked   of the evil Lord –                          90
since that day of dread   to dare his glance
has no mortal Man   had might of soul.
There the mind of Húrin   in a mist of dark

neath gaze unfathomed    groped and foundered,*
yet his heart yielded not    nor his haughty pride.          95
But Lungorthin    Lord of Balrogs
on the mouth smote him,    and Morgoth smiled:
'Nay, fear when thou feelest,    when the flames lick thee
and the whistling whips    thy white body
and wilting flesh    weal and torture!'                     100
Then hung they helpless    Húrin dauntless
in chains by fell    enchantments forged
that with fiery anguish    his flesh devoured,
yet loosed not lips    locked in silence
to pray for pity.    Thus prisoned saw he               105
on the sable walls    the sultry glare
of far-off fires    fiercely burning
down deep corridors    and dark archways
in the blind abysses    of those bottomless halls;
there with mourning mingled    mighty tumult              110
the throb and thunder    of the thudding forges'
brazen clangour;    belched and spouted
flaming furnaces;    there faces sad
through the glooms glided    as the gloating Orcs
their captives herded    under cruel lashes.              115
Many a hopeless glance    on Húrin fell,
for his tearless torment    many tears were spilled.

Lo! Morgoth remembered    the mighty doom,
the weird of old,    that the Elves in woe,
in ruin and wrack    by the reckless hearts               120
of mortal Men    should be meshed at last;
that treason alone    of trusted friend
should master the magic    whose mazes wrapped
the children of Côr,    cheating his purpose,
from defeat fending    Fingolfin's son,                   125
Turgon the terrible,    and the troth-brethren
the sons of Fëanor,    and secret, far,
homes hid darkly    in the hoar forest
where Thingol was throned    in the Thousand Caves.

Then the Lord of Hell    lying-hearted                    130
to where Húrin hung    hastened swiftly,

---

*Here the latest text IID ends, and IIB is followed from this point; see p. 95.

and the Balrogs about him    brazen-handed
with flails of flame    and forgéd iron
there laughed as they looked    on his lonely woe;
but Bauglir said:  'O bravest of Men,                             135
'tis fate unfitting    for thus fellhanded
warrior warfain    that to worthless friends
his sword he should sell,    who seek no more
to free him from fetters    or his fall avenge.
While shrinking in the shadows    they shake fearful        140
in the hungry hills    hiding outcast
their league belying,    lurking faithless,
he by evil lot    in everlasting
dungeons droopeth    doomed to torment
and anguish endless.    That thy arms unchained          145
I had fainer far    should a falchion keen
or axe with edge    eager flaming
wield in warfare    where the wind bloweth
the banners of battle –    such a brand as might
in my sounding smithies    on the smitten anvil           150
of glowing steel    to glad thy soul
be forged and fashioned,    yea, and fair harness
and mail unmatched –    than that marred with flails
my mercy waiving    thou shouldst moan enchained
neath the brazen Balrogs'    burning scourges:            155
who art worthy to win    reward and honour
as a captain of arms    when cloven is mail
and shields are shorn,    when they shake the hosts
of their foes like fire    in fell onset.
Lo! receive my service;    forswear hatred,                   160
ancient enmity    thus ill-counselled –
I am a mild master    who remembers well
his servants' deeds.    A sword of terror
thy hand should hold,    and a high lordship
as Bauglir's champion,    chief of Balrogs,                   165
to lead o'er the lands    my loud armies,
whose royal array    I already furnish;
on Turgon the troll    (who turned to flight
and left thee alone,    now leaguered fast
in waterless wastes    and weary mountains)                170
my wrath to wreak,    and on redhanded
robber-Gnomes, rebels,    and roaming Elves,
that forlorn witless    the Lord of the World

defy in their folly –    they shall feel my might.
I will bid men unbind thee,    and thy body comfort!                175
Go follow their footsteps    with fire and steel,
with thy sword go search    their secret dwellings;
when in triumph victorious    thou returnest hither,
I have hoards unthought-of' –    but Húrin Thalion
suffered no longer    silent wordless;                              180
through clenchéd teeth    in clinging pain,
'O accursed king',    cried unwavering,
'thy hopes build not    so high, Bauglir;
no tool am I    for thy treasons vile,
who tryst nor troth    ever true holdest –                         185
seek traitors elsewhere.'

                        Then returned answer
Morgoth amazed    his mood hiding:
'Nay, madness holds thee;    thy mind wanders;
my measureless hoards    are mountains high
in places secret    piled uncounted                                190
agelong unopened;    Elfin silver
and gold in the gloom    there glister pale;
the gems and jewels    once jealous-warded
in the mansions of the Gods,    who mourn them yet,
are mine, and a meed    I will mete thee thence                    195
of wealth to glut    the Worm of Greed.'

Then Húrin, hanging,    in hate answered:
'Canst not learn of thy lore    when thou look'st on a foe,
O Bauglir unblest?    Bray no longer
of the things thou hast thieved    from the Three Kindreds!        200
In hate I hold thee.    Thou art humbled indeed
and thy might is minished    if thy murderous hope
and cruel counsels    on a captive sad
must wait, on a weak    and weary man.'
To the hosts of Hell    his head then he turned:                  205
'Let thy foul banners    go forth to battle,
ye Balrogs and Orcs;    let your black legions
go seek the sweeping    sword of Turgon.
Through the dismal dales    you shall be driven wailing
like startled starlings    from the stooks of wheat.              210
Minions miserable    of master base,
your doom dread ye,    dire disaster!
The tide shall turn;    your triumph brief

and victory shall vanish.    I view afar
the wrath of the Gods    roused in anger.'                           215

Then tumult awoke,    a tempest wild
in rage roaring    that rocked the walls;
consuming madness    seized on Morgoth,
yet with lowered voice    and leering mouth
thus Thalion Erithámrod    he threatened darkly:             220
'Thou hast said it!    See    how my swift purpose
shall march to its mark    unmarred of thee,
nor thy aid be asked,    overweening
mortal mightless.    I command thee gaze
on my deeds of power    dreadly proven.                       225
Yet if little they like thee,    thou must look thereon
helpless to hinder    or thy hand to raise,
and thy lidless eyes    lit with anguish
shall not shut for ever,    shorn of slumber
like the Gods shall gaze    there grim, tearless,             230
on the might of Morgoth    and the meed he deals
to fools who refuse    fealty gracious.'

To Thangorodrim    was the Thalion borne,
that mountain that meets    the misty skies
on high over the hills    that Hithlum sees                   235
blackly brooding    on the borders of the North.
There stretched on the stone    of steepest peak
in bonds unbreakable    they bound him living;
there the lord of woe    in laughter stood,
there cursed him for ever    and his kindred all              240
that should walk and wander    in woe's shadow
to a doom of death    and dreadful end.
There the mighty man    unmovéd sat,
but unveiled was his vision    that he viewed afar
with eyes enchanted    all earthly things,                    245
and the weird of woe    woven darkly
that fell on his folk –    a fiend's torment.

★

## NOTES

14    After this line IIB had the following:

> how the golden dragon    of the God of darkness
> wrought wrack and ruin    in realms now lost –
> only the mighty of soul,    of Men or Elves,
> doom can conquer,    and in death only.

These lines were struck out in IIB, and do not appear in IIC, IID.

19    Cf. I. 1975:

> where Finweg fell    in flame of swords

with *Finweg* > *Fingon* a later pencilled change in IB. All the texts of II have *Finweg* (IIA *Fingweg*), but *Fingon* appears in a late pencilled emendation to IID.

26    *Nirnaith Únoth* IIB, IIC; *Nirnaith Ornoth* IID, emended in pencil to *Nirnaith Arnediad*. For *Únoth, Ornoth* in the first version see p. 79, notes to lines 1448, 1542–3. I read *Ornoth* here, since *Arnediad* is a form that arose much later.

27    All the texts of II have *the chosen chieftains    of the children of Men*, but IID is emended in pencil to *the seven chieftains    of the sons of Men*.

49    *Fingolfin's son*: see p. 21, note to line 29.
      *Fëanor's children* IID; *and Fëanor's children* IIA, B, C.

76    *'Is it dauntless Húrin,'    quoth Delu-Morgoth* IIB, as in IB (line 51).

157   *as a captain among them* IIB as typed. Cf line 165.

## Commentary on Part I
### of the second version

This part has been expanded to two and a half times its former length, partly through the introduction of descriptions of Angband (42–5, 105–15) – to be greatly enlarged some years later in the *Lay of Leithian*, and of Húrin's last stand (51–61), but chiefly through the much extended account of Morgoth's dealings with Húrin, his attempted seduction of 'the Thalion', and his great rage (not found at all in the first version) at his failure to break his will. The rewritten scene is altogether fiercer, the sense of lying, brutality, and pain (and the heroic power of Húrin's resistance) much stronger.

   There are some interesting details in this opening section. Húrin's dark hair (88) has been referred to above (p. 92). The *thane of Morgoth* who smote him on the mouth (version I, 59) now becomes *Lungorthin, Lord of Balrogs* (96) – which is probably to be interpreted as 'a

Balrog lord', since Gothmog, Lord or Captain of the Balrogs in *The Fall of Gondolin*, soon reappears in the 'Silmarillion' tradition. Notable is the passage (88–94) in which Húrin, thrusting back his long hair, looked into Morgoth's eye, and his mind *in a mist of dark . . . groped and foundered*: the originator of the power of the eye of Glórund his servant, which this poem did not reach.

A line that occurs much later in the first version (1975)

> where Finweg [> Fingon] fell   in flame of swords

is introduced here (19), and there is mention also of his *white banners . . . in blood beaten*, and his *blazing helm*: this is ultimately the origin of the passage in *The Silmarillion* (pp. 193–4):

> a white flame sprang up from the helm of Fingon as it was cloven . . . they beat him into the dust with their maces, and his banner, blue and silver, they trod into the mire of his blood.

At line 26 is the first occurrence of *Nirnaith Arnediad*, but this is a hasty pencilled change to the last text (IID) and belongs to a later phase of nomenclature.

It is said that Turgon guided *seven kindreds* (67) out of the battle; in the tale of *The Fall of Gondolin* there were twelve kindreds of the Gondothlim.

Húrin is named the Prince of Mithrim (37), and his men the Men of Mithrim (59). This may suggest that the meaning of Mithrim, hitherto the name of the lake only, was being extended to the region in which the lake lay; on the earliest 'Silmarillion' map, however, this is not suggested. *The land of Mithrim* occurs at line 248, but the phrase was changed.

The passage in the first version (46–50) saying that Morgoth

> remembered well
> how Men were accounted   all mightless and frail
> by the Elves and their kindred;   how only treason
> could master the magic   whose mazes wrapped
> the children of Corthûn

is changed in the second (118–24) to

> Lo! Morgoth remembered   the mighty doom,
> the weird of old,   that the Elves in woe,
> in ruin and wrack   by the reckless hearts
> of mortal Men   should be meshed at last;
> that treason alone   of trusted friend
> should master the magic   whose mazes wrapped
> the children of Côr

There has been no reference in the *Lost Tales* to any such ancient 'doom' or 'weird'. It is possible that the reference to 'treason' is to the 'Prophecy of the North', spoken by Mandos or his messenger as the host of the

Noldor moved northward up the coast of Valinor after the Kinslaying
(*The Silmarillion* pp. 87–8); in the earliest version of this, in the tale of
*The Flight of the Noldoli* (I. 167), there is no trace of the idea, but it is
already explicit in the 1930 'Silmarillion' that the Gnomes should pay for
the deeds at Swanhaven in 'treachery and the fear of treachery among
their own kindred'. On the other hand, to *the mighty doom, the weird
of old* is ascribed also the ultimate ruin of the Elves which is to come to
pass through Men; and this is not found in any version of the Prophecy of
the North. This passage in the revised version of the poem is echoed in
the same scene in the 1930 'Silmarillion':

> Afterward Morgoth remembering that treachery or the fear of it, and
> especially the treachery of Men, alone would work the ruin of the
> Gnomes, came to Húrin . . .

★

## II
## TÚRIN'S FOSTERING

Lo! the lady Morwen    in the land of shadow
waited in the woodland    for her well-beloved,
but he came never    to clasp her nigh        250
from that black battle.    She abode in vain;
no tidings told her    whether taken or dead
or lost in flight    he lingered yet.
Laid waste his lands    and his lieges slain,
and men unmindful    of that mighty lord        255
in Dorlómin dwelling    dealt unkindly
with his wife in widowhood;    she went with child,
and a son must succour    sadly orphaned,
Túrin Thalion    of tender years.
In days of blackness    was her daughter born,        260
and named Nienor,    a name of tears
that in language of eld    is Lamentation.
Then her thoughts were turned    to Thingol the Elf,
and Lúthien the lissom    with limbs shining,
his daughter dear,    by Dairon loved,        265
who Tinúviel was named    both near and far,
the Star-mantled,    still remembered,
who light as leaf    on linden tree
had danced in Doriath    in days agone,
on the lawns had lilted    in the long moonshine,        270

while deftly was drawn    Dairon's music
with fingers fleet    from flutes of silver.
The boldest of the brave,    Beren Ermabwed,
to wife had won her,    who once of old
had vowed fellowship    and friendly love                    275
with Húrin of Hithlum,    hero dauntless
by the marge of Mithrim's    misty waters.
Thus to her son she said:    'My sweetest child,
our friends are few;    thy father is gone.
Thou must fare afar    to the folk of the wood,              280
where Thingol is throned    in the Thousand Caves.
If he remember Morwen    and thy mighty sire
he will foster thee fairly,    and feats of arms,
the trade he will teach thee    of targe and sword,
that no slave in Hithlum    shall be son of Húrin.           285
A! return my Túrin    when time passeth;
remember thy mother    when thy manhood cometh
or when sorrows snare thee.'    Then silence took her,
for fears troubled    her trembling voice.
Heavy boded the heart    of Húrin's son,                     290
who unwitting of her woe    wondered vaguely,
yet weened her words    were wild with grief
and denied her not;    no need him seemed.

Lo! Mailrond and Halog,    Morwen's henchmen,
were young of yore    ere the youth of Húrin,                295
and alone of the lieges    of that lord of Men
now steadfast in service    stayed beside her:
now she bade them brave    the black mountains
and the woods whose ways    wander to evil;
though Túrin be tender,    to travail unused,                300
they must gird them and go.    Glad they were not,
but to doubt the wisdom    dared not openly
of Morwen who mourned    when men saw not.

Came a day of summer    when the dark silence
of the towering trees    trembled dimly                      305
to murmurs moving    in the milder airs
far and faintly;    flecked with dancing
sheen of silver    and shadow-filtered
sudden sunbeams    were the secret glades
where winds came wayward    wavering softly                  310
warm through the woodland's    woven branches.

Then Morwen stood,    her mourning hidden,
by the gate of her garth    in a glade of Hithlum;
at her breast bore she    her babe unweaned,
crooning lowly    to its careless ears                    315
a song of sweet    and sad cadence,
lest she droop for anguish.    Then the doors opened,
and Halog hastened    neath a heavy burden,
and Mailrond the old    to his mistress led
her gallant Túrin,    grave and tearless,                 320
with heart heavy as stone    hard and lifeless,
uncomprehending    his coming torment.
There he cried with courage,    comfort seeking:
'Lo! quickly will I come    from the courts afar,
I will long ere manhood    lead to Morwen               325
great tale of treasure    and true comrades.'
He wist not the weird    woven of Morgoth,
nor the sundering sorrow    that them swept between,
as farewells they took    with faltering lips.
The last kisses    and lingering words                    330
are over and ended;    and empty is the glen
in the dark forest,    where the dwelling faded
in trees entangled.    Then in Túrin woke
to woe's knowledge    his bewildered heart,
that he wept blindly    awakening echoes               335
sad resounding    in sombre hollows,
as he called: 'I cannot,    I cannot leave thee.
O! Morwen my mother,    why makest me go?
The hills are hateful,    where hope is lost;
O! Morwen my mother,    I am meshed in tears,         340
for grim are the hills    and my home is gone.'
And there came his cries    calling faintly
down the dark alleys    of the dreary trees,
that one there weeping    weary on the threshold
heard how the hills said    'my home is gone.'          345

*        *        *

The ways were weary    and woven with deceit
o'er the hills of Hithlum    to the hidden kingdom
deep in the darkness    of Doriath's forest,
and never ere now    for need or wonder
had children of Men    chosen that pathway,           350
save Beren the brave    who bounds knew not

to his wandering feet    nor feared the woods
or fells or forest    or frozen mountain,
and few had followed    his feet after.
There was told to Túrin    that tale by Halog          355
that in the Lay of Leithian,    Release from Bonds,
in linkéd words    has long been woven,
of Beren Ermabwed,    the boldhearted;
how Lúthien the lissom    he loved of yore
in the enchanted forest    chained with wonder –          360
Tinúviel he named her,    than nightingale
more sweet her voice,    as veiled in soft
and wavering wisps    of woven dusk
shot with starlight,    with shining eyes
she danced like dreams    of drifting sheen,          365
pale-twinkling pearls    in pools of darkness;
how for love of Lúthien    he left the woods
on that quest perilous    men quail to tell,
thrust by Thingol    o'er the thirst and terror
of the Lands of Mourning;    of Lúthien's tresses,          370
and Melian's magic,    and the marvellous deeds
that after happened    in Angband's halls,
and the flight o'er fell    and forest pathless
when Carcharoth    the cruel-fangéd,
the wolf-warden    of the Woeful Gates,          375
whose vitals fire    devoured in torment
them hunted howling    (the hand of Beren
he had bitten from the wrist    where that brave one held
the nameless wonder,    the Gnome-crystal
where light living    was locked enchanted,          380
all hue's essence.    His heart was eaten,
and the woods were filled    with wild madness
in his dreadful torment,    and Doriath's trees
did shudder darkly    in the shrieking glens);
how the hound of Hithlum,    Huan wolf-bane,          385
to the hunt hasted    to the help of Thingol,
and as dawn came dimly    in Doriath's woods
was the slayer slain,    but silent lay
there Beren bleeding    nigh brought to death,
till the lips of Lúthien    in love's despair          390
awoke him to words,    ere he winged afar
to the long awaiting;    thence Lúthien won him,
the Elf-maiden,    and the arts of Melian,

her mother Mablui    of the moonlit hand,
that they dwell for ever    in days ageless                     395
and the grass greys not    in the green forest
where East or West    they ever wander.
Then a song he made them    for sorrow's lightening,
a sudden sweetness    in the silent wood,
that is 'Light as Leaf    on Linden' called,                    400
whose music of mirth    and mourning blended
yet in hearts does echo.    This did Halog sing them:*

   The grass was very long and thin,
     The leaves of many years lay thick,
   The old tree-roots wound out and in,                   405
     And the early moon was glimmering.
   There went her white feet lilting quick,
     And Dairon's flute did bubble thin,
   As neath the hemlock umbels thick
     Tinúviel danced a-shimmering.                        410

   The pale moths lumbered noiselessly,
     And daylight died among the leaves,
   As Beren from the wild country
     Came thither wayworn sorrowing.
   He peered between the hemlock sheaves,                  415
     And watched in wonder noiselessly
   Her dancing through the moonlit leaves
     And the ghostly moths a-following.

   There magic took his weary feet,
     And he forgot his loneliness,                        420
   And out he danced, unheeding, fleet,
     Where the moonbeams were a-glistening.
   Through the tangled woods of Elfinesse
     They fled on nimble fairy feet,
   And left him to his loneliness                         425
     In the silent forest listening,

   Still hearkening for the imagined sound
     Of lissom feet upon the leaves,

*For the textual history of this poem's insertion into the Lay see the Note on pp. 120–2.

For music welling underground
   In the dim-lit caves of Doriath.                          430
But withered are the hemlock sheaves,
   And one by one with mournful sound
Whispering fall the beechen leaves
   In the dying woods of Doriath.

He sought her wandering near and far                           435
   Where the leaves of one more year were strewn,
By winter moon and frosty star
   With shaken light a-shivering.
He found her neath a misty moon,
   A silver wraith that danced afar,                         440
And the mists beneath her feet were strewn
   In moonlight palely quivering.

She danced upon a hillock green
   Whose grass unfading kissed her feet,
While Dairon's fingers played unseen                           445
   O'er his magic flute a-flickering;
And out he danced, unheeding, fleet,
   In the moonlight to the hillock green:
No impress found he of her feet
   That fled him swiftly flickering.                        450

And longing filled his voice that called
   'Tinúviel, Tinúviel,'
And longing sped his feet enthralled
   Behind her wayward shimmering.
She heard as echo of a spell                                   455
   His lonely voice that longing called
'Tinúviel, Tinúviel':
   One moment paused she glimmering.

And Beren caught that elfin maid
   And kissed her trembling starlit eyes,                   460
Tinúviel whom love delayed
   In the woods of evening morrowless.
Till moonlight and till music dies
   Shall Beren by the elfin maid
Dance in the starlight of her eyes                             465
   In the forest singing sorrowless.

Wherever grass is long and thin,
　　And the leaves of countless years lie thick,
And ancient roots wind out and in,
　　As once they did in Doriath,                                    470
Shall go their white feet lilting quick,
　　But never Dairon's music thin
Be heard beneath the hemlocks thick
　　Since Beren came to Doriath.


This for hearts' uplifting　　did Halog sing them          475
as the frowning fortress　　of the forest clasped them
and nethermost night　　in its net caught them.
There Túrin and the twain　　knew torture of thirst
and hunger and fear,　　and hideous flight
from wolfriders　　and wandering Orcs                          480
and the things of Morgoth　　that thronged the woods.
There numbed and wetted　　they had nights of waking
cold and clinging,　　when the creaking winds
summer had vanquished　　and in silent valleys
a dismal dripping　　in the distant shadows                    485
ever splashed and spilt　　over spaces endless
from rainy leaves,　　till arose the light
greyly, grudgingly,　　gleaming thinly
at drenching dawn.　　They were drawn as flies
in the magic mazes;　　they missed their ways               490
and strayed steerless,　　and the stars were hid
and the sun sickened.　　Sombre and weary
had the mountains been;　　the marches of Doriath
bewildered and wayworn　　wound them helpless
in despair and error,　　and their spirits foundered.        495
Without bread or water　　with bleeding feet
and fainting strength　　in the forest straying
their death they deemed it　　to die forwandered,
when they heard a horn　　that hooted afar
and dogs baying.　　Lo! the dreary bents                      500
and hushed hollows　　to the hunt wakened,
and echoes answered　　to eager tongues,
for Beleg the bowman　　was blowing gaily,
who furthest fared　　of his folk abroad
by hill and by hollow　　ahunting far,                        505
careless of comrades　　or crowded halls,
as light as a leaf,　　as the lusty airs

as free and fearless    in friendless places.
He was great of growth    with goodly limbs
and lithe of girth,    and lightly on the ground        510
his footsteps fell    as he fared towards them
all garbed in grey    and green and brown.

'Who are ye?' he asked.    'Outlaws, maybe,
hiding, hunted,    by hatred dogged?'

'Nay, for famine and thirst    we faint,' said Halog,    515
'wayworn and wildered,    and wot not the road.
Or hast not heard    of the hills of slain,
field tear-drenchéd    where in flame and terror
Morgoth devoured    the might and valour
of the hosts of Finweg    and Hithlum's lord?        520
The Thalion Erithámrod    and his thanes dauntless
there vanished from the earth,    whose valiant lady
yet weeps in widowhood    as she waits in Hithlum.
Thou lookest on the last    of the lieges of Morwen,
and the Thalion's child    who to Thingol's court        525
now wend at the word    of the wife of Húrin.'

Then Beleg bade them    be blithe, saying:
'The Gods have guided you    to good keeping;
I have heard of the house    of Húrin undaunted,
and who hath not heard    of the hills of slain,        530
of Nirnaith Ornoth,    Unnumbered Tears!
To that war I went not,    yet wage a feud
with the Orcs unending,    whom mine arrows fleeting
smite oft unseen    swift and deadly.
I am the hunter Beleg    of the hidden people;        535
the forest is my father    and the fells my home.'
Then he bade them drink    from his belt drawing
a flask of leather    full-filled with wine
that is bruised from the berries    of the burning South –
the Gnome-folk know it,    from Nogrod the Dwarves        540
by long ways lead it    to the lands of the North
for the Elves in exile    who by evil fate
the vine-clad valleys    now view no more
in the land of Gods.    There was lit gladly
a fire, with flames    that flared and spluttered,        545
of wind-fallen wood    that his wizard's cunning
rotten, rain-sodden,    to roaring life

there coaxed and kindled    by craft or magic;
there baked they flesh    in the brands' embers;
white wheaten bread    to hearts' delight    550
he haled from his wallet    till hunger waned
and hope mounted,    but their heads were mazed
by that wine of Dor-Winion    that went in their veins,
and they soundly slept    on the soft needles
of the tall pinetrees    that towered above.    555
Then they waked and wondered,    for the woods were light,
and merry was the morn    and the mists rolling
from the radiant sun.    They soon were ready
long leagues to cover.    Now led by ways
devious winding    through the dark woodland,    560
by slade and slope    and swampy thicket,
through lonely days,    long-dragging nights,
they fared unfaltering,    and their friend they blessed,
who but for Beleg    had been baffled utterly
by the magic mazes    of Melian the Queen.    565
To those shadowy shores    he showed the way
where stilly the stream    strikes before the gates
of the cavernous court    of the King of Doriath.
Over the guarded bridge    he gained them passage,
and thrice they thanked him,    and thought in their hearts    570
'the Gods are good' –    had they guessed, maybe,
what the future enfolded,    they had feared to live.

To the throne of Thingol    were the three now come;
there their speech well sped,    and he spake them fair,
for Húrin of Hithlum    he held in honour,    575
whom Beren Ermabwed    as a brother had loved
and remembering Morwen,    of mortals fairest,
he turned not Túrin    in contempt away.
There clasped him kindly    the King of Doriath,
for Melian moved him    with murmured counsel,    580
and he said: 'Lo, O son    of the swifthanded,
the light in laughter,    the loyal in need,
Húrin of Hithlum,    thy home is with me,
and here shalt sojourn    and be held my son.
In these cavernous courts    for thy kindred's sake    585
thou shalt dwell in dear love,    till thou deemest it time
to remember thy mother    Morwen's loneliness;
thou shalt wisdom win    beyond wit of mortals,

and weapons shalt wield     as the warrior-Elves,
nor slave in Hithlum     shall be son of Húrin.'                    590

There the twain tarried     that had tended the child,
till their limbs were lightened     and they longed to fare
through dread and danger     to their dear lady,
so firm their faith.     Yet frore and grey
eld sat more heavy     on the aged head                             595
of Mailrond the old,     and his mistress' love
his might matched not,     more marred by years
than Halog he hoped not     to home again.
Then sickness assailed him     and his sight darkened:
'To Túrin I must turn     my troth and fealty,'                     600
he said and he sighed,     'to my sweet youngling';
but Halog hardened     his heart to go.
An Elfin escort     to his aid was given,
and magics of Melian,     and a meed of gold,
and a message to Morwen     for his mouth to bear,                  605
words of gladness     that her wish was granted,
and Túrin taken     to the tender care
of the King of Doriath;     of his kindly will
now Thingol called her     to the Thousand Caves
to fare unfearing     with his folk again,                          610
there to sojourn in solace     till her son be grown;
for Húrin of Hithlum     was holden in mind
and no might had Morgoth     where Melian dwelt.

Of the errand of the Elves     and of eager Halog
the tale tells not,     save in time they came                      615
to Morwen's threshold.     There Thingol's message
was said where she sat     in her solitary hall,
but she dared not do     as was dearly bidden,
who Nienor her nursling     yet newly weaned
would not leave nor be led     on the long marches                  620
to adventure her frailty     in the vast forest;
the pride of her people,     princes ancient,
had suffered her send     a son to Thingol
when despair urged her,     but to spend her days
an almsguest of others,     even Elfin kings,                       625
it little liked her;     and lived there yet
a hope in her heart     that Húrin would come,
and the dwelling was dear     where he dwelt of old;
at night she would listen     for a knock at the doors

or a footstep falling    that she fondly knew.                630
Thus she fared not forth;    thus her fate was woven.
Yet the thanes of Thingol    she thanked nobly,
nor her shame showed she,    how shorn of glory
to reward their wending    she had wealth too scant,
but gave them in gift    those golden things             635
that last lingered,    and led they thence
a helm of Húrin    once hewn in wars
when he battled with Beren    as brother and comrade
against ogres and Orcs    and evil foes.
Grey-gleaming steel,    with gold adorned             640
wrights had wrought it,    with runes graven
of might and victory,    that a magic sat there
and its wearer warded    from wound or death,
whoso bore to battle    brightly shining
dire dragon-headed    its dreadful crest.             645
This Thingol she bade    and her thanks receive.

Thus Halog her henchman    to Hithlum came,
but Thingol's thanes    thanked her lowly
and girt them to go,    though grey winter
enmeshed the mountains    and the moaning woods,          650
for the hills hindered not    the hidden people.
Lo! Morwen's message    in a month's journey,
so speedy fared they,    was spoken in Doriath.
For Morwen Melian    was moved to ruth,
but courteously the king    that casque received,         655
her golden gift,    with gracious words,
who deeply delved    had dungeons filled
with elvish armouries    of ancient gear,
yet he handled that helm    as his hoard were scant:
'That head were high    that upheld this thing            660
with the token crowned,    the towering crest
to Dorlómin dear,    the dragon of the North,
that Thalion Erithámrod    the thrice renowned
oft bore into battle    with baleful foes.
Would that he had worn it    to ward his head             665
on that direst day    from death's handstroke!'
Then a thought was thrust    into Thingol's heart,
and Túrin was called    and told kindly
that his mother Morwen    a mighty thing
had sent to her son,    his sire's heirloom,             670

o'er-written with runes   by wrights of yore
in dark dwarfland   in the deeps of time,
ere Men to Mithrim   and misty Hithlum
o'er the world wandered;   it was worn aforetime
by the father of the fathers   of the folk of Húrin,      675
whose sire Gumlin   to his son gave it
ere his soul severed   from his sundered heart –
"'Tis Telchar's work   of worth untold,
its wearer warded   from wound or magic,
from glaive guarded   or gleaming axe.      680
Now Húrin's helm   hoard till manhood
to battle bids thee,   then bravely don it,
go wear it well!'   Woeful-hearted
did Túrin touch it   but take it not,
too weak to wield   that mighty gear,      685
and his mind in mourning   for Morwen's answer
was mazed and darkened.

               Thus many a day
it came to pass   in the courts of Thingol
for twelve years long   that Túrin lived.
But seven winters   their sorrows had laid      690
on the son of Húrin   when that summer to the world
came glad and golden   with grievous parting;
nine years followed   of his forest-nurture,
and his lot was lightened,   for he learned at whiles
from faring folk   what befell in Hithlum,      695
and tidings were told   by trusty Elves
how Morwen his mother   knew milder days
and easement of evil,   and with eager voice
all Nienor named   the Northern flower,
the slender maiden   in sweet beauty      700
now graceful growing.   The gladder was he then
and hope yet haunted   his heart at whiles.
He waxed and grew   and won renown
in all lands where Thingol   as lord was held
for his stoutness of heart   and his strong body.      705
Much lore he learned   and loved wisdom,
but fortune followed him   in few desires;
oft wrong and awry   what he wrought turnéd,
what he loved he lost,   what he longed for failed,
and full friendship   he found not with ease,      710

nor was lightly loved,    for his looks were sad;
he was gloomy-hearted    and glad seldom
for the sundering sorrow    that seared his youth.

On manhood's threshold    he was mighty-thewed
in the wielding of weapons;    in weaving song                    715
he had a minstrel's mastery,    but mirth was not in it,
for he mourned the misery    of the Men of Hithlum.
Yet greater his grief    grew thereafter
when from Hithlum's hills    he heard no more
and no traveller told him    tidings of Morwen.                  720
For those days were drawing    to the doom of the Gnomes
and the power of the Prince    of the pitiless kingdom,
of the grim Glamhoth,    was grown apace,
till the lands of the North    were loud with their noise,
and they fell on the folk    with fire and slaughter            725
who bent not to Bauglir    or the borders passed
of dark Dorlómin    with its dreary pines
that Hithlum was called    by the unhappy people.
There Morgoth shut them    in the Shadowy Mountains,
fenced them from Faërie    and the folk of the wood.            730
Even Beleg fared not    so far abroad
as once was his wont,    for the woods were filled
with the armies of Angband    and with evil deeds,
and murder walked    on the marches of Doriath;
only the mighty magic    of Melian the Queen                    735
yet held their havoc    from the hidden people.

To assuage his sorrow    and to sate his rage,
for his heart was hot    with the hurts of his folk,
then Húrin's son    took the helm of his sire
and weapons weighty    for the wielding of men,                 740
and he went to the woods    with warrior-Elves,
and far in the forest    his feet led him
into black battle    yet a boy in years.
Ere manhood's measure    he met and he slew
Orcs of Angband    and evil things                             745
that roamed and ravened    on the realm's borders.
There hard his life,    and hurts he lacked not,
the wounds of shaft    and the wavering sheen
of the sickle scimitars,    the swords of Hell,
the bloodfain blades    on black anvils                        750
in Angband smithied,    yet ever he smote

unfey, fearless,    and his fate kept him.
Thus his prowess was proven    and his praise was noised
and beyond his years    he was yielded honour,
for by him was holden    the hand of ruin                         755
from Thingol's folk,    and Thû feared him,
and wide wandered    the word of Túrin:
'Lo! we deemed as dead    the dragon of the North,
but high o'er the host    its head uprises,
its wings are spread!    Who has waked this spirit          760
and the flame kindled    of its fiery jaws?
Or is Húrin of Hithlum    from Hell broken?'
And Thû who was throned    as thane mightiest
neath Morgoth Bauglir,    whom that master bade
'go ravage the realm    of the robber Thingol              765
and mar the magic    of Melian the Queen',
even Thû feared him,    and his thanes trembled.

One only was there    in war greater,
more high in honour    in the hearts of the Elves
than Túrin son of Húrin,    tower of Hithlum,              770
even the hunter Beleg    of the hidden people,
whose father was the forest    and the fells his home;
to bend whose bow,    Balthronding named,
that the black yewtree    once bore of yore,
had none the might;    unmatched in knowledge         775
of the woods' secrets    and the weary hills.
He was leader beloved    of the light companies
all garbed in grey    and green and brown,
the archers arrowfleet    with eyes piercing,
the scouts that scoured    scorning danger               780
afar o'er the fells    their foemen's lair,
and tales and tidings    timely won them
of camps and councils,    of comings and goings,
all the movements of the might    of Morgoth Bauglir.
Thus Túrin, who trusted    to targe and sword,          785
who was fain of fighting    with foes well seen,
where shining swords    made sheen of fire,
and his corslet-clad    comrades-in-arms
were snared seldom    and smote unlooked-for.

Then the fame of the fights    on the far marches      790
was carried to the courts    of the king of Doriath,
and tales of Túrin    were told in his halls,

of the bond and brotherhood    of Beleg the ageless
with the blackhaired boy    from the beaten people.
Then the king called them    to come before him                    795
did Orc-raids lessen    in the outer lands
ever and often    unasked to hasten,
to rest them and revel    and to raise awhile
in songs and lays    and sweet music
the memory of the mirth    ere the moon was old,                   800
when the mountains were young    in the morning of the world.

On a time was Túrin    at his table seated,
and Thingol thanked him    for his thriving deeds;
there was laughter long    and the loud clamour
of a countless company    that quaffed the mead                    805
and the wine of Dor-Winion    that went ungrudged
in their golden goblets;    and goodly meats
there burdened the boards    neath blazing torches
in those high halls set    that were hewn of stone.
There mirth fell on many;    there minstrels clear                 810
did sing them songs    of the city of Côr
that Taingwethil    towering mountain
o'ershadowed sheerly,    of the shining halls
where the great gods sit    and gaze on the world
from the guarded shores    of the gulf of Faërie.                  815
One sang of the slaying    at the Swans' Haven
and the curse that had come    on the kindreds since

Here the typescript IIB ends abruptly, in the middle of a page; the
manuscript IIA has already ended at line 767.

NOTES

The first page of the typescript of this section of the poem, covering lines
248–95, is duplicated, the one version (b) taking up changes made to the
other (a) and itself receiving further changes. There is no corresponding
text of IIA until line 283.

   248    *in the land of Mithrim* (a), and (b) as typed. The emendation
          in (b) reverts to the reading of the first version (105), *in the
          Land of Shadows*.

265    *Dairon's sister* (a), and (b) as typed.

266–8    These three lines were inserted in (b), with change of *who had danced* 269 to *had danced*. See below, *Note on the poem 'Light as Leaf on Lindentree'*.

273    *Ermabweth* (a), and (b) as typed. The emendation in (b) to *Ermabwed* reverts to the form of the name in the *Lost Tales* and in the first version of the poem (121).

274–8    As typed, (a) was virtually identical with the first version lines 122–5. This was then changed to read:

> did win her to wife,    who once of old
> fellowship had vowed    and friendly love
> Elf with mortal,    even Egnor's son
> with Húrin of Hithlum,    hunting often
> by the marge of Mithrim's    misty waters.
> Thus said she to her son . . .

This passage was then typed in (b), with change of *hunting often* to *hero dauntless*. Subsequently the line *Elf with mortal,    even Egnor's son* was struck out, and other minor changes made to give the text printed.

294    *Mailrond*: *Mailgond* IIA, IIB; I read *Mailrond* in view of the emendations at lines 319, 596.

319    *Mailrond*: *Mailgond* IIA, and IIB as typed, emended in pencil to *Mailrond*; similarly at line 596.

356    *Release from Bondage* IIB as typed (the change to *Release from Bonds* was made for metrical reasons). The reference to the *Lay of Leithian* is not in IIA, but the manuscript is here so scrappy and disjointed as to be of no service.

358–66    These nine lines are typed on a slip pasted into IIB, replacing the following which were struck out:

> how Lúthien the lissom    he loved of yore
> in the enchanted forest    chained with wonder
> as she danced like dreams    of drifting whiteness
> of shadows shimmering    shot with moonlight;

In the first line (358) of the inserted slip *the boldhearted* is an emendation of *brave undaunted*; and above *Ermabwed* is written (later, in pencil) *Er(h)amion*.

374    *Carcharoth*: *Carcharolch* IIA, and IIB as typed.

398–402    These five lines are typed on a slip pasted into IIB at the same time as that giving lines 358–66, but in this case there was nothing replaced in the original typescript. Line 400 as typed read:

> that 'Light as Leaf    on Lind' is called

emended to the reading given.

Beneath the five typed lines my father wrote: 'Here follow
verses "Light as leaf on linden-tree".'

*Note on the poem 'Light as Leaf on Lindentree'*
Lines 266–8 (see note above) were clearly added to the
typescript at the same time as the two pasted-in slips (giving
lines 358–66 and 398–402), in view of line 268 *who light as
leaf   on linden tree*.

This poem, here to be inset into the *Lay of the Children
of Húrin*, is found in three typescripts, here referred to as
(a), (b), and (c), together with a small manuscript page
giving reworkings of the penultimate stanza. These typescripts were made with the same purple ribbon used for the
texts I B and I I B of the Lay and obviously belong to the same
period.

(a), earliest of the three, had no title as typed: the title
*Light as leaf on lind* was written in in ink, and before the
poem begins there is written also in ink:

'Light was Tinúviel as leaf on lind
light as a feather in the laughing wind.'
Tinúviel! Tinúviel!

On this typescript my father wrote some notes on the poem's
dating: 'first beginnings Oxford 1919–20 Alfred St.', 'Leeds
1923, retouched 1924'. (a) is the 1923 version; it differs from
the later (1924) only in the penultimate stanza, on which see
note to lines 459–66 below.

(b) again has no title as typed, but *As Light as Leaf on
Lindentree* was written in ink. This begins with 15 lines of
alliterative verse:

In the Lay of Leithian,    Release from Bondage
in linkéd words    has long been wrought
of Beren Ermabwed,    brave, undaunted;
how Lúthien the lissom    he loved of yore
in the enchanted forest    chained in wonder.          5
Tinúviel he named her,    than nightingale
more sweet her voice,    as veiled in soft
and wavering wisps    of woven dusk
shot with starlight,    with shining eyes
she danced like dreams    of drifting sheen,          10
pale-twinkling pearls    in pools of darkness.
    And songs were raised    for sorrow's lightening,
a sudden sweetness    in a silent hour,
that 'Light as Leaf    on Linden-tree'
were called – here caught    a cadent echo.          15

(c) has the typed title *As Light as Leaf on Lind*, the last word emended to *Linden-tree*. This has only the text of the poem, without the alliterative introduction; and the text is identical to that of (b).

It will be seen that of the alliterative verses in (b) lines 1–2 are very close to lines 356–7 of the Lay (which were original lines in the typescript, not inserted later):

(There was told to Túrin     that tale by Halog)
that in the Lay of Leithian,     Release from Bonds
                                        [< Bondage],
in linkéd words     has long been woven

while lines 3–11 are identical with those on the first pasted-in slip, 358–66 (as typed: *the boldhearted* in line 358 is an emendation from *brave undaunted*). Further, lines 12–15 are close to those on the second pasted-in slip, 398–402:

Then a song he made them     for sorrow's lightening,
a sudden sweetness     in a silent hour,
that is 'Light as Leaf     on Linden' called,
whose music of mirth     and mourning blended
yet in hearts does echo.     This did Halog sing them:

The order of events is very difficult to determine, but the key is probably to be found in the fact that lines 356–7 are found in IIB as originally typed, not in the pasted-in insertion. I think (or perhaps rather guess) that my father composed an alliterative continuation of 13 lines (beginning *of Beren Ermabwed,     brave undaunted*) as an introduction to the poem *Light as Leaf on Lindentree*; and then, at the same time as he typed text (b) of this poem, with the alliterative head-piece, he added them to the typescript of the Lay already in existence.

*Light as Leaf on Lindentree* was published in *The Gryphon* (Leeds University), New Series, Vol. VI, no. 6, June 1925, p. 217. It is here preceded by nine lines of alliterative verse, beginning

'Tis of Beren Ermabwed brokenhearted

and continuing exactly as in (b) above (and in the text of the Lay) as far as *in pools of darkness*; the last four lines do not appear. In his cutting from *The Gryphon* my father changed *broken-hearted* (which is obviously a mere printer's error) to *the boldhearted* (as in the Lay, 358); changed the title to *As Light as Leaf on Lindentree*; and wrote *Erchamion* above *Ermabwed* (see note to lines 358–66).

The text of the inserted poem given in the body of the Lay is that published, which is identical to that of the typescripts (b) and (c). My father made a very few changes to (c) afterwards (i.e. after the poem had been printed) and these are given in the notes that follow, as also are the earlier forms of the penultimate verse.

It may finally be observed that if my deductions are correct the introduction in the Lay of the reference to the *Lay of Leithian* and the outline of the story told by Halog preceded the publication *of Light as Leaf on Lindentree* in June 1925.

———

419    *magic > wonder*, later emendation made to the typescript (c) of *Light as Leaf on Lindentree* after the poem was published.

424    *fairy > elvish*, see note to 419.

459, 464    *elfin > elvish*, see note to 419.

459–66    In the typescript (a) this penultimate stanza reads as follows:

> And Beren caught the elfin maid
>     And kissed her trembling starlit eyes:
> The elfin maid that love delayed
>     In the days beyond our memory.
> Till moon and star, till music dies,
>     Shall Beren and the elfin maid
> Dance to the starlight of her eyes
>     And fill the woods with glamoury.

The single manuscript page (bearing the address 'The University, Leeds') has two versions of the stanza intermediate between that in (a) and the final form. The first of these reads:

> Ere Beren caught the elfin maid
>     And kissed her trembling starlit eyes
> Tinúviel, whom love delayed
>     In the woven woods of Nemorie
>     In the tangled trees of Tramorie.
> Till music and till moonlight dies
>     Shall Beren by the elfin maid
> Dance in the starlight of her eyes
>     And fill the woods with glamoury.

Other variants are suggested for lines 4 and 8:

> In the woven woods of Glamoury
>
>            . . .
>
> O'er the silver glades of Amoury

and

> Ere the birth of mortal memory
>
>            . . .
>
> And fill the woods with glamoury.

I can cast no light on these names.

The second version advances towards the final form, with for lines 4 and 8 of the stanza:

> In the land of laughter sorrowless
> > In spells enchanted sorrowless
>
>            . . .
>
> In eve unending morrowless

The lines finally achieved are also written here. This rewriting of the penultimate stanza is unquestionably the 1924 'retouching' referred to in the note on typescript (a) (see p. 120).

475   *did Halog sing them*: *did Halog recall* IIB as typed. The emendation was made at the same time as the insertion of *Light as Leaf on Lindentree*; as originally written the line followed on 397, at the end of Halog's story.

520   *Finweg* IIB unemended; see note to second version line 19.

531   *Nirnaith Únoth* IIA, and IIB as typed. See note to second version line 26.

551   *haled* underlined in IIB and an illegible word substituted, perhaps *had*.

576   *Ermabweth* IIA, and IIB as typed. Cf. line 273.

596   *Mailrond*: see note to line 319.

658   *elfin* IIA, *elvish* IIB as typed.

767   The manuscript IIA ends here.

811   *Côr* emended in pencil to *Tûn*, but *Tûn* later struck out. In the first version (IB, line 430) the same, but there the emendation *Tûn* not struck out.

812   *Taingwethil*: *Tengwethil* as typed. In the first version IB introduces *Tain-* for *Ten-* at lines 431, 636, but at line 1409 IB has *Ten-* for IA *Tain-*.

A later pencilled note here says: 'English *Tindbrenting*' (see Commentary, p. 127).

## Commentary on Part II
## of the second version
### *'Túrin's Fostering'*

### (i)   *References to the story of Beren and Lúthien*

In this second part of the second version the major innovation is of course
the introduction of the story of Beren and Lúthien, told to Túrin by his
guardian Halog when they were lost in the forest, at once reminiscent of
Aragorn's telling of the same story to his companions on Weathertop
before the attack of the Ringwraiths (*The Fellowship of the Ring*
I. 11); and with the further introduction of the poem *Light as Leaf on
Lindentree*, the original form of the very song that Aragorn chanted on
Weathertop, we realise that the one scene is actually the precursor of the
other.

At line 264 (an original, not an interpolated line) is the first appearance
of the name *Lúthien* for Thingol's daughter, so that Tinúviel becomes
her acquired name (given to her by Beren, line 361). The suggestion of
the interpolated lines 266–7 is that Tinúviel meant 'Starmantled', which
seems likely enough (see I. 269, entry *Tinwë Linto*; the Gnomish
dictionary, contemporary with the *Lost Tales*, rather surprisingly gives
no indication of the meaning of *Tinúviel*). On the other hand, in the
interpolated line 361 the suggestion is equally clear that it meant
'Nightingale'. It is difficult to explain this.*

The original reading at line 265, *Dairon's sister*, goes back to the *Tale
of Tinúviel*, where Dairon was the son of Tinwelint (II. 10).

I noted earlier (p. 25) that lines 178–9 in the first version

> and never ere now    for need or wonder
> had children of Men    chosen that pathway

show that Beren was still an Elf, not a Man; but while these lines are
retained without change in the second version (349–50) their meaning is
reversed by the new line that immediately follows – *save Beren the
brave*, which shows equally clearly that Beren was a Man, not an Elf. At
this time my father was apparently in two minds on this subject. At lines
273 ff. of the second version (referring to Beren's friendship with Húrin)
he originally repeated lines 122–5 of the first, which make no statement
on the matter; but in the first revision of this passage (given in the note to
lines 274–8) he explicitly wrote that Beren was an Elf:

---

* A possible if rather finespun explanation is that lines 266–8 were not in fact written in to
the text at the same time as the two pasted-in slips (giving lines 358–66 and 398–402), as I
have supposed (p. 120), but were earlier. On this view, when 266–8 were written *Tinúviel*
was not yet Beren's name for Lúthien, but was her common *soubriquet*, known *both near
and far* (266), and meant 'Star-mantled'. Later, when 358–66 were added, it had become
the name given to her by Beren (361), and meant 'Nightingale'. If this were so, it could also
be supposed that line 268, *who light as leaf   on linden tree*, gave rise to the title of the
poem.

> (Beren)     who once of old
> fellowship had vowed     and friendly love
> Elf with mortal,     even Egnor's son
> with Húrin of Hithlum . . .

Since this is a rewriting of the original text of IIB it is presumably a withdrawal from the idea (that Beren was a Man) expressed in lines 349–50; while the further rewriting of this passage, getting rid of the line *Elf with mortal,     even Egnor's son*, presumably represents a return to it.

In Halog's recounting of the story of Beren and Lúthien there are some apparent differences from that told in the *Tale of the Nauglafring* and the *Lay of Leithian*. The reference to *Melian's magic* in line 371 is presumably to Melian's knowledge of where Beren was; cf. the *Tale of Tinúviel* II. 17: "'O Gwendeling, my mother,' said she, 'tell me *of thy magic*, if thou canst, how doth Beren fare . . .'" A probable explanation of the mention later in this passage of *the arts of Melian* (393), in association with Lúthien's winning Beren back from death, will be given later. But in no other version of the story is there any suggestion that Carcharoth 'hunted' Beren and Lúthien (377) after he had devoured Beren's hand holding the Silmaril – indeed, the reverse: from the *Tale of Tinúviel* (II. 34) 'Then did Tinúviel and Beren flee like the wind from the gates, *yet was Karkaras far before them*' to *The Silmarillion* (p. 181) 'Howling he fled before them'. (The form *Carcharoth* now first appears, by emendation of *Carcharolch*, which occurs nowhere else; in the *Tale of Tinúviel* the forms are *Karkaras* and (in the second version) *Carcaras*.)

More important, lines 395–7

> that they dwell for ever     in days ageless
> and the grass greys not     in the green forest
> where East or West     they ever wander

seems to represent a conception of the second lives of Beren and Lúthien notably different from that in the *Tale of the Nauglafring* (II. 240), where the doom of mortality that Mandos had spoken fell swiftly upon them (as also in *The Silmarillion*, p. 236):

> nor this time did those twain fare the road together, but when yet was the child of those twain, Dior the Fair, a little one, did Tinúviel slowly fade . . . and she vanished in the woods, and none have seen her dancing ever there again. But Beren searched all the lands of Hithlum and Artanor ranging after her; and never has any of the Elves had more loneliness than his, or ever he too faded from life . . .

However this matter is to be interpreted, the lines in the Lay are clearly to be associated with the end of *Light as Leaf on Lindentree*:

126 THE LAYS OF BELERIAND

> Till moonlight and till music dies
> Shall Beren by the elfin maid
> Dance in the starlight of her eyes
> In the forest singing sorrowless.

Compare the end of the song that Aragorn sang on Weathertop:

> The Sundering Seas between them lay,
> And yet at last they met once more,
> And long ago they passed away
> In the forest singing sorrowless.

### (ii)  *The Dragon-helm and Húrin's ancestors*

The elder of Túrin's guardians, still Gumlin in the first version, is now named (Mailgond >) Mailrond; and Gumlin becomes the name of Húrin's father, who has not been even mentioned before (other than in the reference in the first version to the Dragon-helm being Húrin's *heirloom*, 318). In the second version the Dragon-helm

> was worn aforetime
> by the father of the fathers   of the folk of Húrin,
> whose sire Gumlin   to his son gave it
> ere his soul severed   from his sundered heart.   (674–7)

The last line suggests that a story of Húrin's father had already cóme into existence; and line 675 suggests a long line of ancestors behind Húrin – as also does line 622, *the pride of her people,   princes ancient*, behind Morwen. It is hard to know how my father at this time conceived the earlier generations of Men; and the question must be postponed.

The Dragon-helm itself now begins to gather a history: it was made

> in dark dwarfland   in the deeps of time,
> ere Men to Mithrim   and misty Hithlum
> o'er the world wandered                          (672–4)

and was the work of Telchar (678), now named for the first time. But there is still no indication of the significance attaching to the dragon-crest.

Lines 758–62 (*Lo! we deemed as dead   the dragon of the North . . . Or is Húrin of Hithlum   from Hell broken?*), to which there is nothing corresponding in the first version, clearly foreshadows the *Narn*, p. 79:

> and word ran through the woods, and was heard far beyond Doriath, that the Dragon-helm of Dor-lómin was seen again. Then many wondered, saying: 'Can the spirit of Hador or of Galdor the Tall return from death; or has Húrin of Hithlum escaped indeed from the pits of Angband?'

## (iii)   *Miscellaneous Matters*

The curious references to Beleg in the first version ('son of the wilderness who wist no sire', see p. 25) reappear in the second, but in a changed form, and at one of the occurrences put into Beleg's own mouth: *the forest is my father* 536, cf. 772. *Beleg the ageless* is retained in the second version (793), and at lines 544 ff. he shows a Gandalf-like quality of being able to make fire in wet wood, with *his wizard's cunning* (cf. *The Fellowship of the Ring* II. 3).

The great bow of Beleg is now at last named: *Balthronding* (773; later *Belthronding*).

We learn now that the strong wine of Dor-Winion that Beleg gave to the travellers and which was drunk at the fateful feast in the Thousand Caves was brought to the Northern lands from Nogrod by Dwarves (540–1); and also that there was viticulture in Valinor (543–4), though after the accounts of life in the halls of Tulkas and Oromë in the tale of *The Coming of the Valar* (I. 75) this causes no surprise – indeed it is said that Nessa wife of Tulkas bore 'goblets of the goodliest wine', while Meássë went among the warriors in her house and 'revived the fainting with strong wine' (I. 78).

An interesting detail in the second account of Túrin's reception in Doriath, not found again, is that Melian played a part in the king's graciousness:

for Melian moved him   with murmured counsel.   (580)

From the feast at which Túrin slew Orgof *the songs of the sons of Ing* of the first version (line 421) have now disappeared.

The chronology of Túrin's youth is slightly changed in the second version. In the first, as in the *Tale* (see p. 25), Túrin spent seven years in Doriath while tidings still came from Morwen (line 333); this now becomes nine years (line 693), as in *The Silmarillion* (p. 199).

Lastly, at line 812 a pencilled note against the name *Taingwethil* (Taniquetil) says 'English *Tindbrenting*'. This name is found in notes on the Old English forms of Elvish names (see p. 87), *Tindbrenting þe þa Brega Taniquetil nemnað* ('Tindbrenting which the Valar name Taniquetil'; Old English *bregu* 'king, lord, ruler' = 'Vala'). The name is perhaps to be derived from Old English *tind* 'projecting spike' (Modern English *tine*) and *brenting* (a derivative of *brant* 'steep, lofty', here used in an unrecorded sense (*brenting* occurs only once in recorded Old English, in *Beowulf*, where it means 'ship').

### Verses associated with *The Children of Húrin*

There is a poem found in three manuscripts, all on 'Oxford' paper (see p. 81), in which my father developed elements in the passage lines

2082–2113 in *The Children of Húrin* to a short independent work. The
first text has no title, and reads:

> The high summer
> waned to autumn,    and western gales
> the leaves loosened    from labouring boughs.
> The feet of the forest    in fading gold
> and burnished brown    were buried deeply;          5
> a restless rustle    down the roofless aisles
> sighed and whispered.    The Silver Wherry,
> the sailing moon    with slender mast
> was filled with fires    as of furnace hot;
> its hold hoarded    the heats of summer,          10
> its shrouds were shaped    of shining flame
> uprising ruddy    o'er the rim of Evening
> by the misty wharves    on the margin of the world.
> Then winter hastened    and weathers hardened,
> and sleet and snow    and slanting rain          15
> from glowering heaven,    grey and sunless,
> whistling whiplash    whirled by tempest,
> the lands forlorn    lashed and tortured:
> floods were loosened,    the fallow waters
> sweeping seaward,    swollen, angry,          20
> filled with flotsam,    foaming, turbid
> passed in tumult.    The tempest failed:
> frost descended    from the far mountains,
> steel-cold and still.    Stony-glinting
> icehung evening    was opened wide,          25
> a dome of crystal    over deep silence,
> the windless wastes,    the woods standing
> frozen phantoms    under flickering stars.

Against *deeply* in line 5 is given *thickly* as an alternative reading, and
against *Wherry* in line 7 is given *vessel*.

The first 13 lines of this are almost identical to 2082–94 in the Lay,
with only a few slight changes (mostly for the common purpose in my
father's revisions of his alliterative verse of making the lines more taut).
Then follow in lines 14–16 adaptations of 2102–4; 17 is a new line; 18
contains a part of 2119; 19–22a are based on 2106–9a; 22b–24 are new;
and 25–8 are almost the same as 2110–13.

The second version of the poem bears the title *Storm over Narog*, and is
much developed. This version as written retained lines 14–15 from the
first, but they were changed and expanded to three; and the third text,
entitled *Winter comes to Nargothrond*, is a copy of the second with
this alteration and one or two other very slight changes. I give the third
text here.

*Winter comes to Nargothrond*

The summer slowly    in the sad forest
waned and faded.    In the west arose
winds that wandered    over warring seas.
Leaves were loosened    from labouring boughs:
fallow-gold they fell,    and the feet buried          5
of trees standing    tall and naked,
rustling restlessly    down roofless aisles,
shifting and drifting.
                The shining vessel
of the sailing moon    with slender mast,
with shrouds shapen    of shimmering flame,          10
uprose ruddy    on the rim of Evening
by the misty wharves    on the margin of the world.
With winding horns    winter hunted
in the weeping woods,    wild and ruthless;
sleet came slashing,    and slanting hail          15
from glowering heaven    grey and sunless,
whistling whiplash    whirled by tempest.
The floods were freed    and fallow waters
sweeping seaward,    swollen, angry,
filled with flotsam,    foaming, turbid,          20
passed in tumult.    The tempest died.
Frost descended    from far mountains
steel-cold and still.    Stony-glinting
icehung evening    was opened wide,
a dome of crystal    over deep silence,          25
over windless wastes    and woods standing
as frozen phantoms    under flickering stars.

On the back of *Winter comes to Nargothrond* are written the following verses, which arose from lines 1554–70 of the Lay. The poem has no
title.

With the seething sea    Sirion's waters,
green streams gliding    into grey furrows,
murmurous mingle.    There mews gather,
seabirds assemble    in solemn council,
whitewingéd hosts    whining sadly          5
with countless voices    in a country of sand:
plains and mountains    of pale yellow
sifting softly    in salt breezes,
sere and sunbleached.    At the sea's margin

a shingle lies,    long and shining                              10
with pebbles like pearl    or pale marble:
when the foam of waves    down the wind flieth
in spray they sparkle;    splashed at evening
in the moon they glitter;    moaning, grinding,
in the dark they tumble;    drawing and rolling,             15
when strongbreasted storm    the streams driveth
in a war of waters    to the walls of land.
When the Lord of Ocean    his loud trumpets
in the abyss bloweth    to battle sounding,
longhaired legions    on lathered horses                     20
with backs like whales,    bridles spuming,
charge there snorting,    champing seaweed;
hurled with thunder    of a hundred drums
they leap the bulwarks,    burst the leaguer,
through the sandmountains    sweeping madly             25
up the river roaring    roll in fury.

The last three lines were later placed within brackets.

It may be mentioned here that there exists a poem in rhyming couplets
entitled *The Children of Húrin*. This extends only to 170 lines and
breaks off abruptly, after a short prologue based on the opening of the
later version of the alliterative Lay and an incomplete second section
titled 'The Battle of Unnumbered Tears and Morgoth's Curse'. This
poem comes however from a rather later period – approximately the time
of the abandonment of the *Lay of Leithian* in the same metre, in the
early 1930s, and I do not give it here.

# II

# POEMS EARLY ABANDONED

During his time at the University of Leeds my father embarked on five distinct poetical works concerned with the matter of the mythology; but three of these went no further than the openings. This chapter treats each of them in turn.

## (i)  *The Flight of the Noldoli*

There do not seem to be any certain indications of the date of this brief poem in alliterative verse in relation to *The Children of Húrin* (though it is worth noticing that already in the earliest of the three texts of *The Flight of the Noldoli* Fëanor's son Cranthir is so named, whereas this form only arose by emendation of Cranthor in the typescript text of the Lay (line 1719)). However, both from its general air and from various details it can be seen that it comes from the same time; and since it seems unlikely that (on the one hand) my father would have embarked on a new poem in alliterative verse unless he had laid the other aside, or that (on the other) he would have returned to this mode once he was fully engaged on a long poem in rhyming couplets, I think it very probable that *The Flight of the Noldoli* comes from the earlier part of 1925 (see pp. 3, 81).

Each of the three manuscripts of the poem (A, B, and C) is differently titled: A has *The Flight of the Gnomes as sung in the Halls of Thingol*; B (pencilled in later) *Flight of the Gnomes*; C *The Flight of the Noldoli from Valinor*. A has emendations that are taken up in the text of B, and B has emendations taken up in C; almost all are characteristic metrical/verbal rearrangements, as for example in line 17:

A *in anguish mourning,* emended to the reading of B;
B *and in anguish mourn,* emended to the reading of C;
C *mourning in anguish.*

As generally in this book, earlier variants that have no bearing on names or story are not cited. Each text ends at the same point, but three further lines are roughly written in the margin of A (see note to line 146).

I give now the text of the third version, C.

# THE FLIGHT OF THE NOLDOLI
## FROM VALINOR

A! the Trees of Light,    tall and shapely,
gold and silver,    more glorious than the sun,
than the moon more magical,    o'er the meads of the Gods
their fragrant frith    and flowerladen
gardens gleaming,    once gladly shone.                           5
In death they are darkened,    they drop their leaves
from blackened branches    bled by Morgoth
and Ungoliant the grim    the Gloomweaver.
In spider's form    despair and shadow
a shuddering fear    and shapeless night                         10
she weaves in a web    of winding venom
that is black and breathless.    Their branches fail,
the light and laughter    of their leaves are quenched.
Mirk goes marching,    mists of blackness,
through the halls of the Mighty    hushed and empty,             15
the gates of the Gods    are in gloom mantled.

Lo! the Elves murmur    mourning in anguish,
but no more shall be kindled    the mirth of Côr
in the winding ways    of their walled city,
towercrownëd Tûn,    whose twinkling lamps                        20
are drowned in darkness.    The dim fingers
of fog come floating    from the formless waste
and sunless seas.    The sound of horns,
of horses' hooves    hastening wildly
in hopeless hunt,    they hear afar,                              25
where the Gods in wrath    those guilty ones
through mournful shadow,    now mounting as a tide
o'er the Blissful Realm,    in blind dismay
pursue unceasing.    The city of the Elves
is thickly thronged.    On threadlike stairs                     30
carven of crystal    countless torches
stare and twinkle,    stain the twilight
and gleaming balusters    of green beryl.
A vague rumour    of rushing voices,
as myriads mount    the marble paths,                            35
there fills and troubles    those fair places
wide ways of Tûn    and walls of pearl.

Of the Three Kindreds    to that clamorous throng

are none but the Gnomes    in numbers drawn.
The Elves of Ing    to the ancient halls                    40
and starry gardens    that stand and gleam
upon Timbrenting    towering mountain
that day had climbed    to the cloudy-domed
mansions of Manwë    for mirth and song.
There Bredhil the Blessed    the bluemantled,          45
the Lady of the heights    as lovely as the snow
in lights gleaming    of the legions of the stars,
the cold immortal    Queen of mountains,
too fair and terrible    too far and high
for mortal eyes,    in Manwë's court                        50
sat silently    as they sang to her.

The Foam-riders,    folk of waters,
Elves of the endless    echoing beaches,
of the bays and grottoes    and the blue lagoons,
of silver sands    sown with moonlit,                       55
starlit, sunlit,    stones of crystal,
paleburning gems    pearls and opals,
on their shining shingle,    where now shadows groping
clutched their laughter,    quenched in mourning
their mirth and wonder,    in amaze wandered        60
under cliffs grown cold    calling dimly,
or in shrouded ships    shuddering waited
for the light no more    should be lit for ever.

But the Gnomes were numbered    by name and kin,
marshalled and ordered    in the mighty square       65
upon the crown of Côr.    There cried aloud
the fierce son of Finn.    Flaming torches
he held and whirled    in his hands aloft,
those hands whose craft    the hidden secret
knew, that none    Gnome or mortal                       70
hath matched or mastered    in magic or in skill.
'Lo! slain is my sire    by the sword of fiends,
his death he has drunk    at the doors of his hall
and deep fastness,    where darkly hidden
the Three were guarded,    the things unmatched       75
that Gnome and Elf    and the Nine Valar
can never remake    or renew on earth,
recarve or rekindle    by craft or magic,
not Fëanor Finn's son    who fashioned them of yore –

the light is lost    whence he lit them first,                              80
the fate of Faërie    hath found its hour

Thus the witless wisdom    its reward hath earned
of the Gods' jealousy,    who guard us here
to serve them, sing to them    in our sweet cages,
to contrive them gems    and jewelled trinkets,                             85
their leisure to please    with our loveliness,
while they waste and squander    work of ages,
nor can Morgoth master    in their mansions sitting
at countless councils.    Now come ye all,
who have courage and hope!    My call harken                                90
to flight, to freedom    in far places!
The woods of the world    whose wide mansions
yet in darkness dream    drowned in slumber,
the pathless plains    and perilous shores
no moon yet shines on    nor mounting dawn                                  95
in dew and daylight    hath drenched for ever,
far better were these    for bold footsteps
than gardens of the Gods    gloom-encircled
with idleness filled    and empty days.
Yea! though the light lit them    and the loveliness                        100
beyond heart's desire    that hath held us slaves
here long and long.    But that light is dead.
Our gems are gone,    our jewels ravished;
and the Three, my Three,    thrice-enchanted
globes of crystal    by gleam undying                                       105
illumined, lit    by living splendour
and all hues' essence,    their eager flame –
Morgoth has them    in his monstrous hold,
my Silmarils.    I swear here oaths,
unbreakable bonds    to bind me ever,                                       110
by Timbrenting    and the timeless halls
of Bredhil the Blessed    that abides thereon –
may she hear and heed –    to hunt endlessly
unwearying unwavering    through world and sea,
through leaguered lands,    lonely mountains,                               115
over fens and forest    and the fearful snows,
till I find those fair ones,    where the fate is hid
of the folk of Elfland    and their fortune locked,
where alone now lies    the light divine.'

Then his sons beside him,    the seven kinsmen,                             120

crafty Curufin,    Celegorm the fair,
Damrod and Díriel    and dark Cranthir,
Maglor the mighty,    and Maidros tall
(the eldest, whose ardour    yet more eager burnt
than his father's flame,    than Fëanor's wrath;                125
him fate awaited    with fell purpose),
these leapt with laughter    their lord beside,
with linkëd hands    there lightly took
the oath unbreakable;    blood thereafter
it spilled like a sea    and spent the swords            130
of endless armies,    nor hath ended yet:

'Be he friend or foe    or foul offspring
of Morgoth Bauglir,    be he mortal dark
that in after days    on earth shall dwell,
shall no law nor love    nor league of Gods,            135
no might nor mercy,    not moveless fate,
defend him for ever    from the fierce vengeance
of the sons of Fëanor,    whoso seize or steal
or finding keep    the fair enchanted
globes of crystal    whose glory dies not,            140
the Silmarils.    We have sworn for ever!'

Then a mighty murmuring    was moved abroad
and the harkening host    hailed them roaring:
'Let us go! yea go    from the Gods for ever
on Morgoth's trail    o'er the mountains of the world        145
to vengeance and victory!    Your vows are ours!'

The poem ends here (but see note to line 146).

## NOTES

41    *starry gardens* C, *starlit domes* A, B.
42    *Tengwethil's* A (with *Timbrenting* written in margin), *Tim-brenting's* B, *Timbrenting* C (with *Taingwethil* written in margin). See note to *The Children of Húrin* (second version) line 812.
45    *Bridhil* A, B, C, emended in C to *Bredhil*; so also at line 112.
107    *and all hues' essence*: this half-line (in the form *all hue's*

*essence*) occurs also in the second version of *The Children of Húrin*, line 381, where it is said of the Silmaril of Beren.

111   *Tengwethil* A, *Timbrenting* B, C.

134   *that in after days   on earth shall dwell*: this line bracketed later in pencil in C.

146   There are three roughly-written lines in the margin of the last page of A which were not taken up in B and C, but which presumably follow on line 146:

> But Finweg cried    Fingolfin's son
> when his father found    that fair counsel,
> that wit and wisdom    were of worth no more:
> 'Fools

## Commentary on *The Flight of the Noldoli*

Sad as it is that this poem was abandoned so soon – when in full mastery of the alliterative line my father might have gone on to recount the Kinslaying of Alqualondë, the Prophecy of the North, the crossing of the Helcaraxë, and the burning of the ships, there is nonetheless in its few lines much of interest for the study of the development of the legend. Most notably, there here appears the earliest version of the actual words of the Fëanorian Oath. The Oath was first referred to in the outlines for *Gilfanon's Tale* (I. 238, 240):

> The Seven Sons of Fëanor swore their terrible oath of hatred for ever against all, Gods or Elves or Men, who should hold the Silmarils

but it was there sworn after the coming of the Elves from Valinor, and after the death of Fëanor. In the present poem is the first appearance of the story that the Oath was taken in Valinor before the departure of the Gnomes. It has also been referred to in *The Children of Húrin*, lines 631 ff. of the first version, where it is implied that the mountain of Tain-Gwethil was taken in witness – as it was in *The Silmarillion* (p. 83): here (line 111) Fëanor himself swears by Timbrenting that he will never cease to hunt for the Silmarils.

I cannot explain why line 134

> that in after days    on earth shall dwell

was bracketed (always a mark of exclusion or at least of doubtful retention) in the C-text. The line reappears in identical form in the *Lay of Leithian* (Canto VI, 1636); cf. *The Silmarillion* 'Vala, Demon, Elf or Man as yet unborn'.

The fixed epithets of certain of the Sons of Fëanor are changed from those in *The Children of Húrin* (see p. 86): Celegorm is now 'the fair' and Maidros 'the tall', as they remained; Maglor is 'the mighty' (in *The Silmarillion* 'the mighty singer'). The line concerning Maidros him fate awaited    with fell purpose      (126)

may show that a form of the story of his end was already in being (in the *Tale of the Nauglafring* he survived the attack on Dior the Fair but nothing more is told of him), but I think it much more likely that it refers to his capture and maiming by Morgoth.

In Fëanor's speech occur two interesting references: to *the Nine Valar*, and to his father *Finn*. The number of the Valar is nowhere stated in the *Lost Tales* (where in any case the name includes lesser divine beings; cf. e.g. I. 65–6 'With them came many of those lesser Vali . . . the Mánir and the Súruli, the sylphs of the airs and of the winds'); but 'the Nine Valar' are referred to in the 'Sketch of the Mythology' (1926) and named in the 1930 'Silmarillion': Manwë, Ulmo, Ossë, Aulë, Mandos, Lórien, Tulkas, Oromë, and Melko.

Fëanor's father has not been named since the tale of *The Theft of Melko and the Darkening of Valinor* (I. 145 ff.), where he was called Bruithwir, slain by Melko. In *The Children of Húrin* there is no indication that Fëanor was akin to other princes of the Gnomes – though there can be no doubt that by that time he in fact was so. But the essential features of the Noldorin royal house as it had now emerged and as it was to remain for many years can now be deduced. In the first version of *The Children of Húrin* (line 29 and note) Turgon was the son of Finwë (actually spelt *Finweg*), as he had been in the *Lost Tales* (I. 115), but this was changed to Finwë's heir, with the note 'he was Fingolfin's son'; and in the second version *Turgon the mighty, / Fingolfin's son* is found in the text as written (48–9). We thus have:

Finwë (Finweg)

Fingolfin

Turgon

Further, *Finweg* appears in *The Children of Húrin* (first version 1975, second version 19, 520) as the King of the Gnomes who died in the Battle of Unnumbered Tears; in two of these cases the name was later changed to *Fingon*. In the lines added at the end of the A-text of *The Flight of the Noldoli* (note to line 146) Finweg is Fingolfin's son. We can therefore add:

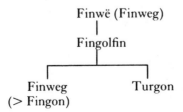

Finwë (Finweg)

Fingolfin

Finweg          Turgon
(> Fingon)

Now in *The Flight of the Noldoli* Fëanor is called Finn's son; and in the 'Sketch of the Mythology' Finn is given as an alternative to Finwë:

> The Eldar are divided into three hosts, one under Ingwë (Ing) . . ., one under Finwë (Finn) after called the Noldoli . . .*

Thus Fëanor has become Fingolfin's brother:

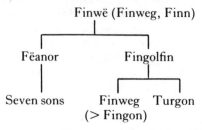

(Only in a later note to lines 1713–20 of *The Children of Húrin* has Finwë's third son Finrod appeared, father of Felagund, Angrod, Egnor, and Orodreth.)

Fëanor's speech also contains a curious foreknowledge of the making of the Sun and Moon (92–6):

> The woods of the world whose wide mansions
> yet in darkness dream drowned in slumber,
> the pathless plains and perilous shores
> no moon yet shines on nor mounting dawn
> in dew and daylight hath drenched for ever

Very notable are Fëanor's concluding words (117–18):

> till I find those fair ones, where the fate is hid
> of the folk of Elfland and their fortune locked

Cf. *The Silmarillion*, p. 67: 'Mandos foretold that the fates of Arda lay locked within them', and Thingol's words to Beren (*ibid.* p. 167): 'though the fate of Arda lie within the Silmarils, yet you shall hold me generous'. It is clear that the Silmarils had already gained greatly in significance since the earliest period of the mythology (see I. 156, 169 note 2; II. 259).

In no other version is Fëanor seen on this occasion holding flaming torches in his hands and whirling them aloft.

The lines (38–9)

> Of the Three Kindreds to that clamorous throng
> are none but the Gnomes in numbers drawn

go back to the tale of *The Flight of the Noldoli* (I. 162): 'Now when . . .

---

* In the 1930 'Silmarillion' it is expressly stated that *Ing* and *Finn* are the Gnomish forms of *Ingwë* and *Finwë*.

Fëanor sees that far the most of the company is of the kin of the Noldor', on which I noted (I. 169) 'It is to be remembered that in the old story the Teleri (i.e. the later Vanyar) had not departed from Kôr.' Later evidence shows that the old story had not been changed; but the fact that in the present poem *the Elves of Ing* (Ingwë) were on Timbrenting (Taniquetil) in the mansions of Manwë and Varda shows the entry of the later narrative (found in the 'Sketch') of the destruction of the Trees. In the old tale of *The Theft of Melko and the Darkening of Valinor* (I. 143 ff. and commentary I. 157) the great festival was the occasion of Melko's attack on the place of the Gnomes' banishment northward in Valinor, the slaying of Fëanor's father, and the theft of the Silmarils; and the destruction of the Trees followed some time afterwards. Now however the festival is the occasion of the attack on the Trees; the First Kindred are on Taniquetil but most of the Gnomes are not.

The name by which Varda is here called, Bridhil the Blessed (changed in C to Bredhil), is found in the old Gnomish dictionary, and also Timbridhil (I. 269, 273, entries *Tinwetári, Varda*). On *Timbrenting* see p. 127, where the form *Tindbrenting* occurring in *The Children of Húrin* (in a note to second version line 812) is discussed. Both forms are found in the 'Sketch':

> Timbrenting or Tindbrenting in English, Tengwethil in Gnomish, Taniquetil in Elfin.

The form with -*m*- is therefore evidently due to a change of pronunciation in English, *ndb* > *mb*.

In line 41 the earlier reading *starlit domes*, changed to *starry gardens*, is probably to be related to the account in the tale of *The Coming of the Valar and the Building of Valinor* of Manwë's abode on Taniquetil (I. 73):

> That house was builded of marbles white and blue and stood amid the fields of snow, and its roofs were made of a web of that blue air called *ilwë* that is above the white and grey. This web did Aulë and his wife contrive, but Varda spangled it with stars, and Manwë dwelt thereunder.

This idea of a roof lit with stars was never lost and appears in a changed form long after, though it is not mentioned in *The Silmarillion*.
The lines (21–3)

>                              The dim fingers
>     of fog came floating    from the formless waste
>     and sunless seas

find an echo in *The Silmarillion* (p. 76):

> it blew chill from the East in that hour, and the vast shadows of the sea were rolled against the walls of the shore.

The lines at the end of the A-text (note to line 146) show that Fingolfin has taken Finwë Nólemë's place as the voice of reason and moderation amid the revolutionary enthusiasm of the Noldoli in the great square of Kôr (see I. 162, 171).

Lastly may be noticed the term 'Foam-riders' used (line 52) of the Third Kindred (the Solosimpi of the *Lost Tales*, later the Teleri); this has been used once before, in *Ælfwine of England* (II. 314), where it is said of Ælfwine's mother Éadgifu that when he was born

> the Foamriders, the Elves of the Sea-marge, whom she had known of old in Lionesse, sent messengers to his birth.

### Analysis of the metre of the poem

At the end of the second text (B) of *The Flight of the Noldoli* my father made an analysis of the metrical forms of the first 20 and certain subsequent lines. For his analysis and explanation of the Old English metre see *On Translating Beowulf*, in *The Monsters and the Critics and Other Essays*, 1983, pp. 61 ff. The letters A, + A, B, C, D, E on the left-hand side of the table refer to the 'types' of Old English half-line; the letters beneath the analyses of 'lifts' and 'dips' are the alliterations employed in each line, with O used for any vowel (since all vowels 'alliterate' with each other) and X for a consonant beginning a lift but not forming part of the alliterative scheme of the line; the words 'full', 'simple', etc. refer to the nature of the alliterative pattern in each case.

| Line | Type | Alliterative pattern |
|------|------|-----------------------|
| 1 | B A | T X ‖ T X — simple |
| 2 | A B | G S ‖ G S — crossed |
| 3 | +A B | M M ‖ M X — full |
| 4 | B C | F F ‖ F X — full |
| 5 | A B | G G ‖ G X — full |
| 6 | +A B | D D ‖ D X — full |
| 7 | C A | B B ‖ B X — full |
| 8 | B C | G G ‖ G X — full |
| 9 | B B | Sp X ‖ Sp X — simple |
| 10 | B B | Sh X ‖ Sh X — simple |
| 11 | B B | W W ‖ W X — full |
| 12 | C B | B B ‖ B X — full |
| 13 | +A B | L L ‖ L X — full |

| 14 | A A | $\frac{/}{M}$ $\overset{x}{-}$ $\frac{/}{M}$ ˘ | ‖ | $\frac{/}{M}$ ˘ $\frac{/}{X}$ ˘ | full |
| 15 | +A A | ˘˘\|$\frac{/}{H}$ ˘˘ $\frac{/}{X}$ ˘ | ‖ | $\frac{/}{H}$ ˘ $\frac{/}{X}$ ˘ | simple |
| 16 | B C | ˘$\frac{/}{G}$ ˘˘ $\frac{/}{G}$ | ‖ | ˘˘ $\frac{/}{G}$ $\frac{/}{X}$ ˘ | full |
| 17 | C A | $\overset{x}{-}$˘$\frac{/}{O}$ $\frac{/}{M}$ ˘ | ‖ | $\frac{/}{M}$ ˘˘ $\frac{/}{O}$ ˘ | double |
| 18 | +A B | ˘˘\|$\frac{/}{M}$ ˘˘ $\frac{/}{K}$ ˘ | ‖ | ˘$\frac{/}{M}$ ˘ $\frac{/}{K}$ | crossed |
| 19 | B C · | ˘˘ $\frac{/}{W}$ ˘ $\frac{/}{W}$ | ‖ | ˘˘ $\frac{/}{W}$ $\frac{/}{X}$ ˘ | full |
| 20 | E B | $\frac{/}{T}$ $\overset{\backslash}{-}$ ˘ $\frac{/}{T}$ | ‖ | ˘$\frac{/}{T}$ ˘ $\frac{/}{X}$ | full |
| 37 | E B | $\frac{/}{W}$ $\overset{\backslash}{(W)}$ ˘ $\frac{/}{X}$ | ‖ | ˘$\frac{/}{W}$ ˘ $\frac{/}{X}$ | simple + |
| 51 | D B | $\frac{/}{S}$ $\frac{/}{S}$ $\overset{\backslash}{-}$ ˘ | ‖ | ˘˘ $\frac{/}{S}$ ˘ $\frac{\backslash}{X}$ | full |
| 57 | E A | $\frac{/}{P}$ $\overset{\backslash}{-}$ ˘ $\frac{/}{X}$ | ‖ | $\frac{/}{P}$ ˘ $\frac{/}{X}$ ˘ | simple |
| 61 | B A | ˘˘ $\frac{/}{K}$ $\overset{x}{-}$ $\frac{/}{K}$ | ‖ | $\frac{/}{K}$ ˘ $\frac{/}{X}$ ˘ | full |
| 67 | +E A | ˘\|$\frac{/}{F}$ $\overset{\backslash}{-}$ ˘ $\frac{/}{F}$ | ‖ | $\frac{/}{F}$ ˘ $\frac{/}{X}$ ˘ | full |
| 79 | +A B | ˘\|$\frac{/}{F}$ ˘ $\frac{/}{F}$ $\overset{x}{-}$ | ‖ | ˘ $\frac{/}{F}$ ˘˘ $\frac{/}{X}$ | full |
| 107 | +A B | ˘\|$\frac{/}{O}$ $\overset{\backslash}{-}$ $\frac{/}{O}$ ˘ | ‖ | ˘$\frac{/}{O}$ ˘ $\frac{/}{X}$ | full |

It may be noticed that the scansion of the first half of line 8 (with the first lift *-goli-*) shows that the primary stress fell on the second syllable of *Ungóliant*; and that *sp* can only alliterate with *sp* (lines 9, 130), as in Old English (the same is of course true of *sh*, which is a separate consonant).

★

## (ii) *Fragment of an alliterative Lay of Eärendel*

There exists one other piece of alliterative verse concerned with the matter of the *Lost Tales*, the opening of a poem that has no title and does not extend far enough to make clear what its subject was to be. The fall of Gondolin, the escape of the fugitives down the secret tunnel, the fight at Cristhorn, and the long wandering in the wilds thereafter, are passed over rapidly in what were to be the introductory lines, and the subject seems about to appear at the end of the fragment:

> all this have others    in ancient stories
> and songs unfolded,    but say I further . . .

and the concluding lines refer to the sojourn of the fugitives in the Land of Willows. But at the end of the text my father wrote several times in different scripts 'Earendel', 'Earendel son of Fengel', 'Earendel Fengelsson'; and I think it extremely likely, even almost certain, that this poem was to be a Lay of Eärendel. (On Fengel see the next section.)

The text is in the first stage of composition and is exceedingly rough, but it contains one line of the utmost interest for the history of Eärendel. It is written on examination paper from the University of Leeds and clearly belongs in time with *The Lay of the Children of Húrin* and *The Flight of the Noldoli*: more than that seems impossible to say.

> Lo! the flame of fire   and fierce hatred
> engulfed Gondolin   and its glory fell,
> its tapering towers   and its tall rooftops
> were laid all low,   and its leaping fountains
> made no music more   on the mount of Gwareth,   5
> and its whitehewn walls   were whispering ash.
> { But Wade of the Helsings   wearyhearted }
> { Túr the earthborn   was tried in battle }
> from the wrack and ruin   a remnant led
> women and children   and wailing maidens
> and wounded men   of the withered folk   10
> down the path unproven   that pierced the hillside,
> neath Tumladin he led them   to the leaguer of hills
> that rose up rugged   as ranged pinnacles
> to the north of the vale.   There the narrow way
> of Cristhorn was cloven,   the Cleft of Eagles,   15
> through the midmost mountains.   And more is told
> in lays and in legend   and lore of others
> of that weary way   of the wandering folk;
> how the waifs of Gondolin   outwitted Melko,
> vanished o'er the vale   and vanquished the hills,   20
> how Glorfindel the golden   in the gap of the Eagles
> battled with the Balrog   and both were slain:
> one like flash of fire   from fangéd rock,
> one like bolted thunder   black was smitten
> to the dreadful deep   digged by Thornsir.   25
> Of the thirst and hunger   of the thirty moons
> when they sought for Sirion   and were sore bestead
> by plague and peril;   of the Pools of Twilight
> and Land of Willows;   when their lamentation
> was heard in the halls   where the high Gods sate   30
> veiled in Valinor   . . the Vanished Isles;
> all this have others   in ancient stories
> and songs unfolded,   but say I further
> how their lot was lightened,   how they laid them down
> in long grasses   of the Land of Willows.   35
> There sun was softer,   . . . the sweet breezes
> and whispering winds,   there wells of slumber
> and the dew enchanted

★

## NOTES

25  The next lines are

> where stony-voicéd    that stream of Eagles
> runs o'er the rocky

but the second of these is struck out and the first left without
continuation.

31  The second half-line was written *in the Vanished Isles*, but *in* was
struck out and replaced by a word that I cannot interpret.

36  The second half-line was written *and the sweet breezes*, but *and*
was struck out and replaced by some other word, possibly *then*.

## Commentary

For the form *Tûr* see II. 148, 260.

In the tale of *The Fall of Gondolin* Cristhorn, the Eagles' Cleft, was in
the Encircling Mountains south of Gondolin, and the secret tunnel led
southwards from the city (II. 167–8 etc.); but from line 14 of this
fragment it is seen that the change to the north had already entered the
legend.

Lines 26–7 (*the thirty moons    when they sought for Sirion*) go
back to the *Fall of Gondolin*, where it is said that the fugitives wandered
'a year and more' in the wastes (see II. 195, 214).

The reading of line 7 as first written (it was not struck out, but *Tûr the
earthborn    was tried in battle* was added in the margins):

> But Wade of the Helsings    wearyhearted

is remarkable. It is taken directly from the very early Old English poem
*Widsith*, where occurs the line *Wada Hælsingum*, sc. *Wada* [*weold*]
*Hælsingum*, 'Wada ruled the Hælsingas'. One may well wonder why the
mysterious figure of Wade should appear here in Tuor's place, and
indeed I cannot explain it: but whatever the reason, the association of
Wade with Tuor is not casual. Of the original story of Wade almost
nothing is known; but he survived in popular recollection through the
Middle Ages and later – he is mentioned by Malory as a mighty being,
and Chaucer refers to 'Wade's boat' in *The Merchant's Tale*; in *Troilus
and Crisyede* Pandare told a 'tale of Wade'. R. W. Chambers (*Widsith*,
Cambridge 1912, p. 95) said that Wade was perhaps 'originally a sea-
giant, dreaded and honoured by the coast tribes of the North Sea and the
Baltic'; and the tribe of the Hælsingas over which he is said to have ruled
in *Widsith* is supposed to have left its name in Helsingör (Elsinore) in
Denmark and in Helsingfors in Finland. Chambers summed up what
few generalities he thought might be made from the scattered references
in English and German as follows:

We find these common characteristics, which we may assume belonged to their ancient prototype, Wada of the Hælsingas:

(1) Power over the sea.
(2) Extraordinary strength – often typified by superhuman stature.
(3) The use of these powers to help those whom Wade favours.

... Probably he grew out of the figure, not of a historic chief, but of a supernatural power, who had no story all his own, and who interested mortal men only when he interfered in their concerns. Hence he is essentially a helper in time of need; and we may be fairly confident that already in the oldest lays he possessed this character.

Most interesting, however, is the fact that in Speght's annotations to Chaucer (1598) he said:

Concerning Wade and his bote *Guingelot*, as also his strange exploits in the same, because the matter is long and fabulous, I passe it over.

The likeness of *Guingelot* to *Wingelot* is sufficiently striking; but when we place together the facts that Wingelot was Eärendel's ship,* that Eärendel was Tuor's son, that Tuor was peculiarly associated with the sea, and that here 'Wade of the Helsings' stands in the place of Tuor, coincidence is ruled out. *Wingelot* was derived from Wade's boat *Guingelot* as certainly, I think, as was Eärendel from the Old English figure (this latter being a fact expressly stated by my father, II. 309).

Why my father should have intruded 'Wade of the Helsings' into the verses at this point is another question. It may conceivably have been unintentional – the words *Wada Hælsingum* were running in his mind (though in that case one might expect that he would have struck the line out and not merely written another line against it as an alternative): but at any rate the reason why they were running in his mind is clear, and this possibility in no way diminishes the demonstrative value of the line that *Wingelot* was derived from *Guingelot*, and that there was a connection of greater significance than the mere taking over of a name – just as in the case of Eärendel.

### (iii)    *The Lay of the Fall of Gondolin*

This was the title that late in his life my father wrote on the bundle of papers constituting the abandoned beginning of this poem; but it seems that it was not conceived on a large scale, since the narrative had reached

---

*In which he undertook 'fabulous exploits'. It is conceivable that there was some connection between Eärendel's great world-girdling voyage and the travels of Wade as described by the twelfth-century English writer Walter Map, who tells how *Gado* (sc. Wade) journeyed in his boat to the furthest Indies.

the dragon-fire arising over the northern heights already within 130 lines. That he composed it while at the University of Leeds is certain, but I strongly suspect that it was the first versification of matter from the *Lost Tales* undertaken, before he turned to the alliterative line. The story, so far as it goes, has undergone virtually no development from the prose tale of *The Fall of Gondolin*, and the closeness of the Lay to the Tale can be seen from this comparison (though the passage is exceptional):

(Tale, II. 158)
Rejoice that ye have found it, for behold before you the City of Seven Names where all who war with Melko may find hope.'
   Then said Tuor: 'What be those names?' And the chief of the Guard made answer: "'Tis said and 'tis sung: "Gondobar am I called and Gondothlimbar, City of Stone and City of the Dwellers in Stone, &c.

(Lay)   Rejoice that ye have found it and rest from endless war,
   For the seven-naméd city 'tis that stands upon the hill,
   Where all who strive with Morgoth find hope and valour still.'
   'What be those names,' said Tuor, 'for I come from long afar?'
   "'Tis said and 'tis sung,' one answered, "'My name is Gondobar
   And Gondothlimbar also, the City hewn of Stone,
   The fortress of the Gnome-folk who dwell in Halls of Stone, &c.

I do not give this poem *in extenso* here, since it does not, so far as the main narrative is concerned, add anything to the Tale; and my father found, as I think, the metrical form unsuitable to the purpose. There are, however, several passages of interest for the study of the larger development of the legends.

In the *Tale*, Tuor was the son of Peleg (who was the son of Indor, II. 160), but here he is the son of Fengel; while on a scrap of paper giving rough workings of the passage cited above* Tuor himself is called Fengel – cf. 'Eärendel son of Fengel' at the end of the fragment of an Eärendel Lay, p. 141. Long afterwards Fengel was the name of the fifteenth King of Rohan in the Third Age, grandfather of Théoden, and there it is the Old English noun *fengel* 'king, prince'.

There are some puzzling statements made concerning Fingolfin, whose appearance here, I feel certain, is earlier than those in the alliterative poems; and the passage in which he appears introduces also the story of Isfin and Eöl.

---

*This is the page referred to in *Unfinished Tales* p. 4: 'some lines of verse in which appear the Seven Names of Gondolin are scribbled on the back of a piece of paper setting out "the chain of responsibility in a battalion".' Not knowing at that time where this isolated scrap came from I took this as an indication of very early date, but this is certainly mistaken: the paper must have survived and been used years later for rough writing.

> Lo, that prince of Gondobar [Meglin]
> dark Eöl's son whom Isfin, in a mountain dale afar
> in the gloom of Doriath's forest, the white-limbed maiden bare,
> the daughter of Fingolfin, Gelmir's mighty heir.
> 'Twas the bent blades of the Glamhoth that drank Fingolfin's life
> as he stood alone by Fëanor; but his maiden and his wife
> were wildered as they sought him in the forests of the night,
> in the pathless woods of Doriath, so dark that as a light
> of palely mirrored moonsheen were their slender elfin limbs
> straying among the black holes where only the dim bat skims
> from Thû's dark-delvéd caverns. There Eöl saw that sheen
> and he caught the white-limbed Isfin, that she ever since hath been
> his mate in Doriath's forest, where she weepeth in the gloam;
> for the Dark Elves were his kindred that wander without home.
> Meglin she sent to Gondolin, and his honour there was high
> as the latest seed of Fingolfin, whose glory shall not die;
> a lordship he won of the Gnome-folk who quarry deep in the earth,
> seeking their ancient jewels; but little was his mirth,
> and dark he was and secret and his hair as the strands of night
> that are tangled in Taur Fuin* the forest without light.

In the *Lost Tales* Finwë Nólemë, first Lord of the Noldoli, was the father of Turgon (and so of Isfin, who was Turgon's sister), I. 115; Finwë Nólemë was slain in the Battle of Unnumbered Tears and his heart cut out by Orcs, but Turgon rescued the body and heart of his father, and the Scarlet Heart became his grim emblem (I. 241, II. 172). Finwë Nólemë is also called Fingolma (I. 238–9, II. 220).

In the alliterative poems Fingolfin is the son of Finwë (Finweg) and the father of Turgon, and also of Finweg (> Fingon), as he was to remain (see p. 137).     Thus:

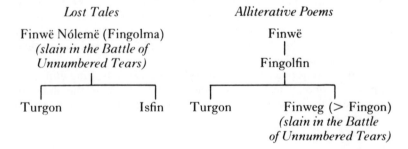

| *Lost Tales* | *Alliterative Poems* |
|---|---|
| Finwë Nólemë (Fingolma) *(slain in the Battle of Unnumbered Tears)* | Finwë \| Fingolfin |
| Turgon          Isfin | Turgon          Finweg (> Fingon) *(slain in the Battle of Unnumbered Tears)* |

But whereas in the *Lay of the Fall of Gondolin* Fingolfin has

---

*\*Taur Fuin* is the form in the *Lost Tales*; it was here emended later to *Taur-na-Fuin*, which is the form from the first in *The Children of Húrin*.

emerged and stepped into Finwë's place as the father of Turgon and Isfin, he is not here the son of Finwë but of one *Gelmir*:

In an early prose text – one of the very few scraps (to be given in the next volume) that bridge the gap in the prose history between the *Lost Tales* and the 'Sketch of the Mythology' – Gelmir appears as the King of the Noldoli at the time of the flight from Valinor, and one of his sons is there named *Golfin*.

There is too little evidence extant (if there ever was any more written down) to penetrate with certainty the earliest evolution of the Noldorin kings. The simplest explanation is that this Gelmir, father of Golfin/ Fingolfin = Fingolma/Finwë Nólemë, father of Fingolfin. But it is also said in this passage that Fingolfin was slain by the Glamhoth 'as he stood alone by Fëanor', and whatever story lies behind this is now vanished (for the earliest, very obscure, references to the death of Fëanor see I. 238–9).

This passage from the *Lay of the Fall of Gondolin* contains the first account of the story of Eöl the Dark Elf, Isfin sister of Turgon, and their son Meglin (for a very primitive form of the legend see II. 220). In the prose tale of *The Fall of Gondolin* the story is dismissed in the words 'that tale of Isfin and Eöl may not here be told', II. 165. In the Lay, Fingolfin's wife and daughter (Isfin) *were seeking for him* when Isfin was taken by Eöl. Since in the 'Sketch' Isfin was lost in Taur-na-Fuin after the Battle of Unnumbered Tears and there trapped by Eöl, it is possible that at this stage Fingolfin was the Elvish king who died (beside Fëanor?) in the great battle. It is also possible that we see here the genesis of the idea of Isfin's wandering in the wilds, although of course with subsequent shifts, whereby Fingolfin died in duel with Morgoth after the Battle of Sudden Flame and Fingon (Isfin's brother) was the Noldorin king slain in the Battle of Unnumbered Tears, the story that she was seeking her father was abandoned. What this passage does certainly show is that the story of Isfin's sending her son to Gondolin is original, but that originally Isfin remained with her captor Eöl and never escaped from him.

Eöl here dwells 'in a mountain dale afar in the gloom of Doriath's forest', 'in the forests of the night', 'where only the dim bat skims from Thû's dark-delvéd caverns'. This must be the earliest reference to Thû, and at any rate in connected writing the earliest to Doriath (Artanor of the *Lost Tales*). I have suggested (II. 63) that in the *Tale of Tinúviel*

'Artanor was conceived as a great region of forest in the heart of which was Tinwelint's cavern', and that the zone of the Queen's protection 'was originally less distinctly bordered, and less extensive, than "the Girdle of Melian" afterwards became'. Here the description of Eöl's habitation in a forest without light (where Thû lives in caverns) suggests rather the forest of Taur-na-Fuin, where

> Never-dawning night  was netted clinging
> in the black branches  of the beetling trees

and where

>                                         goblins even
> (whose deep eyes drill  the darkest shadows)
> bewildered wandered
> >                        (*The Children of Húrin*, p. 34, lines 753 ff.)

The passage also contains an interesting reference to the purpose of the miners of Gondolin: 'seeking their ancient jewels.'

Earlier in this Lay some lines are given to the coming of Tuor to the hidden door beneath the Encircling Mountains:

> Thither Tuor son of Fengel came out of the dim land
> that the Gnomes have called Dor-Lómin, with Bronweg at his hand,
> who fled from the Iron Mountains and had broken Melko's chain
> and cast his yoke of evil, of torment and bitter pain;
> who alone most faithful-hearted led Tuor by long ways
> through empty hills and valleys by dark nights and perilous days,
> till his blue lamp magic-kindled, where flow the shadowy rills
> beneath enchanted alders, found that Gate beneath the hills,
> the door in dark Dungorthin that only the Gnome-folk knew.

In a draft for this passage the name here is *Nan Orwen*, emended to *Dungorthin*. In *The Children of Húrin* (lines 1457 ff.) Túrin and Flinding came to this 'grey valley' after they had passed west over Sirion, and reached the roots of the Shadowy Mountains 'that Hithlum girdle'. For earlier references to Nan Dungorthin and different placings of it see p. 87; the present passage seems to indicate yet another, with the hidden door of Gondolin opening into it.

A few other passages may be noticed. At the beginning there is a reference to old songs telling

> how the Gods in council gathered on the outmost rocky bars
> of the Lonely Island westward, and devised a land of ease
> beyond the great sea-shadows and the shadowy seas;
> how they made the deep gulf of Faërie with long and lonely shore . . .

That the Gods were ferried on an island by Ossë and the Oarni at the time of the fall of the Lamps is told in the tale of *The Coming of the Valar*

(I. 70), and that this isle was afterwards that of the Elves' ferrying (becoming Tol Eressëa) is told in *The Coming of the Elves* (I. 118). When Gondolin was built the people cried 'Côr is built anew!' and the guard who told Tuor the seven names said:

> Loth, the Flower, they name me, saying 'Côr is born again,
> even in Loth-a-ladwen,* the Lily of the Plain.'

I have noticed earlier (II. 208) that whereas it is explicit in *The Silmarillion* that Turgon devised the city to be 'a memorial of Tirion upon Túna', and it became 'as beautiful as a memory of Elven Tirion', this is not said in *The Fall of Gondolin*: Turgon was born in the Great Lands after the return of the Noldoli from Valinor, and had never known Kôr. 'One may feel nonetheless that the tower of the King, the fountains and stairs, the white marbles of Gondolin embody a recollection of Kôr as it is described in *The Coming of the Elves and the Making of Kôr* (I. 122–3).'

There is also a reference to Eärendel

> who passed the Gates of Dread,
> half-mortal and half-elfin, undying and long dead.

The Gates of Dread are probably the gates of the Door of Night, through which Eärendel passed (II. 255).

---

*This is the only point in which the Seven Names differ from their forms in the *Tale* (II. 158). In the *Tale* the name of the city as 'Lily of the Valley' is *Lothengriol*. For *ladwen* 'plain' see II. 344. In a draft of the passage in the lay the name was *Loth Barodrin*.

# III

# THE LAY OF LEITHIAN

My father wrote in his diary that he began 'the poem of Tinúviel' during the period of the summer examinations of 1925 (see p. 3), and he abandoned it in September 1931 (see below), when he was 39. The rough workings for the whole poem are extant (and 'rough' means very rough indeed); from them he wrote a fair copy, which I shall call 'A'.*

On this manuscript A my father most uncharacteristically inserted dates, the first of these being at line 557 (August 23, 1925); and he composed the last hundred-odd lines of the third Canto (ending at line 757) while on holiday at Filey on the Yorkshire coast in September 1925. The next date is two and a half years and 400 lines later, 27–28 March 1928 written against line 1161; and thereafter each day for a further nine days, till 6 April 1928, is marked, during which time he wrote out no less than 1768 lines, to 2929.

Since the dates refer to the copying of verses out fair in the manuscript, not to their actual composition, it might be thought that they prove little; but the rough workings of lines 2497–2504 are written on an abandoned letter dated 1 April 1928, and these lines were written in the fair copy A on 4 April – showing that lines 2505–2929 were actually composed between 1 and 6 April. I think therefore that the dates on A can be taken as effectively indicating the time of composition.

The date November 1929 (at line 3031) is followed by a substantial amount of composition in the last week of September 1930, and again in the middle of September 1931; the last date is 17 September of that year against line 4085 very near the point where the Lay was abandoned. Details of the dates are given in the Notes.

There is also a typescript text ('B') made by my father, of which the last few hundred lines are in manuscript, and this text ends at precisely the same point as does A. This typescript was begun quite early, since my father mentioned in his diary for 16 August 1926 having done 'a little typing of part of *Tinúviel*'; and before the end of 1929 he gave it to C. S. Lewis to read. On 7 December of that year Lewis wrote to him about it, saying:

> I sat up late last night and have read the *Geste* as far as to where Beren and his gnomish allies defeat the patrol of orcs above the sources of the

---

*This was written on the backs of examination-scripts, tied together and prepared as a blank manuscript: it was large enough to last through the six years, and a few scripts at the end of the bundle remained unused.

Narog and disguise themselves in the *rēaf* [Old English: 'garments, weapons, taken from the slain']. I can quite honestly say that it is ages since I have had an evening of such delight: and the personal interest of reading a friend's work had very little to do with it. I should have enjoyed it just as well as if I'd picked it up in a bookshop, by an unknown author. The two things that come out clearly are the sense of reality in the background and the mythical value: the essence of a myth being that it should have no taint of allegory to the maker and yet should suggest incipient allegories to the reader,

Lewis had thus reached in his reading about line 2017. He had evidently received more; it may be that the typescript by this time extended to the attack on Lúthien and Beren by Celegorm and Curufin fleeing from Nargothrond, against which (at line 3031) is the date November 1929 in the manuscript. Some time after this, probably early in 1930, Lewis sent my father 14 pages of detailed criticism, as far as line 1161 (if there was any more it has not survived). This criticism he contrived as a heavily academic commentary on the text, pretending to treat the Lay as an ancient and anonymous work extant in many more or less corrupt manuscripts, overlaid by scribal perversions in antiquity and the learned argumentation of nineteenth-century scholars; and thus entertainingly took the sting from some sharply expressed judgements, while at the same time in this disguise expressing strong praise for particular passages. Almost all the verses which Lewis found wanting for one reason or another are marked for revision in the typescript B if not actually rewritten, and in many cases his proposed emendations, or modifications of them, are incorporated into the text. The greater part of Lewis's commentary is given on pp. 315 ff., with the verses he criticised and the alterations made as a result.

My father abandoned the Lay at the point where the jaws of Carcharoth *crashed together like a trap* on Beren's hand and the Silmaril was engulfed, but though he never advanced beyond that place in the narrative, he did not abandon it for good. When *The Lord of the Rings* was finished he returned to the Lay again and recast the first two Cantos and a good part of the third, and small portions of some others.

To summarise the elements of this history:

(1) Rough workings of the whole poem, composed 1925–31.
(2) Manuscript A of the whole poem, written out progressively during 1925–31.
(3) Typescript B of the whole poem (ending in manuscript), already in progress in 1926.
  This typescript given to C. S. Lewis towards the end of 1929, when it extended probably to about line 3031.

(4)   Recasting of the opening Cantos and parts of some others (after the completion of *The Lord of the Rings*).

———

The manuscript A was emended, both by changes and insertions, at different times, the majority of these alterations being incorporated in the typescript B; while in B, as typed, there are further changes not found in A.

The amount of emendation made to B varies very greatly. My father used it as a basis for the later rewritings, and in these parts the old typescript is entirely covered with new verses; but for long stretches – by far the greater part of the poem – the text is untouched save for very minor and as it were casual modifications to individual lines here and there.

After much experimentation I have concluded that to make a single text, an amalgam derived from the latest writing throughout the poem, would be wholly mistaken. Quite apart from the practical difficulty of changed names in the rewritten parts that do not scan in the old lines, the later verse in its range and technical accomplishment is too distinct; too much time had passed, and in the small amount that my father rewrote of the *Lay of Leithian* after *The Lord of the Rings* we have fragments of a new poem: from which we can gain an idea of what might have been. I have therefore excised these parts, and give them subsequently and separately (Chapter IV).

A further reason for doing so lies in the purpose of this book, which includes the consideration of the Lays as important stages in the evolution of the legends. Some of the revisions to the *Lay of Leithian* are at least 30 years later than the commencement of the poem. From the point of view of the 'history', therefore, the abandonment of the poem in or soon after September 1931 constitutes a terminal point, and I have excluded emendations to names that are (as I believe) certainly later than that, but included those which are earlier.* In a case like that of *Beleriand*, for instance, which was *Broseliand* for much of the poem in B and always later emended to *Beleriand*, but had become *Beleriand* as first written by line 3957, I give *Beleriand* throughout. On the other hand I retain *Gnomes* since my father still used this in *The Hobbit*.

The many small changes made for metrical/stylistic reasons, however, constitute a problem in the attempt to produce a '1931 text', since it is often impossible to be sure to which 'phase' they belong. Some are

———

*This leads to inconsistent treatment of certain names as between the two long Lays, e.g. *Finweg* son of Fingolfin in *The Children of Húrin* but *Fingon* in the *Lay of Leithian*. *Finweg* survived into the 1930 version of 'The Silmarillion' but was early emended to *Fingon*.

demonstrably very early – e.g. *candle flowers* emended to *flowering candles* (line 516), since C. S. Lewis commented on the latter – while others are demonstrably from many years later, and strictly speaking belong with the late rewritings; but many cannot be certainly determined. In any case, such changes – very often made to get rid of certain artifices employed as metrical aids, most notably among these the use of emphatic tenses with *doth* and *did* simply in order to obtain a syllable – such changes have no repercussions beyond the improvement of the individual line; and in such cases it seems a pity, through rigid adherence to the textual basis, to lose such small enhancements, or at any rate to hide them in a trail of tedious textual notes, while letting their less happy predecessors stand in the text. I have thought it justifiable therefore to be frankly inconsistent in these details, and while for example retaining *Gnomes* (for *Elves* or other substitution) or *Thû* (for *Gorthû* or *Sauron*), to introduce small changes of wording that are certainly later than these.

As in the *Lay of the Children of Húrin* there are no numbered notes to the text; the annotation, related to the line-numbers of the poem, is very largely restricted to earlier readings, and these earlier readings are restricted to cases where there is some significant difference, as of name or motive. Citations from the manuscript A are always citations from that text *as first written* (in very many cases it was emended to the reading found in B).

It is to be noticed that while the *Lay of Leithian* was in process of composition the 'Sketch of the Mythology' was written (first in 1926) and rewritten, leading directly into the version of 'The Silmarillion' that I ascribe to 1930, in which many of the essentials, both in narrative and language, of the published work were already present. In my commentaries on each Canto I attempt to take stock of the development in the legends *pari passu* with the text of the poem, and only refer exceptionally to the contemporary prose works.

The A-text has no title, but on the covering page of the bundle of rough workings is written *Tinúviel*, and in his early references to the poem my father called it thus, as he called the alliterative poem *Túrin*. The B-text bears this title:

The
GEST
of
BEREN son of BARAHIR
and
LÚTHIEN the FAY
called
TINÚVIEL the NIGHTINGALE
or the
LAY OF LEITHIAN
Release from Bondage

The 'Gest of Beren and Lúthien' means a narrative in verse, telling of the deeds of Beren and Lúthien. The word *gest* is pronounced as Modern English *jest*, being indeed the 'same word' in phonetic form, though now totally changed in meaning.

My father never explained the name *Leithian* 'Release from Bondage', and we are left to choose, if we will, among various applications that can be seen in the poem. Nor did he leave any comment on the significance – if there is a significance – of the likeness of *Leithian* to *Leithien* 'England'. In the tale of *Ælfwine of England* the Elvish name of England is *Lúthien* (which was earlier the name of Ælfwine himself, England being *Luthany*), but at the first occurrence (only) of this name the word *Leithian* was pencilled above it (II. 330, note 20). In the 'Sketch of the Mythology' England was still *Lúthien* (and at that time Thingol's daughter was also *Lúthien*), but this was emended to *Leithien*, and this is the form in the 1930 version of 'The Silmarillion'. I cannot say (i) what connection if any there was between the two significances of *Lúthien*, nor (ii) whether *Leithien* (once *Leithian*) 'England' is or was related to *Leithian* 'Release from Bondage'. The only evidence of an etymological nature that I have found is a hasty note, impossible to date, which refers to a stem *leth-* 'set free', with *leithia* 'release', and compares *Lay of Leithian*.

★

## The GEST of BEREN and LÚTHIEN

### I

A king there was in days of old:
ere Men yet walked upon the mould
his power was reared in cavern's shade,
his hand was over glen and glade.
His shields were shining as the moon,                5
his lances keen of steel were hewn,
of silver grey his crown was wrought,
the starlight in his banners caught;
and silver thrilled his trumpets long
beneath the stars in challenge strong;               10
enchantment did his realm enfold,
where might and glory, wealth untold,
he wielded from his ivory throne
in many-pillared halls of stone.

There beryl, pearl, and opal pale,                    15
and metal wrought like fishes' mail,
buckler and corslet, axe and sword,
and gleaming spears were laid in hoard –
all these he had and loved them less
than a maiden once in Elfinesse;                    20
for fairer than are born to Men
a daughter had he, Lúthien.

    Such lissom limbs no more shall run
on the green earth beneath the sun;
so fair a maid no more shall be                    25
from dawn to dusk, from sun to sea.
Her robe was blue as summer skies,
but grey as evening were her eyes;
'twas sewn with golden lilies fair,
but dark as shadow was her hair.                    30
Her feet were light as bird on wing,
her laughter lighter than the spring;
the slender willow, the bowing reed,
the fragrance of a flowering mead,
the light upon the leaves of trees,                    35
the voice of water, more than these
her beauty was and blissfulness,
her glory and her loveliness;
and her the king more dear did prize
than hand or heart or light of eyes.                    40

    They dwelt amid Beleriand,
while Elfin power yet held the land,
in the woven woods of Doriath:
few ever thither found the path;
few ever dared the forest-eaves                    45
to pass, or stir the listening leaves
with tongue of hounds a-hunting fleet,
with horse, or horn, or mortal feet.
To North there lay the Land of Dread,
whence only evil pathways led                    50
o'er hills of shadow bleak and cold
or Taur-na-Fuin's haunted hold,
where Deadly Nightshade lurked and lay
and never came or moon or day;
to South the wide earth unexplored;                    55

to West the ancient Ocean roared,
unsailed and shoreless, wide and wild;
to East in peaks of blue were piled
in silence folded, mist-enfurled,
the mountains of the Outer World,								60
beyond the tangled woodland shade,
thorn and thicket, grove and glade,
whose brooding boughs with magic hung
were ancient when the world was young.

 There Thingol in the Thousand Caves,						65
whose portals pale that river laves
Esgalduin that fairies call,
in many a tall and torchlit hall
a dark and hidden king did dwell,
lord of the forest and the fell;								70
and sharp his sword and high his helm,
the king of beech and oak and elm.

 There Lúthien the lissom maid
would dance in dell and grassy glade,
and music merrily, thin and clear,							75
went down the ways, more fair than ear
of mortal Men at feast hath heard,
and fairer than the song of bird.
When leaves were long and grass was green
then Dairon with his fingers lean,							80
as daylight melted into shade,
a wandering music sweetly made,
enchanted fluting, warbling wild,
for love of Thingol's elfin child.

 There bow was bent and shaft was sped,						85
the fallow deer as phantoms fled,
and horses proud with braided mane,
with shining bit and silver rein,
went fleeting by on moonlit night,
as swallows arrow-swift in flight;							90
a blowing and a sound of bells,
a hidden hunt in hollow dells.
There songs were made and things of gold,
and silver cups and jewels untold,
and the endless years of Faëry land							95

rolled over far Beleriand,
until a day beneath the sun,
when many marvels were begun.

# NOTES

The opening of the poem in B is complicated by the fact that my father
partly rewrote, and retyped, the first Canto – a rewriting entirely distinct
from the later fundamental recasting that the early part of the poem
underwent. This first rewriting of the opening Canto was done while the
original composition of the poem was still proceeding, but was fairly far
advanced. The second version was typed in exactly the same form as that
it replaced, whereas the last part of the B-text is not typed; but the name
*Beleriand* appears in it, as typed, and not as an emendation, whereas
elsewhere in B the form is *Broseliand*, always emended in ink to
*Beleriand*.* Moreover it was the first version of Canto I in the B-text that
C. S. Lewis read on the night of 6 December 1929, and I think it very
probable that it was Lewis's criticism that led my father to rewrite the
opening (see pp. 315–16). In the following notes the first version of B is
called B(1), the rewritten text given above being B(2).

1–30   A:   A king was in the dawn of days:
               his golden crown did brightly blaze
               with ruby red and crystal clear;
               his meats were sweet, his dishes dear;
               red robes of silk, an ivory throne,           5
               and ancient halls of archéd stone,
               and wine and music lavished free,
               and thirty champions and three,
               all these he had and heeded not.
               His daughter dear was Melilot:           10
               from dawn to dusk, from sun to sea,
               no fairer maiden found could be.
               Her robe was blue as summer skies,
               but not so blue as were her eyes;
               'twas sewn with golden lilies fair,           15
               but none so golden as her hair.

An earlier draft, after line 12 *found could be*, has the couplet:

               from England unto Eglamar
               o'er folk and field and lands afar.

* Once near the very end (line 3957), in the manuscript conclusion of the B-text, the form
as written is *Beleriand*, not *Broseliand*.

B(1):    A king there was in olden days:
            &c. as A to line 6

          and hoarded gold in gleaming grot,
          all these he had and heeded not.
          But fairer than are born to Men
          a daughter had he, Lúthien:
            &c. as B(2)

14–18   These lines were used afterwards in Gimli's song in Moria (*The Fellowship of the Ring* II. 4); see the Commentary by C. S. Lewis, p. 316.

41–4   A:     They dwelt in dark Broceliand
              while loneliness yet held the land.

       B(1):   They dwelt beyond Broseliand
              while loneliness yet held the land,
              in the forest dark of Doriath.
              Few ever thither found the path;

In B(1) *Ossiriande* is pencilled above *Broseliand*. As noted above, B(2) has *Beleriand* as typed.

48   After this line A and B(1) have:

          Yet came at whiles afar and dim
          beneath the roots of mountains grim
          a blowing and a sound of bells,
          a hidden hunt in hollow dells.

The second couplet reappears at a later point in B(2), lines 91–2.

49–61   A and B(1):

          To North there lay the Land of Dread,
          whence only evil pathways led
          o'er hills of shadow bleak and cold;
          to West and South the oceans rolled
          unsailed and shoreless, wild and wide;
          to East and East the hills did hide
          beneath the tangled woodland shade,

65–6   A:     There Celegorm his ageless days
              doth wear amid the woven ways,
              the glimmering aisles and endless naves
              whose pillared feet that river laves

67   *Esgalduin* A, but *Esgaduin* in the rough workings, which is the form in *The Children of Húrin* (p. 76, line 2164) before correction.

73 A:      There Melilot the lissom maid

79–84 Not in A.

85–93 A and B(1) (with one slight difference):

> There bow was bent and shaft was sped
> and deer as fallow phantoms fled,
> and horses pale with harness bright
> went jingling by on moonlit night;
> there songs were made and things of gold

See note to line 48.

96 A:      rolled over dark Broceliand,
B(1):    rolled over far Broseliand,
In B(1) *Ossiriande* is pencilled against *Broseliand*, as at line 41.

## Commentary on Canto I

An extraordinary feature of the A-version is the name *Celegorm* given to the King of the woodland Elves (Thingol); moreover in the next Canto the rôle of Beren is in A played by *Maglor*, son of Egnor. The only possible conclusion, strange as it is, is that my father was prepared to abandon *Thingol* for *Celegorm* and (even more astonishing) *Beren* for *Maglor*. Both *Celegorm* and *Maglor* as sons of Fëanor have appeared in the *Tale of the Nauglafring* and in the *Lay of the Children of Húrin*.

The name of the king's daughter in A, *Melilot*, is also puzzling (and is it the English plant-name, as in Melilot Brandybuck, a guest at Bilbo Baggins' farewell party?). Already in the second version of *The Children of Húrin* Lúthien has appeared as the 'true' name of Tinúviel (see p. 119, note to 358–66). It is perhaps possible that my father in fact began the *Lay of Leithian* before he stopped work on *The Children of Húrin*, in which case *Melilot* might be the first 'true' name of Tinúviel, displaced by *Lúthien*; but I think that this is extremely unlikely.* In view of *Beren* > *Maglor*, I think *Lúthien* > *Melilot* far more probable. In any event, *Beren* and *Lúthien* soon appear in the original drafts of the *Lay of Leithian*.

It is strange also that in A the king's daughter was blue-eyed and golden-haired, for this would not accord with the robe of darkness that

---

*My father expressly stated in his diary that he began *Tinúviel* in the summer of 1925; and it is to be noted that a reference to the *Lay of Leithian* appears in the alliterative head-piece to one of the typescripts of *Light as Leaf on Lindentree* – which was actually published in June 1925 (see pp. 120–1). Thus the reference in the second version of *The Children of Húrin* to the *Lay of Leithian* (p. 107 line 356) is not evidence that he had in fact begun it.

she spun from her hair: in the *Tale of Tinúviel* her hair was 'dark' (II. 20).

The name *Broceliand* that appears in A (*Broseliand* B) is remarkable, but I can cast no light on my father's choice of this name (the famous Forest of Broceliande in Brittany of the Arthurian legends).\* It would be interesting to know how *Broseliand* led to *Beleriand*, and a clue may perhaps be found on a page of rough working for the opening of the Lay, where he jotted down various names that must be possibilities that he was pondering for the name of the land. The fact that *Ossiriand* occurs among them, while it is also pencilled against *Broseliand* at lines 41 and 96 in B(1), may suggest that these names arose during the search for a replacement of *Broseliand*. The names are:

> *Golodhinand, Noldórinan, Geleriand, Bladorinand, Belaurien,
> Arsiriand, Lassiriand, Ossiriand.*

*Golodhinand* is incidentally interesting as showing *Golodh*, the later Sindarin equivalent of Quenya *Noldo* (in the old Gnomish dictionary *Golda* was the Gnomish equivalent of 'Elvish' *Noldo*, I.262). *Geleriand* I can cast no light on; but *Belaurien* is obviously connected with *Belaurin*, the Gnomish form of *Palúrien* (I.264), and *Bladorinand* with Palúrien's name *Bladorwen* 'the wide earth, Mother Earth' (*ibid.*). It seems at least possible that *Belaurien* lies behind *Beleriand* (which was afterwards explained quite differently).

Another curious feature is the word *beyond* in *They dwelt beyond Broseliand*, the reading of B(1) at line 41, where A has *in* and B(2) has *amid*.

*Esga(l)duin, Taur-na-Fuin* (for *Taur Fuin* of the *Lost Tales*), and *the Thousand Caves* have all appeared in *The Children of Húrin*; but in the mountains that

> to East in peaks of blue were piled
> in silence folded, mist-enfurled

– lines that are absent from A and B(1) – we have the first appearance of the Blue Mountains (*Ered Luin*) of the later legends: fencing Beleriand, as it seems, from *the Outer World*.

In all the texts of the first Canto the King of the woodland Elves is presented as possessing great wealth. This conception appears already in *The Children of Húrin* (see p. 26), in the most marked contrast to all that is told in the *Lost Tales*: cf. the *Tale of Turambar* (II.95) 'the folk of Tinwelint were of the woodlands and had scant wealth', 'his riches were small', and the *Tale of the Nauglafring* (II.227) 'A golden crown

---

\* On the earliest 'Silmarillion' map it is said that 'all the lands watered by Sirion south of Gondolin are called *in English* "Broseliand" '

they [the Dwarves] made for Tinwelint, who yet had worn nought but a
wreath of scarlet leaves.'

## II

Far in the North neath hills of stone
in caverns black there was a throne                    100
by fires illumined underground,
that winds of ice with moaning sound
made flare and flicker in dark smoke;
the wavering bitter coils did choke
the sunless airs of dungeons deep                      105
where evil things did crouch and creep.
There sat a king: no Elfin race
nor mortal blood, nor kindly grace
of earth or heaven might he own,
far older, stronger than the stone                     110
the world is built of, than the fire
that burns within more fierce and dire;
and thoughts profound were in his heart:
a gloomy power that dwelt apart.

Unconquerable spears of steel                          115
were at his nod. No ruth did feel
the legions of his marshalled hate,
on whom did wolf and raven wait;
and black the ravens sat and cried
upon their banners black, and wide                     120
was heard their hideous chanting dread
above the reek and trampled dead.
With fire and sword his ruin red
on all that would not bow the head
like lightning fell. The Northern land                 125
lay groaning neath his ghastly hand.

But still there lived in hiding cold
undaunted, Barahir the bold,
of land bereaved, of lordship shorn,
who once a prince of Men was born                      130
and now an outlaw lurked and lay
in the hard heath and woodland grey,

and with him clung of faithful men
but Beren his son and other ten.
Yet small as was their hunted band                    135
still fell and fearless was each hand,
and strong deeds they wrought yet oft,
and loved the woods, whose ways more soft
them seemed than thralls of that black throne
to live and languish in halls of stone.               140
King Morgoth still pursued them sore
with men and dogs, and wolf and boar
with spells of madness filled he sent
to slay them as in the woods they went;
yet nought hurt them for many years,                  145
until, in brief to tell what tears
have oft bewailed in ages gone,
nor ever tears enough, was done
a deed unhappy; unaware
their feet were caught in Morgoth's snare.            150

    Gorlim it was, who wearying
of toil and flight and harrying,
one night by chance did turn his feet
o'er the dark fields by stealth to meet
with hidden friend within a dale,                     155
and found a homestead looming pale
against the misty stars, all dark
save one small window, whence a spark
of fitful candle strayed without.
Therein he peeped, and filled with doubt              160
he saw, as in a dreaming deep
when longing cheats the heart in sleep,
his wife beside a dying fire
lament him lost; her thin attire
and greying hair and paling cheek                     165
of tears and loneliness did speak.
'A! fair and gentle Eilinel,
whom I had thought in darkling hell
long since emprisoned! Ere I fled
I deemed I saw thee slain and dead                    170
upon that night of sudden fear
when all I lost that I held dear':
thus thought his heavy heart amazed

outside in darkness as he gazed.
But ere he dared to call her name,                                175
or ask how she escaped and came
to this far vale beneath the hills,
he heard a cry beneath the hills!
There hooted near a hunting owl
with boding voice. He heard the howl                              180
of the wild wolves that followed him
and dogged his feet through shadows dim.
Him unrelenting, well he knew,
the hunt of Morgoth did pursue.
Lest Eilinel with him they slay                                   185
without a word he turned away,
and like a wild thing winding led
his devious ways o'er stony bed
of stream, and over quaking fen,
until far from the homes of men                                   190
he lay beside his fellows few
in a secret place; and darkness grew,
and waned, and still he watched unsleeping,
and saw the dismal dawn come creeping
in dank heavens above gloomy trees.                               195
A sickness held his soul for ease,
and hope, and even thraldom's chain
if he might find his wife again.
But all he thought twixt love of lord
and hatred of the king abhorred                                   200
and anguish for fair Eilinel
who drooped alone, what tale shall tell?

    Yet at the last, when many days
of brooding did his mind amaze,
he found the servants of the king,                                205
and bade them to their master bring
a rebel who forgiveness sought,
if haply forgiveness might be bought
with tidings of Barahir the bold,
and where his hidings and his hold                                210
might best be found by night or day.
And thus sad Gorlim, led away
unto those dark deep-dolven halls,
before the knees of Morgoth falls,

and puts his trust in that cruel heart                               215
wherein no truth had ever part.
Quoth Morgoth: 'Eilinel the fair
thou shalt most surely find, and there
where she doth dwell and wait for thee
together shall ye ever be,                                           220
and sundered shall ye sigh no more.
This guerdon shall he have that bore
these tidings sweet, O traitor dear!
For Eilinel she dwells not here,
but in the shades of death doth roam                                 225
widowed of husband and of home –
a wraith of that which might have been,
methinks, it is that thou hast seen!
Now shalt thou through the gates of pain
the land thou askest grimly gain;                                    230
thou shalt to the moonless mists of hell
descend and seek thy Eilinel.'

  Thus Gorlim died a bitter death
and cursed himself with dying breath,
and Barahir was caught and slain,                                    235
and all good deeds were made in vain.
But Morgoth's guile for ever failed,
nor wholly o'er his foes prevailed,
and some were ever that still fought
unmaking that which malice wrought.                                  240
Thus men believed that Morgoth made
the fiendish phantom that betrayed
the soul of Gorlim, and so brought
the lingering hope forlorn to nought
that lived amid the lonely wood;                                     245
yet Beren had by fortune good
long hunted far afield that day,
and benighted in strange places lay
far from his fellows. In his sleep
he felt a dreadful darkness creep                                    250
upon his heart, and thought the trees
were bare and bent in mournful breeze;
no leaves they had, but ravens dark
sat thick as leaves on bough and bark,
and croaked, and as they croaked each neb                            255

let fall a gout of blood; a web
unseen entwined him hand and limb,
until worn out, upon the rim
of stagnant pool he lay and shivered.
There saw he that a shadow quivered                   260
far out upon the water wan,
and grew to a faint form thereon
that glided o'er the silent lake,
and coming slowly, softly spake
and sadly said: 'Lo! Gorlim here,                     265
traitor betrayed, now stands! Nor fear,
but haste! For Morgoth's fingers close
upon thy father's throat. He knows
your secret tryst, your hidden lair',
and all the evil he laid bare                         270
that he had done and Morgoth wrought.
Then Beren waking swiftly sought
his sword and bow, and sped like wind
that cuts with knives the branches thinned
of autumn trees. At last he came,                     275
his heart afire with burning flame,
where Barahir his father lay;
he came too late. At dawn of day
he found the homes of hunted men,
a wooded island in the fen,                           280
and birds rose up in sudden cloud –
no fen-fowl were they crying loud.
The raven and the carrion-crow
sat in the alders all a-row;
one croaked: 'Ha! Beren comes too late',             285
and answered all: 'Too late! Too late!'
There Beren buried his father's bones,
and piled a heap of boulder-stones,
and cursed the name of Morgoth thrice,
but wept not, for his heart was ice.                  290

   Then over fen and field and mountain
he followed, till beside a fountain
upgushing hot from fires below
he found the slayers and his foe,
the murderous soldiers of the king.                   295
And one there laughed, and showed a ring

he took from Barahir's dead hand.
'This ring in far Beleriand,
now mark ye, mates,' he said, 'was wrought.
Its like with gold could not be bought,                    300
for this same Barahir I slew,
this robber fool, they say, did do
a deed of service long ago
for Felagund. It may be so;
for Morgoth bade me bring it back,                         305
and yet, methinks, he has no lack
of weightier treasure in his hoard.
Such greed befits not such a lord,
and I am minded to declare
the hand of Barahir was bare!'                             310
Yet as he spake an arrow sped;
with riven heart he crumpled dead.
Thus Morgoth loved that his own foe
should in his service deal the blow
that punished the breaking of his word.                    315
But Morgoth laughed not when he heard
that Beren like a wolf alone
sprang madly from behind a stone
amid that camp beside the well,
and seized the ring, and ere the yell                      320
of wrath and rage had left their throat
had fled his foes. His gleaming coat
was made of rings of steel no shaft
could pierce, a web of dwarvish craft;
and he was lost in rock and thorn,                         325
for in charméd hour was Beren born;
their hungry hunting never learned
the way his fearless feet had turned.

As fearless Beren was renowned,
as man most hardy upon ground,                             330
while Barahir yet lived and fought;
but sorrow now his soul had wrought
to dark despair, and robbed his life
of sweetness, that he longed for knife,
or shaft, or sword, to end his pain,                       335
and dreaded only thraldom's chain.
Danger he sought and death pursued,

and thus escaped the fate he wooed,
and deeds of breathless wonder dared
whose whispered glory widely fared,                    340
and softly songs were sung at eve
of marvels he did once achieve
alone, beleaguered, lost at night
by mist or moon, or neath the light
of the broad eye of day. The woods                     345
that northward looked with bitter feuds
he filled and death for Morgoth's folk;
his comrades were the beech and oak,
who failed him not, and many things
with fur and fell and feathered wings;                 350
and many spirits, that in stone
in mountains old and wastes alone,
do dwell and wander, were his friends.
Yet seldom well an outlaw ends,
and Morgoth was a king more strong                     355
than all the world has since in song
recorded, and his wisdom wide
slow and surely who him defied
did hem and hedge. Thus at the last
must Beren flee the forest fast                        360
and lands he loved where lay his sire
by reeds bewailed beneath the mire.
Beneath a heap of mossy stones
now crumble those once mighty bones,
but Beren flees the friendless North                   365
one autumn night, and creeps him forth;
the leaguer of his watchful foes
he passes – silently he goes.
No more his hidden bowstring sings,
no more his shaven arrow wings,                        370
no more his hunted head doth lie
upon the heath beneath the sky.
The moon that looked amid the mist
upon the pines, the wind that hissed
among the heather and the fern                         375
found him no more. The stars that burn
about the North with silver fire
in frosty airs, the Burning Briar
that Men did name in days long gone,

were set behind his back, and shone                    380
o'er land and lake and darkened hill,
forsaken fen and mountain rill.

His face was South from the Land of Dread,
whence only evil pathways led,
and only the feet of men most bold                     385
might cross the Shadowy Mountains cold.
Their northern slopes were filled with woe,
with evil and with mortal foe;
their southern faces mounted sheer
in rocky pinnacle and pier,                            390
whose roots were woven with deceit
and washed with waters bitter-sweet.
There magic lurked in gulf and glen,
for far away beyond the ken
of searching eyes, unless it were                      395
from dizzy tower that pricked the air
where only eagles lived and cried,
might grey and gleaming be descried
Beleriand, Beleriand,
the borders of the faëry land.                         400

★

NOTES

128   A:   a lord of Men undaunted, bold
134   A:   Maglor his son and other ten.
141   A:   But the king Bauglir did hunt them sore
177–9 Earlier reading:
              to this far vale among the hills
              a haggard hungry people tills,
              there hooted nigh a hunting owl
205   *found*: earlier reading *sought*
209–10 A:  with tidings of Lord Egnor's band,
              and where their hidings in the land
235   A:   and Egnor was betrayed and slain
246   A:   yet Maglor it was by fortune good
              who hunting &c.
272   A:   till Maglor waking swiftly sought
277   A:   to where his father Egnor lay;
297   A:   he took from Egnor's slaughtered hand:

298 *Broceliand* A, *Broseliand* B emended to *Beleriand*
301 A: for this same Egnor that I slew
304 *Celegorm* A, emended to *Felagoth* and then to *Felagund*
310 A: I found the hand of Egnor bare!'
313–16 These four lines were bracketed, and *that* at line 317 changed
to *Then*, before the B-text went to C. S. Lewis (my father's
numbering of the lines excludes these four, and Lewis's
line-references agree). Lewis did not concur with the exclusion of 313–14, and I have let all four lines stand. See
pp. 318–19.
317, 329 *Maglor* A, *Beren* B
326 A: and deep ghylls in the mountains torn.
331–3 A: ere Egnor in the wilderness
was slain; but now his loneliness,
grief and despair, did rob his life
360 A: proud Maglor fled the forest fast
(*fast* is used in the sense 'secure against attack'; cf. *fastness*).
365 *Maglor* A, *Beren* B
377–81 A: about the North with silver flame
in frosty airs, that men did name
Timbridhil in the days long gone,
he set behind his back, and shone
that sickle of the heavenly field
that Bridhil Queen of stars did wield
o'er land and lake and darkened hill,
The fifth and sixth lines are bracketed, with *and shone* in
the fourth changed to *It shone*.
383–4 Cf. lines 49–50.
399 *Broceliand* A, *Broseliand* B emended to *Beleriand*.

### Commentary on Canto II

In this second Canto the story of the betrayal of the outlaw band is
already in A close to its final form in essentials; but there is no trace of the
story in any form earlier than the first drafts of the *Lay of Leithian*,
composed in the summer of 1925 (see p. 150). In commenting on the
*Tale of Tinúviel* I noted (II. 52):

It seems clear that at this time the history of Beren and his father
(Egnor) was only very sketchily devised; there is in any case no hint of
the story of the outlaw band led by his father and its betrayal by
Gorlim the Unhappy before the first form of the *Lay of Leithian*.

There are indeed differences in the plot of the Lay from the story told
in *The Silmarillion* (pp. 162 ff.): thus the house where Gorlim saw the
phantom of Eilinel was not in the Lay his own; his treachery was far
deeper and more deliberate, in that he sought out the servants of Morgoth

with the intention of revealing the hiding-place of the outlaws; and he came before Morgoth himself (not Thû-Sauron). But these differences are much outnumbered by the similarities, such as the absence of Maglor-Beren on the fatal day, the apparition of Gorlim coming to him in dream across the water of the lake, the carrion-birds in the alder-trees, the cairn, the seizing of the ring, his friendship with birds and beasts.

As regards the names in the A-text: *Gorlim* and *Eilinel* were to remain. Maglor-Beren has already been discussed (p. 159). *Egnor* was still his father, as in the *Lost Tales* (the emendation to *Barahir* in the second version of the *Tale of Tinúviel*, II. 43, was a change made casually years later). *Bauglir* (which entered during the composition of *The Children of Húrin*, see p. 52) is changed throughout to *Morgoth*, but this seems not to have been a rejection of the name, since it appears later in the B-text of the Lay, and survives in *The Silmarillion*.

In A Varda is called *Bridhil* (note to lines 377–81), as she is also in the alliterative poem *The Flight of the Noldoli* (pp. 135, 139); but it is puzzling that the constellation of the Great Bear is in the same passage called *Timbridhil*, for that according to the old Gnomish dictionary is the title of Varda herself (as one would expect: cf. *Tinwetári*, I. 269). The 'Sickle of the Gods' (*Valacirca*) is here the 'sickle of the heavenly field' wielded by Bridhil Queen of Stars. I can cast no light at all on the name *Burning Briar* that appears in B (line 378); it reappears in the 1930 version of 'The Silmarillion':

> Many names have these [the Seven Stars] been called, but in the old days of the North both Elves and Men called them the Burning Briar, and some the Sickle of the Gods.

For the earliest myth of the Great Bear see I. 114, 133.

Indications of geography are sparse, and not increased in the B-text. Taur-na-Fuin has been named earlier in B (line 52), but it is not actually said in the present Canto to be the region where the outlaws lurked, though there is no reason to doubt that this is where my father placed it. Coming southwards Maglor-Beren crossed 'the Shadowy Mountains cold' (386). The Shadowy Mountains were named several times in *The Children of Húrin*, where they are the mountains fencing Hithlum, mirrored in the pools of Ivrin, as they are in *The Silmarillion*. But it would obviously be impossible for Beren to cross the Shadowy Mountains in this application of the name if he were coming out of Taur-na-Fuin and moving south towards Doriath. In the 'Sketch of the Mythology' Beren likewise 'crosses the Shadowy Mountains and after grievous hardships comes to Doriath', and similarly in the 1930 version; in this latter, however, 'Mountains of Shadow' was emended to 'Mountains of Terror'. It is then clear that in the *Lay of Leithian* my father was using 'Shadowy Mountains' in a different sense from that in *The Children of Húrin*, and that the Shadowy Mountains of the present

Canto are the first mention of Ered Gorgoroth, the Mountains of Terror, 'the precipices in which Dorthonion [Taur-nu-Fuin] fell southward' (*The Silmarillion* p. 95); but the other meaning reappears (p. 234). The lake where Egnor-Barahir and his band dwelt in hiding, in *The Silmarillion* (p. 162) *Tarn Aeluin*, is not named in the Lay, where the hiding-place was 'a wooded island in the fen' (280). That the Orc-camp was beside a spring (also unnamed) appears in the Lay, and it is here a hot spring (292–3); in *The Silmarillion* (p. 163) it was *Rivil's Well* above the Fen of Serech.

Most notable of the features of this Canto so far as the development of the legends is concerned, the rescue of Felagund by Barahir in the Battle of Sudden Flame (*The Silmarillion* p. 152) makes its first appearance in the 'service' done to Celegorm by Egnor in A (lines 301–4, where B has Felagund and Barahir). 'Celegorm' has already ceased its brief life as a replacement of Thingol (see p. 159), and is now again that of one of the sons of Fëanor, as it was in *The Children of Húrin*. When these lines in A were written the story was that Celegorm (and Curufin) founded Nargothrond after the breaking of the Leaguer of Angband – a story that seems to have arisen in the writing of *The Children of Húrin*, see pp. 83–5; and it was Celegorm who was rescued by Egnor-Barahir in that battle, and who gave Egnor-Barahir his ring. In the B-text the story has moved forward again, with the emergence of (Felagoth >) Felagund as the one saved by Barahir and the founder of Nargothrond, thrusting Celegorm and Curufin into a very different rôle.

In A Egnor and his son Maglor (Beren) are Men (e.g. Egnor was 'a lord of Men', note to line 128). In the first version of *The Children of Húrin* Beren was still an Elf, while in the second version my father seems to have changed back and forth on this matter (see pp. 124–5). He had not even now, as will appear later, finally settled the question.

# III

There once, and long and long ago,
before the sun and moon we know
were lit to sail above the world,
when first the shaggy woods unfurled,
and shadowy shapes did stare and roam          405
beneath the dark and starry dome
that hung above the dawn of Earth,
the silences with silver mirth
were shaken; the rocks were ringing,

the birds of Melian were singing,                     410
the first to sing in mortal lands,
the nightingales with her own hands
she fed, that fay of garments grey;
and dark and long her tresses lay
beneath her silver girdle's seat                      415
and down unto her silver feet.

   She had wayward wandered on a time
from gardens of the Gods, to climb
the everlasting mountains free
that look upon the outmost sea,                        420
and never wandered back, but stayed
and softly sang from glade to glade.
Her voice it was that Thingol heard,
and sudden singing of a bird,
in that old time when new-come Elves                  425
had all the wide world to themselves.
Yet all his kin now marched away,
as old tales tell, to seek the bay
on the last shore of mortal lands,
where mighty ships with magic hands                   430
they made, and sailed beyond the seas.
The Gods them bade to lands of ease
and gardens fair, where earth and sky
together flow, and none shall die.
But Thingol stayed, enchanted, still,                 435
one moment to hearken to the thrill
of that sweet singing in the trees.
Enchanted moments such as these
from gardens of the Lord of Sleep,
where fountains play and shadows creep,               440
do come, and count as many years
in mortal lands. With many tears
his people seek him ere they sail,
while Thingol listens in the dale.
There after but an hour, him seems,                   445
he finds her where she lies and dreams,
pale Melian with her dark hair
upon a bed of leaves. Beware!
There slumber and a sleep is twined!
He touched her tresses and his mind                   450

was drowned in the forgetful deep,
and dark the years rolled o'er his sleep.

Thus Thingol sailed not on the seas
but dwelt amid the land of trees,
and Melian he loved, divine,                                    455
whose voice was potent as the wine
the Valar drink in golden halls
where flower blooms and fountain falls;
but when she sang it was a spell,
and no flower stirred nor fountain fell.                        460
A king and queen thus lived they long,
and Doriath was filled with song,
and all the Elves that missed their way
and never found the western bay,
the gleaming walls of their long home                           465
by the grey seas and the white foam,
who never trod the golden land
where the towers of the Valar stand,
all these were gathered in their realm
beneath the beech and oak and elm.                              470

In later days when Morgoth first,
fleeing the Gods, their bondage burst,
and on the mortal lands set feet,
and in the North his mighty seat
founded and fortified, and all                                  475
the newborn race of Men were thrall
unto his power, and Elf and Gnome
his slaves, or wandered without home,
or scattered fastnesses walled with fear
upraised upon his borders drear,                                480
and each one fell, yet reigned there still
in Doriath beyond his will
Thingol and deathless Melian,
whose magic yet no evil can
that cometh from without surpass.                               485
Here still was laughter and green grass,
and leaves were lit with the white sun,
and many marvels were begun.

In sunshine and in sheen of moon,
with silken robe and silver shoon,                              490

the daughter of the deathless queen
now danced on the undying green,
half elven-fair and half divine;
and when the stars began to shine
unseen but near a piping woke,                    495
and in the branches of an oak,
or seated on the beech-leaves brown,
Dairon the dark with ferny crown
played with bewildering wizard's art
music for breaking of the heart.                 500
Such players have there only been
thrice in all Elfinesse, I ween:
Tinfang Gelion who still the moon
enchants on summer nights of June
and kindles the pale firstling star;             505
and he who harps upon the far
forgotten beaches and dark shores
where western foam for ever roars,
Maglor whose voice is like the sea;
and Dairon, mightiest of the three.              510

   Now it befell on summer night,
upon a lawn where lingering light
yet lay and faded faint and grey,
that Lúthien danced while he did play.
The chestnuts on the turf had shed               515
their flowering candles, white and red;
there darkling stood a silent elm
and pale beneath its shadow-helm
there glimmered faint the umbels thick
of hemlocks like a mist, and quick               520
the moths on pallid wings of white
with tiny eyes of fiery light
were fluttering softly, and the voles
crept out to listen from their holes;
the little owls were hushed and still;           525
the moon was yet behind the hill.
Her arms like ivory were gleaming,
her long hair like a cloud was streaming,
her feet atwinkle wandered roaming
in misty mazes in the gloaming;                  530
and glowworms shimmered round her feet,

and moths in moving garland fleet
above her head went wavering wan –
and this the moon now looked upon,
uprisen slow, and round, and white,                    535
above the branches of the night.
Then clearly thrilled her voice and rang;
with sudden ecstasy she sang
a song of nightingales she learned
and with her elvish magic turned                       540
to such bewildering delight
the moon hung moveless in the night.
And this it was that Beren heard,
and this he saw, without a word,
enchanted dumb, yet filled with fire                   545
of such a wonder and desire
that all his mortal mind was dim;
her magic bound and fettered him,
and faint he leaned against a tree.
Forwandered, wayworn, gaunt was he,                    550
his body sick and heart gone cold,
grey in his hair, his youth turned old;
for those that tread that lonely way
a price of woe and anguish pay.
And now his heart was healed and slain                 555
with a new life and with new pain.

  He gazed, and as he gazed her hair
within its cloudy web did snare
the silver moonbeams sifting white
between the leaves, and glinting bright                 560
the tremulous starlight of the skies
was caught and mirrored in her eyes.
Then all his journey's lonely fare,
the hunger and the haggard care,
the awful mountains' stones he stained                 565
with blood of weary feet, and gained
only a land of ghosts, and fear
in dark ravines imprisoned sheer –
there mighty spiders wove their webs,
old creatures foul with birdlike nebs                  570
that span their traps in dizzy air,
and filled it with clinging black despair,

and there they lived, and the sucked bones
lay white beneath on the dank stones –
now all these horrors like a cloud                                   575
faded from mind. The waters loud
falling from pineclad heights no more
he heard, those waters grey and frore
that bittersweet he drank and filled
his mind with madness – all was stilled.                             580
He recked not now the burning road,
the paths demented where he strode
endlessly... and ever new
horizons stretched before his view,
as each blue ridge with bleeding feet                                585
was climbed, and down he went to meet
battle with creatures old and strong
and monsters in the dark, and long,
long watches in the haunted night
while evil shapes with baleful light                                 590
in clustered eyes did crawl and snuff
beneath his tree – not half enough
the price he deemed to come at last
to that pale moon when day had passed,
to those clear stars of Elfinesse,                                   595
the hearts-ease and the loveliness.

   Lo! all forgetting he was drawn
unheeding toward the glimmering lawn
by love and wonder that compelled
his feet from hiding; music welled                                   600
within his heart, and songs unmade
on themes unthought-of moved and swayed
his soul with sweetness; out he came,
a shadow in the moon's pale flame –
and Dairon's flute as sudden stops                                   605
as lark before it steeply drops,
as grasshopper within the grass
listening for heavy feet to pass.
'Flee, Lúthien!', and 'Lúthien!'
from hiding Dairon called again;                                     610
'A stranger walks the woods! Away!'
But Lúthien would wondering stay;
fear had she never felt or known,

till fear then seized her, all alone,
seeing that shape with shagged hair          615
and shadow long that halted there.
Then sudden she vanished like a dream
in dark oblivion, a gleam
in hurrying clouds, for she had leapt
among the hemlocks tall, and crept          620
under a mighty plant with leaves
all long and dark, whose stem in sheaves
upheld an hundred umbels fair;
and her white arms and shoulders bare
her raiment pale, and in her hair          625
the wild white roses glimmering there,
all lay like spattered moonlight hoar
in gleaming pools upon the floor.
Then stared he wild in dumbness bound
at silent trees, deserted ground;          630
he blindly groped across the glade
to the dark trees' encircling shade,
and, while she watched with veiléd eyes,
touched her soft arm in sweet surprise.
Like startled moth from deathlike sleep          635
in sunless nook or bushes deep
she darted swift, and to and fro
with cunning that elvish dancers know
about the trunks of trees she twined
a path fantastic. Far behind          640
enchanted, wildered and forlorn
Beren came blundering, bruised and torn:
Esgalduin the elven-stream,
in which amid tree-shadows gleam
the stars, flowed strong before his feet.          645
Some secret way she found, and fleet
passed over and was seen no more,
and left him forsaken on the shore.
'Darkly the sundering flood rolls past!
To this my long way comes at last –          650
a hunger and a loneliness,
enchanted waters pitiless.'

A summer waned, an autumn glowed,
and Beren in the woods abode,

as wild and wary as a faun                              655
that sudden wakes at rustling dawn,
and flits from shade to shade, and flees
the brightness of the sun, yet sees
all stealthy movements in the wood.
The murmurous warmth in weathers good,                  660
the hum of many wings, the call
of many a bird, the pattering fall
of sudden rain upon the trees,
the windy tide in leafy seas,
the creaking of the boughs, he heard;                   665
but not the song of sweetest bird
brought joy or comfort to his heart,
a wanderer dumb who dwelt apart;
who sought unceasing and in vain
to hear and see those things again:                     670
a song more fair than nightingale,
a wonder in the moonlight pale.

An autumn waned, a winter laid
the withered leaves in grove and glade;
the beeches bare were gaunt and grey,                   675
and red their leaves beneath them lay.
From cavern pale the moist moon eyes
the white mists that from earth arise
to hide the morrow's sun and drip
all the grey day from each twig's tip.                  680
By dawn and dusk he seeks her still;
by noon and night in valleys chill,
nor hears a sound but the slow beat
on sodden leaves of his own feet.

The wind of winter winds his horn;                      685
the misty veil is rent and torn.
The wind dies; the starry choirs
leap in the silent sky to fires,
whose light comes bitter-cold and sheer
through domes of frozen crystal clear.                  690

A sparkle through the darkling trees,
a piercing glint of light he sees,
and there she dances all alone
upon a treeless knoll of stone!

Her mantle blue with jewels white                    695
caught all the rays of frosted light.
She shone with cold and wintry flame,
as dancing down the hill she came,
and passed his watchful silent gaze,
a glimmer as of stars ablaze.                        700
And snowdrops sprang beneath her feet,
and one bird, sudden, late and sweet,
shrilled as she wayward passed along.
A frozen brook to bubbling song
awoke and laughed; but Beren stood                   705
still bound enchanted in the wood.
Her starlight faded and the night
closed o'er the snowdrops glimmering white.

    Thereafter on a hillock green
he saw far off the elven-sheen                       710
of shining limb and jewel bright
often and oft on moonlit night;
and Dairon's pipe awoke once more,
and soft she sang as once before.
Then nigh he stole beneath the trees,                715
and heartache mingled with hearts-ease.

    A night there was when winter died;
then all alone she sang and cried
and danced until the dawn of spring,
and chanted some wild magic thing                    720
that stirred him, till it sudden broke
the bonds that held him, and he woke
to madness sweet and brave despair.
He flung his arms to the night air,
and out he danced unheeding, fleet,                  725
enchanted, with enchanted feet.
He sped towards the hillock green,
the lissom limbs, the dancing sheen;
he leapt upon the grassy hill
his arms with loveliness to fill:                    730
his arms were empty, and she fled;
away, away her white feet sped.
But as she went he swiftly came
and called her with the tender name
of nightingales in elvish tongue,                    735

that all the woods now sudden rung:
'Tinúviel! Tinúviel!'
And clear his voice was as a bell;
its echoes wove a binding spell:
'Tinúviel! Tinúviel!'                                    740
His voice such love and longing filled
one moment stood she, fear was stilled;
one moment only; like a flame
he leaped towards her as she stayed
and caught and kissed that elfin maid.                   745

    As love there woke in sweet surprise
the starlight trembled in her eyes.
A! Lúthien! A! Lúthien!
more fair than any child of Men;
O! loveliest maid of Elfinesse,                          750
what madness does thee now possess!
A! lissom limbs and shadowy hair
and chaplet of white snowdrops there;
O! starry diadem and white
pale hands beneath the pale moonlight!                   755
She left his arms and slipped away
just at the breaking of the day.

★

## NOTES

439    Original reading of B:

> from gardens of the God of Sleep,

457    Original reading of B:

> the Gods drink in their golden halls

467–8    Original reading of B:

> who never passed the golden gate
> where doorwards of the Gods do wait,

These three changes are late, and their purpose is to remove
the word *Gods*. The change in line 468 also gets rid of the
purely metrical *do* in *do wait*; similarly *did build and fortify*
> *founded and fortified* 475 and *did raise* > *upraised* 480
look as if they belong to the same time. On the other hand *did*

*flutter* > *were fluttering* 523 and *did waver* > *went wavering* 533 seem to belong with the early emendations (see C. S. Lewis's commentary, pp. 320–1). I mention these changes here to illustrate my remarks on this subject, pp. 152–3.

493 *elfin-* B, emended to *elven-*. Here and subsequently this belongs with the early changes, as does *elfin* to *elvish* at 540, etc.

503 *Tinfang Warble* A, and B as typed; *Gelion* an early change in B.

508 After this line A has a couplet omitted in B:

> from England unto Eglamar
> on rock and dune and sandy bar,

The first of these lines occurs also in an early draft for the opening of the poem, see p. 157, note to lines 1–30.

509 *Maglor* A, B; in the rough draft of this passage *Ivárë* (with *Maglor* written beside it).

527–30 Marked in B with an X (i.e. in need of revision), but with no other verses substituted.

557 This line begins a new page in the A manuscript; at the top of the page is written the date '23/8/25'.

558 *golden* A, and B as typed (no doubt an oversight), early emended to *cloudy*. See note to lines 1–30, and pp. 159–60.

648 After this line the bundle of examination-scripts on which the A manuscript is written (p. 150) is interleaved with other pages, which carry the poem to the end of Canto III. At the bottom of the first of these pages is written *Filey 1925*, where my father was on holiday in September of that year.

743 The couplet lacks its second line. The passage 741–5 is a hasty revision, based on a criticism of Lewis's; see his commentary, p. 325.

### Commentary on Canto III

In this Canto there are many things that derive from the *Tale of Tinúviel* (II. 10 ff.): the chestnut trees, the white moths, the moon rising, the sudden ceasing of Dairon's piping, Tinúviel's unwillingness to flee, her hiding under the hemlocks *like spattered moonlight* (cf. II. 11 'like a spatter of moonlight shimmering'), Beren's touching her arm, her darting between the tree-trunks, and afterwards the 'treeless knoll' where she danced in the winter. But the Canto is also related to the poem *Light as Leaf on Lindentree* (see pp. 108–10, 120–2), which had been published in June 1925, while this part of the *Lay of Leithian* was written a little later in the same year. Echoes of the one poem are heard in the other, and more than an echo in the line *and out he danced unheeding, fleet*, which is found in both (p. 109, line 447; p. 179, line 725).

The aberrant names in the first two Cantos of A have now disappeared from the text. In the second Canto my father had already given back the name *Celegorm* to the son of Fëanor (note to line 304), and now *Thingol* appears in A; *Lúthien* replaces *Melilot*; and *Beren* replaces *Maglor*. *Morgoth* now replaces *Bauglir* in A (see p. 170).

In both texts *Tinúviel* is now explicitly the Elvish word for 'nightingale' (line 735; see p. 124); and *Maglor*, again in both texts, is the name of one of the three greatest singers of Elfinesse:

> he who harps upon the far
> forgotten beaches and dark shores
> where western foam for ever roars,
> Maglor whose voice is like the sea          (506–9)

In the rough draft of this passage the name of this minstrel is however *Ivárë* (though *Maglor* is written beside it), and Ivárë was named in the *Tale of Tinúviel* (II. 10), with Tinfang and Dairon, as one of 'the three most magic players of the Elves', who 'plays beside the sea'. This is the first hint of the after-history of Maglor son of Fëanor, who in the *Tale of the Nauglafring* (II. 241) was slain, as also was Celegorm, in the attack on Dior. The lines in A, omitted in B (note to line 508), are interesting:

> from England unto Eglamar
> on rock and dune and sandy bar

The form *Eglamar* (Gnomish, = *Eldamar*) occurs in the very early poem *The Shores of Faëry* and its prose preface (II. 262, 272); and the same line *from England unto Eglamar* is found in the rough workings of the beginning of the Lay (note to lines 1–30). The mention of *England* is a reminder that at this time the association of the legends with Eriol/Ælfwine was still very much alive, though there is no other indication of it in the *Lay of Leithian*.

*Tinfang Warble* reappears from the *Lost Tales* at line 503, changed to *Tinfang Gelion*; the meaning of *Gelion* is not explained.

In one respect only does the narrative content of the Canto depart in any significant way from the common 'tradition' of the texts, but this is sufficiently remarkable: the Elves departed over the sea to Valinor at the end of the Great Journey in a fleet of ships!

> Yet all his kin now marched away,
> as old tales tell, to seek the bay
> on the last shore of mortal lands,
> where mighty ships with magic hands
> they made, and sailed beyond the seas.          (427–31)

This is very strange (and I am at a loss to account for it, except by the obvious explanation of a passing shift), in that the story of the 'island-car' (Tol Eressëa), which goes back to the *Lost Tales* (I. 118–20), is present in all the versions of 'The Silmarillion'. The Elves are here presented, on the other hand, as great shipbuilders in the beginning of their days. – With the reference in the passage just cited to the *bay* whence the Elves set sail cf. *The Silmarillion* p. 57, where it is told that Ulmo anchored the 'island-car' in the Bay of Balar (and that the eastern horn of the island, breaking off, was the Isle of Balar).

In the description of Beren's journey to Doriath in lines 563 ff. is the first account of the Ered Gorgoroth, the Mountains of Terror (called 'the Shadowy Mountains' in Canto II, see pp. 170–1), with their spiders and their waters that drove mad those who drank from them (cf. *The Silmarillion* p. 121; and with lines 590–1 *evil shapes with baleful light / in clustered eyes* cf. *ibid.* p. 164: 'monsters . . . hunting silently with many eyes').

# IV

He lay upon the leafy mould,
his face upon earth's bosom cold,
aswoon in overwhelming bliss,                          760
enchanted of an elvish kiss,
seeing within his darkened eyes
the light that for no darkness dies,
the loveliness that doth not fade,
though all in ashes cold be laid.                      765
Then folded in the mists of sleep
he sank into abysses deep,
drowned in an overwhelming grief
for parting after meeting brief;
a shadow and a fragrance fair                          770
lingered, and waned, and was not there.
Forsaken, barren, bare as stone,
the daylight found him cold, alone.

'Where art thou gone? The day is bare,
the sunlight dark, and cold the air!                   775
Tinúviel, where went thy feet?
O wayward star! O maiden sweet!
O flower of Elfland all too fair
for mortal heart! The woods are bare!

The woods are bare!' he rose and cried.                    780
'Ere spring was born, the spring hath died!'
And wandering in path and mind
he groped as one gone sudden blind,
who seeks to grasp the hidden light
with faltering hands in more than night.                    785

And thus in anguish Beren paid
for that great doom upon him laid,
the deathless love of Lúthien,
too fair for love of mortal Men;
and in his doom was Lúthien snared,                          790
the deathless in his dying shared;
and Fate them forged a binding chain
of living love and mortal pain.

Beyond all hope her feet returned
at eve, when in the sky there burned                         795
the flame of stars; and in her eyes
there trembled the starlight of the skies,
and from her hair the fragrance fell
of elvenflowers in elven-dell.

Thus Lúthien, whom no pursuit,                               800
no snare, no dart that hunters shoot,
might hope to win or hold, she came
at the sweet calling of her name;
and thus in his her slender hand
was linked in far Beleriand;                                 805
in hour enchanted long ago
her arms about his neck did go,
and gently down she drew to rest
his weary head upon her breast.
A! Lúthien, Tinúviel,                                       810
why wentest thou to darkling dell
with shining eyes and dancing pace,
the twilight glimmering in thy face?
Each day before the end of eve
she sought her love, nor would him leave,                    815
until the stars were dimmed, and day
came glimmering eastward silver-grey.
Then trembling-veiled she would appear
and dance before him, half in fear;

there flitting just before his feet                   820
she gently chid with laughter sweet:
'Come! dance now, Beren, dance with me!
For fain thy dancing I would see.
Come! thou must woo with nimbler feet,
than those who walk where mountains meet       825
the bitter skies beyond this realm
of marvellous moonlit beech and elm.'

   In Doriath Beren long ago
new art and lore he learned to know;
his limbs were freed; his eyes alight,          830
kindled with a new enchanted sight;
and to her dancing feet his feet
attuned went dancing free and fleet;
his laughter welled as from a spring
of music, and his voice would sing             835
as voices of those in Doriath
where paved with flowers are floor and path.
The year thus on to summer rolled,
from spring to a summertime of gold.

   Thus fleeting fast their short hour flies,   840
while Dairon watches with fiery eyes,
haunting the gloom of tangled trees
all day, until at night he sees
in the fickle moon their moving feet,
two lovers linked in dancing sweet,            845
two shadows shimmering on the green
where lonely-dancing maid had been.
   'Hateful art thou, O Land of Trees!
May fear and silence on thee seize!
My flute shall fall from idle hand             850
and mirth shall leave Beleriand;
music shall perish and voices fail
and trees stand dumb in dell and dale!'

   It seemed a hush had fallen there
upon the waiting woodland air;                 855
and often murmured Thingol's folk
in wonder, and to their king they spoke:
'This spell of silence who hath wrought?
What web hath Dairon's music caught?

It seems the very birds sing low;                    860
murmurless Esgalduin doth flow;
the leaves scarce whisper on the trees,
and soundless beat the wings of bees!'

This Lúthien heard, and there the queen
her sudden glances saw unseen.                       865
But Thingol marvelled, and he sent
for Dairon the piper, ere he went
and sat upon his mounded seat –
his grassy throne by the grey feet
of the Queen of Beeches, Hirilorn,                   870
upon whose triple piers were borne
the mightiest vault of leaf and bough
from world's beginning until now.
She stood above Esgalduin's shore,
where long slopes fell beside the door,              875
the guarded gates, the portals stark
of the Thousand echoing Caverns dark.

There Thingol sat and heard no sound
save far off footsteps on the ground;
no flute, no voice, no song of bird,                 880
no choirs of windy leaves there stirred;
and Dairon coming no word spoke,
silent amid the woodland folk.
Then Thingol said: 'O Dairon fair,
thou master of all musics rare,                      885
O magic heart and wisdom wild,
whose ear nor eye may be beguiled,
what omen doth this silence bear?
What horn afar upon the air,
what summons do the woods await?                     890
Mayhap the Lord Tavros from his gate
and tree-propped halls, the forest-god,
rides his wild stallion golden-shod
amid the trumpets' tempest loud,
amid his green-clad hunters proud,                   895
leaving his deer and friths divine
and emerald forests? Some faint sign
of his great onset may have come
upon the Western winds, and dumb
the woods now listen for a chase                     900

that here once more shall thundering race
beneath the shade of mortal trees.
Would it were so! The Lands of Ease
hath Tavros left not many an age,
since Morgoth evil wars did wage,                905
since ruin fell upon the North
and the Gnomes unhappy wandered forth.
But if not he, who comes or what?'
And Dairon answered: 'He cometh not!
No feet divine shall leave that shore,           910
where the Shadowy Seas' last surges roar,
till many things be come to pass,
and many evils wrought. Alas!
the guest is here. The woods are still,
but wait not; for a marvel chill                 915
them holds at the strange deeds they see,
but kings see not – though queens, maybe,
may guess, and maidens, maybe, know.
Where one went lonely two now go!'

    'Whither thy riddle points is plain'         920
the king in anger said, 'but deign
to make it plainer! Who is he
that earns my wrath? How walks he free
within my woods amid my folk,
a stranger to both beech and oak?'               925
But Dairon looked on Lúthien
and would he had not spoken then,
and no more would he speak that day,
though Thingol's face with wrath was grey.
Then Lúthien stepped lightly forth:              930
'Far in the mountain-leaguered North,
my father,' said she, 'lies the land
that groans beneath King Morgoth's hand.
Thence came one hither, bent and worn
in wars and travail, who had sworn               935
undying hatred of that king;
the last of Bëor's sons, they sing,
and even hither far and deep
within thy woods the echoes creep
through the wild mountain-passes cold,           940
the last of Bëor's house to hold

a sword unconquered, neck unbowed,
a heart by evil power uncowed.
No evil needst thou think or fear
of Beren son of Barahir!                               945
If aught thou hast to say to him,
then swear to hurt not flesh nor limb,
and I will lead him to thy hall,
a son of kings, no mortal thrall.'
    Then long King Thingol looked on her            950
while hand nor foot nor tongue did stir,
and Melian, silent, unamazed,
on Lúthien and Thingol gazed.
'No blade nor chain his limbs shall mar'
the king then swore. 'He wanders far,               955
and news, mayhap, he hath for me,
and words I have for him, maybe!'
Now Thingol bade them all depart
save Dairon, whom he called: 'What art,
what wizardry of Northern mist                      960
hath this illcomer brought us? List!
Tonight go thou by secret path,
who knowest all wide Doriath,
and watch that Lúthien – daughter mine,
what madness doth thy heart entwine,               965
what web from Morgoth's dreadful halls
hath caught thy feet and thee enthralls! –
that she bid not this Beren flee
back whence he came. I would him see!
Take with thee woodland archers wise.              970
Let naught beguile your hearts or eyes!'

    Thus Dairon heavyhearted did,
and the woods were filled with watchers hid;
yet needless, for Lúthien that night
led Beren by the golden light                       975
of mounting moon unto the shore
and bridge before her father's door;
and the white light silent looked within
the waiting portals yawning dim.

    Downward with gentle hand she led               980
through corridors of carven dread
whose turns were lit by lanterns hung

or flames from torches that were flung
on dragons hewn in the cold stone
with jewelled eyes and teeth of bone.                    985
Then sudden, deep beneath the earth
the silences with silver mirth
were shaken and the rocks were ringing,
the birds of Melian were singing;
and wide the ways of shadow spread                    990
as into archéd halls she led
Beren in wonder. There a light
like day immortal and like night
of stars unclouded, shone and gleamed.
A vault of topless trees it seemed,                    995
whose trunks of carven stone there stood
like towers of an enchanted wood
in magic fast for ever bound,
bearing a roof whose branches wound
in endless tracery of green                    1000
lit by some leaf-emprisoned sheen
of moon and sun, and wrought of gems,
and each leaf hung on golden stems.
    Lo! there amid immortal flowers
the nightingales in shining bowers                    1005
sang o'er the head of Melian,
while water for ever dripped and ran
from fountains in the rocky floor.
There Thingol sat. His crown he wore
of green and silver, and round his chair                    1010
a host in gleaming armour fair.
Then Beren looked upon the king
and stood amazed; and swift a ring
of elvish weapons hemmed him round.
Then Beren looked upon the ground,                    1015
for Melian's gaze had sought his face,
and dazed there drooped he in that place,
and when the king spake deep and slow:
'Who art thou stumblest hither? Know
that none unbidden seek this throne                    1020
and ever leave these halls of stone!'
no word he answered, filled with dread.
But Lúthien answered in his stead:
'Behold, my father, one who came

pursued by hatred like a flame!                          1025
Lo! Beren son of Barahir!
What need hath he thy wrath to fear,
foe of our foes, without a friend,
whose knees to Morgoth do not bend?'

   'Let Beren answer!' Thingol said.                     1030
'What wouldst thou here? What hither led
thy wandering feet, O mortal wild?
How hast thou Lúthien beguiled
or darest thus to walk this wood
unasked, in secret? Reason good                          1035
'twere best declare now if thou may,
or never again see light of day!'
   Then Beren looked in Lúthien's eyes
and saw a light of starry skies,
and thence was slowly drawn his gaze                     1040
to Melian's face. As from a maze
of wonder dumb he woke; his heart
the bonds of awe there burst apart
and filled with the fearless pride of old;
in his glance now gleamed an anger cold.                 1045
'My feet hath fate, O king,' he said,
'here over the mountains bleeding led,
and what I sought not I have found,
and love it is hath here me bound.
Thy dearest treasure I desire;                           1050
nor rocks nor steel nor Morgoth's fire
nor all the power of Elfinesse
shall keep that gem I would possess.
For fairer than are born to Men
A daughter hast thou, Lúthien.'                          1055

   Silence then fell upon the hall;
like graven stone there stood they all,
save one who cast her eyes aground,
and one who laughed with bitter sound.
Dairon the piper leant there pale                        1060
against a pillar. His fingers frail
there touched a flute that whispered not;
his eyes were dark; his heart was hot.
'Death is the guerdon thou hast earned,
O baseborn mortal, who hast learned                      1065

in Morgoth's realm to spy and lurk
like Orcs that do his evil work!'
'Death!' echoed Dairon fierce and low,
but Lúthien trembling gasped in woe.
'And death,' said Thingol, 'thou shouldst taste,     1070
had I not sworn an oath in haste
that blade nor chain thy flesh should mar.
Yet captive bound by never a bar,
unchained, unfettered, shalt thou be
in lightless labyrinth endlessly                     1075
that coils about my halls profound
by magic bewildered and enwound;
there wandering in hopelessness
thou shalt learn the power of Elfinesse!'
'That may not be!' Lo! Beren spake,                  1080
and through the king's words coldly brake.
'What are thy mazes but a chain
wherein the captive blind is slain?
Twist not thy oaths, O elvish king,
like faithless Morgoth! By this ring –              1085
the token of a lasting bond
that Felagund of Nargothrond
once swore in love to Barahir,
who sheltered him with shield and spear
and saved him from pursuing foe                      1090
on Northern battlefields long ago –
death thou canst give unearned to me,
but names I will not take from thee
of baseborn, spy, or Morgoth's thrall!
Are these the ways of Thingol's hall?'               1095
Proud are the words, and all there turned
to see the jewels green that burned
in Beren's ring. These Gnomes had set
as eyes of serpents twined that met
beneath a golden crown of flowers,                   1100
that one upholds and one devours:
the badge that Finrod made of yore
and Felagund his son now bore.
    His anger was chilled, but little less,
and dark thoughts Thingol did possess,               1105
though Melian the pale leant to his side
and whispered: 'O king, forgo thy pride!

Such is my counsel. Not by thee
shall Beren be slain, for far and free
from these deep halls his fate doth lead,                    1110
yet wound with thine. O king, take heed!'
But Thingol looked on Lúthien.
'Fairest of Elves! Unhappy Men,
children of little lords and kings
mortal and frail, these fading things,                       1115
shall they then look with love on thee?'
his heart within him thought. 'I see
thy ring,' he said, 'O mighty man!
But to win the child of Melian
a father's deeds shall not avail,                            1120
nor thy proud words at which I quail.
A treasure dear I too desire,
but rocks and steel and Morgoth's fire
from all the powers of Elfinesse
do keep the jewel I would possess.                           1125
Yet bonds like these I hear thee say
affright thee not. Now go thy way!
Bring me one shining Silmaril
from Morgoth's crown, then if she will,
may Lúthien set her hand in thine;                           1130
then shalt thou have this jewel of mine.'

Then Thingol's warriors loud and long
they laughed; for wide renown in song
had Fëanor's gems o'er land and sea,
the peerless Silmarils; and three                            1135
alone he made and kindled slow
in the land of the Valar long ago,
and there in Tûn of their own light
they shone like marvellous stars at night,
in the great Gnomish hoards of Tûn,                          1140
while Glingal flowered and Belthil's bloom
yet lit the land beyond the shore
where the Shadowy Seas' last surges roar,
ere Morgoth stole them and the Gnomes
seeking their glory left their homes,                        1145
ere sorrows fell on Elves and Men,
ere Beren was or Lúthien,
ere Fëanor's sons in madness swore

their dreadful oath. But now no more
their beauty was seen, save shining clear          1150
in Morgoth's dungeons vast and drear.
His iron crown they must adorn,
and gleam above Orcs and slaves forlorn,
treasured in Hell above all wealth,
more than his eyes; and might nor stealth          1155
could touch them, or even gaze too long
upon their magic. Throng on throng
of Orcs with reddened scimitars
encircled him, and mighty bars
and everlasting gates and walls,          1160
who wore them now amidst his thralls.
     Then Beren laughed more loud than they
in bitterness, and thus did say:
'For little price do elven-kings
their daughters sell – for gems and rings          1165
and things of gold! If such thy will,
thy bidding I will now fulfill.
On Beren son of Barahir
thou hast not looked the last, I fear.
Farewell, Tinúviel, starlit maiden!          1170
Ere the pale winter pass snowladen,
I will return, not thee to buy
with any jewel in Elfinesse,
but to find my love in loveliness,
a flower that grows beneath the sky.'          1175
Bowing before Melian and the king
he turned, and thrust aside the ring
of guards about him, and was gone,
and his footsteps faded one by one
in the dark corridors. 'A guileful oath          1180
thou sworest, father! Thou hast both
to blade and chain his flesh now doomed
in Morgoth's dungeons deep entombed,'
said Lúthien, and welling tears
sprang in her eyes, and hideous fears          1185
clutched at her heart. All looked away,
and later remembered the sad day
whereafter Lúthien no more sang.
Then clear in the silence the cold words rang
of Melian: 'Counsel cunning-wise,          1190

O king!' she said. 'Yet if mine eyes
lose not their power, 'twere well for thee
that Beren failed his errantry.
Well for thee, but for thy child
a dark doom and a wandering wild.'                    1195

'I sell not to Men those whom I love'
said Thingol, 'whom all things above
I cherish; and if hope there were
that Beren should ever living fare
to the Thousand Caves once more, I swear          1200
he should not ever have seen the air
or light of heaven's stars again.'
But Melian smiled, and there was pain
as of far knowledge in her eyes;
for such is the sorrow of the wise.                      1205

# NOTES

The opening of this Canto is extant in two typescripts (to line 863), the
second version being substantially expanded; it was the first of them that
C. S. Lewis received – indeed, it is clear that the rewriting was in part
due to his criticism.

758–863   The rough drafts for this portion of the Lay (much briefer
          than the later text here printed) were written on the backs of
          booksellers' invoices dated 31 December 1925 and 2 February
          1926.
     761  In this Canto *elvish* rather than *elfin* is found already in A,
          but still *elfin* in both texts at 1164 (emended in B to *elven-*).
          *elven-* 799 occurs in a line found only in the later rewriting,
          B(2).
762–73    These lines are not in A; the B(1) version, severely criticised
          by C. S. Lewis, is given with his commentary, p. 326.
781–841   A:   and the bare woods nor moved nor sighed.
                   Yet ever after when star or moon
                shone clear or misty then came she soon
                just after day before the eve
                and found him, nor his side did leave          5
                until night waned and starlight ceased
                and day came pale o'er the pathless east.
                And there in far Broseliand

he learned the touches of her hand;
his feet grew swift as unseen airs,                                    10
his laughter soft, and far his cares,
his voice like those in Doriath
that wander where there runs no path.
Thus days of golden spring did rise
while Dairon watched with fiery eyes                                   15

The spelling *Broseliand* with *s* has now entered the A-text.

B(1) is as A, except that between lines 7 and 8 above were
inserted ten lines that my father retained in the much longer
B(2) text, 818–27 (*Then trembling-veiled*, &c.)

805     *Broseliand* B(2), emended to *Beleriand*.

849–51   These verses are an emendation to B(2), with *Beleriand*
thus written. For the B(1) version criticised by C. S. Lewis
and the B(2) version before emendation see Lewis's commentary, p. 327.

891, 904   *Tavros* was emended in B to *Tauros*, but this seems to have
been a much later change. The rough workings here had first
the name (*Ormain* >) *Ormaid*, then *Tavros*.

937     Original reading of B: the last of Men, as songs now sing
(with *like echoes* 939)

941     Original reading of B: the last of Men alone to hold

983–5   These lines are marked with an X on the B-text, and the
words *on dragons* underlined and marked with an X –
presumably because the creatures of Morgoth were not
carved on the walls of the Thousand Caves.

987–9   These lines are repeated from Canto III, lines 408–10.

1010     *silver*: original reading of B *gold*.

1059–63   These lines are marked with an X on the B-text, as also are
lines 1068–9. It may be that my father wished to represent
Dairon as less unequivocally hostile to Beren, and also as
ashamed of his words to Thingol (909–19).

1087     A:   that Celegorm of Nargothrond
with *Celegorm* emended first to *Felagoth* and then to
*Felagund* (as at line 304).

1098     *Gnomes*: in the margin of B is written *Elves/smiths*. This is
clearly a late change intended simply to get rid of the word
*Gnomes* (see I.43–4).

1102–3   A:   the badge that Fëanor made of yore
and Celegorm his son now bore.
*Celegorm* is not emended here as it is at line 1087, but the
couplet is enclosed within brackets in the manuscript.

1141     *Glingal, Belthil*: original readings of B *Glingol, Bansil*.
The same changes were made in *The Children of Húrin*
(pp. 80–1, notes to lines 2027–8), where I retain the earlier
forms.

1144-5   These lines are marked with an X on the B-text, perhaps
simply because of the word *Gnomes* which here occurs in
rhyme and cannot be easily replaced (see note to 1098); but
C. S. Lewis criticised the word *their* in line 1145 as obscure
in its reference (see his commentary, p. 329).

1151   A:   in Morgoth Bauglir's dungeons drear. See p. 182.

1161   Here is written in the margin of the A manuscript: 'Mar. 27,
28 1928'.

1175   This line was not originally in A but was pencilled in with
queried indications to place it either after 1172 or (with
irregular rhyming) after 1174, as it is in B.


## Commentary on Canto IV

Comparison of this Canto with the *Tale of Tinúviel* shows that the
narrative has undergone a deepening of significance, and this is largely
brought about by the cardinal change of Beren's being no longer an Elf
but a mortal Man (see p. 171). The story told in the poem is that of
*The Silmarillion* (pp. 165–8); for the prose version, close to the Lay in
every feature large and small, and indeed in many actual phrases, was
based directly on the verses, and in this Canto the verses underwent no
significant later revision. There are some elements in the poem that were
not taken up into the prose version, such as the description of the
Thousand Caves (980 ff.), whose splendour and beauty now first appear
(cf. my remarks on Thingol's wealth, pp. 160–1) – but a description of
Thingol's dwelling is given earlier in *The Silmarillion*, p. 93. In the
original text of the *Silmarillion* version Daeron's part was in fact entirely
excluded, though obviously only for the sake of compression (it was
reintroduced into the published work*). The loud laughter of Thingol's
warriors at Thingol's demand that Beren fetch him a Silmaril is not in the
prose account, and was perhaps deliberately excluded. This feature
harks back rather to the scene in the *Tale of Tinúviel* (II. 13), where
Thingol 'burst into laughter' at the aspect of Beren as suitor for his
daughter, and where the courtiers smiled when Thingol requested a
Silmaril as the bride-price, seeing that he 'treated the matter as an
uncouth jest'. Cf. my commentary on the Tale, II. 53:

> The tone is altogether lighter and less grave than it afterwards became;
> in the jeering laughter of Thingol, who treats the matter as a jest and
> Beren as a benighted fool, there is no hint of what is quite explicit in
> the later story: 'Thus he wrought the doom of Doriath, and was
> ensnared within the curse of Mandos.'

Canto III was in being by the autumn of 1925; while against Canto IV

---

*On pp. 166, 172; but the passage concerning Daeron on p. 183 is original. My father
apparently intended to insert references to Daeron's betrayals of Lúthien, but did not do so.

line 1161 in A there stands the date 27–8 March, 1928. The rough drafts for the opening of IV (lines 758–863) are written on the backs of invoices dated December 1925 and February 1926, but this does not show very much. In any case it seems to me most improbable that my father was writing lines 758–1161 over a period of two and a half years (September 1925 to March 1928): it is far more likely that there was a long gap, and that this fourth Canto was written pretty much at one time. Other evidence in fact suggests that he paused. There exist three pages of notes written on the backs of booksellers' invoices dated February, March, and May 1926, and these pages are of great interest for the development of the legend, for they contain a rapidly-composed plot-outline in which my father is seen working out the narrative of the next Cantos of the Lay.

This outline I will refer to as 'Synopsis I'. I give here its content as far as the end of Canto IV. Contractions used for names are expanded, and passages struck out (done at the time of writing) are included.

Beren and Tinúviel dance in the woods.
Dairon reports to the king.
Beren taken captive to the king.
Dairon will have him slain.
The king will shut him in his dungeons.
Tinúviel pleads.
Melian [*struck out*: says that he must not be slain, and that] refuses to advise but warns Thingol darkly that Beren must not be slain by him, and his coming was not without fate.
Thingol sends him for the Silmaril.
Beren's speech.
Melian says [*struck out*: this was better than his death, but] it were better for Thingol if Beren succeeded not.
Thingol said he would not send him if [he] were going to succeed. Melian smiles.
Flight of Beren.

In the *Tale of Tinúviel* Beren was led by Tinúviel into Thingol's caves (II. 13), and as I noted (II. 52–3):

The betrayal of Beren to Thingol by Daeron . . . has no place in the old story – there is nothing to betray; and indeed it is not shown in the tale that Dairon knew anything whatsoever of Beren before Tinúviel led him into the cave, beyond having once seen his face in the moonlight.

Moreover, in the *Tale* Dairon was Tinúviel's brother (II. 10; see p. 124). In the Lay (lines 909 ff.) Dairon utters strong hints concerning the strange quietness of the forest, which lead directly to a declaration by Lúthien of Beren's presence, and a demand that her father shall not harm him; Thingol swears that he will not, but sends Dairon with archers to prevent Beren's escape – needlessly, for Lúthien brings him that same

night to Thingol's hall. This first part of Synopsis I suggests ideas that
were never given form. Thus Dairon speaks to Thingol of Beren, as in
the Lay, but Beren is actually apprehended and taken to the king as a
prisoner; moreover (while it is of course impossible to be certain of the
precise articulation of the plot from such an extremely compressed
outline) Dairon seems more actively to seek Beren's death than he does in
the poem (despite line 1068), and Tinúviel pleads against her father's
policy.

For explanation of the references in A to Celegorm (notes to lines
1087, 1102–3) see p. 171. According to the earlier story seen in A the ring
given to Barahir was made by Fëanor, Celegorm's father. In B the later
story is present, and the badge of the entwined serpents is that of
Felagund's father Finrod (Finarfin in *The Silmarillion*) who now first
appears (other than in a later note to *The Children of Húrin*, see pp. 80,
138). Barahir now first replaces Egnor as Berin's father in A; and by later
emendation to B (lines 937, 941) Bëor appears, who at this time, as is
seen from the prose texts, was Barahir's father. With exceedingly complex genealogical and chronological restructuring of the houses of the
Elf-friends in later years Bëor came to be removed from Barahir by many
generations.

The name *Tavros* given to Oromë (891, 904) has occurred long before
in the Gnomish dictionary, defined as the 'chief wood-fay, the Blue
Spirit of the Woods' (I. 267, entry *Tavari*). With his *tree-propped halls*
(892) compare the description of Oromë's dwelling in Valmar in the tale
of *The Coming of the Valar and the Building of Valinor*, I. 75–6. At
line 893 is the first mention of the golden hooves of Oromë's horse.

# V

So days drew on from the mournful day;
the curse of silence no more lay
on Doriath, though Dairon's flute
and Lúthien's singing both were mute.
The murmurs soft awake once more                    1210
about the woods, the waters roar
past the great gates of Thingol's halls;
but no dancing step of Lúthien falls
on turf or leaf. For she forlorn,
where stumbled once, where bruised and torn,        1215

with longing on him like a dream,
had Beren sat by the shrouded stream
Esgalduin the dark and strong,
she sat and mourned in a low song:
'Endless roll the waters past!          1220
To this my love hath come at last,
enchanted waters pitiless,
a heartache and a loneliness.'

   The summer turns. In branches tall
she hears the pattering raindrops fall,   1225
the windy tide in leafy seas,
the creaking of the countless trees;
and longs unceasing and in vain
to hear one calling once again
the tender name that nightingales         1230
were called of old. Echo fails.
'Tinúviel! Tinúviel!'
the memory is like a knell,
a faint and far-off tolling bell:
'Tinúviel! Tinúviel!'                      1235

   'O mother Melian, tell to me
some part of what thy dark eyes see!
Tell of thy magic where his feet
are wandering! What foes him meet?
O mother, tell me, lives he still          1240
treading the desert and the hill?
Do sun and moon above him shine,
do the rains fall on him, mother mine?'

   'Nay, Lúthien my child, I fear
he lives indeed in bondage drear.          1245
The Lord of Wolves hath prisons dark,
chains and enchantments cruel and stark,
there trapped and bound and languishing
now Beren dreams that thou dost sing.'

   'Then I alone must go to him             1250
and dare the dread in dungeons dim;
for none there be that will him aid
in all the world, save elven-maid
whose only skill were joy and song,
and both have failed and left her long.'   1255

Then nought said Melian thereto,
though wild the words. She wept anew,
and ran through the woods like hunted deer
with her hair streaming and eyes of fear.
Dairon she found with ferny crown                    1260
silently sitting on beech-leaves brown.
On the earth she cast her at his side.
'O Dairon, Dairon, my tears,' she cried,
'now pity for our old days' sake!
Make me a music for heart's ache,                    1265
for heart's despair, and for heart's dread,
for light gone dark and laughter dead!'

'But for music dead there is no note,'
Dairon answered, and at his throat
his fingers clutched. Yet his pipe he took,          1270
and sadly trembling the music shook;
and all things stayed while that piping went
wailing in the hollows, and there intent
they listened, their business and mirth,
their hearts' gladness and the light of earth        1275
forgotten; and bird-voices failed
while Dairon's flute in Doriath wailed.
Lúthien wept not for very pain,
and when he ceased she spoke again:
'My friend, I have a need of friends,                1280
as he who a long dark journey wends,
and fears the road, yet dare not turn
and look back where the candles burn
in windows he has left. The night
in front, he doubts to find the light                1285
that far beyond the hills he seeks.'
And thus of Melian's words she speaks,
and of her doom and her desire
to climb the mountains, and the fire
and ruin of the Northern realm                       1290
to dare, a maiden without helm
or sword, or strength of hardy limb,
where magic founders and grows dim.
His aid she sought to guide her forth
and find the pathways to the North,                  1295
if he would not for love of her

go by her side a wanderer.
　'Wherefore,' said he, 'should Dairon go
into direst peril earth doth know
for the sake of mortal who did steal　　1300
his laughter and joy? No love I feel
for Beren son of Barahir,
nor weep for him in dungeons drear,
who in this wood have chains enow,
heavy and dark. But thee, I vow,　　1305
I will defend from perils fell
and deadly wandering into hell.'

　No more they spake that day, and she
perceived not his meaning. Sorrowfully
she thanked him, and she left him there.　　1310
A tree she climbed, till the bright air
above the woods her dark hair blew,
and straining afar her eyes could view
the outline grey and faint and low
of dizzy towers where the clouds go,　　1315
the southern faces mounting sheer
in rocky pinnacle and pier
of Shadowy Mountains pale and cold;
and wide the lands before them rolled.
But straightway Dairon sought the king　　1320
and told him his daughter's pondering,
and how her madness might her lead
to ruin, unless the king gave heed.
Thingol was wroth, and yet amazed;
in wonder and half fear he gazed　　1325
on Dairon, and said: 'True hast thou been.
Now ever shall love be us between,
while Doriath lasts; within this realm
thou art a prince of beech and elm!'
He sent for Lúthien, and said:　　1330
'O maiden fair, what hath thee led
to ponder madness and despair
to wander to ruin, and to fare
from Doriath against my will,
stealing like a wild thing men would kill　　1335
into the emptiness outside?'
'The wisdom, father,' she replied;

nor would she promise to forget,
nor would she vow for love or threat
her folly to forsake and meek                        1340
in Doriath her father's will to seek.
This only vowed she, if go she must,
that none but herself would she now trust,
no folk of her father's would persuade
to break his will or lend her aid;                   1345
if go she must, she would go alone
and friendless dare the walls of stone.

In angry love and half in fear
Thingol took counsel his most dear
to guard and keep. He would not bind                 1350
in caverns deep and intertwined
sweet Lúthien, his lovely maid,
who robbed of air must wane and fade,
who ever must look upon the sky
and see the sun and moon go by.                      1355
But close unto his mounded seat
and grassy throne there ran the feet
of Hirilorn, the beechen queen.
Upon her triple boles were seen
no break or branch, until aloft                      1360
in a green glimmer, distant, soft,
the mightiest vault of leaf and bough
from world's beginning until now
was flung above Esgalduin's shores
and the long slopes to Thingol's doors.              1365
Grey was the rind of pillars tall
and silken-smooth, and far and small
to squirrels' eyes were those who went
at her grey feet upon the bent.
Now Thingol made men in the beech,                   1370
in that great tree, as far as reach
their longest ladders, there to build
an airy house; and as he willed
a little dwelling of fair wood
was made, and veiled in leaves it stood              1375
above the first branches. Corners three
it had and windows faint to see,
and by three shafts of Hirilorn

in the corners standing was upborne.
　There Lúthien was bidden dwell,            1380
until she was wiser and the spell
of madness left her. Up she clomb
the long ladders to her new home
among the leaves, among the birds;
she sang no song, she spoke no words.        1385
White glimmering in the tree she rose,
and her little door they heard her close.
The ladders were taken and no more
her feet might tread Esgalduin's shore.

　Thither at whiles they climbed and brought  1390
all things she needed or besought;
but death was his, whoso should dare
a ladder leave, or creeping there
should set one by the tree at night;
a guard was held from dusk to light          1395
about the grey feet of Hirilorn
and Lúthien in prison and forlorn.
There Dairon grieving often stood
in sorrow for the captive of the wood,
and melodies made upon his flute             1400
leaning against a grey tree-root.
Lúthien would from her windows stare
and see him far under piping there,
and she forgave his betraying word
for the music and the grief she heard,       1405
and only Dairon would she let
across her threshold foot to set.
　Yet long the hours when she must sit
and see the sunbeams dance and flit
in beechen leaves, or watch the stars        1410
peep on clear nights between the bars
of beechen branches. And one night
just ere the changing of the light
a dream there came, from the Gods, maybe,
or Melian's magic. She dreamed that she      1415
heard Beren's voice o'er hill and fell
'Tinúviel' call, 'Tinúviel.'
And her heart answered: 'Let me be gone
to seek him no others think upon!'

She woke and saw the moonlight pale                    1420
through the slim leaves. It trembled frail
upon her arms, as these she spread
and there in longing bowed her head,
and yearned for freedom and escape.

    Now Lúthien doth her counsel shape;                1425
and Melian's daughter of deep lore
knew many things, yea, magics more
than then or now know elven-maids
that glint and shimmer in the glades.
She pondered long, while the moon sank                 1430
and faded, and the starlight shrank,
and the dawn opened. At last a smile
on her face flickered. She mused a while,
and watched the morning sunlight grow,
then called to those that walked below.                1435
And when one climbed to her she prayed
that he would in the dark pools wade
of cold Esgalduin, water clear,
the clearest water cold and sheer
to draw for her. 'At middle night,'                    1440
she said, 'in bowl of silver white
it must be drawn and brought to me
with no word spoken, silently.'
Another she begged to bring her wine
in a jar of gold where flowers twine –                 1445
'and singing let him come to me
at high noon, singing merrily.'
Again she spake: 'Now go, I pray,
to Melian the queen, and say:
"thy daughter many a weary hour                         1450
slow passing watches in her bower;
a spinning-wheel she begs thee send."'
Then Dairon she called: 'I prithee, friend,
climb up and talk to Lúthien!'
And sitting at her window then,                         1455
she said: 'My Dairon, thou hast craft,
beside thy music, many a shaft
and many a tool of carven wood
to fashion with cunning. It were good,
if thou wouldst make a little loom                      1460

to stand in the corner of my room.
My idle fingers would spin and weave
a pattern of colours, of morn and eve,
of sun and moon and changing light
amid the beech-leaves waving bright.'          1465
This Dairon did and asked her then:
'O Lúthien, O Lúthien,
What wilt thou weave? What wilt thou spin?'
'A marvellous thread, and wind therein
a potent magic, and a spell                    1470
I will weave within my web that hell
nor all the powers of Dread shall break.'
Then Dairon wondered, but he spake
no word to Thingol, though his heart
feared the dark purpose of her art.            1475

And Lúthien now was left alone.
A magic song to Men unknown
she sang, and singing then the wine
with water mingled three times nine;
and as in golden jar they lay                  1480
she sang a song of growth and day;
and as they lay in silver white
another song she sang, of night
and darkness without end, of height
uplifted to the stars, and flight              1485
and freedom. And all names of things
tallest and longest on earth she sings:
the locks of the Longbeard dwarves; the tail
of Draugluin the werewolf pale;
the body of Glómund the great snake;           1490
the vast upsoaring peaks that quake
above the fires in Angband's gloom;
the chain Angainor that ere Doom
for Morgoth shall by Gods be wrought
of steel and torment. Names she sought,        1495
and sang of Glend the sword of Nan;
of Gilim the giant of Eruman;
and last and longest named she then
the endless hair of Uinen,
the Lady of the Sea, that lies                 1500
through all the waters under skies.

Then did she lave her head and sing
a theme of sleep and slumbering,
profound and fathomless and dark
as Lúthien's shadowy hair was dark –                   1505
each thread was more slender and more fine
than threads of twilight that entwine
in filmy web the fading grass
and closing flowers as day doth pass.

Now long and longer grew her hair,                     1510
and fell to her feet, and wandered there
like pools of shadow on the ground.
Then Lúthien in a slumber drowned
was laid upon her bed and slept,
till morning through the windows crept                 1515
thinly and faint. And then she woke,
and the room was filled as with a smoke
and with an evening mist, and deep
she lay thereunder drowsed in sleep.
Behold! her hair from windows blew                     1520
in morning airs, and darkly grew
waving about the pillars grey
of Hirilorn at break of day.

Then groping she found her little shears,
and cut the hair about her ears,                       1525
and close she cropped it to her head,
enchanted tresses, thread by thread.
Thereafter grew they slow once more,
yet darker than their wont before.
And now was her labour but begun:                      1530
long was she spinning, long she spun;
and though with elvish skill she wrought,
long was her weaving. If men sought
to call her, crying from below,
'Nothing I need,' she answered, 'go!                   1535
I would keep my bed, and only sleep
I now desire, who waking weep.'

Then Dairon feared, and in amaze
he called from under; but three days
she answered not. Of cloudy hair                       1540
she wove a web like misty air
of moonless night, and thereof made

a robe as fluttering-dark as shade
beneath great trees, a magic dress
that all was drenched with drowsiness,                    1545
enchanted with a mightier spell
than Melian's raiment in that dell
wherein of yore did Thingol roam
beneath the dark and starry dome
that hung above the dawning world.                        1550
And now this robe she round her furled,
and veiled her garments shimmering white;
her mantle blue with jewels bright
like crystal stars, the lilies gold,
were wrapped and hid; and down there rolled              1555
dim dreams and faint oblivious sleep
falling about her, to softly creep
through all the air. Then swift she takes
the threads unused; of these she makes
a slender rope of twisted strands                         1560
yet long and stout, and with her hands
she makes it fast unto the shaft
of Hirilorn. Now, all her craft
and labour ended, looks she forth
from her little window facing North.                      1565

    Already the sunlight in the trees
is drooping red, and dusk she sees
come softly along the ground below,
and now she murmurs soft and slow.
Now chanting clearer down she cast                        1570
her long hair, till it reached at last
from her window to the darkling ground.
Men far beneath her heard the sound;
but the slumbrous strand now swung and swayed
above her guards. Their talking stayed,                   1575
they listened to her voice and fell
suddenly beneath a binding spell.

    Now clad as in a cloud she hung;
now down her ropéd hair she swung
as light as squirrel, and away,                           1580
away, she danced, and who could say
what paths she took, whose elvish feet
no impress made a-dancing fleet?

★

## NOTES

1222–3    At lines 651–2 these lines were transposed on C. S. Lewis's suggestion (see p. 323); and *heartache* was emended to *hunger*.

1226    Cf. line 664.

1231    Original reading of B: *are called in elfland. Echo fails.* The change was probably simply to get rid of 'elfland'.

1249    *now*: uncertain (original reading *doth Beren dream* emended to *?now Beren dreams*).

1253    Throughout this Canto *elven-* and *elvish* are emendations of *elfin* made on the B-text.

1260–1    Cf. lines 497–8.

1308–10    Marked *revise* on the B-text.

1312    *her dark hair*: so also in A. See note to line 558.

1316–17    Cf. lines 389–90. The *Shadowy Mountains* (1318) are the Mountains of Terror (Ered Gorgoroth): see pp. 170–1.

1323    This line is marked with an X on the B-text.

1329    As line 1323.

1358    Against *Hirilorn* in A is written *Hiradorn*, and so also at lines 1396, 1523. At line 1563 *Hiradorn* is the form in the text of A.

1362–3    Cf. lines 872–3.

1370    *men > them* A. At 1390, where B has *they*, A had *men > they*; at 1533, 1573 *men* was not changed in either text.

1414–17    Marked with a line on the B-text; in the margin some new verses are written, but so faint and rapid as to be quite illegible.

1488    *locks* B] *beards* A

1489    A:   of Carcharas the wolf-ward pale;
In the original draft the spelling is *Carcaras* as in the typescript version of the *Tale of Tinúviel* (manuscript version *Karkaras*). In the second version of *The Children of Húrin* (p. 107 line 374) the form is *Carcharoth* (emended from *Carcharolch*).

1490    *Glómund* B] *Glórund* A (as in the *Lost Tales*, but there always without accent).

1493    *Angainor* A, B] *Engainor* in the original draft.

1496    *Nan* B] *Nann* A (but *Nan* in the original draft).

1549–50    Cf. lines 406–7.

1563    *Hirilorn* B] *Hiradorn* A. See note to line 1358.

### Commentary on Canto V

The plot-outline 'Synopsis I' covering the narrative of this Canto is very slight:

Mourning of Tinúviel.
Treachery of Dairon.
Building of the Tree House in Hirilorn.
Escape of Tinúviel.
[*Added in*: Repentance, wandering, and loss of Dairon.]

The wandering and loss of Dairon goes back to the *Tale of Tinúviel* (II. 20–1) and survived into *The Silmarillion* (p. 183), but there is no other mention of his 'repentance' (though this is perhaps implied in the Lay, lines 1398 ff.)

In my commentary on the passage in the *Tale of Tinúviel* corresponding to this Canto I remarked (II. 54) that

> the story of her imprisonment in the house in Hirilorn and her escape from it never underwent any significant change. The passage in *The Silmarillion* (p. 172) is indeed very brief, but its lack of detail is due to compression rather than to omission based on dissatisfaction; the *Lay of Leithian*, from which the prose account in *The Silmarillion* directly derives, is in this passage so close, in point of narrative detail, to the *Tale of Tinúviel* as to be almost identical with it.

There is little to add to this here. In one respect the narrative of the Lay is at variance with the story told in *The Silmarillion*. What was 'the curse of silence' (1207)? It was due to Dairon (848–53). In a preliminary, soon abandoned draft for the 'Silmarillion' version, where the story was to be told far more amply (by following the Lay more closely) the matter is made more explicit:

> But Dairon haunted the trees and watched them from afar; and he cried aloud in the bitterness of his heart: 'Hateful is now become the land that I loved, and the trees misshapen. No more shall music here be heard. Let all voices fail in Doriath, and in every dale and upon every hill let the trees stand silent!' And there was a hush and a great stillness; and Thingol's folk were filled with wonder. And they spoke to their king, asking what was the reason of the silence.

Dairon's 'curse' was lifted after Beren's departure, although Lúthien no longer sang and Dairon no longer piped. This is in contrast to *The Silmarillion* (p. 168), where after Beren went

> Lúthien was silent, and from that hour she sang not again in Doriath. *A brooding silence fell upon the woods.*

For the names in the 'lengthening spell' see II. 67–8. A new element among the 'longest things' is introduced in the version in the Lay, the peaks above Angband (1491–2); and in B the name of the great Dragon becomes *Glómund*. The chain with which Morgoth was bound, *Angaino/Angainu* in the *Lost Tales*, becomes *Angainor*; but it is curious that in the Lay it is only spoken of as a punishment awaiting

Morgoth in the future (*ere Doom*, 1493), whereas in the old story of *The Chaining of Melko* (I. 104) it was the shackle with which he was taken prisoner in the original war that led to his captivity in Valinor, and this survived in *The Silmarillion* (p. 51): at the end of the Elder Days 'he was bound with the chain Angainor which he had worn aforetime' (*ibid.* p. 252).

New elements in the story that have yet to appear in the actual narrative of the Lay are seen in *Draugluin*, replacing in B *Carcharas* of A in the 'lengthening spell' (thus Carcharas is no longer the 'father of wolves', see II. 68), and in Melian's reference to Beren's lying in the dungeons of the Lord of Wolves (1246).

Lúthien's dream in which she heard Beren's voice far off is still ascribed, as it was in the *Tale*, to the Gods, if less positively (*a dream there came, from the Gods, maybe,*/*or Melian's magic*, 1414–15); see II. 19, 68. But the passage is marked in B, perhaps indicating dissatisfaction with the idea.

There is curious detail in a marginal note to the B-text. At some time (as I think) long afterwards someone unknown wrote against lines 1331–6: 'Thingol is here being rather obtuse'; and against this remark my father scribbled: 'But he could not believe she *loved* Beren – unless some evil spell had somehow been laid on her.'

# VI

When Morgoth in that day of doom
had slain the Trees and filled with gloom          1585
the shining land of Valinor,
there Fëanor and his sons then swore
the mighty oath upon the hill
of tower-crownéd Tûn, that still
wrought wars and sorrow in the world.          1590
From darkling seas the fogs unfurled
their blinding shadows grey and cold
where Glingal once had bloomed with gold
and Belthil bore its silver flowers.
The mists were mantled round the towers          1595
of the Elves' white city by the sea.
There countless torches fitfully
did start and twinkle, as the Gnomes
were gathered to their fading homes,

and thronged the long and winding stair          1600
that led to the wide echoing square.

There Fëanor mourned his jewels divine,
the Silmarils he made. Like wine
his wild and potent words them fill;
a great host harkens deathly still.          1605
But all he said both wild and wise,
half truth and half the fruit of lies
that Morgoth sowed in Valinor,
in other songs and other lore
recorded is. He bade them flee          1610
from lands divine, to cross the sea,
the pathless plains, the perilous shores
where ice-infested water roars;
to follow Morgoth to the unlit earth
leaving their dwellings and olden mirth;          1615
to go back to the Outer Lands
to wars and weeping. There their hands
they joined in vows, those kinsmen seven,
swearing beneath the stars of Heaven,
by Varda the Holy that them wrought          1620
and bore them each with radiance fraught
and set them in the deeps to flame.
Timbrenting's holy height they name,
whereon are built the timeless halls
of Manwë Lord of Gods. Who calls          1625
these names in witness may not break
his oath, though earth and heaven shake.

Curufin, Celegorm the fair,
Damrod and Díriel were there,
and Cranthir dark, and Maidros tall          1630
(whom after torment should befall),
and Maglor the mighty who like the sea
with deep voice sings yet mournfully.
'Be he friend or foe, or seed defiled
of Morgoth Bauglir, or mortal child          1635
that in after days on earth shall dwell,
no law, nor love, nor league of hell,
not might of Gods, not moveless fate
shall him defend from wrath and hate
of Fëanor's sons, who takes or steals          1640

or finding keeps the Silmarils,
the thrice-enchanted globes of light
that shine until the final night.'

    The wars and wandering of the Gnomes
this tale tells not. Far from their homes                    1645
they fought and laboured in the North.
Fingon daring alone went forth
and sought for Maidros where he hung;
in torment terrible he swung,
his wrist in band of forgéd steel,                           1650
from a sheer precipice where reel
the dizzy senses staring down
from Thangorodrim's stony crown.
The song of Fingon Elves yet sing,
captain of armies, Gnomish king,                             1655
who fell at last in flame of swords
with his white banners and his lords.
They sing how Maidros free he set,
and stayed the feud that slumbered yet
between the children proud of Finn.                          1660
Now joined once more they hemmed him in,
even great Morgoth, and their host
beleaguered Angband, till they boast
no Orc nor demon ever dare
their leaguer break or past them fare.                       1665
    Then days of solace woke on earth
beneath the new-lit Sun, and mirth
was heard in the Great Lands where Men,
a young race, spread and wandered then.
That was the time that songs do call                         1670
the Siege of Angband, when like a wall
the Gnomish swords did fence the earth
from Morgoth's ruin, a time of birth,
of blossoming, of flowers, of growth;
but still there held the deathless oath,                     1675
and still the Silmarils were deep
in Angband's darkly-dolven keep.

    An end there came, when fortune turned,
and flames of Morgoth's vengeance burned,
and all the might which he prepared                          1680
in secret in his fastness flared

and poured across the Thirsty Plain;
and armies black were in his train.
  The leaguer of Angband Morgoth broke;
his enemies in fire and smoke                         1685
were scattered, and the Orcs there slew
and slew, until the blood like dew
dripped from each cruel and crooked blade.
Then Barahir the bold did aid
with mighty spear, with shield and men,              1690
Felagund wounded. To the fen
escaping, there they bound their troth,
and Felagund deeply swore an oath
of friendship to his kin and seed,
of love and succour in time of need.                 1695
But there of Finrod's children four
were Angrod slain and proud Egnor.
Felagund and Orodreth then
gathered the remnant of their men,
their maidens and their children fair;               1700
forsaking war they made their lair
and cavernous hold far in the south.
On Narog's towering bank its mouth
was opened; which they hid and veiled,
and mighty doors, that unassailed                    1705
till Túrin's day stood vast and grim,
they built by trees o'ershadowed dim.
And with them dwelt a long time there
Curufin, and Celegorm the fair;
and a mighty folk grew neath their hands             1710
in Narog's secret halls and lands.

  Thus Felagund in Nargothrond
still reigned, a hidden king whose bond
was sworn to Barahir the bold.
And now his son through forests cold                 1715
wandered alone as in a dream.
Esgalduin's dark and shrouded stream
he followed, till its waters frore
were joined to Sirion, Sirion hoar,
pale silver water wide and free                      1720
rolling in splendour to the sea.
  Now Beren came unto the pools,

wide shallow meres where Sirion cools
his gathered tide beneath the stars,
ere chafed and sundered by the bars                 1725
of reedy banks a mighty fen
he feeds and drenches, plunging then
into vast chasms underground,
where many miles his way is wound.
Umboth-Muilin, Twilight Meres,                      1730
those great wide waters grey as tears
the Elves then named. Through driving rain
from thence across the Guarded Plain
the Hills of the Hunters Beren saw
with bare tops bitten bleak and raw                 1735
by western winds; but in the mist
of streaming rains that flashed and hissed
into the meres he knew there lay
beneath those hills the cloven way
of Narog, and the watchful halls                    1740
of Felagund beside the falls
of Ingwil tumbling from the wold.
An everlasting watch they hold,
the Gnomes of Nargothrond renowned,
and every hill is tower-crowned,                    1745
where wardens sleepless peer and gaze
guarding the plain and all the ways
between Narog swift and Sirion pale;
and archers whose arrows never fail
there range the woods, and secret kill              1750
all who creep thither against their will.
    Yet now he thrusts into that land
bearing the gleaming ring on hand
of Felagund, and oft doth cry:
'Here comes no wandering Orc or spy,                1755
but Beren son of Barahir
who once to Felagund was dear.'
    So ere he reached the eastward shore
of Narog, that doth foam and roar
o'er boulders black, those archers green            1760
came round him. When the ring was seen
they bowed before him, though his plight
was poor and beggarly. Then by night
they led him northward, for no ford

nor bridge was built where Narog poured          1765
before the gates of Nargothrond,
and friend nor foe might pass beyond.
    To northward, where that stream yet young
more slender flowed, below the tongue
of foam-splashed land that Ginglith pens          1770
when her brief golden torrent ends
and joins the Narog, there they wade.
Now swiftest journey thence they made
to Nargothrond's sheer terraces
and dim gigantic palaces.                         1775
    They came beneath a sickle moon
to doors there darkly hung and hewn
with posts and lintels of ponderous stone
and timbers huge. Now open thrown
were gaping gates, and in they strode             1780
where Felagund on throne abode.

    Fair were the words of Narog's king
to Beren, and his wandering
and all his feuds and bitter wars
recounted soon. Behind closed doors               1785
they sat, while Beren told his tale
of Doriath; and words him fail
recalling Lúthien dancing fair
with wild white roses in her hair,
remembering her elven voice that rung             1790
while stars in twilight round her hung.
He spake of Thingol's marvellous halls
by enchantment lit, where fountain falls
and ever the nightingale doth sing
to Melian and to her king.                        1795
The quest he told that Thingol laid
in scorn on him; how for love of maid
more fair than ever was born to Men,
of Tinúviel, of Lúthien,
he must essay the burning waste,                  1800
and doubtless death and torment taste.

    This Felagund in wonder heard,
and heavily spake at last this word:
'It seems that Thingol doth desire
thy death. The everlasting fire                   1805

of those enchanted jewels all know
is cursed with an oath of endless woe,
and Fëanor's sons alone by right
are lords and masters of their light.
He cannot hope within his hoard                    1810
to keep this gem, nor is he lord
of all the folk of Elfinesse.
And yet thou saist for nothing less
can thy return to Doriath
be purchased? Many a dreadful path                 1815
in sooth there lies before thy feet –
and after Morgoth, still a fleet
untiring hate, as I know well,
would hunt thee from heaven unto hell.
Fëanor's sons would, if they could,                1820
slay thee or ever thou reached his wood
or laid in Thingol's lap that fire,
or gained at least thy sweet desire.
Lo! Celegorm and Curufin
here dwell this very realm within,                 1825
and even though I, Finrod's son,
am king, a mighty power have won
and many of their own folk lead.
Friendship to me in every need
they yet have shown, but much I fear               1830
that to Beren son of Barahir
mercy or love they will not show
if once thy dreadful quest they know.'

    True words he spake. For when the king
to all his people told this thing,                 1835
and spake of the oath to Barahir,
and how that mortal shield and spear
had saved them from Morgoth and from woe
on Northern battlefields long ago,
then many were kindled in their hearts             1840
once more to battle. But up there starts
amid the throng, and loudly cries
for hearing, one with flaming eyes,
proud Celegorm with gleaming hair
and shining sword. Then all men stare              1845
upon his stern unyielding face,

and a great hush falls upon that place.

'Be he friend or foe, or demon wild
of Morgoth, Elf, or mortal child,
or any that here on earth may dwell,                    1850
no law, nor love, nor league of hell,
no might of Gods, no binding spell,
shall him defend from hatred fell
of Fëanor's sons, whoso take or steal
or finding keep a Silmaril.                             1855
These we alone do claim by right,
our thrice enchanted jewels bright.'

Many wild and potent words he spoke,
and as before in Tûn awoke
his father's voice their hearts to fire,               1860
so now dark fear and brooding ire
he cast on them, foreboding war
of friend with friend; and pools of gore
their minds imagined lying red
in Nargothrond about the dead,                          1865
did Narog's host with Beren go;
or haply battle, ruin, and woe
in Doriath where great Thingol reigned,
if Fëanor's fatal jewel he gained.
And even such as were most true                         1870
to Felagund his oath did rue,
and thought with terror and despair
of seeking Morgoth in his lair
with force or guile. This Curufin
when his brother ceased did then begin                  1875
more to impress upon their minds;
and such a spell he on them binds
that never again till Túrin's day
would Gnome of Narog in array
of open battle go to war.                               1880
With secrecy, ambush, spies, and lore
of wizardry, with silent leaguer
of wild things wary, watchful, eager,
of phantom hunters, venomed darts,
and unseen stealthy creeping arts,                      1885
with padding hatred that its prey
with feet of velvet all the day

followed remorseless out of sight
and slew it unawares at night –
thus they defended Nargothrond,                    1890
and forgot their kin and solemn bond
for dread of Morgoth that the art
of Curufin set within their heart.

So would they not that angry day
King Felagund their lord obey,                     1895
but sullen murmured that Finrod
nor yet his son were as a god.
Then Felagund took off his crown
and at his feet he cast it down,
the silver helm of Nargothrond:                    1900
'Yours ye may break, but I my bond
must keep, and kingdom here forsake.
If hearts here were that did not quake,
or that to Finrod's son were true,
then I at least should find a few                  1905
to go with me, not like a poor
rejected beggar scorn endure,
turned from my gates to leave my town,
my people, and my realm and crown!'

Hearing these words there swiftly stood            1910
beside him ten tried warriors good,
men of his house who had ever fought
wherever his banners had been brought.
One stooped and lifted up his crown,
and said: 'O king, to leave this town              1915
is now our fate, but not to lose
thy rightful lordship. Thou shalt choose
one to be steward in thy stead.'
Then Felagund upon the head
of Orodreth set it: 'Brother mine,                 1920
till I return this crown is thine.'
Then Celegorm no more would stay,
and Curufin smiled and turned away.

★

# NOTES

| | |
|---|---|
| 1593–4 | Original readings of B *Glingol*, *Bansil*, as at line 1141. |
| 1598–9 | Couplet marked for revision, partly on account of *did start*, partly on account of *Gnomes*. I do not record further instances of this sort, which occur casually throughout. |
| 1619 | Here is written on the B-text: '∧ see the Qenta.' This is the 'Silmarillion' version of 1930, and presumably refers to the form of the Oath as it appears there. |
| 1620 | *Varda the Holy* is written in the margin of the B-text, which like A has *Bridhil the Blessed*. *Bridhil* occurs earlier in A (note to lines 377–81), where B has a different reading. |
| 1632–3 | Cf. lines 506–9. |
| 1647 | *Finweg* A, and B as typed, early emended in B to *Fingon*. |
| 1654 | As line 1647. |
| 1656 | Cf. *The Children of Húrin*, first version line 1975, second version line 19, from which the words (referring to Finweg/Fingon) *fell in flame of swords* are derived; in the second version occur also the king's *white banners*. |
| 1710–11 | A:    a great people were gathered of the Gnomes<br>        in these new-builded secret homes. |
| 1736 | Against the words *by western winds* is written (in such a way as to show that this was the point reached, not the starting-point) the date '29 Mar. 1928', the previous date being 27–28 March 1928 at line 1161. |
| 1859 | *Tûn* B] *Côr* A |
| 1866 | A:    if Felagund should with Beren go; |
| 1891 | A:    and forgot their blood and kinship's bond |
| 1900 | *helm* is an emendation in B for *crown*. |
| 1920 | An X is written against this line, probably long after when Orodreth was moved from his place as Felagund's brother (see p. 91). |
| 1921 | *crown* B] *realm* A |

## Commentary on Canto VI

The plot-outline 'Synopsis I' continues thus:

> Beren goes to Celegorm, who disguises him [*struck out*: and gives him a magic knife. Beren and his Gnomish guides* are captured by Orcs: and a few survivors taken before (Melko >) Morgoth. Beren tells M. he is a 'trapper of the woods'.]

---

* This phrase was changed to: 'Beren gets lost and separated from his Gnomish guides'; and was then struck out with the rest of the passage.

> They go and seek to break into Angband disguised as Orcs, but are captured [*struck out*: and set in chains, and killed one by one. Beren lies wondering which will be his turn.] by the Lord of Wolves, and set in bonds, and devoured one by one.

It is interesting here to see how the relevant features of the story are treated in the 'Sketch of the Mythology' of 1926, as originally written. In this account Beren's father is Barahir, and he 'had been a friend of Celegorm of Nargothrond'. After Thingol's demand that Beren get him a Silmaril:

> Beren sets out to achieve this, is captured, and set in dungeon in Angband, but conceals his real identity, and is given as a slave to Thû the hunter.

This passage is evidently earlier than 'Synopsis I' (at the earliest, the end of May 1926, the date of the latest of the three invoices on which it is written), since the 'Sketch' contains no reference to Celegorm's aid, Beren's companions, their disguising as Orcs, and their capture by the Lord of Wolves. On the contrary, Beren goes to Angband alone just as he did in the *Tale of Tinúviel*, and – most notably – is given to 'Thû the hunter' as a slave, just as in the *Tale* he was given to Tevildo Prince of Cats as a slave. In Synopsis I we see, I think, the very point at which the story of Beren's Gnomish companions came into being, of their disguise as Orcs, and of their deaths one by one in the dungeons of the Lord of Wolves. (Thû appears first in the fragment of the *Lay of the Fall of Gondolin* (p. 146), and in *The Children of Húrin* as Morgoth's most mighty thane: first version line 391, second version line 763).

But already at lines 296 ff. in the A-text of the *Lay of Leithian* (summer 1925) there is a reference to the 'deed of service' done by Egnor Beren's father to Celegorm, and the gift of the ring: while in the 'Sketch' Barahir 'had been a friend of Celegorm of Nargothrond'. Thus:

| | |
|---|---|
| *Lay of Leithian* Canto II (summer 1925) | Egnor Beren's father performed a service for Celegorm, from whom he received a ring. |
| *Sketch of the Mythology* (early in 1926, see p. 3) | Barahir Beren's father was a friend of Celegorm of Nargothrond. |
| | Beren sets out alone and is captured and imprisoned in Angband, but is given as a slave to Thû the hunter. |
| *Synopsis I* (after May 1926) | Beren goes to Celegorm who aids him (story of the Gnomish companions appears). |

The rather surprising conclusion must be that the association of Egnor/Barahir with Celegorm and the gift of the ring *preceded* the emergence of the story of Beren's going to Celegorm for aid.

In the rejected part of Synopsis I here we see a last survival from the

*Tale of Tinúviel*: Beren tells Morgoth that he is a trapper of the woods; cf. the *Tale* (II. 15): 'Beren said therewith that he was a great trapper of small animals and a snarer of birds' – and it was indeed this explanation of Beren's to Melko that got him his post in Tevildo's kitchens. The mention in this rejected passage of a magic knife given to Beren by Celegorm was clearly a passing idea to account for the knife with which Beren would cut the Silmaril from the Iron Crown, since the kitchen-knife with which he did the deed in the *Tale* (II. 33) had been abandoned with the kitchens.

Other loose papers in addition to Synopsis I show the further development of the narrative. The first of these I will refer to as 'Synopsis II'; it begins with the beginning of Canto VI and I cite it here as far as the end of the Canto.

> Beren comes to Felagund at Nargothrond; who receives him well, but warns him of the oath of the sons of Fëanor, and that Curufin and Celegorm dwelling with him have great power in his realm.
>
> Curufin and Celegorm learn of Beren's purpose, and recalling their oath forbid the Gnomes to aid Beren to get the Silmaril for Thingol. The Gnomes fearing war in Nargothrond, or war against Thingol, and in [any] case despairing utterly of reaching the depths of Angband by force or guile will not support Felagund. Felagund mindful of his own oath hands his kingdom over to Orodreth, and with only his own faithful followers of his household (ten in number) goes forth with Beren.

In the *Lay of Leithian* the 'Nargothrond Element' in the story had by this time (the spring of 1928) evolved further (see p. 171). The major figure of (Felagoth >) Felagund, son of Finwë's third son Finrod, had emerged (see p. 91), and by Canto VI was present also in the A-text; it was he, not Celegorm, who was rescued in the battle that ended the Siege of Angband and who then went south with his brother Orodreth to found Nargothrond, and Celegorm with his brother Curufin have been shifted by the movement of the legend into the rôle of Felagund's overpowerful 'guests' (it is not made explicit in the Lay why they were there, though it could be guessed that they also had fled from 'the Northern battlefields'). In the passage from Synopsis II just given my father is seen working out the narrative from this point and on this narrative basis, and many of the motives that are important in the final version now appear: on account of their oath Celegorm and Curufin are the cause of the refusal of the Elves of Nargothrond to support Felagund in the aiding of Beren; Felagund gives the crown to Orodreth; and only ten of Felagund's people go with him.* I think it certain that Synopsis II was written as, and did in fact provide, the outline narrative for this and the following Cantos.

---

*An intermediate stage is seen in a rewritten passage of the 1926 'Sketch of the Mythology', to be given in Vol. IV, where Celegorm has already been displaced by Felagoth (not yet Felagund) but where Celegorm only learns the errand of Felagoth and Beren *after* their departure from Nargothrond, and they leave with a large force.

In Canto VI we meet for the first time several central features of the earlier history of the Gnomes in Beleriand and the North, though these are not necessarily their first occurrences in my father's writings. Thus the story of the rescue of Maidros by (Finweg >) Fingon from his torment on Thangorodrim, where he was hanged by his right hand, is almost certainly implied in *The Children of Húrin*, where it is said that Maidros wielded his sword with his left (see p. 86); and it is fully told in the 'Sketch' as first written early in 1926, some two years before the date of the present Canto (see note to line 1736). Here also are references to the long years of the Siege of Angband after the healing of the feud among the Gnomish princes (the cause of which we do not yet know); and to the bursting of Morgoth's *armies black* (cf. *The Silmarillion* p. 151: 'the black armies of the Orcs') across *the Thirsty Plain* (for which see p. 55). Here we meet for the first time (apart from a later note to *The Children of Húrin*, p. 80) Angrod and Egnor, sons of Finrod and brothers of Felagund and Orodreth, who meet their deaths in the battle; and here it is said that Felagund was wounded (line 1691), and that his rescuers withdrew 'to the fen' – very probably the 'mighty fen' of Sirion referred to at line 1726.

For Finweg > Fingon, and Finn (line 1660) = Finwë, see p. 137–8. The genealogy of the princes of the Gnomes as it had emerged in the 1920s is now complete:

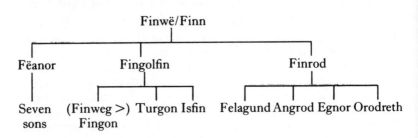

The earliest version of the Fëanorian Oath is found in alliterative verse in *The Flight of the Noldoli* (see pp. 135–6), and that in the *Lay of Leithian* (lines 1634–43) follows it quite closely despite its being in rhyming couplets, with many of the same phrases. Further variations are introduced in Celegorm's version (lines 1848–57). On the name *Timbrenting* of Taniquetil (taken in witness of the Oath) see pp. 127, 139.

Most of the geographical references and names in this Canto are amply explained by Part III 'Failivrin' of *The Children of Húrin*. For the Hills of the Hunters, the rivers Ginglith and Ingwil, and the Guarded Plain see pp. 88–9. It is now made clear that Umboth-Muilin, the Twilight Meres, were north of Sirion's fall and passage underground (to which there is a reference in *The Children of Húrin*, line 1467), whereas in the

*Lost Tales* the reverse was the case (see II. 217); and also that Esgalduin was a tributary of Sirion (lines 1717–20). In the verses describing Nargothrond the *Lay of Leithian* looks back to and echoes *The Children of Húrin*; compare

> Doors there darkly    dim gigantic
> were hewn in the hillside;    huge their timbers
> and their posts and lintels    of ponderous stone
>                                        (p. 68, 1828–30)

with

> Nargothrond's sheer terraces
> and dim gigantic palaces                              (1774–5)

and

> doors there darkly hung and hewn
> with posts and lintels of ponderous stone
> and timbers huge.                                     (1777–9)

I have mentioned earlier (pp. 88, 90) the drawing and watercolour of the entrance to Nargothrond. The drawing is inscribed 'Lyme 1928' (a summer holiday at Lyme Regis in Dorset) and the watercolour was very likely done at the same time: thus a few months after the writing of Canto VI of the *Lay of Leithian*. In both are seen the bare Hills of the Hunters beyond (*with bare tops bitten bleak and raw*, 1735), and in the watercolour *Nargothrond's sheer terraces* (1774); but neither picture suggests that the entrance was *hid and veiled* (1704), *by trees o'er-shadowed dim* (1707) – a feature of the description that goes back to the *Tale of Turámbar* ('the doors of the caves . . . were cunningly concealed by trees', II. 81).

I noticed in my commentary on the *Tale of Turambar* (II. 124 and footnote) that 'the policy of secrecy and refusal of open war pursued by the Elves of Nargothrond was always an essential element', but that from *The Silmarillion* p. 168 'it seems that when Beren came to Nargothrond the "secret" policy was already pursued under Felagund', whereas from p. 170 'it seems that it came into being from the potent rhetoric of Curufin after Beren went there'. From this Canto it is seen that this contradiction, if contradiction it is, has its source in the two passages lines 1743–51 and 1877–93.

In this latter passage there are again strong echoes of *The Children of Húrin*; compare

> a leaguer silent
> unseen, stealthy,    beset the stranger,
> as of wild things wary    that watch moveless,
> then follow fleetly    with feet of velvet
> their heedless prey    with padding hatred (p. 66, 1749–53)

with
>        with silent leaguer
> of wild things wary, watchful, eager,
> of phantom hunters, venomed darts,
> and unseen stealthy creeping arts,
> with padding hatred that its prey
> with feet of velvet all the day
> followed remorseless . . .                              (1882–8)

There remain a couple of points concerning names. The Great Lands are still so called (1668); but at 1616 the expression 'Outer Lands' occurs. This was used in *The Cottage of Lost Play* as first written in the sense of the Great Lands, but was subsequently applied to the lands beyond the Western Sea (see I. 21, 81–2). 'Outer Lands' = Middle-earth is frequent in *The Silmarillion*.

The name of the river, Narog, is used, as often later, to refer to the realm of Nargothrond: the King of Nargothrond is the King of Narog (see lines 1782, 1866).

# VII

> Thus twelve alone there ventured forth
> from Nargothrond, and to the North                    1925
> they turned their silent secret way,
> and vanished in the fading day.
> No trumpet sounds, no voice there sings,
> as robed in mail of cunning rings
> now blackened dark with helmets grey                  1930
> and sombre cloaks they steal away.
>      Far-journeying Narog's leaping course
> they followed till they found his source,
> the flickering falls, whose freshets sheer
> a glimmering goblet glassy-clear                      1935
> with crystal waters fill that shake
> and quiver down from Ivrin's lake,
> from Ivrin's mere that mirrors dim
> the pallid faces bare and grim
> of Shadowy Mountains neath the moon.                  1940
>
>      Now far beyond the realm immune
> from Orc and demon and the dread

of Morgoth's might their ways had led.
In woods o'ershadowed by the heights
they watched and waited many nights,                    1945
till on a time when hurrying cloud
did moon and constellation shroud,
and winds of autumn's wild beginning
soughed in the boughs, and leaves went spinning
down the dark eddies rustling soft,                    1950
they heard a murmur hoarsely waft
from far, a croaking laughter coming;
now louder; now they heard the drumming
of hideous stamping feet that tramp
the weary earth. Then many a lamp                    1955
of sullen red they saw draw near,
swinging, and glistening on spear
and scimitar. There hidden nigh
they saw a band of Orcs go by
with goblin-faces swart and foul.                    1960
Bats were about them, and the owl,
the ghostly forsaken night-bird cried
from trees above. The voices died,
the laughter like clash of stone and steel
passed and faded. At their heel                    1965
the Elves and Beren crept more soft
than foxes stealing through a croft
in search of prey. Thus to the camp
lit by flickering fire and lamp
they stole, and counted sitting there                    1970
full thirty Orcs in the red flare
of burning wood. Without a sound
they one by one stood silent round,
each in the shadow of a tree;
each slowly, grimly, secretly                    1975
bent then his bow and drew the string.

Hark! how they sudden twang and sing,
when Felagund lets forth a cry;
and twelve Orcs sudden fall and die.
Then forth they leap casting their bows.                    1980
Out their bright swords, and swift their blows!
The stricken Orcs now shriek and yell
as lost things deep in lightless hell.

Battle there is beneath the trees
bitter and swift; but no Orc flees;                    1985
there left their lives that wandering band
and stained no more the sorrowing land
with rape and murder. Yet no song
of joy, or triumph over wrong,
the Elves there sang. In peril sore                    1990
they were, for never alone to war
so small an Orc-band went, they knew.
Swiftly the raiment off they drew
and cast the corpses in a pit.
This desperate counsel had the wit                     1995
of Felagund for them devised:
as Orcs his comrades he disguised.

    The poisoned spears, the bows of horn,
the crooked swords their foes had borne
they took; and loathing each him clad                  2000
in Angband's raiment foul and sad.
They smeared their hands and faces fair
with pigment dark; the matted hair
all lank and black from goblin head
they shore, and joined it thread by thread             2005
with Gnomish skill. As each one leers
at each dismayed, about his ears
he hangs it noisome, shuddering.
    Then Felagund a spell did sing
of changing and of shifting shape;                     2010
their ears grew hideous, and agape
their mouths did start, and like a fang
each tooth became, as slow he sang.
Their Gnomish raiment then they hid,
and one by one behind him slid,                        2015
behind a foul and goblin thing
that once was elven-fair and king.

    Northward they went; and Orcs they met
who passed, nor did their going let,
but hailed them in greeting; and more bold             2020
they grew as past the long miles rolled.
    At length they came with weary feet
beyond Beleriand. They found the fleet
young waters, rippling, silver-pale

of Sirion hurrying through that vale                                    2025
where Taur-na-Fuin, Deadly Night,
the trackless forest's pine-clad height,
falls dark forbidding slowly down
upon the east, while westward frown
the northward-bending Mountains grey                                    2030
and bar the westering light of day.

   An isléd hill there stood alone
amid the valley, like a stone
rolled from the distant mountains vast
when giants in tumult hurtled past.                                     2035
Around its feet the river looped
a stream divided, that had scooped
the hanging edges into caves.
There briefly shuddered Sirion's waves
and ran to other shores more clean.                                     2040
   An elven watchtower had it been,
and strong it was, and still was fair;
but now did grim with menace stare
one way to pale Beleriand,
the other to that mournful land                                        2045
beyond the valley's northern mouth.
Thence could be glimpsed the fields of drouth,
the dusty dunes, the desert wide;
and further far could be descried
the brooding cloud that hangs and lowers                                2050
on Thangorodrim's thunderous towers.

   Now in that hill was the abode
of one most evil; and the road
that from Beleriand thither came
he watched with sleepless eyes of flame.                                2055
(From the North there led no other way,
save east where the Gorge of Aglon lay,
and that dark path of hurrying dread
which only in need the Orcs would tread
through Deadly Nightshade's awful gloom                                 2060
where Taur-na-Fuin's branches loom;
and Aglon led to Doriath,
and Fëanor's sons watched o'er that path.)

   Men called him Thû, and as a god

in after days beneath his rod                              2065
bewildered bowed to him, and made
his ghastly temples in the shade.
Not yet by Men enthralled adored,
now was he Morgoth's mightiest lord,
Master of Wolves, whose shivering howl         2070
for ever echoed in the hills, and foul
enchantments and dark sigaldry
did weave and wield. In glamoury
that necromancer held his hosts
of phantoms and of wandering ghosts,          2075
of misbegotten or spell-wronged
monsters that about him thronged,
working his bidding dark and vile:
the werewolves of the Wizard's Isle.

   From Thû their coming was not hid;      2080
and though beneath the eaves they slid
of the forest's gloomy-hanging boughs,
he saw them afar, and wolves did rouse:
'Go! fetch me those sneaking Orcs,' he said,
'that fare thus strangely, as if in dread,    2085
and do not come, as all Orcs use
and are commanded, to bring me news
of all their deeds, to me, to Thû.'

   From his tower he gazed, and in him grew
suspicion and a brooding thought,              2090
waiting, leering, till they were brought.
Now ringed about with wolves they stand,
and fear their doom. Alas! the land,
the land of Narog left behind!
Foreboding evil weights their mind,            2095
as downcast, halting, they must go
and cross the stony bridge of woe
to Wizard's Isle, and to the throne
there fashioned of blood-darkened stone.

   'Where have ye been? What have ye seen?'     2100

   'In Elfinesse; and tears and distress,
the fire blowing and the blood flowing,
these have we seen, there have we been.
Thirty we slew and their bodies threw

in a dark pit. The ravens sit                                  2105
and the owl cries where our swath lies.'

'Come, tell me true, O Morgoth's thralls,
what then in Elfinesse befalls?
What of Nargothrond? Who reigneth there?
Into that realm did your feet dare?'                           2110

'Only its borders did we dare.
There reigns King Felagund the fair.'

'Then heard ye not that he is gone,
that Celegorm sits his throne upon?'

'That is not true! If he is gone,                              2115
then Orodreth sits his throne upon.'

'Sharp are your ears, swift have they got
tidings of realms ye entered not!
What are your names, O spearmen bold?
Who your captain, ye have not told.'                           2120

'Nereb and Dungalef and warriors ten,
so we are called, and dark our den
under the mountains. Over the waste
we march on an errand of need and haste.
Boldog the captain awaits us there                             2125
where fires from under smoke and flare.'

'Boldog, I heard, was lately slain
warring on the borders of that domain
where Robber Thingol and outlaw folk
cringe and crawl beneath elm and oak                           2130
in drear Doriath. Heard ye not then
of that pretty fay, of Lúthien?
Her body is fair, very white and fair.
Morgoth would possess her in his lair.
Boldog he sent, but Boldog was slain:                          2135
strange ye were not in Boldog's train.
    Nereb looks fierce, his frown is grim.
Little Lúthien! What troubles him?
Why laughs he not to think of his lord
crushing a maiden in his hoard,                                2140
that foul should be what once was clean,
that dark should be where light has been?'

Whom do ye serve, Light or Mirk?
Who is the maker of mightiest work?
Who is the king of earthly kings,                    2145
the greatest giver of gold and rings?
Who is the master of the wide earth?
Who despoiled them of their mirth,
the greedy Gods? Repeat your vows,
Orcs of Bauglir! Do not bend your brows!             2150
Death to light, to law, to love!
Cursed be moon and stars above!
May darkness everlasting old
that waits outside in surges cold
drown Manwë, Varda, and the sun!                     2155
May all in hatred be begun,
and all in evil ended be,
in the moaning of the endless Sea!'

But no true Man nor Elf yet free
would ever speak that blasphemy,                     2160
and Beren muttered: 'Who is Thû
to hinder work that is to do?
Him we serve not, nor to him owe
obeisance, and we now would go.'

Thû laughed: 'Patience! Not very long               2165
shall ye abide. But first a song
I will sing to you, to ears intent.'
Then his flaming eyes he on them bent,
and darkness black fell round them all.
Only they saw as through a pall                      2170
of eddying smoke those eyes profound
in which their senses choked and drowned.
He chanted a song of wizardry,
of piercing, opening, of treachery,
revealing, uncovering, betraying.                    2175
Then sudden Felagund there swaying
sang in answer a song of staying,
resisting, battling against power,
of secrets kept, strength like a tower,
and trust unbroken, freedom, escape;                2180
of changing and of shifting shape,
of snares eluded, broken traps,
the prison opening, the chain that snaps.

Backwards and forwards swayed their song.
Reeling and foundering, as ever more strong          2185
Thû's chanting swelled, Felagund fought,
and all the magic and might he brought
of Elfinesse into his words.
Softly in the gloom they heard the birds
singing afar in Nargothrond,                         2190
the sighing of the sea beyond,
beyond the western world, on sand,
on sand of pearls in Elvenland.

Then the gloom gathered: darkness growing
in Valinor, the red blood flowing                    2195
beside the sea, where the Gnomes slew
the Foamriders, and stealing drew
their white ships with their white sails
from lamplit havens. The wind wails.
The wolf howls. The ravens flee.                     2200
The ice mutters in the mouths of the sea.
The captives sad in Angband mourn.
Thunder rumbles, the fires burn,
a vast smoke gushes out, a roar –
and Felagund swoons upon the floor.                  2205

Behold! they are in their own fair shape,
fairskinned, brighteyed. No longer gape
Orclike their mouths; and now they stand
betrayed into the wizard's hand.
Thus came they unhappy into woe,                     2210
to dungeons no hope nor glimmer know,
where chained in chains that eat the flesh
and woven in webs of strangling mesh
they lay forgotten, in despair.

Yet not all unavailing were                          2215
the spells of Felagund; for Thû
neither their names nor purpose knew.
These much he pondered and bethought,
and in their woeful chains them sought,
and threatened all with dreadful death,              2220
if one would not with traitor's breath
reveal this knowledge. Wolves should come
and slow devour them one by one

before the others' eyes, and last
should one alone be left aghast,                    2225
then in a place of horror hung
with anguish should his limbs be wrung,
in the bowels of the earth be slow
endlessly, cruelly, put to woe
and torment, till he all declared.                  2230

Even as he threatened, so it fared.
From time to time in the eyeless dark
two eyes would grow, and they would hark
to frightful cries, and then a sound
of rending, a slavering on the ground,              2235
and blood flowing they would smell.
But none would yield, and none would tell.

# NOTES

1943    Against the end of this line is written the date 'March 30
        1928'. The previous date was 29 March 1928 at line 1736.
2023    (and subsequently) *Broseliand* A, and B as typed.
2026    *Deadly Night*] *Tangled Night* A, and B as typed. Cf.
        *Deadly Nightshade* as a name of Taur-na-Fuin in *The
        Children of Húrin* (p. 55) and at line 2060 in the present
        Canto.
2047    *fields of drouth*: the expression *Plains of Drouth* occurs in
        *The Children of Húrin*, p. 36, line 826.
2056–63 These lines are marked with an X and a sign for deletion in
        the B-text, probably not on account of anything in their
        content but because my father felt them to be intrusive.
2064–6  Emended in B to:

> Gnomes called him Gorthû, as a god
> in after days beneath his rod
> bewildered they bowed to him, and made

(*Sauron* was first substituted for *Thû*. *Men* is written beside
*they* in line 2066.) *Thû* > *Gorthû* at all subsequent occurrences in this Canto, or the name avoided by substitution of
pronoun or article; thus 2088 *of all their deeds to me,
Gorthû*; 2161–2 *Doth Gorthû / now hinder work*; 2165
*He laughed*; 2186 *the chanting*; etc.

This change is difficult to date, but was made when
*Gnomes* was still employed (2064). In Canto VIII *Thû* was
left unchanged, and subsequently, until 3290, which was
emended to *where Gorthû reigned*; at the end of the poem
(3947, 3951) *Thû* was changed to *Sauron*.

2100–6   On the changed metre of these lines see the Commentary.

2114   After this line is written the date 'March 31st' (i.e. 1928).
The previous date was 30 March 1928 at line 1943.

2121   *Nereb and Dungalef*: emended in B to *Wrath and Hate*, at
the same time as *Thû* > *Gorthû*.

2137   *Nereb looks fierce*: emended in B to *Fierce is your chief*.

2155   *Bridhil* A, and B as typed; the change to *Varda* made at the
same time as *Thû* to *Gorthû*. Cf. note to line 1620.

2175–7   The three rhyming lines go back through A to the original
draft.

2193   *Elvenland* is an emendation to B *Fairyland*.

## Commentary on Canto VII

The plot-outline 'Synopsis I' for the narrative in this Canto has already
been given (pp. 219–20). 'Synopsis II' continues from the point reached
on p. 221.

They ambush an Orc-band, and disguising themselves in the raiment and fashion of the slain, march on Northward. Between the
Shadowy Mountains and the Forest of Night, where the young Sirion
flows in the narrowing valley, they come upon the *werewolves*, and
the host of Thû Lord of Wolves. They are taken before Thû, and after
a contest of riddling questions and answers are revealed as spies, but
Beren is taken as a Gnome, and that Felagund is King of Nargothrond
remains hidden.

They are placed in a deep dungeon. Thû desires to discover their
purpose and real names and vows death, one by one, and torment to
the last one, if they will not reveal them. From time to time a great
werewolf [*struck through*: Thû in disguise] comes and devours one
of the companions.

This is obviously the narrative basis for Canto VII, and the story here
reaches its final form. There may seem to be a difference between the
outline and the Lay, in that the former says that 'after a contest of
riddling questions and answers they are revealed as spies', whereas in the
latter Felagund is overcome by song of greater power. In fact, the
riddling contest is present, but seems not to have been fully developed.
In the original draft my father scribbled the following note before he
wrote the passage lines 2100 ff.:

Riddling questions. Where have you been, who have you slain? Thirty men. Who reigns in Nargothrond? Who is captain of Orcs? Who wrought the world? Who is king &c. They show Elfin [?bias] and too little knowledge of Angband, too much of Elfland. Thû and Felagund . . . . . enchantments against one another and Thû's slowly win, till they stand revealed as Elves.

Lines 2100–6 are in a changed metre, especially suitable to a riddle contest, and their content (the reply to Thû's question 'Where have ye been? What have ye seen?') is riddling ('misleading accuracy'). But after this the verse returns to the common metre, and the riddling element disappears (except in *dark our den / under the mountains*). The name *Dungalef* (2121), though it sounds Orcish enough, was an oddly transparent device, since *Felagund* had just been mentioned; but it succeeded (2217). No doubt Thû's ponderings on the matter were too subtle.

This is the first full portrait of Thû, who emerges as a being of great power, far advanced in sorcery, and is indeed here called 'necromancer' (2074). Here also is the first suggestion that his history would extend far beyond the tale of Beren and Lúthien, when 'in after days' Men would worship him, and build 'his ghastly temples in the shade'.

It is in this Canto, also, that the island in the river Sirion (not actually mentioned in Synopsis II) makes its first appearance, together with a mention of the origin of the fortress:

> An elven watchtower had it been,
> and strong it was, and still was fair.          (2041–2)

My father's drawing (*Pictures by J. R. R. Tolkien*, no. 36) was made at Lyme Regis in Dorset in July 1928, less than four months after these lines were written; and in the drawing the caves scooped by the waters in the edges of the island (lines 2037–8) can be seen.

The Shadowy Mountains referred to in Synopsis II and in the poem are no longer the Mountains of Terror (Ered Gorgoroth), as they were at lines 386, 1318 (see pp. 170–1). In Synopsis II it is said that the young Sirion flows in the narrowing valley between the Shadowy Mountains and the Forest of Night (Taur-na-Fuin), and in the poem Ivrin's lake mirrors

> the pallid faces bare and grim
> of Shadowy Mountains neath the moon          (1939–40)

as in *The Children of Húrin* (p. 62, lines 1581–2). Thus the term now reverts to its meaning in the alliterative poem, a meaning that it would henceforward retain. It is also to be noted that this mountain-range is 'northward-bending' (2030).

The lines concerning Ivrin in *The Children of Húrin* (1594–7):

> newborn Narog,     nineteen fathoms
> o'er a flickering force     falls in wonder,

>     and a glimmering goblet    with glass-lucent
>     fountains fills he    by his freshets carven

are echoed in *The Lay of Leithian* (1934–6):

>     the flickering falls, whose freshets sheer
>     a glimmering goblet glassy-clear
>     with crystal waters fill . . .

A new feature of the northern lands appears in this Canto: the Gorge of Aglon (2057), already placed (as other evidence shows) at the eastern end of Taur-na-Fuin; and line 2063 gives the first indication that this region was the territory of the Fëanorians.

The raid of the Orc-captain Boldog into Doriath, seeking to capture Lúthien for Morgoth, was an important element in the history of this time, though later it disappeared and there is no trace of it in *The Silmarillion*. Discussion of it is postponed till later in the *Lay of Leithian*, but it may be noticed here that an early reference to it is found in *The Children of Húrin* (p. 16 lines 392–4, p. 117 lines 764–6). There it was Thû himself who was bidden by Morgoth *go ravage the realm    of the robber Thingol.*

The term *Foamriders*, used of the Third Kindred of the Elves in line 2197, is found earlier in the alliterative *Flight of the Noldoli* (see p. 140).

# VIII

>     Hounds there were in Valinor
>     with silver collars. Hart and boar,
>     the fox and hare and nimble roe                    2240
>     there in the forests green did go.
>     Oromë was the lord divine
>     of all those woods. The potent wine
>     went in his halls and hunting song.
>     The Gnomes anew have named him long              2245
>     Tavros, the God whose horns did blow
>     over the mountains long ago;
>     who alone of Gods had loved the world
>     before the banners were unfurled
>     of Moon and Sun; and shod with gold              2250
>     were his great horses. Hounds untold
>     baying in woods beyond the West

of race immortal he possessed:
grey and limber, black and strong,
white with silken coats and long,                    2255
brown and brindled, swift and true
as arrow from a bow of yew;
their voices like the deeptoned bells
that ring in Valmar's citadels,
their eyes like living jewels, their teeth            2260
like ruel-bone. As sword from sheath
they flashed and fled from leash to scent
for Tavros' joy and merriment.

In Tavros' friths and pastures green
had Huan once a young whelp been.                     2265
He grew the swiftest of the swift,
and Oromë gave him as a gift
to Celegorm, who loved to follow
the great God's horn o'er hill and hollow.
Alone of hounds of the Land of Light,                 2270
when sons of Fëanor took to flight
and came into the North, he stayed
beside his master. Every raid
and every foray wild he shared,
and into mortal battle dared.                         2275
Often he saved his Gnomish lord
from Orc and wolf and leaping sword.
A wolf-hound, tireless, grey and fierce
he grew; his gleaming eyes would pierce
all shadows and all mist, the scent                   2280
moons old he found through fen and bent,
through rustling leaves and dusty sand;
all paths of wide Beleriand
he knew. But wolves, he loved them best;
he loved to find their throats and wrest              2285
their snarling lives and evil breath.
The packs of Thû him feared as Death.
No wizardry, nor spell, nor dart,
no fang, nor venom devil's art
could brew had harmed him; for his weird              2290
was woven. Yet he little feared
that fate decreed and known to all:
before the mightiest he should fall,

before the mightiest wolf alone
that ever was whelped in cave of stone.                    2295

Hark! afar in Nargothrond,
far over Sirion and beyond,
there are dim cries and horns blowing,
and barking hounds through the trees going.
    The hunt is up, the woods are stirred.      2300
Who rides to-day? Ye have not heard
that Celegorm and Curufin
have loosed their dogs? With merry din
they mounted ere the sun arose,
and took their spears and took their bows.                 2305
The wolves of Thû of late have dared
both far and wide. Their eyes have glared
by night across the roaring stream
of Narog. Doth their master dream,
perchance, of plots and counsels deep,                     2310
of secrets that the Elf-lords keep,
of movements in the Gnomish realm
and errands under beech and elm?

    Curufin spake: 'Good brother mine,
I like it not. What dark design                            2315
doth this portend? These evil things,
we swift must end their wanderings!
And more, 'twould please my heart full well
to hunt a while and wolves to fell.'
And then he leaned and whispered low                       2320
that Orodreth was a dullard slow;
long time it was since the king had gone,
and rumour or tidings came there none.
    'At least thy profit it would be
to know whether dead he is or free;                        2325
to gather thy men and thy array.
"I go to hunt" then thou wilt say,
and men will think that Narog's good
ever thou heedest. But in the wood
things may be learned; and if by grace,                    2330
by some blind fortune he retrace
his footsteps mad, and if he bear
a Silmaril – I need declare
no more in words; but one by right

is thine (and ours), the jewel of light;                    2335
another may be won – a throne.
The eldest blood our house doth own.'

    Celegorm listened. Nought he said,
but forth a mighty host he led;
and Huan leaped at the glad sounds,                         2340
the chief and captain of his hounds.
    Three days they ride by holt and hill
the wolves of Thû to hunt and kill,
and many a head and fell of grey
they take, and many drive away,                             2345
till nigh to the borders in the West
of Doriath a while they rest.

    There were dim cries and horns blowing,
and barking dogs through the woods going.
The hunt was up. The woods were stirred,                    2350
and one there fled like startled bird,
and fear was in her dancing feet.
She knew not who the woods did beat.
Far from her home, forwandered, pale,
she flitted ghostlike through the vale;                     2355
ever her heart bade her up and on,
but her limbs were worn, her eyes were wan.
    The eyes of Huan saw a shade
wavering, darting down a glade
like a mist of evening snared by day                        2360
and hasting fearfully away.
He bayed, and sprang with sinewy limb
to chase the shy thing strange and dim.
On terror's wings, like a butterfly
pursued by a sweeping bird on high,                         2365
she fluttered hither, darted there,
now poised, now flying through the air –
in vain. At last against a tree
she leaned and panted. Up leaped he.
No word of magic gasped with woe,                           2370
no elvish mystery she did know
or had entwined in raiment dark
availed against that hunter stark,
whose old immortal race and kind
no spells could ever turn or bind.                          2375

Huan alone that she ever met
she never in enchantment set
nor bound with spells. But loveliness
and gentle voice and pale distress
and eyes like starlight dimmed with tears          2380
tamed him that death nor monster fears.

    Lightly he lifted her, light he bore
his trembling burden. Never before
had Celegorm beheld such prey:
'What hast thou brought, good Huan say!          2385
Dark-elvish maid, or wraith, or fay?
Not such to hunt we came today.'

    ''Tis Lúthien of Doriath,'
the maiden spake. 'A wandering path
far from the Wood-Elves' sunny glades          2390
she sadly winds, where courage fades
and hope grows faint.' And as she spoke
down she let slip her shadowy cloak,
and there she stood in silver and white.
Her starry jewels twinkled bright          2395
in the risen sun like morning dew;
the lilies gold on mantle blue
gleamed and glistened. Who could gaze
on that fair face without amaze?
Long did Curufin look and stare.          2400
The perfume of her flower-twined hair,
her lissom limbs, her elvish face,
smote to his heart, and in that place
enchained he stood. 'O maiden royal,
O lady fair, wherefore in toil          2405
and lonely journey dost thou go?
What tidings dread of war and woe
In Doriath have betid? Come tell!
For fortune thee hath guided well;
friends thou hast found,' said Celegorm,          2410
and gazed upon her elvish form.

    In his heart him thought her tale unsaid
he knew in part, but nought she read
of guile upon his smiling face.
    'Who are ye then, the lordly chase          2415

that follow in this perilous wood?'
she asked; and answer seeming-good
they gave. 'Thy servants, lady sweet,
lords of Nargothrond thee greet,
and beg that thou wouldst with them go          2420
back to their hills, forgetting woe
a season, seeking hope and rest.
And now to hear thy tale were best.'

So Lúthien tells of Beren's deeds
in northern lands, how fate him leads          2425
to Doriath, of Thingol's ire,
the dreadful errand that her sire
decreed for Beren. Sign nor word
the brothers gave that aught they heard
that touched them near. Of her escape          2430
and the marvellous mantle she did shape
she lightly tells, but words her fail
recalling sunlight in the vale,
moonlight, starlight in Doriath,
ere Beren took the perilous path.          2435
        'Need, too, my lords, there is of haste!
No time in ease and rest to waste.
For days are gone now since the queen,
Melian whose heart hath vision keen,
looking afar me said in fear          2440
that Beren lived in bondage drear.
The Lord of Wolves hath prisons dark,
chains and enchantments cruel and stark,
and there entrapped and languishing
doth Beren lie – if direr thing          2445
hath not brought death or wish for death':
then gasping woe bereft her breath.

        To Celegorm said Curufin
apart and low: 'Now news we win
of Felagund, and now we know          2450
wherefore Thû's creatures prowling go',
and other whispered counsels spake,
and showed him what answer he should make.
        'Lady,' said Celegorm, 'thou seest
we go a-hunting roaming beast,          2455
and though our host is great and bold,

'tis ill prepared the wizard's hold
and island fortress to assault.
Deem not our hearts or wills at fault.
Lo! here our chase we now forsake                    2460
and home our swiftest road we take,
counsel and aid there to devise
for Beren that in anguish lies.'

To Nargothrond they with them bore
Lúthien, whose heart misgave her sore.               2465
Delay she feared; each moment pressed
upon her spirit, yet she guessed
they rode not as swiftly as they might.
Ahead leaped Huan day and night,
and ever looking back his thought                    2470
was troubled. What his master sought,
and why he rode not like the fire,
why Curufin looked with hot desire
on Lúthien, he pondered deep,
and felt some evil shadow creep                      2475
of ancient curse o'er Elfinesse.
His heart was torn for the distress
of Beren bold, and Lúthien dear,
and Felagund who knew no fear.

In Nargothrond the torches flared                    2480
and feast and music were prepared.
Lúthien feasted not but wept.
Her ways were trammelled; closely kept
she might not fly. Her magic cloak
was hidden, and no prayer she spoke                  2485
was heeded, nor did answer find
her eager questions. Out of mind,
it seemed, were those afar that pined
in anguish and in dungeons blind
in prison and in misery.                             2490
Too late she knew their treachery.
It was not hid in Nargothrond
that Fëanor's sons her held in bond,
who Beren heeded not, and who
had little cause to wrest from Thû                   2495
the king they loved not and whose quest
old vows of hatred in their breast

had roused from sleep. Orodreth knew
the purpose dark they would pursue:
King Felagund to leave to die,                                    2500
and with King Thingol's blood ally
the house of Fëanor by force
or treaty. But to stay their course
he had no power, for all his folk
the brothers had yet beneath their yoke,                          2505
and all yet listened to their word.
Orodreth's counsel no man heard;
their shame they crushed, and would not heed
the tale of Felagund's dire need.

    At Lúthien's feet there day by day                            2510
and at night beside her couch would stay
Huan the hound of Nargothrond;
and words she spoke to him soft and fond:
'O Huan, Huan, swiftest hound
that ever ran on mortal ground,                                  2515
what evil doth thy lords possess
to heed no tears nor my distress?
Once Barahir all men above
good hounds did cherish and did love;
once Beren in the friendless North,                              2520
when outlaw wild he wandered forth,
had friends unfailing among things
with fur and fell and feathered wings,
and among the spirits that in stone
in mountains old and wastes alone                               2525
still dwell. But now nor Elf nor Man,
none save the child of Melian,
remembers him who Morgoth fought
and never to thraldom base was brought.'

    Nought said Huan; but Curufin                                2530
thereafter never near might win
to Lúthien, nor touch that maid,
but shrank from Huan's fangs afraid.
    Then on a night when autumn damp
was swathed about the glimmering lamp                            2535
of the wan moon, and fitful stars
were flying seen between the bars
of racing cloud, when winter's horn

already wound in trees forlorn,
lo! Huan was gone. Then Lúthien lay                 2540
fearing new wrong, till just ere day,
when all is dead and breathless still
and shapeless fears the sleepless fill,
a shadow came along the wall.
Then something let there softly fall                2545
her magic cloak beside her couch.
Trembling she saw the great hound crouch
beside her, heard a deep voice swell
as from a tower a far slow bell.

    Thus Huan spake, who never before               2550
had uttered words, and but twice more
did speak in elven tongue again:
'Lady beloved, whom all Men,
whom Elfinesse, and whom all things
with fur and fell and feathered wings              2555
should serve and love – arise! away!
Put on thy cloak! Before the day
comes over Nargothrond we fly
to Northern perils, thou and I.'
And ere he ceased he counsel wrought               2560
for achievement of the thing they sought.
There Lúthien listened in amaze,
and softly on Huan did she gaze.
Her arms about his neck she cast –
in friendship that to death should last.           2565

# NOTES

2246    *Tavros* not emended, nor at lines 2263–4 (see p. 195, note to
        lines 891, 904).
2248    *of Gods had loved* B] *of Valar loved* A
2283    *Beleriand*] *Broseliand* A, and B as typed.
2385    After this line is written the date 'April 2nd'. The previous
        date was 31 March 1928 at line 2114.
2423    After this line is written the date 'April 3rd'. The previous
        date was 2 April 1928 at line 2385.
2442–4  Cf. lines 1246–8.

2484–5    The reference to the hiding of Lúthien's cloak is not in A.
2522–6    Cf. lines 349–53. Line 2523 is repeated at 2555.
  2551    *But twice more* emendation in B; *nor ever more* A, *but once more* B as typed.
  2552    *elven*: *elfin* B, but since *elfin* is changed at almost every occurrence I have done so here.

## Commentary on Canto VIII

The development of the narrative of this Canto from the *Tale of Tinúviel* to *The Silmarillion* can be followed step by step. The first stage is seen in the very brief words of the 'Sketch', following on the passage given on p. 220.

> Lúthien is imprisoned by Thingol, but escapes and goes in search of Beren. With the aid of Huan lord of dogs she rescues Beren [i.e. from 'Thû the hunter'], and gains entrance to Angband . . .

This is too compressed to reveal what ideas underlay it; but at least it is clear that Huan was still independent of any master. In the earliest map Huan is assigned a territory (south and east of Ivrin), and this clearly belongs with the old conception.

Synopsis I, a little later than the 'Sketch' (see p. 220), continues from the point reached on pp. 219–20:

> Tinúviel flies in her magic robe, she meets Celegorm out hunting, and is pursued by him and captured by Huan his dog and hurt. [*Struck out*: In redress he offers to help] He offers redress – but cannot help; he lent his Gnomes to Beren and all perished, and so must Beren. Huan goes with her.

A little later in the outline it is said:

> It was written in the fate of Huan that he could only be slain by a wolf.

At this stage, where Celegorm was the ruler of Nargothrond to whom Beren went in his trouble, Celegorm 'lent his Gnomes' to Beren;* Lúthien fleeing from Doriath was pursued by Celegorm while out hunting and was hurt by Huan, who now first appears as Celegorm's hound. Here there is no suggestion of evil behaviour towards her (and no mention of Curufin); Celegorm is unable to assist her, further than he has already assisted Beren, but Huan goes with her on her quest: was this the 'redress' for her hurt that Celegorm offered her? It is not said. It is clear that the position of the ruler of Nargothrond as a son of Fëanor,

---

* If the previous passage of Synopsis I (p. 219) is strictly interpreted Celegorm went with Beren from Nargothrond, but this is obviously not meant: my father must have struck out more than he intended to. It is now clear that in this form of the story Celegorm disguised Beren and gave him guides.

1344444444444

444

bound by the Oath, must have developed quite differently if this form of the story had been retained, since he was also sworn to aid the kin of Barahir (see below, p. 247).

In Synopsis II, given on p. 233 to the point equivalent to the end of Canto VII, the plot reaches almost to its development in the present Canto of the Lay; but this was achieved in stages, and the original text of the outline was so much changed and extended by later alterations that it would be extremely difficult to follow if set out as hitherto. I give it therefore in two forms. As first written it read:

> Curufin and Celegorm go hunting with all their hounds. Huan the sleepless is the chief. He is proof against magic sleep or death – it is his fate to be slain only by the 'greatest wolf'. They espy Lúthien who flees, but is caught by Huan whom she cannot enchant. The hound bears her to Celegorm, who learns her purpose. Hearing who she is, and falling in love with her he takes away her magic cloak, and holds her captive.
>
> At last he yields to her tears to let her free and give her back her cloak, but he will not aid her because of his oath. Nor does he desire to rescue Felagund, since he is now all-powerful in Nargothrond. She departs from Celegorm. But Huan has become devoted to her, and goes with her.

At this stage, the hunting evidently had no significance in itself: it was the device by which Huan (already in Synopsis I the hound of Celegorm, and with a peculiar fate) was to be brought to accompany Lúthien, an essential feature going back to the *Tale of Tinúviel*. There is no mention of her being hurt by Huan, as there is in Synopsis I (and so no question of 'redress'); and here Celegorm falls in love with her and therefore holds her captive. But this is only for a time; he yields to her prayer and gives her back her cloak, though because of his oath he will not aid her; and the evil motive of his desiring to let Felagund perish so that he may retain power in Nargothrond appears. Lúthien leaves Celegorm; Huan goes with her, as in Synopsis I, but the motive is now explicitly the hound's love for her.

After emendation the outline read as follows:

> Because of the disguise of Felagund Thû is suspicious and his wolves fare far abroad. Celegorm seizes pretext for a wolfhunt.
>
> Curufin and Celegorm go wolf-hunting guilefully (really to intercept Felagund*) with all their hounds. Huan the sleepless is the chief. (Huan came with him [i.e. Celegorm] from Tavros' halls.) He is proof against magic sleep or death – it is his fate to be slain only by the

---

*i.e., if he should return to Nargothrond; see lines 2330ff.

'greatest wolf'. They espy Lúthien who flees, but is caught by Huan whom she cannot enchant. The hound bears her to Celegorm, who learns her purpose. Hearing who she is, and falling in love with her, Curufin takes away her magic cloak, and holds her captive. Although she tells him Melian's words and that Felagund and Beren are in Thû's power he won't attempt a rescue even of Felagund. (*Marginal note*: It is Curufin who put evil into Celegorm's heart.)

In spite of her tears to let her free and give her back her cloak he will not aid her because of his oath and love. Nor does he desire to rescue Felagund, since he is now all-powerful in Nargothrond. But Huan has become devoted to her, and aids her to escape *without her cloak*.

The hunting of Celegorm and Curufin is now given a sinister import, and is related to the wolves of Thû who 'fare far abroad'. Huan's Valinórean ancestry appears; and Curufin becomes the evil genius of the brothers, and also the lover of Lúthien. Lúthien is now held prisoner in Nargothrond until she escapes by the aid of Huan – but she does not get back her cloak.

Which of the brothers is referred to in the latter part of the emended outline is not clear: as originally written it was Celegorm throughout, but by the change of 'falling in love with her he takes away her magic cloak' to 'falling in love with her Curufin takes away her magic cloak' Curufin becomes the antecedent to all that follows. Whether my father really intended this is hard to say.

When he came to write Canto VIII, on the basis of this emended outline, some further change took place – notably, the return to Lúthien by Huan of her cloak before they left Nargothrond; and the element added to the outline 'It is Curufin who put evil into Celegorm's heart' is expanded. It is now Curufin who suggests the wolfhunt, with its secret intention, and line 2453 shows him as the subtler and more longheaded schemer, standing behind his brother and prompting him – it is clear from lines 2324 ff. that Celegorm has some authority – or is felt by Curufin to have some authority – that Curufin lacks.

Curufin expresses his contempt for Orodreth ('a dullard slow', 2321), and this is the first hint of that weakening of Orodreth's character to which I referred earlier (p. 91). Of course the emergence of Felagund pushed him in any case into a subordinate rôle, as the younger brother of the founder of Nargothrond, and the concomitant development whereby Celegorm and Curufin remained in Nargothrond as powerful interlopers weakened his position still further. It may be that the position imposed on him by the movements in the legend led to the conclusion that he cannot have been made of very stern stuff.

These subtleties in the relationship between Celegorm and Curufin are passed over in the prose version (*The Silmarillion* pp. 172–3), and there is no suggestion that Curufin was the more sinister of the pair, and the prime mover in their machinations. Celegorm recovers his earlier rôle as the one who was enamoured of Lúthien. In the Lay appears the motive, not mentioned in Synopsis II, of the intention of Celegorm and Curufin to ally themselves with 'King Thingol's blood' by the forced marriage of Lúthien (lines 2498–2503); and this reappears in *The Silmarillion*, where it is to Celegorm that Thingol is to be compelled to give her.

The process whereby the legends of Beren and Lúthien on the one hand and of Nargothrond on the other became entwined is now (to this point in the story) almost complete, and this is a convenient point to recapitulate the main shifts in its evolution.

In the *Lost Tales* Orodreth was lord of the Rodothlim, a people of the Gnomes, in the caves that were to become Nargothrond, but Beren had no connection with the Rodothlim (and Huan had no master). Then Celegorm appeared as the Gnomish prince rescued by Beren's father (Egnor > Barahir) in the battle that afterwards became the Battle of Sudden Flame, to whom he swore an oath of abiding friendship and aid; and Celegorm and Curufin became the founders of Nargothrond after the battle (p. 84). It was to Celegorm that Beren therefore came seeking aid; and Celegorm plays the later role of Felagund in Synopsis I to the extent that he gives him Gnomish guides. Lúthien fleeing from Doriath is caught by Huan, now the hound of Celegorm, and hurt, but this has no outcome beyond the departure of Lúthien in Huan's company (Synopsis I).

The most major change came with the emergence of Felagund and his taking over Celegorm's part both as founder of Nargothrond and as the one rescued by Barahir. Orodreth became his younger brother, the only other son of Finrod to survive the battle in which the Siege of Angband ended. But Celegorm's association with Nargothrond was not abandoned; and his powerful presence there together with that of his brother Curufin – again as a result of the battle – introduces the motive of conflict between the Fëanorians and the King, each held by their own oaths. This conflict had been present in the earlier plot, but there it was a conflict within Celegorm's mind alone, since he had sworn both oaths; there is however no real evidence as to how my father would have treated this, unless we assume from his giving Gnomish guides to Beren in Synopsis I that he gave precedence to his oath to Barahir.

When Lúthien is captured by Huan and taken to Nargothrond she is caught up in the ambitions of Celegorm and Curufin, and indeed her capture itself is made to come about from their evil intentions towards Felagund and determination to prevent his return.

Of Huan it is told in the Lay that he was the only hound of Valinor to come east over the sea (2270). His fate that he should meet death only when 'he encountered the mightiest wolf that would ever walk the world'

(*The Silmarillion* p. 173) appears (already referred to in Synopsis II, pp. 245–6), but it is not said as it is in *The Silmarillion* that this was because as the hound of Celegorm he came under the Doom of the Noldor. In the A-text of the Lay (note to line 2551) he spoke only once in his life, in the B-text twice; but this was emended to three times, as still in *The Silmarillion*.

The statement in lines 2248–50 that Oromë

> alone of Gods had loved the world
> before the banners were unfurled
> of Moon and Sun

seems to forget Yavanna: see the tale of *The Chaining of Melko* (I. 98–9) and *The Silmarillion* pp. 40–1.

The *dim cries and horns blowing, / and barking hounds through the trees going* (lines 2298–9, repeated with variations in lines 2348–9) derive from the Middle English Lay of Sir Orfeo:

> With dim cri & bloweing
> & houndes also wiþ him berking.*

# IX

> In Wizard's Isle still lay forgot,
> enmeshed and tortured in that grot
> cold, evil, doorless, without light,
> and blank-eyed stared at endless night
> two comrades. Now alone they were.    2570
> The others lived no more, but bare
> their broken bones would lie and tell
> how ten had served their master well.
>
> To Felagund then Beren said:
> "Twere little loss if I were dead,    2575
> and I am minded all to tell,
> and thus, perchance, from this dark hell
> thy life to loose. I set thee free

---

*Auchinleck manuscript lines 285–6 (ed. A. J. Bliss, Oxford 1954, p. 26); cf. my father's translation (*Sir Gawain and the Green Knight, Pearl, and Sir Orfeo*, 1975):

> with blowing far and crying dim
> and barking hounds that were with him

from thine old oath, for more for me
hast thou endured than e'er was earned.'                    2580

    'A! Beren, Beren hast not learned
that promises of Morgoth's folk
are frail as breath. From this dark yoke
of pain shall neither ever go,
whether he learn our names or no,                    2585
with Thû's consent. Nay more, I think
yet deeper of torment we should drink,
knew he that son of Barahir
and Felagund were captive here,
and even worse if he should know                    2590
the dreadful errand we did go.'

    A devil's laugh they ringing heard
within their pit. 'True, true the word
I hear you speak,' a voice then said.
''Twere little loss if he were dead,                    2595
the outlaw mortal. But the king,
the Elf undying, many a thing
no man could suffer may endure.
Perchance, when what these walls immure
of dreadful anguish thy folk learn,                    2600
their king to ransom they will yearn
with gold and gem and high hearts cowed;
or maybe Celegorm the proud
will deem a rival's prison cheap,
and crown and gold himself will keep.                    2605
Perchance, the errand I shall know,
ere all is done, that ye did go.
The wolf is hungry, the hour is nigh;
no more need Beren wait to die.'

    The slow time passed. Then in the gloom                    2610
two eyes there glowed. He saw his doom,
Beren, silent, as his bonds he strained
beyond his mortal might enchained.
Lo! sudden there was rending sound
of chains that parted and unwound,                    2615
of meshes broken. Forth there leaped
upon the wolvish thing that crept
in shadow faithful Felagund,

careless of fang or venomed wound.
There in the dark they wrestled slow,                          2620
remorseless, snarling, to and fro,
teeth in flesh, gripe on throat,
fingers locked in shaggy coat,
spurning Beren who there lying
heard the werewolf gasping, dying.                             2625
Then a voice he heard: 'Farewell!
On earth I need no longer dwell,
friend and comrade, Beren bold.
My heart is burst, my limbs are cold.
Here all my power I have spent                                 2630
to break my bonds, and dreadful rent
of poisoned teeth is in my breast.
I now must go to my long rest
neath Timbrenting in timeless halls
where drink the Gods, where the light falls                    2635
upon the shining sea.' Thus died the king,
as elvish singers yet do sing.

There Beren lies. His grief no tear,
his despair no horror has nor fear,
waiting for footsteps, a voice, for doom.                      2640
Silences profounder than the tomb
of long-forgotten kings, neath years
and sands uncounted laid on biers
and buried everlasting-deep,
slow and unbroken round him creep.                             2645

The silences were sudden shivered
to silver fragments. Faint there quivered
a voice in song that walls of rock,
enchanted hill, and bar and lock,
and powers of darkness pierced with light.                     2650
He felt about him the soft night
of many stars, and in the air
were rustlings and a perfume rare;
the nightingales were in the trees,
slim fingers flute and viol seize                              2655
beneath the moon, and one more fair
than all there be or ever were
upon a lonely knoll of stone
in shimmering raiment danced alone.

Then in his dream it seemed he sang,                    2660
and loud and fierce his chanting rang,
old songs of battle in the North,
of breathless deeds, of marching forth
to dare uncounted odds and break
great powers, and towers, and strong walls shake; 2665
and over all the silver fire
that once Men named the Burning Briar,
the Seven Stars that Varda set
about the North, were burning yet,
a light in darkness, hope in woe,                    2670
the emblem vast of Morgoth's foe.

'Huan, Huan! I hear a song
far under welling, far but strong;
a song that Beren bore aloft.
I hear his voice, I have heard if oft                    2675
in dream and wandering.' Whispering low
thus Lúthien spake. On the bridge of woe
in mantle wrapped at dead of night
she sat and sang, and to its height
and to its depth the Wizard's Isle,                    2680
rock upon rock and pile on pile,
trembling echoed. The werewolves howled,
and Huan hidden lay and growled
watchful listening in the dark,
waiting for battle cruel and stark.                    2685

Thû heard that voice, and sudden stood
wrapped in his cloak and sable hood
in his high tower. He listened long,
and smiled, and knew that elvish song.
'A! little Lúthien! What brought                    2690
the foolish fly to web unsought?
Morgoth! a great and rich reward
to me thou wilt owe when to thy hoard
this jewel is added.' Down he went,
and forth his messengers he sent.                    2695

Still Lúthien sang. A creeping shape
with bloodred tongue and jaws agape
stole on the bridge; but she sang on
with trembling limbs and wide eyes wan.

The creeping shape leaped to her side,                          2700
and gasped, and sudden fell and died.
   And still they came, still one by one,
and each was seized, and there were none
returned with padding feet to tell
that a shadow lurketh fierce and fell                           2705
at the bridge's end, and that below
the shuddering waters loathing flow
o'er the grey corpses Huan killed.
   A mightier shadow slowly filled
the narrow bridge, a slavering hate,                            2710
an awful werewolf fierce and great:
pale Draugluin, the old grey lord
of wolves and beasts of blood abhorred,
that fed on flesh of Man and Elf
beneath the chair of Thû himself.                               2715

   No more in silence did they fight.
Howling and baying smote the night,
till back by the chair where he had fed
to die the werewolf yammering fled.
'Huan is there' he gasped and died,                             2720
and Thû was filled with wrath and pride.
'Before the mightiest he shall fall,
before the mightiest wolf of all',
so thought he now, and thought he knew
how fate long spoken should come true.                          2725
   Now there came slowly forth and glared
into the night a shape long-haired,
dank with poison, with awful eyes
wolvish, ravenous; but there lies
a light therein more cruel and dread                            2730
than ever wolvish eyes had fed.
More huge were its limbs, its jaws more wide,
its fangs more gleaming-sharp, and dyed
with venom, torment, and with death.
The deadly vapour of its breath                                 2735
swept on before it. Swooning dies
the song of Lúthien, and her eyes
are dimmed and darkened with a fear,
cold and poisonous and drear.

   Thus came Thû, as wolf more great                          2740

than e'er was seen from Angband's gate
to the burning south, than ever lurked
in mortal lands or murder worked.
Sudden he sprang, and Huan leaped
aside in shadow. On he swept                    2745
to Lúthien lying swooning faint.
To her drowning senses came the taint
of his foul breathing, and she stirred;
dizzily she spake a whispered word,
her mantle brushed across his face.             2750
He stumbled staggering in his pace.
Out leaped Huan. Back he sprang.
Beneath the stars there shuddering rang
the cry of hunting wolves at bay,
the tongue of hounds that fearless slay.        2755
Backward and forth they leaped and ran
feinting to flee, and round they span,
and bit and grappled, and fell and rose.
   Then suddenly Huan holds and throws
his ghastly foe; his throat he rends,           2760
choking his life. Not so it ends.
From shape to shape, from wolf to worm,
from monster to his own demon form,
Thû changes, but that desperate grip
he cannot shake, nor from it slip.              2765
No wizardry, nor spell, nor dart,
no fang, nor venom, nor devil's art
could harm that hound that hart and boar
had hunted once in Valinor.

   Nigh the foul spirit Morgoth made            2770
and bred of evil shuddering strayed
from its dark house, when Lúthien rose
and shivering looked upon his throes.

   'O demon dark, O phantom vile
of foulness wrought, of lies and guile,         2775
here shalt thou die, thy spirit roam
quaking back to thy master's home
his scorn and fury to endure;
thee he will in the bowels immure
of groaning earth, and in a hole               2780
everlastingly thy naked soul

shall wail and gibber – this shall be,
unless the keys thou render me
of thy black fortress, and the spell
that bindeth stone to stone thou tell,                2785
and speak the words of opening.'

   With gasping breath and shuddering
he spake, and yielded as he must,
and vanquished betrayed his master's trust.

   Lo! by the bridge a gleam of light,            2790
like stars descended from the night
to burn and tremble here below.
There wide her arms did Lúthien throw,
and called aloud with voice as clear
as still at whiles may mortal hear                    2795
long elvish trumpets o'er the hill
echo, when all the world is still.
   The dawn peered over mountains wan,
their grey heads silent looked thereon.
The hill trembled; the citadel                        2800
crumbled, and all its towers fell;
the rocks yawned and the bridge broke,
and Sirion spumed in sudden smoke.
   Like ghosts the owls were flying seen
hooting in the dawn, and bats unclean                 2805
went skimming dark through the cold airs
shrieking thinly to find new lairs
in Deadly Nightshade's branches dread.
The wolves whimpering and yammering fled
like dusky shadows. Out there creep                   2810
pale forms and ragged as from sleep,
crawling, and shielding blinded eyes:
the captives in fear and in surprise
from dolour long in clinging night
beyond all hope set free to light.                    2815

   A vampire shape with pinions vast
screeching leaped from the ground, and passed,
its dark blood dripping on the trees;
and Huan neath him lifeless sees
a wolvish corpse – for Thû had flown                  2820

to Taur-na-Fuin, a new throne
and darker stronghold there to build.
    The captives came and wept and shrilled
their piteous cries of thanks and praise.
But Lúthien anxious-gazing stays.           2825
Beren comes not. At length she said:
'Huan, Huan, among the dead
must we then find him whom we sought,
for love of whom we toiled and fought?'
    Then side by side from stone to stone     2830
o'er Sirion they climbed. Alone
unmoving they him found, who mourned
by Felagund, and never turned
to see what feet drew halting nigh.
'A! Beren, Beren!' came her cry,        2835
'almost too late have I thee found?
Alas! that here upon the ground
the noblest of the noble race
in vain thy anguish doth embrace!
Alas! in tears that we should meet      2840
who once found meeting passing sweet!'

    Her voice such love and longing filled
he raised his eyes, his mourning stilled,
and felt his heart new-turned to flame
for her that through peril to him came.    2845

    'O Lúthien, O Lúthien,
more fair than any child of Men,
O loveliest maid of Elfinesse,
what might of love did thee possess
to bring thee here to terror's lair!     2850
O lissom limbs and shadowy hair,
O flower-entwinéd brows so white,
O slender hands in this new light!'

    She found his arms and swooned away
just at the rising of the day.       2855

★

## NOTES

2637  *elfin* B, not here emended, but it is clear that the intention
was to change *elfin* to *elvish (elven)* in all cases.

2666–7  Cf. lines 377–9 and note. In the present passage A's reading
is as B.

2699  Line marked with an X on the B-text.

2712–13  These lines (referring to Draugluin) not in A.

2722–3  Cf. lines 2293–4.

2755  Line marked with an X on the B-text.

2766–7  Cf. lines 2288–9.

2769  After this line is written the date 'April 4th'. The previous
date was 3 April 1928 at line 2423.

2842  Cf. line 741.

2854–5  Cf. the ending of Canto III, lines 756–7.


### Commentary on Canto IX

Synopsis I continues from the point reached on p. 244:

> Huan goes with her. She goes to the castle of the Lord of Wolves and
> sings for him. The captives in the dungeons hear her.
>     It was written in the fate of Huan that he could only be slain by a
> wolf.
>     She tells (by arrangement) of the sickness of Huan and so induces
> the Lord of Wolves to go werewolf and seek him. The wolf-battle
> of the glade. The 'words of opening' wrung from the Lord of Wolves
> and the castle broken. Rescue of Beren.

Synopsis II is here less affected by later changes and can be given in a
single text (taking it up from the point reached on p. 246).

> But Huan has become devoted to her, and aids her to escape *without
> her cloak*. [*Bracketed*: He trails Beren and Felagund to the House of
> Thû.]
>     At last only Felagund and Beren remain. It is Beren's turn to be
> devoured. But Felagund bursts his bonds and wrestles with the were-
> wolf and slays him, but is killed. Beren is reserved for torment.
>     Lúthien sings outside the house [*added*: on the bridge of woe] of
> Thû and Beren hears her voice, and his answering song comes up from
> underground to Huan's ears.
>     Thû takes her inside. She tells him a twisted tale – by the desire of
> Huan, and because without her cloak she cannot enchant him. She
> tells of her bondage to Celegorm and her capture by Huan of whom she
> feigns hatred. Of all things in the world Thû hates Huan most. His
> weird to be slain only by the 'greatest wolf' is known. Lúthien says
> Huan is lying sick in the woods. Thû disguises himself as a mighty

werewolf and is led by her to where Huan is lying in ambush. [*Added*: But he purposes to make her a thrall.] There follows the battle of the werewolf. Huan slays Thû's companions and with his teeth in Thû's throat wrests in return for life 'the words of opening' from him. The house of Thû is broken, and the captives set free. Beren is found [*struck out*: and borne back to Nargothrond.]

There is also to be considered now another outline, 'Synopsis III', very hastily written and not entirely legible. This outline begins here and I follow it to the end of the narrative in this Canto.

Thû lies choking under Huan. Lúthien arouses. She says 'thou phantom made of foulness by Morgoth, thou shalt die and thy spirit go back in fear to Angband to meet thy master's scorn and languish in the dark bosom of the world, if the "spoken keys" of thy fortress are not yielded.'

With his gasping breath he says them. Lúthien standing on the bridge with her arms spread calls them aloud. The dawn comes pale over the mountains. The hill quivers and gapes, the towers fall, the bridge falls and block[s] Sirion on one side, the dungeons gape. The owls flee away like phantoms in the first light, great bats are seen skimming away to Taur-na-Fuin shrieking thinly. [*Added*: and one as large as an eagle leads them. The spirit of Thû. His body has a . . . . . . . . . . . . a wolf.] The wolves flee whimpering and yammering. Pale captives blinking in the light creep and crawl into the light. [*Struck out*: Beren comes forth.] No Beren. They seek for him and find him sitting beside Felagund.

These outlines are of great interest, since they show very clearly an intermediate stage in the evolution of the legend, between the original story of Tevildo Prince of Cats in the *Tale of Tinúviel* and the story of Thû in the *Lay of Leithian*. Still present is Lúthien's untrue tale that Huan is lying sick in the woods (see II. 26), and in Synopsis II Thû retains the (originally feline) Tevildo-trait of hating Huan more than any other creature in the world (II. 21). The old element of Tinúviel's entering the castle alone in order to inveigle Tevildo out of it, so that he may be attacked by Huan, was not yet abandoned – but in Synopsis II she does not have her cloak, and so cannot enchant Thû, whereas in the *Tale* the drowsiness which came upon the doorkeeper cat Umuiyan, and afterwards on Tevildo himself, is ascribed to her 'robe of sable mist' (II. 24–5). In the Lay, as in the account in *The Silmarillion* based on the Lay, Lúthien's sleep-bearing cloak has come back into the story at this juncture, since Huan retrieved it before they left Nargothrond, and she used it against Thû in the battle on the bridge.

A new element enters in Synopsis I with the singing of Lúthien before Thû, and the captives in the dungeons hearing her; in the old *Tale*

Tinúviel merely spoke very loudly so that Beren might hear her in the kitchen where he toiled. In Synopsis II this element is developed to the final form, with Lúthien singing on the bridge leading to the Wizard's Isle; but she still enters the castle by herself, before 'the battle of the werewolf'.

The sentence added in Synopsis II saying that Thû 'purposes to make her a thrall' goes back to the *Tale* (II. 26), and survived into the Lay and *The Silmarillion* ('he thought to make her captive and hand her over to the power of Morgoth, for his reward would be great').

The statement in II that 'Huan slays Thû's companions' doubtless proceeds from the story in the *Tale*, where when Tevildo set out to find Huan he was accompanied by two of his 'thanes', though in the *Tale* only Oikeroi was slain by Huan, and the other (unnamed) cat fled up a tree, as also did Tevildo himself (II. 28). In II, and in more detail in III, Thû is at Huan's mercy on the ground. In neither I nor II (III only takes up after this point) is there any suggestion of the wolves coming out from the castle and being slain by Huan one by one and silently, until at last Draugluin came forth; but as I noted in my commentary on the *Tale* (II. 54–5) 'the killing of the cat Oikeroi is the germ of Huan's fight with Draugluin – the skin of Huan's dead opponent is put to the same use in either case'. This element of the procession of wolves before Thû comes only enters with the poem. The verses naming Draugluin as the last and greatest of them (2712–13) are not in A, but in Lúthien's 'lengthening spell' *Draugluin the werewolf pale* is named in B (1489), where A has *Carcharas*.

Most interesting of all the features of this part of the story is that of the 'words of opening' or 'spoken keys', which goes back to the *Tale* (II. 28–9). I have discussed there (II. 55) the implications of this element in the enlarged context (the fortress of Thû had been an Elvish watchtower): the consequent 'displacement' of the spell that held the stones together.

In Synopsis III appear other features of the final story: the flight of Thû as a great bat; the finding of Beren sitting beside the body of Felagund. The pale captives who creep blinking into the light go back ultimately to the host of cats, reduced by the breaking of Tevildo's spell to puny size, who came forth from the castle in the *Tale* (II. 29, 55).

In Canto IX the story reaches its final form, and the passage in *The Silmarillion* derives from it closely, with only minor differences – the chief being the omission of all mention of Thû's voice in the dungeon, which is only found in the poem (lines 2592–2609). The old element still present in Synopsis II of Lúthien entering the castle alone has at last disappeared.

There remain a few matters of interest apart from the development of the story. Felagund's dying words (2633–6):

> I now must go to my long rest
> neath Timbrenting in timeless halls
> where drink the Gods, where the light falls
> upon the shining sea

are closely similar to Túrin's words of parting to Beleg dead (p. 58, 1408–11):

> Now fare well, Beleg,    to feasting long
> neath Tengwethil    in the timeless halls
> where drink the Gods,    neath domes golden
> o'er the sea shining.

As I have said (p. 94), Túrin foresees for Beleg an afterlife in Valinor, in the halls of the Gods, and does not speak, as does Beleg himself in Túrin's dream, of a time of 'waiting':

> my life has winged    to the long waiting
> in the halls of the Moon    o'er the hills of the sea.
>
> (p. 65, 1696–7)

Very notable are the words about Thû: 'the foul spirit Morgoth *made*' (line 2770).

In the passage (2666–71) referring to the constellation of the Great Bear is the first suggestion of the idea that Varda set the Seven Stars in the sky as an emblem of hope against Morgoth. Cf. *The Silmarillion* (p. 174):

[Beren] sang a song of challenge that he had made in praise of the Seven Stars, the Sickle of the Valar that Varda hung above the North as a sign for the fall of Morgoth.

## X

> Songs have recalled the Elves have sung
> in old forgotten elven tongue
> how Lúthien and Beren strayed
> by the banks of Sirion. Many a glade
> they filled with joy, and there their feet          2860
> passed by lightly, and days were sweet.
> Though winter hunted through the wood,
> still flowers lingered where she stood.
> Tinúviel! Tinúviel!
> the birds are unafraid to dwell          2865

and sing beneath the peaks of snow
where Beren and where Lúthien go.

The isle in Sirion they left behind;
but there on hill-top might one find
a green grave, and a stone set,                     2870
and there there lie the white bones yet
of Felagund, of Finrod's son –
unless that land is changed and gone,
or foundered in unfathomed seas,
while Felagund laughs beneath the trees             2875
in Valinor, and comes no more
to this grey world of tears and war.

To Nargothrond no more he came;
but thither swiftly ran the fame
of their king dead, of Thû o'erthrown,              2880
of the breaking of the towers of stone.
For many now came home at last,
who long ago to shadow passed;
and like a shadow had returned
Huan the hound, and scant had earned                2885
or praise or thanks of master wroth;
yet loyal he was, though he was loath.
The halls of Narog clamours fill
that vainly Celegorm would still.
There men bewailed their fallen king,               2890
crying that a maiden dared that thing
which sons of Fëanor would not do.
'Let us slay these faithless lords untrue!'
the fickle folk now loudly cried
with Felagund who would not ride.                   2895
Orodreth spake: 'The kingdom now
is mine alone. I will allow
no spilling of kindred blood by kin.
But bread nor rest shall find herein
these brothers who have set at nought               2900
the house of Finrod.' They were brought.
Scornful, unbowed, and unashamed
stood Celegorm. In his eye there flamed
a light of menace. Curufin
smiled with his crafty mouth and thin.              2905

'Be gone for ever – ere the day
shall fall into the sea. Your way
shall never lead you hither more,
nor any son of Fëanor;
nor ever after shall be bond                    2910
of love twixt yours and Nargothrond.'

'We will remember it,' they said,
and turned upon their heels, and sped,
and took their horses and such folk
as still them followed. Nought they spoke       2915
but sounded horns, and rode like fire,
and went away in anger dire.

Towards Doriath the wanderers now
were drawing nigh. Though bare the bough,
though cold the wind, and grey the grasses      2920
through which the hiss of winter passes,
they sang beneath the frosty sky
uplifted o'er them pale and high.
They came to Mindeb's narrow stream
that from the hills doth leap and gleam         2925
by western borders where begin
the spells of Melian to fence in
King Thingol's land, and stranger steps
to wind bewildered in their webs.

There sudden sad grew Beren's heart:            2930
'Alas, Tinúviel, here we part
and our brief song together ends,
and sundered ways each lonely wends!'

'Why part we here? What dost thou say,
just at the dawn of brighter day?'              2935

'For safe thou'rt come to borderlands
o'er which in the keeping of the hands
of Melian thou wilt walk at ease
and find thy home and well-loved trees.'

'My heart is glad when the fair trees          2940
far off uprising grey it sees
of Doriath inviolate.
Yet Doriath my heart did hate,
and Doriath my feet forsook,

my home, my kin. I would not look                    2945
on grass nor leaf there evermore
without thee by me. Dark the shore
of Esgalduin the deep and strong!
Why there alone forsaking song
by endless waters rolling past                        2950
must I then hopeless sit at last,
and gaze at waters pitiless
in heartache and in loneliness?'

    'For never more to Doriath
can Beren find the winding path,                      2955
though Thingol willed it or allowed;
for to thy father there I vowed
to come not back save to fulfill
the quest of the shining Silmaril,
and win by valour my desire.                          2960
"Not rock nor steel nor Morgoth's fire
nor all the power of Elfinesse,
shall keep the gem I would possess":
thus swore I once of Lúthien
more fair than any child of Men.                      2965
My word, alas! I must achieve,
though sorrow pierce and parting grieve.'

    'Then Lúthien will not go home,
but weeping in the woods will roam,
nor peril heed, nor laughter know.                    2970
And if she may not by thee go
against thy will thy desperate feet
she will pursue, until they meet,
Beren and Lúthien, love once more
on earth or on the shadowy shore.'                    2975

    'Nay, Lúthien, most brave of heart,
thou makest it more hard to part.
Thy love me drew from bondage drear,
but never to that outer fear,
that darkest mansion of all dread,                    2980
shall thy most blissful light be led.'

    'Never, never!' he shuddering said.
But even as in his arms she pled,
a sound came like a hurrying storm.

There Curufin and Celegorm                                         2985
in sudden tumult like the wind
rode up. The hooves of horses dinned
loud on the earth. In rage and haste
madly northward they now raced
the path twixt Doriath to find                                     2990
and the shadows dreadly dark entwined
of Taur-na-Fuin. That was their road
most swift to where their kin abode
in the east, where Himling's watchful hill
o'er Aglon's gorge hung tall and still.                            2995

They saw the wanderers. With a shout
straight on them swung their hurrying rout,
as if neath maddened hooves to rend
the lovers and their love to end.
But as they came the horses swerved                                3000
with nostrils wide and proud necks curved;
Curufin, stooping, to saddlebow
with mighty arm did Lúthien throw,
and laughed. Too soon; for there a spring
fiercer than tawny lion-king                                       3005
maddened with arrows barbéd smart,
greater than any hornéd hart
that hounded to a gulf leaps o'er,
there Beren gave, and with a roar
leaped on Curufin; round his neck                                  3010
his arms entwined, and all to wreck
both horse and rider fell to ground;
and there they fought without a sound.
Dazed in the grass did Lúthien lie
beneath bare branches and the sky;                                 3015
the Gnome felt Beren's fingers grim
close on his throat and strangle him,
and out his eyes did start, and tongue
gasping from his mouth there hung.
Up rode Celegorm with his spear,                                   3020
and bitter death was Beren near.
With elvish steel he nigh was slain
whom Lúthien won from hopeless chain,
but baying Huan sudden sprang
before his master's face with fang                                 3025

white-gleaming, and with bristling hair,
as if he on boar or wolf did stare.
    The horse in terror leaped aside,
and Celegorm in anger cried:
'Curse thee, thou baseborn dog, to dare                    3030
against thy master teeth to bare!'
But dog nor horse nor rider bold
would venture near the anger cold
of mighty Huan fierce at bay.
Red were his jaws. They shrank away,                       3035
and fearful eyed him from afar:
nor sword nor knife, nor scimitar,
no dart of bow, nor cast of spear,
master nor man did Huan fear.

    There Curufin had left his life,                       3040
had Lúthien not stayed that strife.
Waking she rose and softly cried
standing distressed at Beren's side:
'Forbear thy anger now, my lord!
nor do the work of Orcs abhorred;                          3045
for foes there be of Elfinesse
unnumbered, and they grow not less,
while here we war by ancient curse
distraught, and all the world to worse
decays and crumbles. Make thy peace!'                      3050

    Then Beren did Curufin release;
but took his horse and coat of mail,
and took his knife there gleaming pale,
hanging sheathless, wrought of steel.
No flesh could leeches ever heal                           3055
that point had pierced; for long ago
the dwarves had made it, singing slow
enchantments, where their hammers fell
in Nogrod ringing like a bell.
Iron as tender wood it cleft,                              3060
and sundered mail like woollen weft.
But other hands its haft now held;
its master lay by mortal felled.
Beren uplifting him, far him flung,
and cried 'Begone!', with stinging tongue;                 3065
'Begone! thou renegade and fool,

and let thy lust in exile cool!
Arise and go, and no more work
like Morgoth's slaves or curséd Orc;
and deal, proud son of Fëanor,                        3070
in deeds more proud than heretofore!'
Then Beren led Lúthien away,
while Huan still there stood at bay.

'Farewell,' cried Celegorm the fair.
'Far get you gone! And better were                    3075
to die forhungered in the waste
than wrath of Fëanor's sons to taste,
that yet may reach o'er dale and hill.
No gem, nor maid, nor Silmaril
shall ever long in thy grasp lie!                     3080
We curse thee under cloud and sky,
we curse thee from rising unto sleep!
Farewell!' He swift from horse did leap,
his brother lifted from the ground;
then bow of yew with gold wire bound                  3085
he strung, and shaft he shooting sent,
as heedless hand in hand they went;
a dwarvish dart and cruelly hooked.
They never turned nor backward looked.
Loud bayed Huan, and leaping caught                   3090
the speeding arrow. Quick as thought
another followed deadly singing;
but Beren had turned, and sudden springing
defended Lúthien with his breast.
Deep sank the dart in flesh to rest.                  3095
He fell to earth. They rode away,
and laughing left him as he lay;
yet spurred like wind in fear and dread
of Huan's pursuing anger red.
Though Curufin with bruised mouth laughed,            3100
yet later of that dastard shaft
was tale and rumour in the North,
and Men remembered at the Marching Forth,
and Morgoth's will its hatred helped.

Thereafter never hound was whelped                    3105
would follow horn of Celegorm
or Curufin. Though in strife and storm,

though all their house in ruin red
went down, thereafter laid his head
Huan no more at that lord's feet,                          3110
but followed Lúthien, brave and fleet.
Now sank she weeping at the side
of Beren, and sought to stem the tide
of welling blood that flowed there fast.
The raiment from his breast she cast;                      3115
from shoulder plucked the arrow keen;
his wound with tears she washed it clean.
    Then Huan came and bore a leaf,
of all the herbs of healing chief,
that evergreen in woodland glade                           3120
there grew with broad and hoary blade.
The powers of all grasses Huan knew,
who wide did forest-paths pursue.
Therewith the smart he swift allayed,
while Lúthien murmuring in the shade                        3125
the staunching song, that Elvish wives
long years had sung in those sad lives
of war and weapons, wove o'er him.

    The shadows fell from mountains grim.
Then sprang about the darkened North                       3130
the Sickle of the Gods, and forth
each star there stared in stony night
radiant, glistering cold and white.
But on the ground there is a glow,
a spark of red that leaps below:                           3135
under woven boughs beside a fire
of crackling wood and sputtering briar
there Beren lies in drowsing deep,
walking and wandering in sleep.
Watchful bending o'er him wakes                            3140
a maiden fair; his thirst she slakes,
his brow caresses, and softly croons
a song more potent than in runes
or leeches' lore hath since been writ.
Slowly the nightly watches flit.                           3145
The misty morning crawleth grey
from dusk to the reluctant day.

    Then Beren woke and opened eyes,

and rose and cried: 'Neath other skies,
in lands more awful and unknown,                    3150
I wandered long, methought, alone
to the deep shadow where the dead dwell;
but ever a voice that I knew well,
like bells, like viols, like harps, like birds,
like music moving without words,                    3155
called me, called me through the night,
enchanted drew me back to light!
Healed the wound, assuaged the pain!
Now are we come to morn again,
new journeys once more lead us on –                    3160
to perils whence may life be won,
hardly for Beren; and for thee
a waiting in the wood I see,
beneath the trees of Doriath,
while ever follow down my path                    3165
the echoes of thine elvish song,
where hills are haggard and roads are long.'

   'Nay, now no more we have for foe
dark Morgoth only, but in woe,
in wars and feuds of Elfinesse                    3170
thy quest is bound; and death, no less,
for thee and me, for Huan bold
the end of weird of yore foretold,
all this I bode shall follow swift,
if thou go on. Thy hand shall lift                    3175
and lay in Thingol's lap the dire
and flaming jewel, Fëanor's fire,
never, never! A why then go?
Why turn we not from fear and woe
beneath the trees to walk and roam                    3180
roofless, with all the world as home,
over mountains, beside the seas,
in the sunlight, in the breeze?'

   Thus long they spoke with heavy hearts;
and yet not all her elvish arts,                    3185
nor lissom arms, nor shining eyes
as tremulous stars in rainy skies,
nor tender lips, enchanted voice,
his purpose bent or swayed his choice.

Never to Doriath would he fare                        3190
save guarded fast to leave her there;
never to Nargothrond would go
with her, lest there came war and woe;
and never would in the world untrod
to wander suffer her, worn, unshod,                   3195
roofless and restless, whom he drew
with love from the hidden realms she knew.
'For Morgoth's power is now awake;
already hill and dale doth shake,
the hunt is up, the prey is wild:                     3200
a maiden lost, an elven child.
Now Orcs and phantoms prowl and peer
from tree to tree, and fill with fear
each shade and hollow. Thee they seek!
At thought thereof my hope grows weak,                3205
my heart is chilled. I curse mine oath,
I curse the fate that joined us both
and snared thy feet in my sad doom
of flight and wandering in the gloom!
Now let us haste, and ere the day                     3210
be fallen, take our swiftest way,
till o'er the marches of thy land
beneath the beech and oak we stand
in Doriath, fair Doriath
whither no evil finds the path,                       3215
powerless to pass the listening leaves
that droop upon those forest-eaves.'

Then to his will she seeming bent.
Swiftly to Doriath they went,
and crossed its borders. There they stayed           3220
resting in deep and mossy glade;
there lay they sheltered from the wind
under mighty beeches silken-skinned,
and sang of love that still shall be,
though earth be foundered under sea,                  3225
and sundered here for evermore
shall meet upon the Western Shore.

One morning as asleep she lay
upon the moss, as though the day
too bitter were for gentle flower                     3230

to open in a sunless hour,
Beren arose and kissed her hair,
and wept, and softly left her there.
   'Good Huan,' said he, 'guard her well!
In leafless field no asphodel,              3235
in thorny thicket never a rose
forlorn, so frail and fragrant blows.
Guard her from wind and frost, and hide
from hands that seize and cast aside;
keep her from wandering and woe,       3240
for pride and fate now make me go.'

   The horse he took and rode away,
nor dared to turn; but all that day
with heart as stone he hastened forth
and took the paths toward the North.     3245

## NOTES

2877    Against this line is written the date 'April 5th'. The previous
date was 4 April 1928 at line 2769.

2929    At the end of this line is written the date 'April 6th'.

2950–3  Cf. lines 649–52, 1220–3.

2998    Against this line is written the date 'April 27th 1928'.

3031    Before this line is written the date 'Nov. 1929'. This date may
refer forward or backward; but both it and the text that
follows are written with a slightly finer nib than that used for
the preceding portion of the poem. The previous date was 27
April 1928 at line 2998.

3076–84  Against these seven lines, as first written in the margin of the
manuscript A, is the date 'Sept. 1930'.

3119    Against this line my father wrote in the margin of the B-text
the word *athelas*. In *The Fellowship of the Ring* (I. 12)
Aragorn said that it was brought to Middle-earth by the
Númenóreans.

3220    After the word *borders* is written the date '25 September
1930'.

3242–5  These last four lines of the Canto are only found in A, but I
suspect that they were omitted inadvertently.

## Commentary on Canto X

The development of the story in this Canto can again be followed step by step in the outlines. In the *Tale of Tinúviel* (II. 30–1) Beren and Tinúviel wandered away with Huan after the defeat of Tevildo, and it was her desire to return to Artanor but unwillingness to part from Beren that led to their resolve to try to gain a Silmaril. The catskin of Oikeroi, thane of Tevildo, was carried by Huan as a trophy, and they begged it from him; it was in the guise of a cat that Beren went to Angband. Synopsis I says no more of this part of the narrative than 'Tinúviel and Beren disguised as a werewolf go to Angband', and apart from the fact that the skin was that of a werewolf and not of a cat there had probably been no development from the *Tale*.

Synopsis II continues from the point reached on p. 257 as follows:

> Lúthien tends Beren in the wood. Huan brings news to Nargothrond. The Gnomes drive forth Curufin and Celegorm, grieving for Felagund, and send the cloak back to Lúthien. Lúthien takes her cloak again and led by Huan they go to Angband. By his guidance and her magic they escape capture. Huan dare not come any further. Beren is disguised as a werewolf. They enter Angband.

The sentences 'and send the cloak back to Lúthien. Lúthien takes her cloak again' were changed at the time of writing to read: 'and send to succour Beren and Lúthien. Huan brings Lúthien back her cloak again.' (This outline was written of course before my father reached Canto VIII, at the end of which Huan brought Lúthien her cloak before she escaped from Nargothrond.)

Here Synopsis II ends. At the bottom of the page is written very roughly:

> Celegorm's embassy to Thingol so that Thingol knows or thinks he knows Beren dead and Lúthien in Nargothrond.
> Why Celegorm and Curufin hated by Thingol . .  . . . . .
> The loss of Dairon.

While the expulsion of Celegorm and Curufin from Nargothrond is now first mentioned, it is clear that the story of their attack on Beren and Lúthien did not exist. Huan brings the news of the destruction of the Wizard's Tower, but it seems that he does not leave Nargothrond with Celegorm and brings back the cloak to Lúthien independently.

Synopsis III has been given on p. 257 to the point where Lúthien and Huan find Beren 'sitting beside Felagund'. I give the next portion of this outline as it was first written:

> They hallow the isle and bury Felagund on its top, and no wolf or evil creature will ever come there again. Beren is led into the woods. [*The following sentence was bracketed with a marginal direction that it should come later*: Morgoth hearing of the breaking of

the Wizard's Tower sends out an army of Orcs; finding the wolves are
slain with . . . . . . throats he thinks it is Huan and fashions a vast wolf –
Carcharas – mightiest of all wolves to guard his door.]
    They hide in Taur-na-Fuin careful not to lose sight of light at edge.
Lúthien bids Beren desist. He cannot, he says, return to Doriath.
Then, she says, she will live in the woods with Beren and Huan. But he
has spoken his word; he has vowed not to fear Morgoth . . . hell. Then
she says [that she] fears that their lives will all be forfeit. But life
perchance lies after death. Where Beren goes she goes. This gives him
pause. They ask Huan. He speaks for second and last time. 'No more
may Huan go with you – what you see at the gate, he will see later – his
fate does not lead to Angband. Perchance, though his eyes are dim,
[?thy] paths lead out of it again.' He goes to Nargothrond. They will
not return to Nargothrond with him.
    Lúthien and Beren leave Taur-na-Fuin and wander about together a
while. Longing to look on Doriath seizes her and Beren thinks of the
quest unaccomplished. Beren offers to lead her to the borders of
Doriath, but they cannot bear to part.
    They go to the Wizard's Isle and take a 'wolf-ham' and a bat-robe.
Thus they trembling inwardly set forth. The journey to Angband over
Dor-na-Fauglith and into the dark ravines of the hills.

Here first appears the burial of Felagund on the summit of the isle, and
its hallowing. This outline makes no mention of the events in Nargothrond, and concentrates exclusively on Beren and Lúthien. They are in
Taur-na-Fuin, and Huan is with them; and we have the first version of
Huan's counsel to them, and his foreseeing that what they meet at the
Gate of Angband he will himself see later. Since the attack by Celegorm
and Curufin had still not been devised, the story is briefer than it was to
become; thus Huan speaks to them in Taur-na-Fuin soon after the
destruction of the Wizard's Tower, and then departs to Nargothrond,
while they after a while go to the Isle and take the 'wolf-ham' ('wolf-hame'
in *The Silmarillion* p. 178, Old English *hama*) and 'bat-robe', which
now first appear (though the 'wolf-hame' derives from the catskin of
Oikeroi in the *Tale*). From the words 'They will not return to Nargothrond with him' and from the fact that as the outline was written he is
not mentioned again, it is clear that Huan was now out of the story (until
his reappearance in a later episode). His speech is here called 'the second
and last time' that he spoke with words. Afterwards the story was
changed in this point, for he spoke to Beren a third time at his death (see
note to line 2551).
    Pencilled changes were made to this passage of Synopsis III, and these
move the narrative a long way to the final version:

    They hallow the isle and bury Felagund on its top, and no wolf or
    evil creature will ever come there again.
    Lúthien and Beren leave Taur-na-Fuin and wander about together a

while. Longing to look on Doriath seizes her and Beren thinks of the quest unaccomplished. Beren offers to lead her to the borders of Doriath, but they cannot bear to part.

News by captives and Huan is brought to Nargothrond. Celegorm and Curufin    in a revulsion of feeling the Nargothronders wish to slay them. Orodreth will not. They are exiled and all Fëanorians from Nargothrond for ever. They ride off. Assault of Celegorm and Curufin in wood on Beren and Lúthien. Rescue by Huan. Beren wrestles with Curufin and gets his magic knife – [eight further words illegible]

Huan brings them a wolf-ham. Thus they trembling inwardly set forth. Huan speaks for last time and says farewell. He will not come. The journey to Angband, &c.

Here more is told of the expulsion of Celegorm and Curufin from Nargothrond, and Orodreth's refusal to allow them to be slain, and here at last is mention – probably written here at the very time of its devising – of the attack on Beren and Lúthien as the Fëanorians rode from Nargothrond. The desertion of Celegorm by Huan is implied; Beren gets Curufin's knife, which is to replace the knife from Tevildo's kitchens as the implement with which Beren cut the Silmaril from the Iron Crown; and it is Huan who gets the wolfskin, and then utters his parting speech.

An extremely difficult page in pencil ('Synopsis IV') shows these new elements being developed further:

Beren's heart grows sad. He says he has led Tinúviel back to the border of her land where she is safe. Alas for their second parting. She says but from this land she herself escaped and fled only to be with him – yet she admits that her heart longs for Doriath and Melian too, but not Doriath without him. He quotes his own words to Thingol: 'Not Morgoth's fire &c.' – and says he cannot (even if Thingol would allow) return emptyhanded. . . . . . she will not go back. She will wander in the woods – and if he will not take her with him she will follow his feet against his will. He protests – at this moment Celegorm and Curufin ride up seeking the way North [struck out at time of writing: round Doriath by the Gorgoroth] between Doriath and Taur-na-Fuin to the Gorge of Aglon and their own kin.

They ride straight on and seek to ride Beren down. Curufin stoops and lifts Lúthien to his saddle. Beren leaps aside and leaps at Curufin's neck [?hurling] him down. Celegorm with his spear rides up to slay Beren. Huan intervenes scattering the [?brothers'] folk and dogs and holds Celegorm at bay while Beren wrestles with Curufin and chokes him senseless. Beren takes his weapons – especially his magic knife, and bids him get on horse and be gone. They ride off. Huan stays with Beren and Lúthien and forsakes his master [?for ever]. Celegorm suddenly turns and shoots an arrow at Huan which of course falls harmless from him, but Curufin shoots at Beren (and Lúthien) [*changed to*: shoots at Lúthien] and wounds Beren.

Lúthien heals Beren. They tell Huan of their doubts and debate and he goes off and brings the wolfham and batskin from the Wizard's Isle. Then he speaks for the last time.

They prepare to go to Angband.

This was certainly prepared as an outline for Canto 10 of the Lay, for the section of the synopsis that follows is headed '11'.

There is here the further development that Beren and Lúthien have come to the borders of Doriath; but the solitary departure of Beren after his healing, leaving Lúthien with Huan, has still not emerged. There are a few differences in the account of the fight with Celegorm and Curufin from the final form, but for the most part the detail of the events was never changed from its first writing down (as I believe it to be) on this page. There is here no mention of Beren's taking Curufin's horse, on which he was later to ride north by himself to Anfauglith; and the detail of the shooting is different – in the synopsis Celegorm aimed at Huan, and Curufin (who seems to have retained his bow, though Beren took all his weapons) at (Beren and) Lúthien. There is also mention of 'folk' accompanying the brothers on their journey from Nargothrond.

In this outline is the first occurrence of the name *Gorgoroth*.

There is one further outline ('Synopsis V'), consisting of four pages that are the concluding part of a text of which the beginning has disappeared: it begins with a heading '10 continued', which is certainly a Canto number, though the content extends much beyond the end of Canto X in the Lay.* The text takes up with the healing of Beren's wound.

Huan brings a herb of healing, and Lúthien and the hound tend Beren in the forest, building a hut of boughs. Beren mending will still go on his quest. But Lúthien foretells that all their lives will be forfeit if they pursue. Beren will not go back to Doriath otherwise. Nor will he or Huan go to Nargothrond, or keep Lúthien in Thingol's despite, for war would certainly arise twixt Elf and Elf, [?even] if Orodreth harboured them. 'Then why shall we not dwell here in the wood?' saith Lúthien. Because of danger outside Doriath, and the Orcs, and the knowledge Morgoth must now possess of Lúthien's wandering.

One morning early Beren steals away on Curufin's horse and reaches the eaves of Taur-na-Fuin.

Here at last is the element of Beren's solitary departure.

---

* It is also possible that '10 continued' means only that my father began Synopsis V at this point, i.e. he had already reached about line 3117 in the actual composition of the Lay when he began the outline.

The casting out of Celegorm and Curufin from Nargothrond in the Lay is very closely followed in *The Silmarillion* (even to phrases, as 'neither bread nor rest'); in the Lay, however, there are some who will go with them (lines 2914–15), a detail found in Synopsis IV, whereas in *The Silmarillion* it is explicit that they went alone.*

The debate between Beren and Lúthien which was interrupted by the coming of Celegorm and Curufin (lines 2930–82) is clearly based on the scheme of it given in Synopsis IV (p. 272); in *The Silmarillion* it reappears, though much reduced and changed. The fight with Celegorm and Curufin is likewise derived from Synopsis IV, and is followed in the prose of *The Silmarillion* – with such detail as the cursing of Beren 'under cloud and sky', and Curufin's knife that would cut iron as if it were green wood, hanging sheathless by his side. In the Lay the knife becomes a dwarf-made weapon from Nogrod, though neither it nor its maker is yet named. In the Lay the shooter of the treacherous shafts is Celegorm; in *The Silmarillion* it is Curufin, using Celegorm's bow, and the vile act is settled on the wickeder (as he was certainly also the cleverer) of the brothers – in this Canto he is given the proper visage of a cunning villain: 'with his crafty mouth and thin' (2905). The reference of line 3103 'and Men remembered at the Marching Forth' is to the Union of Maidros before the Battle of Unnumbered Tears.

The second debate between Beren and Lúthien after his recovery from the wound is derived from Synopsis V; it is not present at all in *The Silmarillion*, though it is not without its importance in its representation of Beren's utter determination in the face of Lúthien's persuasions to abandon the quest.

Two new elements in the geography appear in this Canto: the Hill of Himling (later Himring) rising to the east of the Gorge of Aglon (2994), and the river Mindeb: lines 2924–5 (and the rewritten verses given on p. 360) seem to be the only description of it anywhere.

The curious element of Morgoth's particular interest in Lúthien (so that he sent the Orc-captain Boldog to Doriath to capture her, lines 2127–36) reappears in this Canto (3198–3201).

At the beginning of the Canto the burial of Felagund leads to a further reference to his fate after death without mention of Mandos (see p. 259):

> while Felagund laughs beneath the trees
> in Valinor, and comes no more
> to this grey world of tears and war.

---

* The reference in *The Silmarillion* to Celebrimbor son of Curufin remaining in Nargothrond at this time and renouncing his father was a much later development.

# XI

Once wide and smooth a plain was spread,
where King Fingolfin proudly led
his silver armies on the green,
his horses white, his lances keen;
his helmets tall of steel were hewn,                    3250
his shields were shining as the moon.
    There trumpets sang both long and loud,
and challenge rang unto the cloud
that lay on Morgoth's northern tower,
while Morgoth waited for his hour.                      3255

    Rivers of fire at dead of night
in winter lying cold and white
upon the plain burst forth, and high
the red was mirrored in the sky.
From Hithlum's walls they saw the fire,                 3260
the steam and smoke in spire on spire
leap up, till in confusion vast
the stars were choked. And so it passed,
the mighty field, and turned to dust,
to drifting sand and yellow rust,                       3265
to thirsty dunes where many bones
lay broken among barren stones.
    Dor-na-Fauglith, Land of Thirst,
they after named it, waste accurst,
the raven-haunted roofless grave                        3270
of many fair and many brave.
Thereon the stony slopes look forth
from Deadly Nightshade falling north,
from sombre pines with pinions vast,
black-plumed and drear, as many a mast                  3275
of sable-shrouded ships of death
slow wafted on a ghostly breath.

    Thence Beren grim now gazes out
across the dunes and shifting drought,
and sees afar the frowning towers                       3280
where thunderous Thangorodrim lowers.
    The hungry horse there drooping stood,
proud Gnomish steed; it feared the wood;
upon the haunted ghastly plain

no horse would ever stride again. 3285
'Good steed of master ill,' he said,
'farewell now here! Lift up thy head,
and get thee gone to Sirion's vale,
back as we came, past island pale
where Thû once reigned, to waters sweet 3290
and grasses long about thy feet.
And if Curufin no more thou find,
grieve not! but free with hart and hind
go wander, leaving work and war,
and dream thee back in Valinor, 3295
whence came of old thy mighty race
from Tavros' mountain-fencéd chase.'

There still sat Beren, and he sang,
and loud his lonely singing rang.
Though Orc should hear, or wolf a-prowl, 3300
or any of the creatures foul
within the shade that slunk and stared
of Taur-na-Fuin, nought he cared,
who now took leave of light and day,
grim-hearted, bitter, fierce and fey. 3305

'Farewell now here, ye leaves of trees,
your music in the morning-breeze!
Farewell now blade and bloom and grass
that see the changing seasons pass;
ye waters murmuring over stone, 3310
and meres that silent stand alone!
Farewell now mountain, vale, and plain!
Farewell now wind and frost and rain,
and mist and cloud, and heaven's air;
ye star and moon so blinding-fair 3315
that still shall look down from the sky
on the wide earth, though Beren die –
though Beren die not, and yet deep,
deep, whence comes of those that weep
no dreadful echo, lie and choke 3320
in everlasting dark and smoke.
'Farewell sweet earth and northern sky,
for ever blest, since here did lie,
and here with lissom limbs did run,
beneath the moon, beneath the sun, 3325

Lúthien Tinúviel
more fair than mortal tongue can tell.
Though all to ruin fell the world,
and were dissolved and backward hurled
unmade into the old abyss,                                    3330
yet were its making good, for this –
the dawn, the dusk, the earth, the sea –
that Lúthien on a time should be!'

His blade he lifted high in hand,
and challenging alone did stand                               3335
before the threat of Morgoth's power;
and dauntless cursed him, hall and tower,
o'ershadowing hand and grinding foot,
beginning, end, and crown and root;
then turned to stride forth down the slope                    3340
abandoning fear, forsaking hope.

'A, Beren, Beren!' came a sound,
'almost too late have I thee found!
O proud and fearless hand and heart,
not yet farewell, not yet we part!                            3345
Not thus do those of elven race
forsake the love that they embrace.
A love is mine, as great a power
as thine, to shake the gate and tower
of death with challenge weak and frail                        3350
that yet endures, and will not fail
nor yield, unvanquished were it hurled
beneath the foundations of the world.
Beloved fool! escape to seek
from such pursuit; in might so weak                           3355
to trust not, thinking it well to save
from love thy loved, who welcomes grave
and torment sooner than in guard
of kind intent to languish, barred,
wingless and helpless him to aid                              3360
for whose support her love was made!'

Thus back to him came Lúthien:
they met beyond the ways of Men;
upon the brink of terror stood
between the desert and the wood.                              3365

He looked on her, her lifted face
beneath his lips in sweet embrace:
'Thrice now mine oath I curse,' he said,
'that under shadow thee hath led!
But where is Huan, where the hound                    3370
to whom I trusted, whom I bound
by love of thee to keep thee well
from deadly wandering unto hell?'

'I know not! But good Huan's heart
is wiser, kinder than thou art,                       3375
grim lord, more open unto prayer!
Yet long and long I pleaded there,
until he brought me, as I would,
upon thy trail – a palfrey good
would Huan make, of flowing pace:                     3380
thou wouldst have laughed to see us race,
as Orc on werewolf ride like fire
night after night through fen and mire,
through waste and wood! But when I heard
thy singing clear – (yea, every word                  3385
of Lúthien one rashly cried,
and listening evil fierce defied) –,
he set me down, and sped away;
but what he would I cannot say.'

Ere long they knew, for Huan came,                    3390
his great breath panting, eyes like flame,
in fear lest her whom he forsook
to aid some hunting evil took
ere he was nigh. Now there he laid
before their feet, as dark as shade,                  3395
two grisly shapes that he had won
from that tall isle in Sirion:
a wolfhame huge – its savage fell
was long and matted, dark the spell
that drenched the dreadful coat and skin,             3400
the werewolf cloak of Draugluin;
the other was a batlike garb
with mighty fingered wings, a barb
like iron nail at each joint's end –
such wings as their dark cloud extend                 3405
against the moon, when in the sky

from Deadly Nightshade screeching fly
Thû's messengers.

              'What hast thou brought,
good Huan? What thy hidden thought?
Of trophy of prowess and strong deed,         3410
when Thû thou vanquishedst, what need
here in the waste?' Thus Beren spoke,
and once more words in Huan woke:
his voice was like the deeptoned bells
that ring in Valmar's citadels:             3415

   'Of one fair gem thou must be thief,
Morgoth's or Thingol's, loath or lief;
thou must here choose twixt love and oath!
If vow to break is still thee loath,
then Lúthien must either die            3420
alone, or death with thee defie
beside thee, marching on your fate
that hidden before you lies in wait.
Hopeless the quest, but not yet mad,
unless thou, Beren, run thus clad        3425
in mortal raiment, mortal hue,
witless and redeless, death to woo.
   'Lo! good was Felagund's device,
but may be bettered, if advice
of Huan ye will dare to take,           3430
and swift a hideous change will make
to forms most curséd, foul and vile,
of werewolf of the Wizard's Isle,
of monstrous bat's envermined fell
with ghostly clawlike wings of hell.       3435
   'To such dark straits, alas! now brought
are ye I love, for whom I fought.
Nor further with you can I go –
whoever did a great hound know
in friendship at a werewolf's side       3440
to Angband's grinning portals stride?
Yet my heart tells that at the gate
what there ye find, 'twill be my fate
myself to see, though to that door
my feet shall bear me nevermore.        3445
Darkened is hope and dimmed my eyes,

I see not clear what further lies;
yet maybe backwards leads your path
beyond all hope to Doriath,
and thither, perchance, we three shall wend,          3450
and meet again before the end.'

They stood and marvelled thus to hear
his mighty tongue so deep and clear;
then sudden he vanished from their sight
even at the onset of the night.                       3455

His dreadful counsel then they took,
and their own gracious forms forsook;
in werewolf fell and batlike wing
prepared to robe them, shuddering.
With elvish magic Lúthien wrought,                    3460
lest raiment foul with evil fraught
to dreadful madness drive their hearts;
and there she wrought with elvish arts
a strong defence, a binding power,
singing until the midnight hour.                      3465

Swift as the wolvish coat he wore,
Beren lay slavering on the floor,
redtongued and hungry; but there lies
a pain and longing in his eyes,
a look of horror as he sees                           3470
a batlike form crawl to its knees
and drag its creased and creaking wings.
Then howling under moon he springs
fourfooted, swift, from stone to stone,
from hill to plain – but not alone:                   3475
a dark shape down the slope doth skim,
and wheeling flitters over him.

Ashes and dust and thirsty dune
withered and dry beneath the moon,
under the cold and shifting air                       3480
sifting and sighing, bleak and bare;
of blistered stones and gasping sand,
of splintered bones was built that land,
o'er which now slinks with powdered fell
and hanging tongue a shape of hell.                   3485
Many parching leagues lay still before

when sickly day crept back once more;
many choking miles yet stretched ahead
when shivering night once more was spread
with doubtful shadow and ghostly sound          3490
that hissed and passed o'er dune and mound.
    A second morning in cloud and reek
struggled, when stumbling, blind and weak,
a wolvish shape came staggering forth
and reached the foothills of the North;          3495
upon its back there folded lay
a crumpled thing that blinked at day.

    The rocks were reared like bony teeth,
and claws that grasped from opened sheath,
on either side the mournful road                 3500
that onward led to that abode
far up within the Mountain dark
with tunnels drear and portals stark.
    They crept within a scowling shade,
and cowering darkly down them laid.              3505
Long lurked they there beside the path,
and shivered, dreaming of Doriath,
of laughter and music and clean air,
in fluttered leaves birds singing fair.
    They woke, and felt the trembling sound,     3510
the beating echo far underground
shake beneath them, the rumour vast
of Morgoth's forges; and aghast
they heard the tramp of stony feet
that shod with iron went down that street:       3515
the Orcs went forth to rape and war,
and Balrog captains marched before.

    They stirred, and under cloud and shade
at eve stepped forth, and no more stayed;
as dark things on dark errand bent               3520
up the long slopes in haste they went.
Ever the sheer cliffs rose beside,
where birds of carrion sat and cried;
and chasms black and smoking yawned,
whence writhing serpent-shapes were spawned;     3525
until at last in that huge gloom,
heavy as overhanging doom,

that weighs on Thangorodrim's foot
like thunder at the mountain's root,
they came, as to a sombre court                                  3530
walled with great towers, fort on fort
of cliffs embattled, to that last plain
that opens, abysmal and inane,
before the final topless wall
of Bauglir's immeasurable hall,                                  3535
whereunder looming awful waits
the gigantic shadow of his gates.

# NOTES

3249–53   Cf. the opening of the Lay, lines 5–10.
3267   Against this line is written the date 'Sep. 26 1930'. The
       previous date was 25 Sept. 1930 at line 3220.
3297   *Tavros* > *Tauros* B: see notes to lines 891, 904; 2246.
3303   *Taur-na-Fuin* > *Taur-nu-Fuin* B (a late change).
3401   *Draugluin* appears here in the A-text (see p. 258).
3414–15   Cf. lines 2258–9.
3419–23   The shift from *thee* to *your* and *you* is intentional, and
       indicates that Huan now refers to both Beren and Lúthien.
3478   Against this line is written the date 'Sep. 27 1930'.

## Commentary on Canto XI

The earliest version of the narrative of this Canto describes Tinúviel's
sewing of Beren into the catskin of Oikeroi and teaching him some
aspects of feline behaviour; she herself was not disguised. Very little is
made of the journey to Angamandi, but the approach to the gates is
described:

> At length however they drew near to Angamandi, as indeed the
> rumblings and deep noises, and the sound of mighty hammerings of
> ten thousand smiths labouring unceasingly, declared to them. Nigh
> were the sad chambers where the thrall-Noldoli laboured bitterly
> under the Orcs and goblins of the hills, and here the gloom and
> darkness was great so that their hearts fell . . . (II. 31).

Synopses I and II have virtually nothing here beyond the bare event
(p. 270). In its emended form Synopsis III comes near to the final

story of the 'wolfhame' and the parting from Huan (p. 272); and this outline continues:

> Thangorodrim towers above them. There are rumblings, steam and vapours burst from fissures in the rock. Ten thousand smiths are hammering – they pass the vaults where the thrall-Gnomes are labouring without rest. The gloom sinks into their hearts.

This is remarkably close to the passage cited above from the *Tale of Tinúviel*.

Synopsis IV (p. 273) adds no more, for after 'They prepare to go to Angband' it continues with events in Doriath and the embassy to Thingol from Celegorm, which at this stage my father was going to introduce before the Angband adventure, and in this outline virtually nothing is said of that.

There remains Synopsis V, whose outline for Canto '10' has been given on p. 273 as far as 'One morning early Beren steals away on Curufin's horse and reaches the eaves of Taur-na-Fuin', and it is here that Beren's solitary departure first enters. This outline continues, still under the heading 'Canto 10':

> There he looks upon Thangorodrim and sings a song of farewell to earth and light, and to Lúthien. In the midst up come Lúthien and Huan! With the hound's aid she has followed him; and moreover from the Wizard's Isle Huan has brought a wolf-ham and a bat-coat. [*Struck through at time of writing*: Beren sets Lúthien upon the horse and they ride through Taur-na-Fuin.*] Beren sets Curufin's horse to gallop free and he speeds away. Now Beren takes the shape of werewolf and Tinúviel of bat. Then Huan bids farewell. And speaks. No hound can walk with werewolf – more peril should I be than help in Morgoth's land. Yet what ye shall see at Angband's gate I perchance too shall see, though my fate doth not lead to those doors. Darkened is all hope, and dimmed my eyes, yet perchance I see thy paths leading from that place once more. Then he vanishes. They make a grievous journey. Thangorodrim looms over them, . . . . . . . . in its smoky foothills.

This ends the outline for 'Canto 10' in Synopsis V.

There is a notable difference in the structure of the story in the Lay from that in *The Silmarillion* (pp. 178–9): in the Lay Huan is absent (gone to the Wizard's Isle for the wolfcoat and batskin) when Lúthien finds Beren – she does not know where he has gone – but he comes up a little later; whereas in the prose account Huan and Lúthien came together, and they were clad in 'the ghastly wolf-hame of Draugluin and the bat-fell of Thuringwethil' – an apparition that filled Beren with

---

*Beren must in fact have been on the northern edge of Taur-na-Fuin when Lúthien and Huan came up with him, since 'he looks upon Thangorodrim'.

dismay. The story in *The Silmarillion* is a reversion, at least in so far as Huan and Lúthien arrive together, to that of Synopsis V ('In the midst up come Lúthien and Huan', p. 283).

In the Lay the bat-wings are only said to be such as bear up Thû's messengers, and are not associated with a particular or chief messenger (Thuringwethil, 'messenger of Sauron').

But the prose version in other respects follows that of the Lay closely, with as before retention of phrases ('between the desert and the wood', 'Thrice now I curse my oath', 'fingered wings . . . barbed at each joint's end', 'the bat wheeled and flittered above him'); and the speech of Huan is closely modelled on that in the Lay.

From Beren's words to the horse (3288–90)

> get thee gone to Sirion's vale,
> back as we came, past island pale
> where Thû once reigned

it is clear that as in *The Silmarillion* 'he rode northward again with all speed to the Pass of Sirion, and coming to the skirts of Taur-nu-Fuin he looked out across the waste of Anfauglith'. It is not said in the Lay how Lúthien and Huan came there, but in *The Silmarillion* 'clad in these dreadful garments' they 'ran through Taur-nu-Fuin, and all things fled before them'.

The Battle of Sudden Flame (lines 3256 ff.) has been described earlier in the Lay (lines 1678 ff.), but it has not been actually stated before that the northern plain was once green and grassy (3246–8), and became a desert after the 'rivers of fire . . . upon the plain burst forth'.

With Beren's words to Curufin's horse (3295–7):

> dream thee back in Valinor,
> whence came of old thy mighty race

cf. *The Silmarillion* p. 119, where it is told that 'many of the sires' of the horses of the Noldor of Hithlum who rode on Ard-galen came from Valinor.

# XII

> In that vast shadow once of yore
> Fingolfin stood: his shield he bore
> with field of heaven's blue and star          3540
> of crystal shining pale afar.
> In overmastering wrath and hate
> desperate he smote upon that gate,

the Gnomish king, there standing lone,
while endless fortresses of stone                    3545
engulfed the thin clear ringing keen
of silver horn on baldric green.
His hopeless challenge dauntless cried
Fingolfin there: 'Come, open wide,
dark king, your ghastly brazen doors!                3550
Come forth, whom earth and heaven abhors!
Come forth, O monstrous craven lord,
and fight with thine own hand and sword,
thou wielder of hosts of banded thralls,
thou tyrant leaguered with strong walls,             3555
thou foe of Gods and elvish race!
I wait thee here. Come! Show thy face!'

Then Morgoth came. For the last time
in those great wars he dared to climb
from subterranean throne profound,                   3560
the rumour of his feet a sound
of rumbling earthquake underground.
Black-armoured, towering, iron-crowned
he issued forth; his mighty shield
a vast unblazoned sable field                        3565
with shadow like a thundercloud;
and o'er the gleaming king it bowed,
as huge aloft like mace he hurled
that hammer of the underworld,
Grond. Clanging to ground it tumbled                 3570
down like a thunder-bolt, and crumbled
the rocks beneath it; smoke up-started,
a pit yawned, and a fire darted.

Fingolfin like a shooting light
beneath a cloud, a stab of white,                    3575
sprang then aside, and Ringil drew
like ice that gleameth cold and blue,
his sword devised of elvish skill
to pierce the flesh with deadly chill.
With seven wounds it rent his foe,                   3580
and seven mighty cries of woe
rang in the mountains, and the earth quook,
and Angband's trembling armies shook.
Yet Orcs would after laughing tell

of the duel at the gates of hell;                              3585
though elvish song thereof was made
ere this but one – when sad was laid
the mighty king in barrow high,
and Thorndor, Eagle of the sky,
the dreadful tidings brought and told            3590
to mourning Elfinesse of old.
Thrice was Fingolfin with great blows
to his knees beaten, thrice he rose
still leaping up beneath the cloud
aloft to hold star-shining, proud,               3595
his stricken shield, his sundered helm,
that dark nor might could overwhelm
till all the earth was burst and rent
in pits about him. He was spent.
His feet stumbled. He fell to wreck              3600
upon the ground, and on his neck
a foot like rooted hills was set,
and he was crushed – not conquered yet;
one last despairing stroke he gave:
the mighty foot pale Ringil clave                3605
about the heel, and black the blood
gushed as from smoking fount in flood.

   Halt goes for ever from that stroke
great Morgoth; but the king he broke,
and would have hewn and mangled thrown           3610
to wolves devouring. Lo! from throne
that Manwë bade him build on high,
on peak unscaled beneath the sky,
Morgoth to watch, now down there swooped
Thorndor the King of Eagles, stooped,            3615
and rending beak of gold he smote
in Bauglir's face, then up did float
on pinions thirty fathoms wide
bearing away, though loud they cried,
the mighty corse, the Elven-king;                3620
and where the mountains make a ring
far to the south about that plain
where after Gondolin did reign,
embattled city, at great height
upon a dizzy snowcap white                        3625
in mounded cairn the mighty dead

he laid upon the mountain's head.
Never Orc nor demon after dared
that pass to climb, o'er which there stared
Fingolfin's high and holy tomb,                              3630
till Gondolin's appointed doom.

    Thus Bauglir earned the furrowed scar
that his dark countenance doth mar,
and thus his limping gait he gained;
but afterward profound he reigned                            3635
darkling upon his hidden throne;
and thunderous paced his halls of stone,
slow building there his vast design
the world in thraldom to confine.
Wielder of armies, lord of woe,                              3640
no rest now gave he slave or foe;
his watch and ward he thrice increased,
his spies were sent from West to East
and tidings brought from all the North,
who fought, who fell; who ventured forth,                    3645
who wrought in secret; who had hoard;
if maid were fair or proud were lord;
well nigh all things he knew, all hearts
well nigh enmeshed in evil arts.
    Doriath only, beyond the veil                          3650
woven by Melian, no assail
could hurt or enter; only rumour dim
of things there passing came to him.
A rumour loud and tidings clear
of other movements far and near                              3655
among his foes, and threat of war
from the seven sons of Fëanor,
from Nargothrond, from Fingon still
gathering his armies under hill
and under tree in Hithlum's shade,                           3660
these daily came. He grew afraid
amidst his power once more; renown
of Beren vexed his ears, and down
the aisléd forests there was heard
great Huan baying.

                Then came word          3665
most passing strange of Lúthien

wild-wandering by wood and glen,
and Thingol's purpose long he weighed,
and wondered, thinking of that maid
so fair, so frail. A captain dire,                                    3670
Boldog, he sent with sword and fire
to Doriath's march; but battle fell
sudden upon him: news to tell
never one returned of Boldog's host,
and Thingol humbled Morgoth's boast.                                  3675
Then his heart with doubt and wrath was burned:
new tidings of dismay he learned,
how Thû was o'erthrown and his strong isle
broken and plundered, how with guile
his foes now guile beset; and spies                                   3680
he feared, till each Orc to his eyes
was half suspect. Still ever down
the aisléd forests came renown
of Huan baying, hound of war
that Gods unleashed in Valinor.                                       3685

    Then Morgoth of Huan's fate bethought
long-rumoured, and in dark he wrought.
Fierce hunger-haunted packs he had
that in wolvish form and flesh were clad,
but demon spirits dire did hold;                                      3690
and ever wild their voices rolled
in cave and mountain where they housed
and endless snarling echoes roused.
From these a whelp he chose and fed
with his own hand on bodies dead,                                     3695
on fairest flesh of Elves and Men,
till huge he grew and in his den
no more could creep, but by the chair
of Morgoth's self would lie and glare,
nor suffer Balrog, Orc, nor beast                                     3700
to touch him. Many a ghastly feast
he held beneath that awful throne,
rending flesh and gnawing bone.
There deep enchantment on him fell,
the anguish and the power of hell;                                    3705
more great and terrible he became
with fire-red eyes and jaws aflame,

with breath like vapours of the grave,
than any beast of wood or cave,
than any beast of earth or hell                                   3710
that ever in any time befell,
surpassing all his race and kin,
the ghastly tribe of Draugluin.

Him Carcharoth, the Red Maw, name
the songs of Elves. Not yet he came                               3715
disastrous, ravening, from the gates
of Angband. There he sleepless waits;
where those great portals threatening loom
his red eyes smoulder in the gloom,
his teeth are bare, his jaws are wide;                            3720
and none may walk, nor creep, nor glide,
nor thrust with power his menace past
to enter Morgoth's dungeon vast.

Now, lo! before his watchful eyes
a slinking shape he far descries                                  3725
that crawls into the frowning plain
and halts at gaze, then on again
comes stalking near, a wolvish shape
haggard, wayworn, with jaws agape;
and o'er it batlike in wide rings                                 3730
a reeling shadow slowly wings.
Such shapes there oft were seen to roam,
this land their native haunt and home;
and yet his mood with strange unease
is filled, and boding thoughts him seize.                         3735

'What grievous terror, what dread guard
hath Morgoth set to wait, and barred
his doors against all entering feet?
Long ways we have come at last to meet
the very maw of death that opes                                   3740
between us and our quest! Yet hopes
we never had. No turning back!'
Thus Beren speaks, as in his track
he halts and sees with werewolf eyes
afar the horror that there lies.                                  3745
Then onward desperate he passed,
skirting the black pits yawning vast,

where King Fingolfin ruinous fell
alone before the gates of hell.

Before those gates alone they stood,                    3750
while Carcharoth in doubtful mood
glowered upon them, and snarling spoke,
and echoes in the arches woke:
'Hail! Draugluin, my kindred's lord!
'Tis very long since hitherward                         3755
thou camest. Yea, 'tis passing strange
to see thee now: a grievous change
is on thee, lord, who once so dire,
so dauntless, and as fleet as fire,
ran over wild and waste, but now                        3760
with weariness must bend and bow!
'Tis hard to find the struggling breath
when Huan's teeth as sharp as death
have rent the throat? What fortune rare
brings thee back living here to fare —                  3765
if Draugluin thou art? Come near!
I would know more, and see thee clear.'

'Who art thou, hungry upstart whelp,
to bar my ways whom thou shouldst help?
I fare with hasty tidings new                           3770
to Morgoth from forest-haunting Thû.
Aside! for I must in; or go
and swift my coming tell below!'

Then up that doorward slowly stood,
eyes shining grim with evil mood,                       3775
uneasy growling: 'Draugluin,
if such thou be, now enter in!
But what is this that crawls beside,
slinking as if 'twould neath thee hide?
Though wingéd creatures to and fro                      3780
unnumbered pass here, all I know.
I know not this. Stay, vampire, stay!
I like not thy kin nor thee. Come, say
what sneaking errand thee doth bring,
thou wingéd vermin, to the king!                        3785
Small matter, I doubt not, if thou stay
or enter, or if in my play

I crush thee like a fly on wall,
or bite thy wings and let thee crawl.'

    Huge-stalking, noisome, close he came.     3790
In Beren's eyes there gleamed a flame;
the hair upon his neck uprose.
Nought may the fragrance fair enclose,
the odour of immortal flowers
in everlasting spring neath showers     3795
that glitter silver in the grass
in Valinor. Where'er did pass
Tinúviel, such air there went.
From that foul devil-sharpened scent
its sudden sweetness no disguise     3800
enchanted dark to cheat the eyes
could keep, if near those nostrils drew
snuffling in doubt. This Beren knew
upon the brink of hell prepared
for battle and death. There threatening stared     3805
those dreadful shapes, in hatred both,
false Draugluin and Carcharoth
when, lo! a marvel to behold:
some power, descended from of old,
from race divine beyond the West,     3810
sudden Tinúviel possessed
like inner fire. The vampire dark
she flung aside, and like a lark
cleaving through night to dawn she sprang,
while sheer, heart-piercing silver, rang     3815
her voice, as those long trumpets keen
thrilling, unbearable, unseen
in the cold aisles of morn. Her cloak
by white hands woven, like a smoke,
like all-bewildering, all-enthralling,     3820
all-enfolding evening, falling
from lifted arms, as forth she stepped,
across those awful eyes she swept,
a shadow and a mist of dreams
wherein entangled starlight gleams.     3825

    'Sleep, O unhappy, tortured thrall!
Thou woebegotten, fail and fall
down, down from anguish, hatred, pain,

---

from lust, from hunger, bond and chain,
to that oblivion, dark and deep,     3830
the well, the lightless pit of sleep!
For one brief hour escape the net,
the dreadful doom of life forget!'

His eyes were quenched, his limbs were loosed;
he fell like running steer that noosed     3835
and tripped goes crashing to the ground.
Deathlike, moveless, without a sound
outstretched he lay, as lightning stroke
had felled a huge o'ershadowing oak.

★

## NOTES

3554    *banded* A, B; > *branded* B, but I think that the *r* was written in by somebody else.

3589    *Thorndor* emended to *Thorondor* in B, but I think that this was a late correction.

3606    *pinned it to earth* A, B; *about the heel* apparently a late emendation to B.

3615    *Thorndor* later emended to *Thorondor* in B, see 3589.

3623    *after* > *secret* B, a late emendation when Gondolin's foundation had been made much earlier.

3638–9    A:    nor ever again to war came forth
          until the last battle of the North,
          but builded slow his mighty thought
          of pride and lust unfathomed wrought.

3650    Against this line is written the date 'Sep. 28'. The previous date was 27 Sept. 1930 against line 3478.

3658    *Finweg* A, B, emended to *Fingon* B, as at lines 1647, 1654.

3712–13    This couplet not in A, as originally written.

3714    A (as originally written):

       Him Carcharos, the Knife-fang, name

*Carcharos* then > *Carcharas*, and then > *Carcharoth* (see notes to lines 3751, 3807). In the margin of A is written *Red Maw*, and *Caras* with another, illegible, word beginning *Car-*; also *Gargaroth*; and *Fearphantom Draugluin is his name*. This may mean that my father was thinking of using the name *Draugluin* for the Wolf of Angband, though

> *Draugluin* had by now appeared in the A-text (3401) for the
> great wolf of the Wizard's Isle.

3751 *Carcharas* A, not emended to *Carcharoth* (see note to 3714).

3790 Against this line is written the date 'Sep. 30 1930'. The
previous date was 28 Sept. 1930 against line 3650.

3807 *Carcharoth* A (rhyming with *both*); see notes to 3714,
3751.

## Commentary on Canto XII

The greater part of this Canto is retrospective: beginning with the death
of Fingolfin in combat with Morgoth, it passes to Morgoth's doubts and
fears and his rearing of Carcharoth. By this time (September 1930) a
large part, at any rate, of the prose 'Silmarillion' developed out of the
'Sketch of the Mythology' had been written, as I hope to demonstrate
later, and it seems certain that the story of Fingolfin's duel with Morgoth
as it appears in this Canto followed the prose version, though we meet it
here for the first time (together with the names *Grond*, the Hammer of
the Underworld, and *Ringil*, Fingolfin's sword). The text in *The Silmarillion* (pp. 153–4) was largely based on the Lay, which it follows in
the structure of the account and from which derive many phrases;[*] but
independent traces of the 'prose tradition' are also present. The account
in the poem gives no indication of when the duel took place, or of what
led Fingolfin to challenge Morgoth. For the much earlier mention of
Fingolfin's death (now very obscure, but certainly quite differently
conceived) see pp. 146–7.

The further mention in this Canto of Boldog's raid (lines 3665–75)
will be discussed at the end of the poem (pp. 310–13).

Turning to the 'foreground' narrative, a passage in Synopsis III
already given (pp. 270–1) bears on the content of Canto XII: it was
bracketed and marked 'Later'.

> Morgoth hearing of the breaking of the Wizard's Tower sends out an
> army of Orcs; finding the wolves are slain with . . . . . . throats he
> thinks it is Huan and fashions a vast wolf – Carcharas – mightiest of all
> wolves to guard his door.

Synopsis III continues from the point reached on p. 283:

> The hideous gates of Angband. There lay *Carcharoth knifefang*.
> He gets slowly to his feet and bars the gate. 'Growl not O Wolf for I go
> to seek Morgoth with news of Thû.' He approached to snuff the air of

---

[*] For example: 'the rumour of his feet' (cf. line 3561); Morgoth 'like a tower, iron-
crowned' (cf. 3563); he swung Grond down 'like a bolt of thunder' (cf. 3571); 'smoke and
fire darted' (cf. 3572–3); 'the blood gushed forth black and smoking' (cf. 3606–7); &c.

her, for faint suspicion moved in his wicked heart, and he fell into
slumber.

The interpretation of the wolf's name as 'Knife-fang' goes back to the
*Tale of Tinúviel* and survived into the A-text of the Lay (see note to line
3714), but was replaced in B by the translation 'Red Maw'. The words
'red maw' are used of Karkaras in the *Tale*, but not as his name (II. 34).
The idea of Carcharoth's approaching Lúthien 'to snuff the air of her'
is also derived, in these same words, from the *Tale* (II. 31).

Synopsis IV does not here concern us (see p. 283); Synopsis V, after
the point reached on p. 283, now has a heading '11', and is clearly the
basis for the story in Canto XII of the Lay:

[*Added in pencil*: Battle of Morgoth and Fingolfin.]
    Morgoth hears of the ruin of Thû's castle. His mind is filled with
misgiving and anger. The gates of Angband strengthened; because of
the rumour of Huan he [*struck out at time of writing*: fashions the
greatest] chooses the fiercest wolf from all the whelps of his packs, and
feeds him on flesh of Men and Elves, and enchants him so that he
becomes the most great and terrible of all beasts that ever have been –
Carcharos.
    Beren and Lúthien approach. [*Added in pencil*: the pitted plain of
Fingolfin's fight.] The enchanting of Carcharos.

# XIII

Into the vast and echoing gloom,                    3840
more dread than many-tunnelled tomb
in labyrinthine pyramid
where everlasting death is hid,
down awful corridors that wind
down to a menace dark enshrined;                    3845
down to the mountain's roots profound,
devoured, tormented, bored and ground
by seething vermin spawned of stone;
down to the depths they went alone.
    The arch behind of twilit shade                 3850
they saw recede and dwindling fade;
the thunderous forges' rumour grew,
a burning wind there roaring blew
foul vapours up from gaping holes.

Huge shapes there stood like carven trolls          3855
enormous hewn of blasted rock
to forms that mortal likeness mock;
monstrous and menacing, entombed,
at every turn they silent loomed
in fitful glares that leaped and died.               3860
There hammers clanged, and tongues there cried
with sound like smitten stone; there wailed
faint from far under, called and failed
amid the iron clink of chain
voices of captives put to pain.                      3865

    Loud rose a din of laughter hoarse,
self-loathing yet without remorse;
loud came a singing harsh and fierce
like swords of terror souls to pierce.
Red was the glare through open doors                 3870
of firelight mirrored on brazen floors,
and up the arches towering clomb
to glooms unguessed, to vaulted dome
swathed in wavering smokes and steams
stabbed with flickering lightning-gleams.            3875
To Morgoth's hall, where dreadful feast
he held, and drank the blood of beast
and lives of Men, they stumbling came:
their eyes were dazed with smoke and flame.
The pillars, reared like monstrous shores            3880
to bear earth's overwhelming floors,
were devil-carven, shaped with skill
such as unholy dreams doth fill:
they towered like trees into the air,
whose trunks are rooted in despair,                  3885
whose shade is death, whose fruit is bane,
whose boughs like serpents writhe in pain.
    Beneath them ranged with spear and sword
stood Morgoth's sable-armoured horde:
the fire on blade and boss of shield                 3890
was red as blood on stricken field.
Beneath a monstrous column loomed
the throne of Morgoth, and the doomed
and dying gasped upon the floor:
his hideous footstool, rape of war.                  3895

About him sat his awful thanes,
the Balrog-lords with fiery manes,
redhanded, mouthed with fangs of steel;
devouring wolves were crouched at heel.
And o'er the host of hell there shone    3900
with a cold radiance, clear and wan,
the Silmarils, the gems of fate,
emprisoned in the crown of hate.

Lo! through the grinning portals dread
sudden a shadow swooped and fled;    3905
and Beren gasped – he lay alone,
with crawling belly on the stone:
a form bat-wingéd, silent, flew
where the huge pillared branches grew,
amid the smokes and mounting steams.    3910
And as on the margin of dark dreams
a dim-felt shadow unseen grows
to cloud of vast unease, and woes
foreboded, nameless, roll like doom
upon the soul, so in that gloom    3915
the voices fell, and laughter died
slow to silence many-eyed.
A nameless doubt, a shapeless fear,
had entered in their caverns drear,
and grew, and towered above them cowed,    3920
hearing in heart the trumpets loud
of gods forgotten. Morgoth spoke,
and thunderous the silence broke:
'Shadow, descend! And do not think
to cheat mine eyes! In vain to shrink    3925
from thy Lord's gaze, or seek to hide.
My will by none may be defied.
Hope nor escape doth here await
those that unbidden pass my gate.
Descend! ere anger blast thy wing,    3930
thou foolish, frail, bat-shapen thing,
and yet not bat within! Come down!'

Slow-wheeling o'er his iron crown,
reluctantly, shivering and small,
Beren there saw the shadow fall,    3935
and droop before the hideous throne,

a weak and trembling thing, alone.
And as thereon great Morgoth bent
his darkling gaze, he shuddering went,
belly to earth, the cold sweat dank                3940
upon his fell, and crawling shrank
beneath the darkness of that seat,
beneath the shadow of those feet.
 Tinúviel spake, a shrill, thin, sound
piercing those silences profound:                 3945
'A lawful errand here me brought;
from Thû's dark mansions have I sought,
from Taur-na-Fuin's shade I fare
to stand before thy mighty chair!'

 'Thy name, thou shrieking waif, thy name!         3950
Tidings enough from Thû there came
but short while since. What would he now?
Why send such messenger as thou?'

 'Thuringwethil I am, who cast
a shadow o'er the face aghast                      3955
of the sallow moon in the doomed land
of shivering Beleriand.'

 'Liar art thou, who shalt not weave
deceit before mine eyes. Now leave
thy form and raiment false, and stand              3960
revealed, and delivered to my hand!'

 There came a slow and shuddering change:
the batlike raiment dark and strange
was loosed, and slowly shrank and fell
quivering. She stood revealed in hell.             3965
About her slender shoulders hung
her shadowy hair, and round her clung
her garment dark, where glimmered pale
the starlight caught in magic veil.
Dim dreams and faint oblivious sleep               3970
fell softly thence, in dungeons deep
an odour stole of elven-flowers
from elven-dells where silver showers
drip softly through the evening air;
and round there crawled with greedy stare          3975
dark shapes of snuffling hunger dread.

With arms upraised and drooping head
then softly she began to sing
a theme of sleep and slumbering,
wandering, woven with deeper spell          3980
than songs wherewith in ancient dell
Melian did once the twilight fill,
profound, and fathomless, and still.

The fires of Angband flared and died,
smouldered into darkness; through the wide          3985
and hollow halls there rolled unfurled
the shadows of the underworld.
All movement stayed, and all sound ceased,
save vaporous breath of Orc and beast.
One fire in darkness still abode:          3990
the lidless eyes of Morgoth glowed;
one sound the breathing silence broke:
the mirthless voice of Morgoth spoke.

'So Lúthien, so Lúthien,
a liar like all Elves and Men!          3995
Yet welcome, welcome, to my hall!
I have a use for every thrall.
What news of Thingol in his hole
shy lurking like a timid vole?
What folly fresh is in his mind,          4000
who cannot keep his offspring blind
from straying thus? or can devise
no better counsel for his spies?'

She wavered, and she stayed her song.
'The road,' she said, 'was wild and long,          4005
but Thingol sent me not, nor knows
what way his rebellious daughter goes.
Yet every road and path will lead
Northward at last, and here of need
I trembling come with humble brow,          4010
and here before thy throne I bow;
for Lúthien hath many arts
for solace sweet of kingly hearts.'

'And here of need thou shalt remain
now, Lúthien, in joy or pain –          4015
or pain, the fitting doom for all,

*The Lay of Leithian*, lines 3994–4027

for rebel, thief, and upstart thrall.
Why should ye not in our fate share
of woe and travail? Or should I spare
to slender limb and body frail                          4020
breaking torment? Of what avail
here dost thou deem thy babbling song
and foolish laughter? Minstrels strong
are at my call. Yet I will give
a respite brief, a while to live,                        4025
a little while, though purchased dear,
to Lúthien the fair and clear,
a pretty toy for idle hour.
In slothful gardens many a flower
like thee the amorous gods are used                      4030
honey-sweet to kiss, and cast then bruised,
their fragrance loosing, under feet.
But here we seldom find such sweet
amid our labours long and hard,
from godlike idleness debarred.                          4035
And who would not taste the honey-sweet
lying to lips, or crush with feet
the soft cool tissue of pale flowers,
easing like gods the dragging hours?
A! curse the Gods! O hunger dire,                        4040
O blinding thirst's unending fire!
One moment shall ye cease, and slake
your sting with morsel I here take!'

    In his eyes the fire to flame was fanned,
and forth he stretched his brazen hand.                  4045
Lúthien as shadow shrank aside.
'Not thus, O king! Not thus!' she cried,
'do great lords hark to humble boon!
For every minstrel hath his tune;
and some are strong and some are soft,                   4050
and each would bear his song aloft,
and each a little while be heard,
though rude the note, and light the word.
But Lúthien hath cunning arts
for solace sweet of kingly hearts.                       4055
Now hearken!' And her wings she caught
then deftly up, and swift as thought

slipped from his grasp, and wheeling round,
fluttering before his eyes, she wound
a mazy-wingéd dance, and sped                    4060
about his iron-crownéd head.
Suddenly her song began anew;
and soft came dropping like a dew
down from on high in that domed hall
her voice bewildering, magical,                  4065
and grew to silver-murmuring streams
pale falling in dark pools in dreams.

She let her flying raiment sweep,
enmeshed with woven spells of sleep,
as round the dark void she ranged and reeled.    4070
From wall to wall she turned and wheeled
in dance such as never Elf nor fay
before devised, nor since that day;
than swallow swifter, than flittermouse
in dying light round darkened house              4075
more silken-soft, more strange and fair
than sylphine maidens of the Air
whose wings in Varda's heavenly hall
in rhythmic movement beat and fall.
Down crumpled Orc, and Balrog proud;             4080
all eyes were quenched, all heads were bowed;
the fires of heart and maw were stilled,
and ever like a bird she thrilled
above a lightless world forlorn
in ecstasy enchanted borne.                      4085
All eyes were quenched, save those that glared
in Morgoth's lowering brows, and stared
in slowly wandering wonder round,
and slow were in enchantment bound.
Their will wavered, and their fire failed,       4090
and as beneath his brows they paled,
the Silmarils like stars were kindled
that in the reek of Earth had dwindled
escaping upwards clear to shine,
glistening marvellous in heaven's mine.          4095

Then flaring suddenly they fell,
down, down upon the floors of hell.
The dark and mighty head was bowed;

like mountain-top beneath a cloud
the shoulders foundered, the vast form            4100
crashed, as in overwhelming storm
huge cliffs in ruin slide and fall;
and prone lay Morgoth in his hall.
His crown there rolled upon the ground,
a wheel of thunder; then all sound                4105
died, and a silence grew as deep
as were the heart of Earth asleep.

Beneath the vast and empty throne
the adders lay like twisted stone,
the wolves like corpses foul were strewn;         4110
and there lay Beren deep in swoon:
no thought, no dream nor shadow blind
moved in the darkness of his mind.
    'Come forth, come forth! The hour hath knelled,
and Angband's mighty lord is felled!              4115
Awake, awake! For we two meet
alone before the aweful seat.'
This voice came down into the deep
where he lay drowned in wells of sleep;
a hand flower-soft and flower-cool                4120
passed o'er his face, and the still pool
of slumber quivered. Up then leaped
his mind to waking; forth he crept.
The wolvish fell he flung aside
and sprang unto his feet, and wide                4125
staring amid the soundless gloom
he gasped as one living shut in tomb.
There to his side he felt her shrink,
felt Lúthien now shivering sink,
her strength and magic dimmed and spent,          4130
and swift his arms about her went.

Before his feet he saw amazed
the gems of Fëanor, that blazed
with white fire glistening in the crown
of Morgoth's might now fallen down.               4135
To move that helm of iron vast
no strength he found, and thence aghast
he strove with fingers mad to wrest
the guerdon of their hopeless quest,

till in his heart there fell the thought                    4140
of that cold morn whereon he fought
with Curufin; then from his belt
the sheathless knife he drew, and knelt,
and tried its hard edge, bitter-cold,
o'er which in Nogrod songs had rolled                       4145
of dwarvish armourers singing slow
to hammer-music long ago.
Iron as tender wood it clove
and mail as woof of loom it rove.
The claws of iron that held the gem,                        4150
it bit them through and sundered them;
a Silmaril he clasped and held,
and the pure radiance slowly welled
red glowing through the clenching flesh.
Again he stooped and strove afresh                          4155
one more of the holy jewels three
that Fëanor wrought of yore to free.
But round those fires was woven fate:
not yet should they leave the halls of hate.
The dwarvish steel of cunning blade                         4160
by treacherous smiths of Nogrod made
snapped; then ringing sharp and clear
in twain it sprang, and like a spear
or errant shaft the brow it grazed
of Morgoth's sleeping head, and dazed                       4165
their hearts with fear. For Morgoth groaned
with voice entombed, like wind that moaned
in hollow caverns penned and bound.
There came a breath; a gasping sound
moved through the halls, as Orc and beast                   4170
turned in their dreams of hideous feast;
in sleep uneasy Balrogs stirred,
and far above was faintly heard
an echo that in tunnels rolled,
a wolvish howling long and cold.                            4175

★

# NOTES

3840    At the beginning of the Canto is written the date 'Oct. 1 1930'.
        The previous date was 30 Sept. 1930 at line 3790.

3860    With this line the B typescript comes to an end, and the text
        continues to the end in fine manuscript.

3881    This line is dated 'Sept. 14 1931'. The previous date was 1 Oct.
        1930 at line 3840.

3887    This line is dated 'Sept. 15' (1931).

3947    Late change in B: *from Sauron's mansions have I sought*. See
        p. 232, note to lines 2064–6.

3951    Late change in B: *Tidings enough from Sauron came*.

3954    In the margin of B is written against *Thuringwethil*, at the
        time of the writing out of the text, 'sc. she of hidden shadow'.

3957    *Beleriand* A and B (i.e. not *Broseliand* emended).

3962    This line is dated 'Sep. 16 1931'.

3969    *magic* > *elvish* in B, but this is doubtless a late change, when
        my father no longer used this once favourite word.

4029    Against this line is written the date 'Sep. 14', duplicating that
        given to line 3881.

4045    Against this line is written the date 'Sep. 16', duplicating that
        given to line 3962.

4085    After this line is written the last date in the A manuscript,
        'Sept. 17 1931'.

4092–3  These lines were written in the margin of B, but the original
        lines:

            the Silmarils were lit like stars
            that fume of Earth upreeking mars

        were not struck out.

4163–6  A:   in twain it sprang; and quaking fear
             fell on their hearts, for Morgoth groaned


## Commentary on Canto XIII

There is not much to be learnt from the Synopses concerning this part of
the narrative, but the Angband scene was never greatly changed from its
original form in the *Tale of Tinúviel* (II. 31 ff.). Synopsis I is at the end
reduced to mere headings, II has given out, and IV does not deal with the
entry into Angband. III, given on pp. 293–4 as far as the enchantment of
Carcharoth, continues:

    After endless wanderings in corridors they stumble into the pres-
    ence of Morgoth. Morgoth speaks. 'Who art thou that flittest about my
    halls as a bat, but art not a bat? Thou dost not belong here, nor wert
    thou summoned. Who has ever come here unsummoned? None!' 'But

I was summoned. I am Lúthien daughter of Thingol.' Then Morgoth laughed, but he was moved with suspicion, and said that her accursed race would get no soft words or favour in Angband. What could she do to give him pleasure, and save herself from the lowest dungeons? He reached out his mighty brazen hand but she shrank away. He is angry but she offers to dance.

[*The remainder of the outline is in pencil and in places indecipherable*:] She lets fall her bat-garb. Her hair falls about. The lights of Angband die. Impenetrable dark falls: only the eyes of Morgoth and the faint glimmer of Tinúviel . . . . . . . . . . . . . . Her fragrance causes all to draw near greedily. Tinúviel flies [?in at] door leaving Beren struck with horror. . . . . . . . . . . . .

Here this outline ends. Morgoth's words 'Who art thou that flittest about my halls as a bat' occur also in the *Tale of Tinúviel* (II. 32) – this outline several times adopts directly the wording of the *Tale*, see pp. 283, 294. This is a curious point, for in the *Tale* Tinúviel was not attired in a bat-skin, whereas in Synopsis III she was. It is conceivable that Melko's words actually gave rise to this element in the story.

In the *Tale* Tinúviel lied to Melko, saying that Tinwelint her father had driven her out, and in reply he said that she need not hope for 'soft words'– this too is a phrase that recurs in Synopsis III. But the remainder of this outline does not relate closely to the *Tale*.

Synopsis V is here very brief. After 'the enchanting of Carcharos' (p. 294) it has only (still under the heading '11'):

> The cozening of Morgoth and the rape of the Silmaril.
> The dwarvish knife of Curufin breaks.

It is clear that the concluding passage of Synopsis III, given above, was a direct precursor of Canto XIII; but some elements – and actual wording – in the scene go back to the *Tale* without being mentioned in the Synopsis. Lúthien's words 'his rebellious daughter' (4007) seem to echo 'he is an overbearing Elf and I give not my love at his command' (II, 32); there is a clear relation between the words of the *Tale* (*ibid.*):

> Then did Tinúviel begin such a dance as neither she nor other sprite or fay or elf danced ever before or has done since

and lines 4072–3

> in dance such as never Elf nor fay
> before devised, nor since that day;

and with 'the adders lay like twisted stone' (4109) cf. 'Beneath his chair the adders lay like stones.' It is interesting to see the idea of the shard of the knife-blade striking Morgoth's brow (in *The Silmarillion* his cheek) emerging in the composition of this Canto; as first written (see note to lines 4163–6) it seems to have been the sound of the knife snapping that disturbed the sleepers, as it was expressly in the *Tale* (II. 33). With the 'treacherous smiths of Nogrod' (4161) who made Curufin's knife cf. the passage in *The Children of Húrin* concerning *the bearded Dwarves of troth unmindful* who made the knife of Flinding that slipped from its sheath (p. 44, lines 1142 ff.): that was made by the Dwarves of Belegost, and like Curufin's

> [its] edge would eat    through iron noiseless
> as a clod of clay    is cleft by the share.

The account in *The Silmarillion* (pp. 180–1) is clearly based on Canto XIII, from which it derives many features, though it is reduced, notably by compressing the two episodes of Lúthien singing (3977 ff., 4062 ff.) into one; and the prose here owes less to the verses than in other places.

Lúthien's naming herself *Thuringwethil* to Morgoth (line 3954) is notable. In *The Silmarillion* (p. 178) the bat-fell which Huan brought from Tol-in-Gaurhoth was that of Thuringwethil: 'she was the messenger of Sauron, and was wont to fly in vampire's form to Angband'; whereas in the Lay (lines 3402 ff.), as I have noticed (p. 284), 'the bat-wings are only said to be such as bear up Thû's messengers, and are not associated with a particular or chief messenger'. It seems possible that in the Lay Lúthien devised this name ('she of hidden shadow') as a riddling description of herself, and that this led to the conception of the bat-messenger from the Wizard's Isle to Angband named Thuringwethil; but there is no proof of this.

With the

> sylphine maidens of the Air
> whose wings in Varda's heavenly hall
> in rhythmic movement beat and fall          (4077–9)

cf. the tale of *The Coming of the Valar and the Building of Valinor* (I. 65–6), where it is said that with Manwë and Varda there entered the world 'many of those lesser Vali who loved them and had played nigh them and attuned their music to theirs, and these are the Mánir and the Súruli, *the sylphs of the airs and of the winds*'.

# XIV

> Up through the dark and echoing gloom
> as ghosts from many-tunnelled tomb,
> up from the mountains' roots profound
> and the vast menace underground,
> their limbs aquake with deadly fear,          4180

terror in eyes, and dread in ear,
together fled they, by the beat
affrighted of their flying feet.

    At last before them far away
they saw the glimmering wraith of day,          4185
the mighty archway of the gate –
and there a horror new did wait.
Upon the threshold, watchful, dire,
his eyes new-kindled with dull fire,
towered Carcharoth, a biding doom:              4190
his jaws were gaping like a tomb,
his teeth were bare, his tongue aflame;
aroused he watched that no one came,
no flitting shade nor hunted shape,
seeking from Angband to escape.                 4195
Now past that guard what guile or might
could thrust from death into the light?

    He heard afar their hurrying feet,
he snuffed an odour strange and sweet;
he smelled their coming long before             4200
they marked the waiting threat at door.
His limbs he stretched and shook off sleep,
then stood at gaze. With sudden leap
upon them as they sped he sprang,
and his howling in the arches rang.             4205
    Too swift for thought his onset came,
too swift for any spell to tame;
and Beren desperate then aside
thrust Lúthien, and forth did stride
unarmed, defenceless to defend                  4210
Tinúviel until the end.
With left he caught at hairy throat,
with right hand at the eyes he smote –
his right, from which the radiance welled
of the holy Silmaril he held.                   4215
As gleam of swords in fire there flashed
the fangs of Carcharoth, and crashed
together like a trap, that tore
the hand about the wrist, and shore
through brittle bone and sinew nesh,            4220
devouring the frail mortal flesh;

and in that cruel mouth unclean
engulfed the jewel's holy sheen.

### The Unwritten Cantos

There was virtually no change in the narrative from the *Tale* to the Lay in
the opening passage of Canto XIV, but the account in *The Silmarillion*
differs, in that there Beren did not strike at the eyes of the wolf with his
right hand holding the Silmaril, but held the jewel up before Carcharoth
to daunt him. My father intended to alter the Lay here, as is seen from a
marginal direction to introduce the element of 'daunting'.

   *The Lay of Leithian* ends here, in both the A and B texts, and also in
the pages of rough draft, but an isolated sheet found elsewhere gives a
few further lines, together with variants, in the first stage of composition:

> Against the wall then Beren reeled
> but still with his left he sought to shield
> fair Lúthien, who cried aloud
> to see his pain, and down she bowed
> in anguish sinking to the ground.

   There is also a short passage, found on a separate sheet at the end of the
B-text, which is headed 'a piece from the end of the poem':

> Where the forest-stream went through the wood,
> and silent all the stems there stood
> of tall trees, moveless, hanging dark
> with mottled shadows on their bark
> above the green and gleaming river,                        5
> there came through leaves a sudden shiver,
> a windy whisper through the still
> cool silences; and down the hill,
> as faint as a deep sleeper's breath,
> an echo came as cold as death:                            10
> 'Long are the paths, of shadow made
> where no foot's print is ever laid,
> over the hills, across the seas!
> Far, far away are the Lands of Ease,
> but the Land of the Lost is further yet,                  15
> where the Dead wait, while ye forget.
> No moon is there, no voice, no sound
> of beating heart; a sigh profound
> once in each age as each age dies
> alone is heard. Far, far it lies,                         20

> the Land of Waiting where the Dead sit,
> in their thought's shadow, by no moon lit.

With the last lines compare the passage at the end of the tale of Beren and Lúthien in *The Silmarillion* (p. 186):

> But Lúthien came to the halls of Mandos, which are the appointed places of the Eldalië, beyond the mansions of the West upon the confines of the world. There those that wait sit in the shadow of their thought.

There is nothing else, and I do not think that there ever was anything else. All my father's later work on the poem was devoted to the revision of what was already in existence; and the *Lay of Leithian* ends here.

Of the five synopses that have been given in sections in previous pages, only the fifth bears on the escape of Beren and Lúthien from Angband. This outline was last quoted on p. 305 ('the dwarvish knife of Curufin breaks'). It continues:

> Beren and Lúthien flee in fear. Arousing of Carcharos. Beren's hand is bitten off in which he holds the Silmaril. Madness of Carcharos. Angband awakes. Flight of Beren and Lúthien towards the waters of Sirion. Canto [i.e. Canto 11, see p. 305] ends as they hear the pursuing wolves behind. Wrapped in Lúthien's cloak they flit beneath the stars.

Thus the rescue of Beren and Lúthien by Thorondor and his vassals was not yet present, and the story was still in this respect unchanged from the *Tale of Tinúviel* (II. 34); cf. especially:

> Tinúviel wrapped part of her dark mantle about Beren, and so for a while flitting by dusk and dark amid the hills they were seen by none.

The first record of the changed story of the escape from Angband is found on an isolated slip, written hastily in pencil and very difficult to decipher:

> Carcharoth goes mad and drives all [?orcs] before him like a wind. The sound of his awful howling causes rocks to split and fall. There is an earthquake underground. Morgoth's wrath on waking. The gateway [?falls] in and hell is blocked, and great fires and smokes burst from Thangorodrim. Thunder and lightning. Beren lies dying before the gate. Tinúviel's song as she kisses his hand and prepares to die. Thorondor comes down and bears them amid the lightning that [?stabs] at them like spears and a hail of arrows from the battlements. They pass above Gondolin and Lúthien sees the white city far below, [?gleaming] like a lily in the valley. Thorondor sets her down in Brethil.

This is very close in narrative structure to the story in *The Silmarillion* (p. 182), with the earthquake, fire and smoke from Thangorodrim, Beren's lying near death at the Gate, Lúthien's kissing his hand (staunching the wound), the descent of Thorondor, and the passage of the eagle(s) over Gondolin. This last shows that this brief outline is relatively late, since Gondolin was already in existence before the Battle of Unnumbered Tears (II. 208). But in this text they are set down in Brethil (a name that does not appear in the works until several years later); in *The Silmarillion* they are set down 'upon the borders of Doriath', in 'that same dell whence Beren had stolen in despair and left Lúthien asleep'. – On the reference to Gondolin as 'a lily in the valley' see I. 172.

Synopsis V has more to tell subsequently of the wanderings of Beren and Lúthien before they returned to Doriath, but I now set out the remaining materials in their entirety before commenting on them. First it is convenient to cite the end of Synopsis II, which has been given already (p. 270):

> Celegorm's embassy to Thingol so that Thingol knows or thinks he knows Beren dead and Lúthien in Nargothrond.
> Why Celegorm and Curufin hated by Thingol . .  . . . . .
> The loss of Dairon.

Synopsis IV has been given (p. 273) only as far as 'They prepare to go to Angband', since the outline then turns away from the story of Beren and Lúthien themselves, according to my father's projection at that time for the further course of the Lay, and continues as follows:

II

> Doriath. The hunt for Lúthien and the loss of Dairon. War on the borders. Boldog slain. So Thingol knows Lúthien not yet dead is caught, but fears that Boldog's raid means that Morgoth has got wind of her wandering. Actually it means no more than the legend of her beauty.
> An embassy comes from Celegorm. Thingol learns that Beren is dead, and Lúthien at Nargothrond. He is roused to wrath by the hints of the letter that Celegorm will leave Felagund to die, and will usurp the throne of Nargothrond. And so Thingol had better let Lúthien stay where she is.
> Thingol prepares an army to go against Nargothrond, but learns that Lúthien has left, and Celegorm and Curufin have fled to Aglon. He sends an embassy to Aglon. It is routed and put to flight by the sudden onslaught of Carcharas. Mablung escapes to tell the tale. The devastation of Doriath by Carcharas.

12

The rape of the Silmaril and the home-coming of Beren and Lúthien.

13

The wolf-hunt and death of Huan and Beren.

14

The recall of Beren and Huan.

Synopsis V continues as a more substantial preparation for the end of the poem never to be written, which my father at this stage conceived in three further Cantos.

12

Sorrow in Doriath at flight of Lúthien. Thingol's heart hardened against Beren, despite words of Melian. A mighty hunt is made throughout the realm, but many of the folk strayed north and west and south of Doriath beyond the magic of Melian and were lost. Dairon became separated from his comrades and wandered away into the East of the world, where some say he pipes yet seeking Lúthien in vain.

The embassy of Celegorm tells Thingol that Beren and Felagund are dead, that Celegorm will make himself king of Narog, and while telling him that Lúthien is safe in Nargothrond and treating for her hand, hints that she will not return: it also warns him to trouble not the matter of the Silmarils. Thingol is wroth – and is moved to think better of Beren, while yet blaming [him] for the woes that followed his coming to Doriath, and most for loss of Dairon.

Thingol arms for war against Celegorm. Melian says she would forbid this evil war of Elf with Elf, but that never shall Thingol cross blade with Celegorm. Thingol's army meets with the host of Boldog on the borders of Doriath. Morgoth has heard of the beauty of Lúthien, and the rumour of her wandering. He has ordered Thû and the Orcs to capture her. A battle is fought and Thingol is victorious. The Orcs are driven into Taur-na-Fuin or slain. Thingol himself slays Boldog. Mablung Heavyhand was Thingol's chief warrior and fought at his side; Beleg was the chief of his scouts. Though victorious Thingol is filled with still more disquiet at Morgoth's hunt for Lúthien. Beleg goes forth from the camp on Doriath's borders and journeys, unseen by the archers, to Narog. He brings tidings of the flight of Lúthien, the rescue of Beren, and the exile of Celegorm and Curufin. He [read Thingol] goes home and sends an embassy to Aglon to demand recompense, and aid in the rescue of Lúthien. He renews his vow to imprison Beren for ever if he does not return with a Silmaril, though Melian warns him that he knows not what he says.

The embassy meets the onslaught of Carcharos who by fate or the power of the Silmaril bursts into Doriath. All perish save Mablung who brings the news. Devastation of the woods. The wood-elves flee to the caves.

### 13

Beren and Lúthien escape to the Shadowy Mountains, but become lost and bewildered in the dreads of Nan Dungorthin, and are hunted by phantoms, and snared at last by the great spiders. Huan rescues them, and guides them down Sirion, and so they reach Doriath from the south, and find the woods silent and empty till they come to the guarded bridge.

Huan, Beren, and Lúthien come before Thingol. They tell their tale; yet Thingol will not relent. The brave words of Beren, revealing the mystery of Carcharos. Thingol relents. The wolf-hunt is prepared. Huan, Thingol, Beren, and Mablung depart. Lúthien abides with Melian in foreboding. Carcharos is slain, but slew Huan who defended Beren. Yet Beren is mortally hurt, though he lived to place the Silmaril on Thingol's hand which Mablung cut from the wolf's belly.

The meeting and farewell of Beren and Tinúviel beneath Hirilorn. Burial of Huan and Beren.

### 14

Fading of Lúthien. Her journey to Mandos. The song of Lúthien in Mandos' halls, and the release of Beren. They dwelt long in Broseliand, but spake never more to mortal Men, and Lúthien became mortal.

This concludes all the material in the outlines. For the references to Boldog's raid, and Morgoth's interest in Lúthien, in the Lay itself see lines 2127–36, 2686–94, 3198–3201, and 3665–75.

In Synopsis IV (p. 310) Boldog's raid takes place earlier in the story, before the coming of Celegorm's embassy to Thingol, but its narrative value is obscure. It is not clear why the raid must inform Thingol that 'Lúthien not yet dead is caught', nor why he should conclude that 'Morgoth has got wind of her wandering'. Moreover the statement that 'actually it means no more than the legend of her beauty' can only mean (if Morgoth had *not* heard of her wandering forth from Doriath) that he sent out Boldog's warband with the express intention of seizing her from the fastness of the Thousand Caves.

In Synopsis V the raid was moved to a later point, and the host out of Doriath that destroyed Boldog was actually moving against Nargothrond. In *The Silmarillion* the embassy from Celegorm survived, but of Boldog's raid there is no hint, and Thingol does no more than 'think to make war' on Nargothrond:

But Thingol learned that Lúthien had journeyed far from Doriath, for messages came secretly from Celegorm, . . . saying that Felagund was dead, and Beren was dead, but Lúthien was in Nargothrond, and that Celegorm would wed her. Then Thingol was wrathful, and he sent forth spies, thinking to make war upon Nargothrond; and thus he learned that Lúthien was again fled, and that Celegorm and Curufin were driven from Nargothrond. Then his counsel was in doubt, for he had not the strength to assail the seven sons of Fëanor; but he sent messengers to Himring to summon their aid in seeking for Lúthien, since Celegorm had not sent her to the house of her father, nor had he kept her safely (pp. 183–4).

The 'spies' of this passage were derived from Beleg's secret mission to Nargothrond in Synopsis V (p. 311). It seems probable that my father actually discarded Boldog's raid; and with it went all suggestion that Lúthien's wandering had been reported to Morgoth (cf. lines 3665 ff.) and that Thû was given orders to capture her (Synopsis V). The passage in Canto IX of the Lay (2686–94) where Thû recognised Lúthien's voice – or, at least, knew that it must be she who was singing – does not, indeed, at all suggest that Thû was actively seeking her. These lines were the source for the passage in *The Silmarillion*, where Sauron standing in the tower of Tol-in-Gaurhoth

> smiled hearing her voice, for he knew that it was the daughter of Melian. The fame of the beauty of Lúthien, and the wonder of her song had long gone forth from Doriath; and he thought to make her captive and hand her over to the power of Morgoth, for his reward would be great.

But the idea that the beauty and singing of Lúthien had come to the ears of Sauron survives from the stage when Morgoth's interest in her was an important motive.

As noticed earlier (p. 209), the wandering and loss of Dairon goes back to the *Tale of Tinúviel* (II. 20–1) and survived into *The Silmarillion* (p. 183), where it is said that Daeron passed over the Blue Mountains 'into the East of Middle-earth, where for many ages he made lament beside dark waters for Lúthien'. Less is made in the later story of the great hunt for Lúthien, and nothing is said of the changing moods and intentions of Thingol towards Beren referred to in Synopsis V. The 'political' element of the ambitions of Celegorm and Curufin and the attempted browbeating and blackmail of Thingol is of course a new element that first appears in the Synopses (other than the earlier reference in the Lay, 2501–3, to the brothers' intentions in this regard), since the 'Nargothrond Element' is wholly absent from the *Tale of Tinúviel*; and similarly the interception of the embassy from Thingol to Aglon by Carcharoth, from which Mablung alone survived. This also remains in *The Silmarillion*.

In Synopsis V, where the bearing away of Beren and Lúthien from
Angband by Thorondor is not yet present, they flee from Angband
'towards the waters of Sirion' (p. 309), and (p. 312) 'escape to the
Shadowy Mountains, but become lost and bewildered in the dreads of
Nan Dungorthin, and are hunted by phantoms, and snared at last by the
great spiders. Huan rescues them, and guides them down Sirion . . .'
In the *Tale* likewise (II. 34–5), Huan rescued them from 'Nan
Dumgorthin'. This is a point of geography and shifting nomenclature of
great perplexity. I have shown (pp. 170–1, 234) that the meaning of
'Shadowy Mountains' changes in the course of the *Lay of Leithian*:
whereas at first (lines 386, 1318) the reference is to the Mountains
of Terror (Ered Gorgoroth), subsequently (line 1940) it is to Ered
Wethrin, the range fencing Hithlum. The Mountains of Terror, with the
great spiders, are described in lines 563 ff.

   In the present passage of Synopsis V the statements that Beren and
Lúthien escaping from Angband fled towards Sirion, and that Huan
rescuing them from Nan Dungorthin guided them down Sirion, very
strongly suggests that the Shadowy Mountains are here again, as might
be expected, Ered Wethrin. Nan Dungorthin must then be placed as in
*The Children of Húrin*, west of Sirion, in a valley of the southern slopes
of the Shadowy Mountains. But this means that the great spiders are
found in both places.

   It is difficult to suggest a satisfactory explanation of this. A possibility
is that when Beren crossed the Mountains of Terror and encountered the
spiders (lines 569–74) 'Nan Dungorthin' was placed in that region,
though it is not named; in Synopsis V however it is again placed, with its
spiders, west of Sirion.

   In the later story the eagles set Beren and Lúthien down on the borders
of Doriath, and Huan came to them there.

   In the conclusion of Synopsis V there is very little that is at variance
with the story of the wolf-hunt and the death of Beren in *The Silmarillion*, so far as can be seen from the very compressed outline; but Beleg
was not present at the hunt in the Synopsis, as he was not in the *Tale*
(II. 38).

   The sentence that concludes Synopsis IV is curious: 'The recall of
Beren and Huan' (p. 311). 'Recall' obviously refers to the return from
Mandos (the last heading of Synopsis I is 'Tinúviel goes to Mandos and
recalls Beren'); in which case my father must have intended to have
Huan return from the dead with Beren and Lúthien. In the *Tale of
Tinúviel* Huan was not slain (II. 39), and there was no prophecy con-
cerning his fate to fall before the mightiest wolf that should ever walk the
world; but he became the companion of Mablung (II. 41), and in the
*Tale of the Nauglafring* he returned to Beren and Lúthien in the land of
i·Guilwarthon after the death of Thingol and the sack of the Thousand
Caves.

★

# APPENDIX

*C. S. Lewis's Commentary on the Lay of Leithian*

I give here the greater part of this commentary, for which see pp. 150–1.*
Lewis's line-references are of course changed throughout to those in this
book. The letters H, J, K, L, P, R refer to the imaginary manuscripts of
the ancient poem.

For the text criticised in the first entry of the commentary see
pp. 157–8, i.e. text B(1).

4 *Meats were sweet.* This is the reading of PRK. Let
any one believe if he can that our author gave such a
cacophany. J *His drink was sweet his dishes dear.*
L *His drink was sweet his dish was dear.* (Many
scholars have rejected lines 1–8 altogether as unworthy of the poet. 'They were added by a later hand
to supply a gap in the archtype,' says Peabody; and
adds 'The more melodious movement and surer narrative stride of the passage beginning with line 9 [*But
fairer than are born to Men*] should convince the
dullest that here, and here only, the authentic work of
the poet begins.' I am not convinced that H, which
had better be quoted in full, does not give the true
opening of the *Geste.*

> *That was long since in ages old*
> *When first the stars in heaven rolled,*
> *There dwelt beyond Broseliand,*
> *While loneliness yet held the land,*
> *A great king comely under crown,*
> *The gold was woven in his gown,*
> *The gold was clasped about his feet,*
> *The gold about his waist did meet.*
> *And in his many-pillared house*
> *Many a gold bee and ivory mouse*
> *And amber chessmen on their field*
> *Of copper, many a drinking horn*
> *Dear purchased from shy unicorn*
> *Lay piled, with gold in gleaming grot.*
> *All these he had* etc.)

*An account of it, with some citation, has been given by Humphrey Carpenter in *The
Inklings*, pp. 29–31, where the view expressed in his *Biography*, p. 145, that 'Tolkien did
not accept any of Lewis's suggestions', is corrected.

[It seems virtually certain that it was Lewis's criticism that led my father to rewrite the opening (the B (2) text, p. 154). If the amber chessmen and ivory mice found no place in the new version, it is notable that in Lewis's lines occur the words 'And in his many-pillared house'. These are not derived from the B(1) text which Lewis read, but in B(2) appears the line (14) *in many-pillared halls of stone*. It seems then that Durin's *many-pillared* halls in Gimli's song in Moria were originally so called by C. S. Lewis, thinking of the halls of Thingol in Doriath.]

40    The description of Lúthien has been too often and too justly praised to encourage the mere commentator in intruding.

68    *tall*. Thus PRKJH. L *vast*. Schick's complimentary title of 'internal rime' for these cacophanies does not much mend matters. 'The poet of the *Geste* knew nothing of internal rime, and its appearance (so called) is an infallible mark of corruption' (Pumpernickel). But cf. 209, 413.

71–2    The reader who wishes to acquire a touchstone for the true style of the *Geste* had better learn by heart this faultless and characteristic distych.

77        HL    *Of mortal men at feast has heard*

[The line in B(1) was *of mortal feaster ever heard*. With *hath* for *has* Lewis's line was adopted.]

99–150    This is considered by all critics one of the noblest passages in the *Geste*.

112    Notice the double sense of within (macrocosmic and microcosmic). That the original poet may have been unconscious of this need not detract from our pleasure.

[Lewis was clearly right to suspect that the original poet had no such double sense in mind.]

117          H   *The legions of his marching hate*

[Lewis was criticising the original line in B *his evil legions' marshalled hate*. With retention of *marshalled* for *marching* Lewis's line was adopted.]


[In the following comment the reading criticised was:

> *swift ruin red of fire and sword*
> *leapt forth on all denied his word,*
> *and all the lands beyond the hills*                    125
> *were filled with sorrow and with ills.*]

124     The relative understood. I suspect both the construction and the word *denied*, neither of which has the true ring. H reads:

> *And ruin of red fire and sword*
> *To all that would not hail him lord*
> *Came fast, and far beyond the hills*
> *Spread Northern wail and iron ills.*
> *And therefore in wet woods and cold* etc.


130     'A weak line' (Peabody).

[The original reading in B which Lewis criticised was *who had this king once held in scorn*, changed to *who once a prince of Men was born*]


137     Some emend. The rhythm, however, is good, and probably would occur more often if the syllabic prudery of scribes had not elsewhere 'emended' it.


172        LH   *When I lost all*

[No alteration made to the text.]


173–4        L   *Thus, out of wet night while he gazed,*
                   *he thought, with heavy heart amazed*

[No alteration made to the text.]


[In the following comment the reading criticised was:

> *But ere he dared to call her name*
> *or ask how she escaping came*]

175–6    *she escaping*. A Latinised phrase, at once betraying
very late corruption. The ugly assonance *ere . . . dared*
confirms my suspicion of the distych. No satisfactory
emendation has been proposed.

[*she escaping came* was changed to *she escaped and came*]

196    H    *Whining, his spirit ached for ease*. Peabody
observes of the whole passage: 'The combination
of extreme simplicity, with convincing truth of
psychology, and the pathos which, without comment, makes us aware that Gorlim is at once
pardonable and unpardonable, render this part
of the story extremely affecting.'

[No alteration made to line 196]

208    *haply*.    LH    *chance*.

[No alteration made to the text.]

209–10    One of the few passages in which Schick's theory of
deliberate internal rime finds some support.

[See the comment on line 68.]

215    *that*.    H    *the*.

[No alteration made to the text.]

[The lines 313–16 referred to in the following comment had been
bracketed for exclusion, and *that* at 317 changed to *Then*, before the text
went to Lewis.]

313    H reads    *Thus Morgoth loved that his own foe*
*Should in his service deal the blow.*
*Then Beren . . .*

'Our scribe is right in his erasure of the second distych,
but wrong in his erasure of the first' (Peabody). The
first erased couplet certainly deserves to remain in the
text; indeed its loss seriously impairs the reality of
Morgoth. I should print as in H, enclosing *Thus . . .*
*blow* in brackets or dashes.

[My father ticked the first two lines (313–14), which may show that he accepted this suggestion. I have let all four stand in the text.]

400   Of Canto 2 as a whole Peabody writes: 'If this is not good romantic narrative, I confess myself ignorant of the meaning of the words.'

401   et seq. A more philosophical account of the period is given in the so called *Poema Historiale*, probably contemporary with the earliest MSS of the *Geste*. The relevant passage runs as follows:

> *There was a time before the ancient sun*
> *And swinging wheels of heaven had learned*
> *   to run*
> *More certainly than dreams; for dreams*
> *   themselves*
> *Had bodies then and filled the world with elves.*
> *The starveling lusts whose walk is now*
> *   confined*
> *To darkness and the cellarage of the mind,*
> *And shudderings and despairs and shapes of sin*
> *Then walked at large, and were not cooped*
> *   within.*
> *Thought cast a shadow: brutes could speak:*
> *   and men*
> *Get children on a star. For spirit then*
> *Kneaded a fluid world and dreamed it new*
> *Each moment. Nothing yet was false or true.*

[Humphrey Carpenter, who cites these verses in *The Inklings*, says (p. 30): 'Sometimes Lewis actually suggested entirely new passages to replace lines he thought poor, and here too he ascribed his own versions to supposedly historical sources. For example, he suggested that the lines about the "elder days" [401 ff.] could be replaced by the following stanza of his own, which he described as "the so called *Poema Historiale* [&c.]".' But he cannot have intended these lines, which not only, as Humphrey Carpenter says, show 'how greatly Lewis's poetic imagination differed from Tolkien's', but are in a different metre, as a replacement; see Lewis's comment on lines 438–42.]

413   Another instance where the 'internal rime' theory is justified.

438–42     Almost certainly spurious. This abstract philosophi-
           cal statement – which would not surprise us in the
           scholastic verse of the period, such as the *Poema
           Historiale* – is quite foreign to the manner of the *Geste*.
           L reads:

> *. . . singing in the wood*
> *And long he stood and long he stood*
> *Till, many a day, with hound and hail*
> *His people seek him ere they sail,*
> *Then, finding not, take ship with tears.*
> *But after a long tale of years*
> *(Though but an hour to him it seemed)*
> *He found her where she lay and dreamed.*

[My father marked lines 438 ff. in the typescript, but made no change to
the text.]

516     *Flowering candles*. The reader should notice how the
        normally plain style of the *Geste* has yet the power of
        rising into such expressions as this without losing its
        unity.

[In the following comment the reading criticised was:

> *the silent elms stood dark and tall,*
> *and round their boles did shadows fall*                     518
> *where glimmered faint . . .*]

518     *did* PRK, *let* JL. Though neither is good, PRK seems
        the better reading. Its slight clumsiness may be
        passed over by a reader intent on the story: the 'neat'
        evasion *let*, with its purely formal attribution of an
        active rôle to the trees, is much worse, as cheap
        scenery is worse than a plain backcloth. H reads:

> *The silent elms stood tall and grey*
> *And at the roots long shadows lay*

519–42     'This passage', Peabody observes, 'amply atones for
           the poet's lapse (*dormitat Homerus*) in 518. *Ipsa
           mollities*.'

[I do not understand why Lewis picked particularly on *did* at line 518: the

use of *did* as a metrical aid was very common in the B-text as Lewis saw it
– it occurred twice, for instance, in the passage here praised: *did flutter*
523, *did waver* 533, both subsequently changed.]

555–6 'O si sic omnia!* Does not our poet show glimpses of
the true empyrean of poesy, however, in his work-
manlike humility, he has chosen more often to
inhabit the milder and aerial (not aetherial) middle
heaven?' (Pumpernickel). Some have seen in the
conception of death-into-life a late accretion. But cf.
the very early lyric preserved in the MS N3057, now
in the public library at Narrowthrode (the ancient
*Nargothrond*), which is probably as early as the *Geste*,
though like all the scholastic verse it strikes a more
modern note:

> *Because of endless pride*
> *Reborn with endless error,*
> *Each hour I look aside*
> *Upon my secret mirror,*
> *And practice postures there*
> *To make my image fair.*

> *You give me grapes, and I,*
> *Though staring, turn to see*
> *How dark the cool globes lie*
> *In the white hand of me,*
> *And stand, yet gazing thither,*
> *Till the live clusters wither.*

> *So should I quickly die*
> *Narcissus-like for want,*
> *Save that betimes my eye*
> *Sees there such shapes as haunt*
> *Beyond nightmare and make*
> *Pride humble for pride's sake.*

> *Then, and then only, turning*
> *The stiff neck round, I grow*
> *A molten man all burning*
> *And look behind, and know*
> *Who made the flaw, what light makes dark,*
> *    what fair*

> *Makes foul my shadowy form reflected there,*
> *That self-love, big with love, dying, its child*
>     *may bear.*

[It is a matter for speculation, what the author of Nargothrond thought of the public library at Narrowthrode. – This poem, with some alterations, was included in *The Pilgrim's Regress* (1933).]

563–92    *Sic* in all MSS. The passage is, of course, genuine, and truly worthy of the *Geste*. But surely it must originally have stood at 391 or 393? The artificial insertion of Beren's journey in its present place – where it appears as retrospect not as direct narrative, though defensible, belongs to a kind of art more sophisticated than that of the *Geste*: it is just such a transposition as a late Broseliandic literary redactor would make under the influence of the classical epic.

[A quarter of a century later, or more, my father rewrote this part of the poem; and he took Lewis's advice. See p. 352.]

[The original reading of B criticised in the next comment (lines 629 ff.) was:

> *Then stared he wild in dumbness bound*
> *at silent trees, deserted ground;*
> *the dizzy moon was twisted grey*
> *in tears, for she had fled away.*]

629–30    Thus in PRKJ. The Latinised adverbial use of the adjective in *wild* and the omitted articles in the next line are suspicious.

L    *But wildly Beren gazed around*
      *On silent trees (and)\* empty ground.*
      *The dizzy moon etc.*

\*Peabody supplies *and*. But the monosyllabic foot is quite possible. Cf. 687.

H    *But wildly Beren gazed around.*
      *Emptied the tall trees stood. The ground*
      *Lay empty. A lonely moon looked grey*
      *Upon the untrodden forest way.*

I prefer H because it gets rid of the conceit (it is little more) about the moon. (This sort of half-hearted personification is, of course, to be distinguished from genuine mythology.)

[Against this my father scribbled on Lewis's text: 'Not so!! The moon was dizzy and twisted because of the tears in his eyes.' Nonetheless he struck the two lines out heavily in the typescript, and I have excluded them from the text.]

635–6    An excellent simile.

641    Peabody, though a great friend to metrical resolutions in general, finds this particular resolution (*Bewildered enchanted*) 'singularly harsh'. Perhaps the original text read *wildered*.

[The reading in B was *bewildered, enchanted and forlorn*. My father then changed *bewildered* to *wildered* and placed it after *enchanted*.]

651–2    JHL transpose.

[This was done. Cf. lines 1222–3, where these lines are repeated but left in the original sequence.]

[After line 652 B had:

> *Thus thought his heart. No words would come*
> *from his fast lips, for smitten dumb*
> *a spell lay on him, as a dream*
> *in longing chained beside the stream.*

After seeing Lewis's comment my father marked this passage 'revise', and also with a deletion mark, on which basis I have excluded the four lines from the text.]

Only in PR. Almost undoubtedly spurious. 'The latest redactors', says Pumpernickel, 'were always needlessly amplifying, as if the imagination of their readers could do nothing for itself, and thus blunting the true force and energy of the *Geste*. . . .' Read:

> *A heartache and a loneliness*
> *– Enchanted waters pitiless.'*
> *A summer waned* etc.

[*heartache* was the original reading of B at 651, changed later to *hunger*, but retained at 1223.]

653–72     Of this admirable passage Peabody remarks: 'It is as if the wood itself were speaking.'

677–9     LH     *From her dim cave the damp moon eyed*
*White mists that float from earth to hide*
*The sluggard morrow's sun and drip*

[No alteration made to the text.]

683     *Beat*, which is utterly inappropriate to the sound described, must be a corruption. No plausible emendation has been suggested.

[My father scribbled in a hesitant substitute for *beat* and a different form for line 684 (*of his own feet on leafy* . . . .) but I cannot read the rhyming words.]

685–708     In praise of this passage I need not add to the innumerable eulogies of my predecessors.

710     Bentley read *saw far off*, to avoid the ugliness that always results from w-final followed by an initial vowel in the next word.

[The reading criticised was *saw afar*, and the line was changed as suggested.]

715     *Stole he* PRK. *He stole* JHL. PRK looks like the metrical 'improvement' of a scribe: dearly bought by a meaningless inversion.

[The reading criticised was *Then stole he nigh*, changed to *Then nigh he stole*.]

727–45     This passage, as it stands, is seriously corrupt, though the beauty of the original can still be discerned.

[See the following notes.]

[The original reading of B in lines 729–30 was:

> *the hillock green he leapt upon –*
> *the elfin loveliness was gone*;]

729    Intolerable bathos and prose in a passage of such tension.

[The original reading of B in line 739 was:

> *its echoes wove a halting spell*:]

739    Why *halting*? 'Let the amanuensis take back his rubbish' (Bentley).

[Against this my father wrote 'A spell to halt anyone', but in the margin of B he wrote *staying/binding*, and I have adopted *binding* in the text.]

[The original reading of B in lines 741–5 was:

> *His voice such love and longing fill*        741
> *one moment stood she, touched and still;*
> *one moment only, but he came*
> *and all his heart was burned with flame.*      744]

741–2    The historic present is always to be suspected. The second verse is hopelessly corrupt. *Touched* in this sense is impossible in the language of the *Geste*: and if the word were possible, the conception is fitter for a nineteenth century drawing-room in Narrowthrode than for the loves of heroes. HL read:

> *And clear his voice came as a bell*
> *Whose echoes wove a wavering spell*
> *Tinúviel. Tinúviel.*
> *Such love and longing filled his voice*
> *That, one moment, without choice,*
> *One moment without fear or shame,*
> *Tinúviel stood; and like a flame*
> *He leapt towards her as she stayed*
> *And caught and kissed that elfin maid.*

[My father marked the passage 'revise', and very roughly corrected it (adopting the concluding verses of Lewis's version) to the form which I have given in the text, despite the defective couplet.]

[The original reading of B was:

> aswoon in mingled grief and bliss,
> enchantment of an elvish kiss.]

760–1    L    *Aswoon with grief, aswoon with bliss,*
*Enchanted of an elvish kiss.*

[*enchanted* for *enchantment* was adopted.]

[The original reading – the text B(1) seen by Lewis, see p. 194 – of lines 762–73 was:

> *and saw within his blinded eyes*
> *a light that danced like silver flies*
> *a starlit face of tenderness*
> *crowned by the stars of Elfinesse.*
> *A mist was in his face like hair,*                          5
> *and laughing whispers moved the air –*
> *'O! dance with me now, Beren. Dance!' –*
> *a silver laugh, a mocking glance:*
> *'Come dance the wild and headlong maze*
> *those dance, we're told, beyond the ways*          10
> *who dwell that lead to lands of Men!*
> *Come teach the feet of Lúthien!'*
> *The shadows wrapped her. Like a stone*
> *the daylight found him cold and lone.*

On line 8 of this passage Lewis commented:]

L    *a silver laughter, an arch glance*

'Whether *mocking* or *arch* is the more intolerably miss-ish I care not to decide' (Peabody).

[The line was abandoned in the B(2) version. On lines 9–12 Lewis commented:]

JHL omit. Is not the whole passage [from the beginning of the Canto to the end of the passage from B(1) given above] unworthy of the poet?

[It is clear that this severe criticism led to the rewriting of the opening of the Canto.]

775    The chiasmus is suspiciously classical. H gives *Dark is the sun, cold is the air.*

[Against this my father scribbled: 'But classics did not invent chiasmus! —it is perfectly natural.' (*Chiasmus:* a grammatical figure by which the order of words in one of two parallel clauses is inverted in the other.)]

[The passage criticised by Lewis in the following comment was:

> *Hateful art thou, O Land of Trees!*
> *My flute shall finger no more seize;*
> *may music perish* etc.]

849    Clearly corrupt. HJL *Oh hateful land of trees be mute! My fingers, now forget the flute!*

[Against this my father wrote: 'Frightful 18th century!!!' But he reordered the second line to: *my fingers the flute shall no more seize*, and subsequently rewrote the passage to the form given in the text, lines 849–52.]

849–83    'These lines are very noble' (Pumpernickel).

909    *cometh.* HJL *comes.* HJL is certainly the more emphatic rhythm.

[No alteration made to the text.]

[The original reading of B at line 911 was:

> . . . *those shores,*
> *those white rocks where the last tide roars*]

911    'Where *eight* dull words oft creep in one low line.' Lines of monosyllables are often to be found in the *Geste*, but rarely so clustered with consonants as this. No satisfactory emendation has been suggested. I suspect this is a garbled version of 1142–3: our scribes do not always accept or understand epic repetition.

[The emendation made to B and given in the text is derived from lines 1142–3 as Lewis suggested. His reference is to Pope, *An Essay on Criticism*, line 347: *And ten low words oft creep in one dull line.*]

978–9    In *Gestestudien* Vol. XIII pp. 9–930 the reader will find a summary of the critical war that has raged round the possibility of the assonance (or rime) of *within-dim*. Perhaps a great deal of ink would have been saved if the scholars of the last century had been familiar with the L reading *Where out of yawning arches came A white light like unmoving flame*. 'My own conclusion is that *if* the assonance in the *textus receptus* is correct, the same phenomenon must originally have occurred often, and have been suppressed elsewhere by the scribes. Editorial effort might profitably be devoted to restoring it' (Schuffer). But cf. 1140–1.

[The original reading of B in lines 980–1 was:

> With gentle hand there she him led
> down corridors etc.]

980  J   *Downward with gentle hand she him led*, which explains the corruption. The verse originally ran *Downward with gentle hand she led*. The scribe of J, wrongly believing an object to be needed, inserted *him*. *Vulg.* then 'emends' the metre by dropping *Downward* and inserting *there*: thus giving a clumsy line.

[In this note *Vulg.* = *Vulgate*, the common or usual form of a literary work. My father wrote in Lewis's line on the B-text with his initials, and made the consequent change of *down* to *through* in line 981.]

[The original reading of B was: *as into archéd halls was led*]

991  HJL   *she led*

996  L   *in old stone carven stood*
[No alteration made to the text.]

[The original reading in B was: *while waters endless dripped and ran*]

1007  H   *While water forever dript and ran*

[The original reading in B was: *in lightless labyrinths endlessly*]

1075  *Labyrinths.*    HJL  *Labyrinth.*

[Lewis corrected his spelling to *Laborynth(s)*, against which my father queried: 'Why this spelling?']

980–1131  The whole of this passage has always been deservedly regarded as one of the gems of the *Geste*.

1132–61  I suspect that this passage has been greatly expanded by the late redactors who found their audience sometimes very ignorant of the myths. It is, as it stands, far from satisfactory. On the one hand it is too long an interruption of the action: on the other it is too succinct for a reader who knows nothing of the mythology. It is also obscure: thus in 1145 few readers can grasp that *their* means 'the Silmarils'. The shorter version of H and L, though not good, may in some respects be nearer the original:

> *Then Thingol's warriors loud and long*
> *Laughed: for wide renown in song*
> *Had Fëanor's gems o'er land and sea,*
> *The Silmarils, the shiners three,*
> *Three only, and in every one*
> *The light that was before the sun*
> *And moon, shone yet. But now no more*
> *Those leavings of the lights of yore*
> *Were seen on earth's back: in the drear*
> *Abysm of Morgoth blazing clear*
> *His iron crown they must adorn*
> *And glitter on orcs and slaves forlorn* etc.

[My father put an exclamation mark against *the shiners three*; and he wrote an X against lines 1144–5 (see note to these lines).]

★

Here C. S. Lewis's commentary on *The Gest of Beren and Lúthien* ends, and no more is recorded of the opinions of Peabody, Pumpernickel, Schuffer and Schick in the volumes of *Gestestudien* – nor indeed, on this subject, of those of their generous-minded inventor.

# IV

# THE LAY OF LEITHIAN
# RECOMMENCED

When my father began the *Lay of Leithian* again from the beginning, he did not at first intend much more, perhaps, than a revision, an improvement of individual lines and short passages, but all on the original plan and structure. This, at least, is what he did with Canto I; and he carried out the revisions on the old B typescript. But with Canto II he was quickly carried into a far more radical reconstruction, and was virtually writing a new poem on the same subject and in the same metre as the old. This, it is true, was partly because the story of Gorlim had changed, but it is also clear that a new impulse had entered, seeking a new rather than merely altered expression. The old typescript was still used at least as a physical basis for the new writing, but for a long stretch the typed verses were simply struck through and the new written on inserted pages and slips.

The old Canto II of just over 300 lines was expanded to 500, and divided into new Cantos 2 and 3 (the old and the new can be conveniently distinguished by Roman and Arabic numerals).

The rewriting on the old typescript continues for a short distance into Canto III (new Canto 4) and then stops. On the basis of this now extremely chaotic text my father wrote out a fine, decorated manuscript, 'C', inevitably introducing some further changes; and this stops only a few lines short of the point where the rewriting on the B-text stops. Subsequently, an amanuensis typescript ('D') was made, in two copies, apparently with my father's supervision, but for the moment nothing need be said of this beyond noticing that he made certain changes to these texts at a later time.

The rewriting on the B-text was no doubt a secondary stage, of which the preliminary workings no longer exist; for in the case of the new Canto 4 such preliminary drafts are extant. On one of these pages, and quite obviously done at the same time as the verse-drafts, my father drew a floor-plan of part of the house 99 Holywell Street, Oxford, to which he removed in 1950. He doubtless drew the plan shortly before moving house, while pondering its best arrangement. It is clear then that a new start on the *Lay of Leithian* was one of the first things that he turned to when *The Lord of the Rings* was complete.

I give below the text of the manuscript C in its final form (that is, after certain changes had been made to it) so far as it goes (line 624), incor-

porating one or two very minor alterations made later to the D type-
script(s), followed by a further short section (lines 625–60) found only in
draft before being added to D. Brief Notes and Commentary are given on
pp. 348 ff.

# THE LAY OF LEITHIAN

## I.   OF THINGOL IN DORIATH

A king there was in days of old:
ere Men yet walked upon the mould
his power was reared in caverns' shade,
his hand was over glen and glade.
Of leaves his crown, his mantle green,                        5
his silver lances long and keen;
the starlight in his shield was caught,
ere moon was made or sun was wrought.
   In after-days, when to the shore
of Middle-earth from Valinor                                  10
the Elven-hosts in might returned,
and banners flew and beacons burned,
when kings of Eldamar went by
in strength of war, beneath the sky
then still his silver trumpets blew                           15
when sun was young and moon was new.
Afar then in Beleriand,
in Doriath's beleaguered land,
King Thingol sat on guarded throne
in many-pillared halls of stone:                              20
there beryl, pearl, and opal pale,
and metal wrought like fishes' mail,
buckler and corslet, axe and sword,
and gleaming spears were laid in hoard:
all these he had and counted small,                           25
for dearer than all wealth in hall,
and fairer than are born to Men,
a daughter had he, Lúthien.

## OF LÚTHIEN THE BELOVED

Such lissom limbs no more shall run
on the green earth beneath the sun;                           30

so fair a maid no more shall be
from dawn to dusk, from sun to sea.
Her robe was blue as summer skies,
but grey as evening were her eyes;
her mantle sewn with lilies fair,                    35
but dark as shadow was her hair.
Her feet were swift as bird on wing,
her laughter merry as the spring;
the slender willow, the bowing reed,
the fragrance of a flowering mead,                   40
the light upon the leaves of trees,
the voice of water, more than these
her beauty was and blissfulness,
her glory and her loveliness.

   She dwelt in the enchanted land         45
while elven-might yet held in hand
the woven woods of Doriath:
none ever thither found the path
unbidden, none the forest-eaves
dared pass, or stir the listening leaves.            50
To North there lay a land of dread,
Dungorthin where all ways were dead
in hills of shadow bleak and cold;
beyond was Deadly Nightshade's hold
in Taur-nu-Fuin's fastness grim,                     55
where sun was sick and moon was dim.
To South the wide earth unexplored;
to West the ancient Ocean roared,
unsailed and shoreless, wide and wild;
to East in peaks of blue were piled,                 60
in silence folded, mist-enfurled,
the mountains of the outer world.

   Thus Thingol in his dolven hall
amid the Thousand Caverns tall
of Menegroth as king abode:                          65
to him there led no mortal road.
Beside him sat his deathless queen,
fair Melian, and wove unseen
nets of enchantment round his throne,
and spells were laid on tree and stone:              70
sharp was his sword and high his helm,

the king of beech and oak and elm.
When grass was green and leaves were long,
when finch and mavis sang their song,
there under bough and under sun                    75
in shadow and in light would run
fair Lúthien the elven-maid,
dancing in dell and grassy glade.

### OF DAIRON MINSTREL OF THINGOL

When sky was clear and stars were keen,
then Dairon with his fingers lean,                 80
as daylight melted into eve,
a trembling music sweet would weave
on flutes of silver, thin and clear
for Lúthien, the maiden dear.

There mirth there was and voices bright;           85
there eve was peace and morn was light;
there jewel gleamed and silver wan
and red gold on white fingers shone,
and elanor and niphredil
bloomed in the grass unfading still,               90
while the endless years of Elven-land
rolled over far Beleriand,
until a day of doom befell,
as still the elven-harpers tell.

★

### 2.   OF MORGOTH & THE SNARING OF GORLIM

Far in the Northern hills of stone                 95
in caverns black there was a throne
by flame encircled; there the smoke
in coiling columns rose to choke
the breath of life, and there in deep
and gasping dungeons lost would creep             100
to hopeless death all those who strayed
by doom beneath that ghastly shade.
   A king there sat, most dark and fell

of all that under heaven dwell.
Than earth or sea, than moon or star                105
more ancient was he, mightier far
in mind abysmal than the thought
of Eldar or of Men, and wrought
of strength primeval; ere the stone
was hewn to build the world, alone                  110
he walked in darkness, fierce and dire,
burned, as he wielded it, by fire.

He 'twas that laid in ruin black
the Blessed Realm and fled then back
to Middle-earth anew to build                       115
beneath the mountains mansions filled
with misbegotten slaves of hate:
death's shadow brooded at his gate.
His hosts he armed with spears of steel
and brands of flame, and at their heel              120
the wolf walked and the serpent crept
with lidless eyes. Now forth they leapt,
his ruinous legions, kindling war
in field and frith and woodland hoar.
Where long the golden elanor                        125
had gleamed amid the grass they bore
their banners black, where finch had sung
and harpers silver harps had wrung
now dark the ravens wheeled and cried
amid the reek, and far and wide                     130
the swords of Morgoth dripped with red
above the hewn and trampled dead.
Slowly his shadow like a cloud
rolled from the North, and on the proud
that would not yield his vengeance fell;            135
to death or thraldom under hell
all things he doomed: the Northern land
lay cowed beneath his ghastly hand.

But still there lived in hiding cold
Bëor's son, Barahir the bold,                       140
of land bereaved and lordship shorn
who once a prince of Men was born,
and now an outlaw lurked and lay
in the hard heath and woodland grey.

OF THE SAVING OF KING INGLOR FELAGUND BY THE XII BËORINGS

Twelve men beside him still there went,                    145
still faithful when all hope was spent.
Their names are yet in elven-song
remembered, though the years are long
since doughty Dagnir and Ragnor,
Radhruin, Dairuin and Gildor,                              150
Gorlim Unhappy, and Urthel,
and Arthad and Hathaldir fell;
since the black shaft with venomed wound
took Belegund and Baragund,
the mighty sons of Bregolas;                               155
since he whose doom and deeds surpass
all tales of Men was laid on bier,
fair Beren son of Barahir.
For these it was, the chosen men
of Bëor's house, who in the fen                            160
of reedy Serech stood at bay
about King Inglor in the day
of his defeat, and with their swords
thus saved of all the Elven-lords
the fairest; and his love they earned.                     165
And he escaping south, returned
to Nargothrond his mighty realm,
where still he wore his crownëd helm;
but they to their northern homeland rode,
dauntless and few, and there abode                         170
unconquered still, defying fate,
pursued by Morgoth's sleepless hate.

OF TARN AELUIN THE BLESSED

Such deeds of daring there they wrought
that soon the hunters that them sought
at rumour of their coming fled.                            175
Though price was set upon each head
to match the weregild of a king,
no soldier could to Morgoth bring
news even of their hidden lair;
for where the highland brown and bare                      180
above the darkling pines arose
of steep Dorthonion to the snows

and barren mountain-winds, there lay
a tarn of water, blue by day,
by night a mirror of dark glass                                185
for stars of Elbereth that pass
above the world into the West.
Once hallowed, still that place was blest:
no shadow of Morgoth, and no evil thing
yet thither came; a whispering ring                            190
of slender birches silver-grey
stooped on its margin, round it lay
a lonely moor, and the bare bones
of ancient Earth like standing stones
thrust through the heather and the whin;                       195
and there by houseless Aeluin
the hunted lord and faithful men
under the grey stones made their den.

### OF GORLIM UNHAPPY

Gorlim Unhappy, Angrim's son,
as the tale tells, of these was one                            200
most fierce and hopeless. He to wife,
while fair was the fortune of his life,
took the white maiden Eilinel:
dear love they had ere evil fell.
To war he rode; from war returned                              205
to find his fields and homestead burned,
his house forsaken roofless stood,
empty amid the leafless wood;
and Eilinel, white Eilinel,
was taken whither none could tell,                             210
to death or thraldom far away.
Black was the shadow of that day
for ever on his heart, and doubt
still gnawed him as he went about
in wilderness wandring, or at night                            215
oft sleepless, thinking that she might
ere evil came have timely fled
into the woods: she was not dead,
she lived, she would return again
to seek him, and would deem him slain.                         220
Therefore at whiles he left the lair,

and secretly, alone, would peril dare,
and come to his old house at night,
broken and cold, without fire or light,
and naught but grief renewed would gain,          225
watching and waiting there in vain.

In vain, or worse – for many spies
had Morgoth, many lurking eyes
well used to pierce the deepest dark;
and Gorlim's coming they would mark              230
and would report. There came a day
when once more Gorlim crept that way,
down the deserted weedy lane
at dusk of autumn sad with rain
and cold wind whining. Lo! a light               235
at window fluttering in the night
amazed he saw; and drawing near,
between faint hope and sudden fear,
he looked within. 'Twas Eilinel!
Though changed she was, he knew her well.        240
With grief and hunger she was worn,
her tresses tangled, raiment torn;
her gentle eyes with tears were dim,
as soft she wept: 'Gorlim, Gorlim!
Thou canst not have forsaken me.                 245
Then slain, alas! thou slain must be!
And I must linger cold, alone,
and loveless as a barren stone!'

One cry he gave – and then the light
blew out, and in the wind of night               250
wolves howled; and on his shoulder fell
suddenly the griping hands of hell.
There Morgoth's servants fast him caught
and he was cruelly bound, and brought
to Sauron captain of the host,                   255
the lord of werewolf and of ghost,
most foul and fell of all who knelt
at Morgoth's throne. In might he dwelt
on Gaurhoth Isle; but now had ridden
with strength abroad, by Morgoth bidden          260
to find the rebel Barahir.
He sat in dark encampment near,

and thither his butchers dragged their prey.
There now in anguish Gorlim lay:
with bond on neck, on hand and foot,                    265
to bitter torment he was put,
to break his will and him constrain
to buy with treason end of pain.
But naught to them would he reveal
of Barahir, nor break the seal                          270
of faith that on his tongue was laid;
until at last a pause was made,
and one came softly to his stake,
a darkling form that stooped, and spake
to him of Eilinel his wife.                             275
    'Wouldst thou,' he said, 'forsake thy life,
who with few words might win release
for her, and thee, and go in peace,
and dwell together far from war,
friends of the King? What wouldst thou more?'          280
And Gorlim, now long worn with pain,
yearning to see his wife again
(whom well he weened was also caught
in Sauron's net), allowed the thought
to grow, and faltered in his troth.                     285
Then straight, half willing and half loath,
they brought him to the seat of stone
where Sauron sat. He stood alone
before that dark and dreadful face,
and Sauron said: 'Come, mortal base!                    290
What do I hear? That thou wouldst dare
to barter with me? Well, speak fair!
What is thy price?' And Gorlim low
bowed down his head, and with great woe,
word on slow word, at last implored                     295
that merciless and faithless lord
that he might free depart, and might
again find Eilinel the White,
and dwell with her, and cease from war
against the King. He craved no more.                    300

    Then Sauron smiled, and said: 'Thou thrall!
The price thou askest is but small
for treachery and shame so great!

I grant it surely! Well, I wait:
Come! Speak now swiftly and speak true!'                315
Then Gorlim wavered, and he drew
half back; but Sauron's daunting eye
there held him, and he dared not lie:
as he began, so must he wend
from first false step to faithless end:                  310
he all must answer as he could,
betray his lord and brotherhood,
and cease, and fall upon his face.

    Then Sauron laughed aloud. 'Thou base,
thou cringing worm! Stand up,                            315
and hear me! And now drink the cup
that I have sweetly blent for thee!
Thou fool: a phantom thou didst see
that I, I Sauron, made to snare
thy lovesick wits. Naught else was there.                320
Cold 'tis with Sauron's wraiths to wed!
Thy Eilinel! She is long since dead,
dead, food of worms less low than thou.
And yet thy boon I grant thee now:
to Eilinel thou soon shalt go,                           325
and lie in her bed, no more to know
of war – or manhood. Have thy pay!'

    And Gorlim then they dragged away,
and cruelly slew him; and at last
in the dank mould his body cast,                         330
where Eilinel long since had lain
in the burned woods by butchers slain.
    Thus Gorlim died an evil death,
and cursed himself with dying breath,
and Barahir at last was caught                           335
in Morgoth's snare; for set at naught
by treason was the ancient grace
that guarded long that lonely place,
Tarn Aeluin: now all laid bare
were secret paths and hidden lair.                       340

★

### 3. OF BEREN SON OF BARAHIR & HIS ESCAPE

Dark from the North now blew the cloud;
the winds of autumn cold and loud
hissed in the heather; sad and grey
Aeluin's mournful water lay.
'Son Beren', then said Barahir,                          345
'Thou knowst the rumour that we hear
of strength from the Gaurhoth that is sent
against us; and our food nigh spent.
On thee the lot falls by our law
to go forth now alone to draw                            350
what help thou canst from the hidden few
that feed us still, and what is new
to learn. Good fortune go with thee!
In speed return, for grudgingly
we spare thee from our brotherhood,                      355
so small: and Gorlim in the wood
is long astray or dead. Farewell!'
As Beren went, still like a knell
resounded in his heart that word,
the last of his father that he heard.                    360

    Through moor and fen, by tree and briar
he wandered far: he saw the fire
of Sauron's camp, he heard the howl
of hunting Orc and wolf a-prowl,
and turning back, for long the way,                      365
benighted in the forest lay.
In weariness he then must sleep,
fain in a badger-hole to creep,
and yet he heard (or dreamed it so)
nearby a marching legion go                              370
with clink of mail and clash of shields
up towards the stony mountain-fields.
He slipped then into darkness down,
until, as man that waters drown
strives upwards gasping, it seemed to him                375
he rose through slime beside the brim
of sullen pool beneath dead trees.
Their livid boughs in a cold breeze
trembled, and all their black leaves stirred:
each leaf a black and croaking bird,                     380

whose neb a gout of blood let fall.
He shuddered, struggling thence to crawl
through winding weeds, when far away
he saw a shadow faint and grey
gliding across the dreary lake.                     385
Slowly it came, and softly spake:
'Gorlim I was, but now a wraith
of will defeated, broken faith,
traitor betrayed. Go! Stay not here!
Awaken, son of Barahir,                             390
and haste! For Morgoth's fingers close
upon thy father's throat; he knows
your trysts, your paths, your secret lair.'
     Then he revealed the devil's snare
in which he fell, and failed; and last              395
begging forgiveness, wept, and passed
out into darkness. Beren woke,
leapt up as one by sudden stroke
with fire of anger filled. His bow
and sword he seized, and like the roe               400
hotfoot o'er rock and heath he sped
before the dawn. Ere day was dead
to Aeluin at last he came,
as the red sun westward sank in flame;
but Aeluin was red with blood,                      405
red were the stones and trampled mud.
Black in the birches sat a-row
the raven and the carrion crow;
wet were their nebs, and dark the meat
that dripped beneath their griping feet.            410
One croaked: 'Ha, ha, he comes too late!'
'Ha, ha!' they answered, 'ha! too late!'
     There Beren laid his father's bones
in haste beneath a cairn of stones;
no graven rune nor word he wrote                    415
o'er Barahir, but thrice he smote
the topmost stone, and thrice aloud
he cried his name. 'Thy death', he vowed,
'I will avenge. Yea, though my fate
should lead at last to Angband's gate.'             420
And then he turned, and did not weep:
too dark his heart, the wound too deep.

Out into night, as cold as stone,
loveless, friendless, he strode alone.

Of hunter's lore he had no need                               425
the trail to find. With little heed
his ruthless foe, secure and proud,
marched north away with blowing loud
of brazen horns their lord to greet,
trampling the earth with grinding feet.                       430
Behind them bold but wary went
now Beren, swift as hound on scent,
until beside a darkling well,
where Rivil rises from the fell
down into Serech's reeds to flow,                             435
he found the slayers, found his foe.
From hiding on the hillside near
he marked them all: though less than fear,
too many for his sword and bow
to slay alone. Then, crawling low                             440
as snake in heath, he nearer crept.
There many weary with marching slept,
but captains, sprawling on the grass,
drank and from hand to hand let pass
their booty, grudging each small thing                        445
raped from dead bodies. One a ring
held up, and laughed: 'Now, mates,' he cried
'here's mine! And I'll not be denied,
though few be like it in the land.
For I 'twas wrenched it from the hand                         450
of that same Barahir I slew,
the robber-knave. If tales be true,
he had it of some elvish lord,
for the rogue-service of his sword.
No help it gave to him – he's dead.                           455
They're parlous, elvish rings, 'tis said;
still for the gold I'll keep it, yea
and so eke out my niggard pay.
Old Sauron bade me bring it back,
and yet, methinks, he has no lack                             460
of weightier treasures in his hoard:
the greater the greedier the lord!
So mark ye, mates, ye all shall swear

the hand of Barahir was bare!'
And as he spoke an arrow sped                              465
from tree behind, and forward dead
choking he fell with barb in throat;
with leering face the earth he smote.
  Forth, then as wolfhound grim there leapt
Beren among them. Two he swept                            470
aside with sword; caught up the ring;
slew one who grasped him; with a spring
back into shadow passed, and fled
before their yells of wrath and dread
of ambush in the valley rang.                             475
Then after him like wolves they sprang,
howling and cursing, gnashing teeth,
hewing and bursting through the heath,
shooting wild arrows, sheaf on sheaf,
at trembling shade or shaken leaf.                        480
  In fateful hour was Beren born:
he laughed at dart and wailing horn;
fleetest of foot of living men,
tireless on fell and light on fen,
elf-wise in wood, he passed away,                         485
defended by his hauberk grey
of dwarvish craft in Nogrod made,
where hammers rang in cavern's shade.

  As fearless Beren was renowned:
when men most hardy upon ground                           490
were reckoned folk would speak his name,
foretelling that his after-fame
would even golden Hador pass
or Barahir and Bregolas;
but sorrow now his heart had wrought                      495
to fierce despair, no more he fought
in hope of life or joy or praise,
but seeking so to use his days
only that Morgoth deep should feel
the sting of his avenging steel,                          500
ere death he found and end of pain:
his only fear was thraldom's chain.
Danger he sought and death pursued,
and thus escaped the doom he wooed,

and deeds of breathless daring wrought                505
alone, of which the rumour brought
new hope to many a broken man.
They whispered 'Beren', and began
in secret swords to whet, and soft
by shrouded hearths at evening oft                    510
songs they would sing of Beren's bow,
of Dagmor his sword: how he would go
silent to camps and slay the chief,
or trapped in his hiding past belief
would slip away, and under night                      515
by mist or moon, or by the light
of open day would come again.
Of hunters hunted, slayers slain
they sang, of Gorgol the Butcher hewn,
of ambush in Ladros, fire in Drûn,                    520
of thirty in one battle dead,
of wolves that yelped like curs and fled,
yea, Sauron himself with wound in hand.
Thus one alone filled all that land
with fear and death for Morgoth's folk;               525
his comrades were the beech and oak
who failed him not, and wary things
with fur and fell and feathered wings
that silent wander, or dwell alone
in hill and wild and waste of stone                   530
watched o'er his ways, his faithful friends.

   Yet seldom well an outlaw ends;
and Morgoth was a king more strong
than all the world has since in song
recorded: dark athwart the land                       535
reached out the shadow of his hand,
at each recoil returned again;
two more were sent for one foe slain.
New hope was cowed, all rebels killed;
quenched were the fires, the songs were stilled,      540
tree felled, heath burned, and through the waste
marched the black host of Orcs in haste.
   Almost they closed their ring of steel
round Beren; hard upon his heel
now trod their spies; within their hedge              545

of all aid shorn, upon the edge
of death at bay he stood aghast
and knew that he must die at last,
or flee the land of Barahir,
his land beloved. Beside the mere          550
beneath a heap of nameless stones
must crumble those once mighty bones,
forsaken by both son and kin,
bewailed by reeds of Aeluin.

In winter's night the houseless North          555
he left behind, and stealing forth
the leaguer of his watchful foe
he passed – a shadow on the snow,
a swirl of wind, and he was gone,
the ruin of Dorthonion,          560
Tarn Aeluin and its water wan,
never again to look upon.
No more shall hidden bowstring sing,
no more his shaven arrows wing,
no more his hunted head shall lie          565
upon the heath beneath the sky.
The Northern stars, whose silver fire
of old Men named the Burning Briar,
were set behind his back, and shone
o'er land forsaken: he was gone.          570

Southward he turned, and south away
his long and lonely journey lay,
while ever loomed before his path
the dreadful peaks of Gorgorath.
Never had foot of man most bold          575
yet trod those mountains steep and cold,
nor climbed upon their sudden brink,
whence, sickened, eyes must turn and shrink
to see their southward cliffs fall sheer
in rocky pinnacle and pier          580
down into shadows that were laid
before the sun and moon were made.
In valleys woven with deceit
and washed with waters bitter-sweet
dark magic lurked in gulf and glen;          585
but out away beyond the ken

of mortal sight the eagle's eye
from dizzy towers that pierced the sky
might grey and gleaming see afar,
as sheen on water under star,                          590
Beleriand, Beleriand,
the borders of the Elven-land.


★


4.   OF THE COMING OF BEREN TO DORIATH; BUT FIRST IS TOLD OF
        THE MEETING OF MELIAN AND THINGOL

There long ago in Elder-days
ere voice was heard or trod were ways,
the haunt of silent shadows stood                      595
in starlit dusk Nan Elmoth wood.
In Elder-days that long are gone
a light amid the shadows shone,
a voice was in the silence heard:
the sudden singing of a bird.                          600
There Melian came, the Lady grey,
and dark and long her tresses lay
beneath her silver girdle-seat
and down unto her silver feet.
The nightingales with her she brought,                 605
to whom their song herself she taught,
who sweet upon her gleaming hands
had sung in the immortal lands.
     Thence wayward wandering on a time
from Lórien she dared to climb                         610
the everlasting mountain-wall
of Valinor, at whose feet fall
the surges of the Shadowy Sea.
Out away she went then free,
to gardens of the Gods no more                         615
returning, but on mortal shore,
a glimmer ere the dawn she strayed,
singing her spells from glade to glade.
     A bird in dim Nan Elmoth wood
trilled, and to listen Thingol stood                   620
amazed; then far away he heard

a voice more fair than fairest bird,
a voice as crystal clear of note
as thread of silver glass remote.

Here the manuscript C ends. Of the next short section there are no less
than five rough drafts, with endless small variations of wording (and the
first ten lines of it were written onto the B-text). The final form was then
added, in type, to the D typescript:

Of folk and kin no more he thought;                625
of errand that the Eldar brought
from Cuiviénen far away,
of lands beyond the Seas that lay
no more he recked, forgetting all,
drawn only by that distant call                    630
till deep in dim Nan Elmoth wood
lost and beyond recall he stood.
And there he saw her, fair and fay:
Ar-Melian, the Lady grey,
as silent as the windless trees,                    635
standing with mist about her knees,
and in her face remote the light
of Lórien glimmered in the night.
No word she spoke; but pace by pace,
a halting shadow, towards her face                  640
forth walked the silver-mantled king,
tall Elu Thingol. In the ring
of waiting trees he took her hand.
One moment face to face they stand
alone, beneath the wheeling sky,                    645
while starlit years on earth go by
and in Nan Elmoth wood the trees
grow dark and tall. The murmuring seas
rising and falling on the shore
and Ulmo's horn he heeds no more.                   650

But long his people sought in vain
their lord, till Ulmo called again,
and then in grief they marched away,
leaving the woods. To havens grey
upon the western shore, the last                    655
long shore of mortal lands, they passed,
and thence were borne beyond the Sea

in Aman, the Blessed Realm, to be
by evergreen Ezellohar
in Valinor, in Eldamar.                                    660

★

52    On one of the copies of D *Dungorthin* was changed to
      *Dungortheb*, but this belongs to a later layer of nomen-
      clature and I have not introduced it into the text.

55    *Taur-nu-Fuin* C: the line as written on the B-text still had
      *Taur-na-Fuin*.

140   *Bëor's son*: changed on one of the copies of D to *the
      Bëoring*, i.e. a man of Bëor's house. This was a change made
      when the genealogy had been greatly extended and Barahir
      was no longer Bëor's son but his remote descendant (see
      p. 198).

249–330 In this section of the Canto the rewriting on (or inserted into)
      the B-text exists in two versions, one the immediate fore-
      runner of the other. The difference between them is that in
      the earlier Gorlim was still, as in the earlier Lay, taken to
      Angband and to Morgoth himself. Thus the passage in the
      first rewriting corresponding to lines 255–66 reads:

              to Angband and the iron halls
              where laboured Morgoth's hopeless thralls;
              and there with bonds on hand and foot
              to grievous torment he was put

      In what follows the two versions are the same, except that
      in the first it is Morgoth, not Sauron: precisely the same lines
      are used of each. But at lines 306–11 the first version has:

              Then Gorlim wavered, and he drew
              half back; but Morgoth's daunting eyes
              there held him. To the Lord of Lies
              'tis vain in lies the breath to spend:
              as he began, so he must end,
              and all must answer as he could

      and at lines 318–21 Morgoth says:

              Thou fool! A phantom thou didst see
              that Sauron my servant made to snare
              thy lovesick wits. Naught else was there.
              Cold 'tis with Sauron's wraiths to wed!

547   The word *aghast* is marked with an X in C (because Beren
      was not aghast).

567-8   At first the passage in B (p. 167, lines 369-82) beginning *No
        more his hidden bowstring sings* was scarcely changed in
        the rewriting, but as first written C had (old lines 376-9):

> found him no more. The stars that burn
> about the North with silver fire
> that Varda wrought, the Burning Briar
> as Men it called in days long gone

Old lines 373-5 were then cut out and 376-9 rewritten:

> The stars that burn with silver fire
> about the North, the Burning Briar
> that Varda lit in ages gone

This was in turn changed to the text given, lines 567-8.

581     In one of the copies of D an X is placed against this line. I
        think this was probably very late and marks my father's
        changed ideas concerning the making of the Sun and Moon.

596     *Nan Elmoth*: in the preliminary draft the name of the wood
        was first *Glad-uial*, emended to *Glath-uial*; then *Gilam-
        moth*, emended to *Nan Elmoth*. It was here that the name
        *Nan Elmoth* emerged.

627     In one of the drafts of this passage the line is *from Waking
        Water far away*.

634     In one of the drafts of this passage *Tar-Melian* stands in the
        margin as an alternative.


Commentary on lines 1-660

A strictly chronological account of the evolution of the legends of the
Elder Days would have to consider several other works before the
revisions to the *Lay of Leithian* were reached. By treating the Lay
revised and unrevised as an entity and not piecemeal I jump these stages,
and names which had in fact emerged a good while before appear here for
the first time in this 'History'. I do little more than list them:

65      *Menegroth*
89      *elanor* and *niphredil*. At line 125 is a reference to *the
        golden elanor*.
115     *Middle-earth*
149 ff. The names of the men of Barahir's band, beside Beren and
        Gorlim: *Dagnir, Ragnor, Radhruin, Dairuin, Gildor,
        Urthel, Arthad, Hathaldir*; *Belegund* and *Baragund*.
            Belegund and Baragund are the sons of *Bregolas* (Barahir's
        brother); and Gorlim is the son of *Angrim* (199).
            All these names appear in *The Silmarillion* (pp. 155, 162).

161    'the fen of reedy *Serech*.' Beren came on the Orcs at the well of *Rivil*, which 'rises from the fell / down into Serech's reeds to flow' (434–5).

162    Felagund is called *Inglor* (*Inglor Felagund* in the sub-title, p. 335).

182, 560    *Dorthonion*

186    *Elbereth*

196, etc.    (*Tarn*) *Aeluin*

255, etc.    *Sauron*

259, 347    *Gaurhoth*. Cf. *Tol-in-Gaurhoth* 'Isle of Werewolves' in *The Silmarillion*.

434    *Rivil*

493    *Hador*

512    *Dagmor*. Beren's sword is named nowhere else.

519    *Gorgol the Butcher*. He is named nowhere else.

520    *Ladros* (the lands to the north-east of Dorthonion that were granted by the Noldorin kings to the Men of the House of Bëor).

520    *Drûn*. This name is marked on the later of the 'Silmarillion' maps (that on which the published map was based) as north of Aeluin and west of Ladros, but is named in no other place.

574    *Gorgorath*. This has occurred in the prose outline for Canto X of the Lay, but in the form *Gorgoroth* (p. 272).

596, etc.    *Nan Elmoth*. See note to line 596.

634    *Ar-Melian* (*Tar-Melian*). The name is not found elsewhere with either prefix.

659    *Ezellohar* (the Green Mound of the Two Trees in Valinor).

In addition may be noted here *Dungorthin* (52), where the new version changes the old lines 49–50

> To North there lay the Land of Dread
> whence only evil pathways led

to

> To North there lay a land of dread,
> Dungorthin where all ways were dead

In the old version 'the Land of Dread' clearly meant, simply, 'the land of Morgoth'. Here Dungorthin is placed as it is in *The Silmarillion* (p. 121), between the Mountains of Terror and the northern bound of the Girdle of Melian; see p. 314.

In the revised Lay the story of Gorlim was greatly developed. In the old (see pp. 162–4, 169–70), Gorlim left his companions and went 'to meet / with hidden friend within a dale'; he found 'a homestead looming pale', and within it he saw a phantom of Eilinel. He left the house, in fear of Morgoth's hunters and wolves, and returned to his companions; but after some days he deliberately sought out Morgoth's servants and offered to betray his fellows. He was taken to the halls of Morgoth – who does not say that the wraith was set to decoy Gorlim:

> a wraith of that which might have been,
> methinks, it is that thou hast seen!

(But in lines 241–2 it is said that 'men believed that Morgoth made/the fiendish phantom'.)

There is also a remarkable development in the revised Lay, in that 'the XII Bëorings' (one would expect XIII, including Barahir himself) of Dorthonion were the very men who saved King Felagund in the Battle of Sudden Flame:

> For these it was, the chosen men
> of Bëor's house, who in the fen
> of reedy Serech stood at bay
> about King Inglor in the day
> of his defeat . . .                     (159–63)

In *The Silmarillion* the story is that 'Morgoth pursued [Barahir] to the death, until at last there remained to him only twelve companions' (p. 162): there is no suggestion that these survivors were a picked band, already joined as companions in an earlier heroic deed.

Felagund (Inglor) is now said to have *returned* to Nargothrond (lines 166–7) after his rescue by Barahir and his men (see pp. 85–6).

From this point onwards substantial rewriting of the poem is restricted to a few sections.

## Canto III continued

From the end of the rewritten opening of the poem (line 660 above) the D typescript continues as a copy of B to the end of the poem, but though it was certainly made under my father's supervision it is of very minor textual value in itself.

The passage in the original text (p. 173) lines 453 (*Thus Thingol sailed not on the seas*) to 470 was left unchanged; but for lines 471 (*In later days when Morgoth first*) to approximately 613 my father substituted 142 lines of new verse (omitting the long retrospective passage lines 563 ff. concerning Beren's journey over the Mountains of Terror), in which there is very little of the old Lay, and as the passage proceeds progressively less. There is no doubt that these lines are (relatively) very late: an apparently contemporaneous piece of rewriting in Canto X is certainly post-1955 (see p. 360), and they may well be considerably later than that. There is a quantity of rough draft material in manuscript, but also a typescript made by my father of the first 103 lines, inserted into the D-text.

In later days, when Morgoth fled
from wrath and raised once more his head
and Iron Crown, his mighty seat
beneath the smoking mountain's feet
founded and fortified anew,     5
then slowly dread and darkness grew:
the Shadow of the North that all
the Folk of Earth would hold in thrall.

    The lords of Men to knee he brings,
the kingdoms of the Exiled Kings     10
assails with ever-mounting war:
in their last havens by the shore
they dwell, or strongholds walled with fear
defend upon his borders drear,
till each one falls. Yet reign there still     15
in Doriath beyond his will
the Grey King and immortal Queen.
No evil in their realm is seen;
no power their might can yet surpass:
there still is laughter and green grass,     20
there leaves are lit by the white sun,
and many marvels are begun.

    There went now in the Guarded Realm
beneath the beech, beneath the elm,
there lightfoot ran now on the green     25
the daughter of the king and queen:
of Arda's eldest children born
in beauty of their elven-morn
and only child ordained by birth
to walk in raiment of the Earth     30
from Those descended who began
before the world of Elf and Man.

    Beyond the bounds of Arda far
still shone the Legions, star on star,
memorials of their labour long,     35
achievement of Vision and of Song;

and when beneath their ancient light
on Earth below was cloudless night,
music in Doriath awoke,
and there beneath the branching oak,                    40
or seated on the beech-leaves brown,
Daeron the dark with ferny crown
played on his pipes with elvish art
unbearable by mortal heart.
    No other player has there been,           45
no other lips or fingers seen
so skilled, 'tis said in elven-lore,
save Maelor* son of Fëanor,
forgotten harper, singer doomed,
who young when Laurelin yet bloomed                     50
to endless lamentation passed
and in the tombless sea was cast.†
    But Daeron in his heart's delight
yet lived and played by starlit night,
until one summer-eve befell,                            55
as still the elven harpers tell.
Then merrily his piping trilled;
the grass was soft, the wind was stilled,
the twilight lingered faint and cool
in shadow-shapes upon the pool‡                         60
beneath the boughs of sleeping trees
standing silent. About their knees
a mist of hemlocks glimmered pale,
and ghostly moths on lace-wings frail
went to and fro. Beside the mere                        65
quickening, rippling, rising clear
the piping called. Then forth she came,
as sheer and sudden as a flame
of peerless white the shadows cleaving,
her maiden-bower on white feet leaving;                 70
and as when summer stars arise

---

*Both *Maglor* and *Maelor* appear in the draft manuscripts of this passage. The final typescript has *Maelor*, changed to *Maglor*, but not I think by my father.

† In *The Silmarillion* (p. 254) it is not said that Maglor ended his life in the sea: he cast the Silmaril into the sea, 'and thereafter he wandered ever upon the shores, singing in pain and regret beside the waves'.

‡There is no other reference to a 'pool' or 'mere' at the place in the woods where Beren came upon Lúthien.

radiant into darkened skies,
her living light on all was cast
in fleeting silver as she passed.
There now she stepped with elven pace,                    75
bending and swaying in her grace,
as half-reluctant; then began
to dance, to dance: in mazes ran
bewildering, and a mist of white
was wreathed about her whirling flight.                   80
Wind-ripples on the water flashed,
and trembling leaf and flower were plashed
with diamond-dews, as ever fleet
and fleeter went her wingéd feet.

Her long hair as a cloud was streaming                    85
about her arms uplifted gleaming,
as slow above the trees the Moon
in glory of the plenilune
arose, and on the open glade
its light serene and clear was laid.                      90
Then suddenly her feet were stilled,
and through the woven wood there thrilled,
half wordless, half in elven-tongue,
her voice upraised in blissful song
that once of nightingales she learned                     95
and in her living joy had turned
to heart-enthralling loveliness,
unmarred, immortal, sorrowless.

*Ir Ithil ammen Eruchín*
  *menel-vîr síla díriel*                                 100
*si loth a galadh lasto dîn!*
  *A Hîr Annûn gilthoniel,*
*le linnon im Tinúviel!*

The typescript ends here, but the final manuscript draft continues:

O elven-fairest Lúthien
what wonder moved thy dances then?                        105
That night what doom of Elvenesse
enchanted did thy voice possess?
Such marvel shall there no more be
on Earth or west beyond the Sea,

at dusk or dawn, by night or noon                              110
or neath the mirror of the moon!
On Neldoreth was laid a spell;
the piping into silence fell,
for Daeron cast his flute away,
unheeded on the grass it lay,                                   115
in wonder bound as stone he stood
heart-broken in the listening wood.
And still she sang above the night,
as light returning into light
upsoaring from the world below                                 120
when suddenly there came a slow
dull tread of heavy feet on leaves,
and from the darkness on the eaves
of the bright glade a shape came out
with hands agrope, as if in doubt                              125
or blind, and as it stumbling passed
under the moon a shadow cast
bended and darkling. Then from on high
as lark falls headlong from the sky
the song of Lúthien fell and ceased;                           130
but Daeron from the spell released
awoke to fear, and cried in woe:
'Flee Lúthien, ah Lúthien go!
An evil walks the wood! Away!'
Then forth he fled in his dismay                               135
ever calling her to follow him,
until far off his cry was dim
'Ah flee, ah flee now, Lúthien!'
But silent stood she in the glen
unmoved, who never fear had known,                             140
as slender moonlit flower alone,
white and windless with upturned face
waiting

Here the manuscript comes to an end.


Canto IV

A small section of this Canto was partly rewritten at some late date. Lines
884 ff. were changed to:

> Then Thingol said: 'O Dairon wise,
> with wary ears and watchful eyes,
> who all that passes in this land
> dost ever heed and understand,
> what omen doth this silence bear?

This was written rapidly on the B-text and was primarily prompted, I think, by the wish to get rid of the word 'magic' at line 886, which is underlined and marked with an X on the D typescript. At the same time 'wild stallion' at 893 was changed to 'great stallion', and *Tavros* to *Tauros* at 891. A little further on, lines 902–19 were changed, also at this time:

> beneath the trees of Ennorath.*
> Would it were so! An age now hath
> gone by since Nahar trod this earth
> in days of our peace and ancient mirth,
> ere rebel lords of Eldamar
> pursuing Morgoth from afar
> brought war and ruin to the North.
> Doth Tauros to their aid come forth?
> But if not he, who comes or what?'
> And Dairon said: 'He cometh not!
> No feet divine shall leave that shore
> where the Outer Seas' last surges roar,
> till many things be come to pass,
> and many evils wrought. Alas!
> the guest is here. The woods are still,
> but wait not; for a marvel chill
> them holds at the strange deeds they see,
> though king sees not – yet queen, maybe,
> can guess, and maiden doubtless knows
> who ever now beside her goes.'

Lines 926–9 were rewritten:

> But Dairon looked on Lúthien's face
> and faltered, seeing his disgrace
> in those clear eyes. He spoke no more,
> and silent Thingol's anger bore.

But these rewritings were hasty, at the level of rough draft, and in no way comparable to what has preceded.

---

*Ennorath*: 'Middle-earth'; cf. *The Lord of the Rings*, Appendix E (III.393, footnote 1).

Cantos V–IX

There is no later recasting in these Cantos save for four lines in Canto IX:
the dying words of Felagund to Beren (2633 ff.):

> I now must go to my long rest
> in Aman, there beyond the shore
> of Eldamar for ever more
> in memory to dwell.' Thus died the king,
> as still the elven harpers sing.

At this point my father wrote on one of the copies of the D-text:
'He should give ring back to Beren' (for the later history of the ring see
*Unfinished Tales* p. 171 note 2, and *The Lord of the Rings* Appendix A,
III. 322 note 1 and 338). But in fact it is nowhere said that Beren had
returned the ring to Felagund.

Canto X

With the beginning of this Canto a substantial passage of new writing
begins, at first written on the B-text, and then, with further change, in a
typescript made by my father, to all appearance at the same time as that
given on pp. 352–5 (but in this case the new verse was retyped as part
of the D-text).

> Songs have recalled, by harpers sung
> long years ago in elven tongue,
> how Lúthien and Beren strayed
> in Sirion's vale; and many a glade
> they filled with joy, and there their feet          5
> passed by lightly, and days were sweet.
> Though winter hunted through the wood,
> still flowers lingered where they stood.
> Tinúviel! Tinúviel!
> Still unafraid the birds now dwell          10
> and sing on boughs amid the snow
> where Lúthien and Beren go.
>
> From Sirion's Isle they passed away,
> but on the hill alone there lay
> a green grave, and a stone was set,          15
> and there there lie the white bones yet
> of Finrod fair, Finarfin's son,

unless that land be changed and gone,
or foundered in unfathomed seas,
while Finrod walks beneath the trees          20
in Eldamar* and comes no more
to the grey world of tears and war.

    To Nargothrond no more he came
but thither swiftly ran the fame
of their dead king and his great deed,        25
how Lúthien the Isle had freed:
the Werewolf Lord was overthrown,
and broken were his towers of stone.
For many now came home at last
who long ago to shadow passed;                30
and like a shadow had returned
Huan the hound, though scant he earned
or praise or thanks of Celegorm.
    There now arose a growing storm,
a clamour of many voices loud,               35
and folk whom Curufin had cowed
and their own king had help denied,
in shame and anger now they cried:
'Come! Slay these faithless lords untrue!
Why lurk they here? What will they do,       40
but bring Finarfin's kin to naught,
treacherous cuckoo-guests unsought?
Away with them!' But wise and slow
Orodreth spoke: 'Beware, lest woe
and wickedness to worse ye bring!            45
Finrod is fallen. I am king.
But even as he would speak, I now
command you. I will not allow
in Nargothrond the ancient curse
from evil unto evil worse                    50
to work. With tears for Finrod weep
repentant! Swords for Morgoth keep!
No kindred blood shall here be shed.
Yet here shall neither rest nor bread
the brethren find who set at naught          55

*Eldamar: earlier reading the Blessed Realm. – With these lines cf. the revised version of Felagund's dying words in Canto IX (p. 357).

Finarfin's house. Let them be sought,
unharmed to stand before me! Go!
The courtesy of Finrod show!'

In scorn stood Celegorm, unbowed,
with glance of fire in anger proud                    60
and menacing; but at his side
smiling and silent, wary-eyed,
was Curufin, with hand on haft
of his long knife. And then he laughed,
and 'Well?' said he. 'Why didst thou call           65
for us, Sir Steward? In thy hall
we are not wont to stand. Come, speak,
if aught of us thou hast to seek!'

Cold words Orodreth answered slow:
'Before the king ye stand. But know,                 70
of you he seeks for naught. His will
ye come to hear, and to fulfil.
Be gone for ever, ere the day
shall fall into the sea! Your way
shall never lead you hither more,                    75
nor any son of Fëanor;
of love no more shall there be bond
between your house and Nargothrond!'

'We will remember it,' they said,
and turned upon their heels, and sped,               80
saddled their horses, trussed their gear,
and went with hound and bow and spear,
alone; for none of all the folk
would follow them. No word they spoke,
but sounded horns, and rode away                     85
like wind at end of stormy day.

The typescript made by my father ends here, but the revision written on
the B-text continues (and was incorporated in the D typescript).

Towards Doriath the wanderers now
were drawing nigh. Though bare was bough,
and winter through the grasses grey
went hissing chill, and brief was day,               90
they sang beneath the frosty sky

above them lifted clear and high.
They came to Mindeb swift and bright
that from the northern mountains' height
to Neldoreth came leaping down                    95
with noise among the boulders brown,
but into sudden silence fell,
passing beneath the guarding spell
that Melian on the borders laid
of Thingol's land. There now they stayed;        100
for silence sad on Beren fell.
Unheeded long, at last too well
he heard the warning of his heart:
alas, beloved, here we part.
'Alas, Tinúviel,' he said,                        105
'this road no further can we tread
together, no more hand in hand
can journey in the Elven-land.'
    'Why part we here? What dost thou say,
even at dawn of brighter day?'                    110

From lines 2936 to 2965 no further changes were made (except
*Elfinesse* to *Elvenesse* at 2962). In the preceding passage, Inglor
Felagund son of Finrod has become Finrod Felagund son of Finarfin,
which dates the revision to, at earliest, 1955, for the change had not been
made in the first edition of *The Lord of the Rings*.

A further short stretch of rewriting begins at 2966, returning to the
original text two lines later:

My word, alas! I now must keep,
and not the first of men must weep
for oath in pride and anger sworn.
Too brief the meeting, brief the morn,
too soon comes night when we must part!           5
All oaths are for breaking of the heart,
with shame denied, with anguish kept.
Ah! would that now unknown I slept
with Barahir beneath the stone,
and thou wert dancing still alone,                10
unmarred, immortal, sorrowless,
singing in joy of Elvenesse.'

    'That may not be. For bonds there are
stronger than stone or iron bar,

more strong than proudly spoken oath.        15
Have I not plighted thee my troth?
Hath love no pride nor honour then?
Or dost thou deem then Lúthien
so frail of purpose, light of love?
By stars of Elbereth above!        20
If thou wilt here my hand forsake
and leave me lonely paths to take,
then Lúthien will not go home . . .

At the same time line 2974 was changed to

beyond all hope in love once more

and 2988 ff. to

In rage and haste
thus madly eastward they now raced,
to find the old and perilous path
between the dreadful Gorgorath
and Thingol's realm. That was their road
most swift to where their kin abode
far off, where Himring's watchful hill
o'er Aglon's gorge hung tall and still.

They saw the wanderers. With a shout
straight on them turned their steeds about . . .


### Cantos XI–XIII

There is no rewriting in Cantos XI and XII, but a little towards the end
of XIII. Lines 4092–5 were replaced by:

the Silmarils with living light
were kindled clear, and waxing bright
shone like the stars that in the North
above the reek of earth leap forth.

Lines 4150–9 were replaced by:

In claws of iron the gem was caught;
the knife them rent, as they were naught

but brittle nails on a dead hand.
Behold! the hope of Elvenland,
the fire of Fëanor, Light of Morn                    5
before the sun and moon were born,
thus out of bondage came at last,
from iron to mortal hand it passed.
There Beren stood. The jewel he held,
and its pure radiance slowly welled               10
through flesh and bone, and turned to fire
with hue of living blood. Desire
then smote his heart their doom to dare,
and from the deeps of Hell to bear
all three immortal gems, and save                15
the elven-light from Morgoth's grave.
Again he stooped; with knife he strove;
through band and claw of iron it clove.
But round the Silmarils dark Fate
was woven: they were meshed in hate,           20
and not yet come was their doomed hour
when wrested from the fallen power
of Morgoth in a ruined world,
regained and lost, they should be hurled
in fiery gulf and groundless sea,                  25
beyond recall while Time shall be.


Canto XIV

Lines 4184–90 were rewritten:

At last before them far away
they saw a glimmer, faint and grey
of ghostly light that shivering fell
down from the yawning gates of Hell.
Then hope awoke, and straightway died –
the doors were open, gates were wide;
but on the threshold terror walked.
{ The dreadful wolf awake there stalked }
{ The wolf awake there watchful stalked }
and in his eyes the red fire glowered;
there Carcharoth in menace towered,
a waiting death, a biding doom:

Lines 4208–11 were rewritten:

> and Beren in despair then strode
> past Lúthien to bar the road,
> unarmed, defenceless, to defend
> the elven-maid until the end.

Of the original Lay scarcely more than a sixth is represented in the rewriting, and the proportion of new verse to old is less than a quarter; so that Humphrey Carpenter's statement in *The Inklings*, p. 31, that 'Eventually, indeed, he came to rewrite the whole poem' must, alas, be corrected.

# Note on the original submission of the
## Lay of Leithian and The Silmarillion
### in 1937

In the wake of the immediate success of *The Hobbit*, which was published on 21 September 1937, Stanley Unwin, the chairman of George Allen & Unwin, was naturally anxious that my father should produce a sequel or successor – about hobbits. The result of the first meeting between them, not long after the publication of the book, was that my father sent in various manuscripts, among them the *Lay of Leithian* (referred to in the correspondence of that time as the *Gest(e) of Beren and Lúthien*) and *The Silmarillion*.

Humphrey Carpenter says in his *Biography* (p. 183) that 'the manuscript [of *The Silmarillion*] – or rather, the bundle of manuscripts – had arrived in a somewhat disordered state, and the only clearly continuous section seemed to be the long poem "The Gest of Beren and Lúthien".' Rayner Unwin has told me that in the record kept by Allen & Unwin of incoming manuscripts the works delivered on 15 November 1937 were listed as:

1  Farmer Giles of Ham
2  Long Poem
3  Mr Bliss
4  The Gnomes Material
5  The Lost Road

Notes of my father's show that together with *The Silmarillion* 'proper' he sent at this time *Ainulindalë* (The Music of the Ainur), *Ambarkanta* (The Shape of the World), and *The Fall of the Númenoreans*. I think that this is why the fourth item in the record book was written down as 'The Gnomes Material'. It may be that the different manuscripts were not very clearly differentiated, while the title-pages of the different works would certainly seem obscure; and 'The Gnomes Material' was a convenient covering phrase.* But perhaps one may detect in it a note of helplessness as well, apparent also in the description of item 2 as a 'Long Poem'. – On the other hand, it should be mentioned that the text of *The Silmarillion* was at that time a fine, simple, and very legible manuscript.

---

*There is no question that *The Silmarillion* itself did go to Allen & Unwin at this time. My father made a note while it was gone about changes to be made to it when it came back to him, and he specifically acknowledged the return of it (*Letters* p. 27): 'I have received safely . . . the *Geste* (in verse) and the *Silmarillion* and related fragments.'

There is no evidence that *The Silmarillion* and the other Middle-earth prose works were submitted to the publishers' reader. In his report on the poem he referred only to 'a few pages' and 'some pages' in prose, and Stanley Unwin, when he returned the manuscripts on 15 December 1937, mentioned 'the pages of a prose version' which accompanied the poem. Humphrey Carpenter seems certainly right in his suggestion (*Biography* p. 184) that these pages were attached 'for the purpose of completing the story, for the poem itself was unfinished'; they were pages from the story of Beren and Lúthien as told in *The Silmarillion*. But it is also obvious from the reader's report that he saw nothing else of *The Silmarillion*. He headed his report: '*The Geste of Beren and Lúthien* (Retold in Verse by ? )', and began:

> I am rather at a loss to know what to do with this – it doesn't even seem to have an author! – or any indication of sources, etc. Publishers' readers are rightly supposed to be of moderate intelligence and reading; but I confess my reading has not extended to early Celtic Gestes, and I don't even know whether this is a famous Geste or not, or, for that matter, whether it is authentic. I presume it is, as the unspecified versifier has included some pages of a prose-version (which is far superior).

By the last sentence he meant, I think, that the *story*, as represented in what he took to be a close prose translation, was authentic 'Celtic Geste', and that 'the unspecified versifier' had proceeded to make a poem out of it.

However, he was a critic positive in his taste, and he contrasted the poem, greatly to its disadvantage, with 'the few pages of (presumably) prose transcript from the original'. In the poem, he said, 'the primitive strength is gone, the clear colours are gone' – a notable conclusion, even if the actual evolution of the Matter of Beren and Lúthien was thus turned onto its head.

It may seem odd that the reader who was given the poem should have had so little to go on; even odder, that he wrote with some enthusiasm about the fragment of prose narrative that accompanied it, yet never saw the work from which the fragment came, though that was the most important manuscript sent in by the author: he had indeed no reason to suspect its existence. But I would guess that my father had not made it sufficiently clear at the outset what the Middle-earth prose works were and how they related to each other, and that as a result 'the Gnomes Material' had been set aside as altogether too peculiar and difficult.

At the bottom of the reader's report Charles Furth of Allen & Unwin wrote: 'What do we do?'; and it was left to the tact of Stanley Unwin to devise a way. When he returned the manuscripts to my father he said:

> As you yourself surmised, it is going to be a difficult task to do anything with the *Geste of Beren and Lúthien* in verse form, but our

reader is much impressed with the pages of a prose version that accompanied it

– and he quoted from the report *only* the approving (if misdirected) remarks which the reader had made about the *Silmarillion* fragment, and which Humphrey Carpenter quotes – 'It has something of that mad, bright-eyed beauty that perplexes all Anglo-Saxons in the face of Celtic art,' &c. But Stanley Unwin then went on to say:

> *The Silmarillion* contains plenty of wonderful material; in fact it is a mine to be explored in writing further books like *The Hobbit* rather than a book in itself.

These words effectively show in themselves that *The Silmarillion* had not been given to a reader and reported on. At that time it was an extremely coherent work, though unfinished in that version.* Beyond question, Stanley Unwin's object was to save my father's feelings, while (relying on the reader's report – which concerned the poem) rejecting the material submitted, and to persuade him to write a book that would continue the success of *The Hobbit*. But the result was that my father was entirely misled; for in his reply of 16 December 1937 (given in full in *Letters* pp. 26–7) – three days before he wrote saying that he had completed the first chapter, 'A Long-expected Party', of 'a new story about Hobbits' – he said:

> My chief joy comes from learning that the Silmarillion is not rejected with scorn ... I do not mind about the verse-form [i.e. the verse-form of the tale of Beren and Lúthien, the *Lay of Leithian*] which in spite of certain virtuous passages has grave defects, for it is only for me the rough material.† But I shall certainly now hope one day to be able, or to be able to afford, to publish the Silmarillion!

He was quite obviously under the impression that *The Silmarillion* had been given to a reader and reported on (no doubt he saw no significance in Stanley Unwin's phrase '*the pages of* a prose version'); whereas so far as the existing evidence goes (and it seems sufficiently complete) this was not the case at all. He thought it had been read and rejected, whereas it had merely been rejected. The reader had certainly rejected the *Lay of Leithian*; he had not rejected *The Silmarillion*, of which he had only seen a few pages (not knowing what they were), and in any case enjoyed them – granting the difficulties that an Anglo-Saxon finds in appreciating Celtic art.

*There was not in fact a great deal more to be done in reworking the 1930 text: the new version extended (in some 40,000 words) to part way through Chapter XXI, *Of Túrin Turambar*.

†This may seem a rather surprising thing to say; but it is to be remembered that he had abandoned the poem six years before, and was at this time absorbed in the perfecting of the prose *Silmarillion*.

It is strange to reflect on what the outcome might conceivably have been if *The Silmarillion* actually had been read at that time, and if the reader had maintained the good opinion he formed from those few pages; for while there is no necessary reason to suppose even so that it would have been accepted for publication, it does not seem absolutely out of the question. And if it had been? My father wrote long after (in 1964, *Letters* p. 346):

I then [after the publication of *The Hobbit*] offered them the legends of the Elder Days, but their readers turned that down. They wanted a sequel. But I wanted heroic legends and high romance. The result was *The Lord of the Rings*.

# GLOSSARY OF OBSOLETE, ARCHAIC, AND RARE WORDS AND MEANINGS

In this list words occurring in the *Lay of the Children of Húrin* (H, and the second version H ii) and in the *Lay of Leithian* (L, and the continuous part of the later rewriting L ii) are referenced to the lines; words from other poems or passages are referenced to the pages on which they occur.

Both Lays, but especially *The Children of Húrin*, make use of some totally lost words (and lost meanings), but the list includes also a good many that remain well-known literary archaisms, and some words that are neither but are of very limited currency.

**an**   if, H 63, 485
**as**   as if, H 310, ii. 659
**astonied**   astounded, H 578
**bade**   H ii. 646. If *This Thingol she bade* means 'This she *offered* to Thingol' the word is used in two senses within the line: she *bade* (offered) him the helm, and *bade* (asked) him to receive her thanks'; but more probably the line means 'she asked him to receive it, and her thanks' (cf. H 301).
**bale**   evil, woe, torment, H 56, ii. 81
**balusters**   the pillars of a balustrade, p. 132
**bated**   restrained, held in, H 1121
**bent**   open place covered with grass, H 1032, 1517, 1539, ii. 500; L 1369, 2281
**betid**   come to pass, L 2408
**blent**   mingled, H 453, 583; L ii. 317
**boots**   in **it boots not**, it is of no use, H 1871
**bosmed**   (in **bare-bosmed**) bosomed, H 1198
**brand**   blade, sword, H 1340, ii. 149
**carping**   talk, chatter, H 477; **carped** H 506
**casque**   helmet, H ii. 655
**chaplet**   garland, L 753
**chase**   hunting-grounds, L 3297
**clomb**   old past tense of *climb*, H 1494; L 1382, 3872
**corse**   corpse, H 1295, 1404; L 3620
**cozening**   beguiling or defrauding, p. 305
**croft**   enclosed plot of arable land, L 1968
**dear**   precious, valuable, H 480
**dolour**   suffering, L 2814
**dolven**   (also in **dark(ly)-**, **deep-dolven**) delved, dug, H 2052; L 213, 1677, ii. 63

**dreed** endured, suffered, H 531

**drouth** (the same word in origin as *drought*) dryness, H 946, 972; **(plains of, fields of) drouth**, thirst, H 826; L 2047

**eld** old age, H ii. 595; **of eld**, of old, H 118, ii. 262

**enfurled** (in **mist-enfurled**) enveloped, swathed (in something twisted or folded), L 59, ii. 61. The word is not recorded with the prefix *en-*. Cf. **furled**, wrapped, L 1551, **unfurled**, opened out, L 404, 1591, 3986

**enow** enough, L 1304

**error** (probably) wandering, H ii. 495

**fain** gladly, H 130; L 823; glad, L ii. 368; **fain of** eager for, or well-pleased with, H 410, 458, ii. 786; **warfain** eager for war, H 386, 1664, ii. 137, **bloodfain** ii. 750; **I had fainer** I would like it better, H ii. 146

**falchion** (broad) sword, H 1217, ii. 63, 146

**fallow** golden brown, H 2106; pp. 128–9; **fallow-gold** p. 129; **fallow deer** L 86. (A distinct word from *fallow* of ground.)

**fare** journeying, H 2184

**fast** fixedly, unmovingly, H 1614 (or perhaps adjective qualifying *pondering*, deep, unbroken, cf. *fast asleep*); secure against attack, L 360

**fell** hide, L 2344, 3398, 3458, 3484, 3941, 4124, ii. 528

**fey** death-bound, L 3305; see **unfey**.

**flittermouse** bat, L 4074

**fold** land, H 765; **folds** H 533, 1632 probably the same, but perhaps 'windings'.

**force** waterfall, H 1595

**forhungered** starved, L 3076

**forwandered** worn out by wandering, H 190, 897, ii. 498; L 550, 2354

**freshets** small streams of fresh water, H 1597; L 1934

**frith** wood, woodland, H 1795; p. 132; L 896, 2264, ii. 124

**frore** frosty, H ii. 594; very cold, L 578, 1718

**garth** enclosed ground beside a house, garden, yard, H 149, ii. 313

**ghyll** deep rocky ravine, H 1498

**glaive** lance, or sword, H 322, 1210, ii. 680

**glamoury** magic, enchantment, pp. 122–3; L 2073

**gloam** twilight, p. 146

**grasses** plants, herbs, L 3122

**guerdon** recompense, H 658; L 222, 1064, 4139

**haggard** (of clothes) ragged, disordered, H 466; (of hills) wild, H 2120, L 3167; modern meaning H 1890, L 3720 (in transferred sense, **haggard hunger**, **haggard care** H 1437, L 564)

**haled** drew, pulled out, H ii. 551

**hap** fortune, lot, condition, H 340

**hest** command, H 86, 689

**hie**   hasten, H 838
**hight**   called, named, H 366, 863
**hold**   fastness, stronghold, L 52, 1702, 2457; p. 134 (or perhaps 'grasp'); refuge, L 210
**holt**   wood, copse, L 2342
**inane**   empty, void, L 3533
**keep**   central part of the stronghold, L 1677
**lambent**   of flame, playing on a surface without burning, H 1217
**lapped**   hemmed in, H 690; enfolded, H 709
**lea**   grassland, H 35, 1797, ii. 66
**leasows**   meadows, H 1797
**leeches**   physicians, L 3055, 3144
**let**   hinder, L 2019
**levin**   lightning, H 1681
**lief**   willing, L 3417; **liever** better, more delightful, H 78
**like**   please, H 90, 286, 598, 1376, ii. 226, 626 (but 'like' H 616)
**lind**   linden, lime-tree, p. 120
**loath**   hateful to, L 3419; unwilling, L 3417
**lode**   path, road, H 798
**louted**   bent, bowed, H 1520
**march**   borderland, H ii. 493; L 3672
**marge**   margin, H 1555
**mavis**   song-thrush, L ii. 74
**meed**   reward, requital, H 81, 268, 701, 793, ii. 195, 231, 604
**meet**   fitting, H 487
**mete**   deal out (used in the construction *I shall mete thee a meed, his meed was meted*) H 81, 532, 701, 1092, ii. 195
**mews**   seagulls, p. 129; **seamew** H 1551
**neb**   beak, bill, L 255, 570, ii. 381, 409
**nesh**   soft, tender, L 4220
**opes**   opens, L 3740; **oped** H 550
**or ever**   before ever, L 1821
**or . . . or**   either . . . or, H 439–40; L 54, 2886; p. 359
**outer**   utter, uttermost (?), L 2979
**palfrey**   small saddle-horse, L 3379
**parlous**   perilous, dangerous, L ii. 456
**pled**   old past tense of *plead*, L 2983
**plenilune**   full moon, p. 354
**prate**   chatter, talk to no purpose, H 501
**quick**   living, alive, H ii. 78
**quod**   (quoth), said, H 88
**quook**   old past tense of *quake*, L 3582
**recked**   cared, H 619; L ii. 629; **unrecked** unheeded, disregarded, H 1799
**redeless**   without resource, devoid of counsel, L 3427
**rive**   cleave, H 1211; past tense **rove**, L 4149

**roamed** wandered, went (of a path or journey), H 1432; extended (?) (of regions), H 1577. (These usages appear to be unrecorded.)

**rout** company, troop, band, L 2997

**rove** see **rive**.

**ruel-bone** some kind of ivory, L 2261 (cf. J. R. R. Tolkien, *Sir Gawain, Pearl, and Sir Orfeo*, translation of *Pearl* stanza 18: *And her hue as rewel ivory wan*).

**ruth** pity, compassion, H 306, 1941, 1969, 2134, ii.654; L 116; remorse, H 509; sorrow, H 1661

**shaws** woods, thickets, H 647 (cf. the *Trollshaws* west of Rivendell).

**sheer** (of light) bright, L 689; (of water) clear and pure, L 1439

**shoon** old plural of *shoe*, L 490

**shores** supports, props, L 3880

**sigaldry** sorcery, L 2072 (cf. stanza 3 of the poem *Errantry*, in J. R. R. Tolkien, *The Adventures of Tom Bombadil*, 1962).

**slade** valley, dell, H 235, 1150, 2171, ii.561; **slades of death** H 685, 886

**slot** track, trail (of a hunted creature), H 745, 1314

**slough** mire, mud, H 881

**sped** availed (attained his purpose), H 41; prospered (transitive), H 247, (intransitive) ii.574; pressed, urged on, H 284; sent with haste, H 654

**stared** (probably) shone, L 3132, a meaning of the verb found in the mediaeval alliterative poems: cf. J. R. R. Tolkien, *Sir Gawain, Pearl, and Sir Orfeo*, translation of *Pearl* stanza 10: *stars stare in the welkin in winter night*, where the original has *staren* with this meaning.

**strikes** runs, flows, H 240, 520, ii.567

**suage** assuage, relieve, H 612

**sued** petitioned for, appealed for, H 857

**swath** 'the space covered by a sweep of the mower's scythe' (O.E.D.), H 33, ii.64; L 2106

**swinking** toiling, H 784

**sylphine** of the nature of a sylph (spirit inhabiting the air, see p. 306), L 4077. (This adjective to *sylph* is not recorded.)

**tale** count, amount, sum, H 159, 471, ii.326. Cf. **untold** uncounted, H ii.678, L 12, 2251

**targe** shield, H 131, 409, 2153, ii.284, 785

**thewed** in **mighty-thewed**, of great strength, with mighty sinews, H ii.714

**thirled** pierced, H 697

**tilth** cultivated land, H 1798

**tors** rocky hill-tops, H 2119

**travail** hardship (as endured on a journey, i.e. both *travail* and *travel*), H 143, ii.300

**unfey** not 'fey', not fated to die, H ii.752 (or possibly the meaning is 'not feeble, not timid', reversing another sense of *fey*). This word is apparently not recorded in English, but *ú-feigr* 'unfey' is found in Old Norse.

**unkempt**  uncombed, H 490

**unrecked**  see **recked**.

**wading**  going, passing, H 1605

**waiving**  refusing, rejecting, H ii. 154

**wallet**  bag for provisions, H 228, ii. 551

**wan**  dark, L 261, ii. 561

**wanhope**  despair, H 188

**web**  woven fabric, L 1471; used of ring-mail L 324, and of the 'weavings' of fate H ii. 13

**weeds**  clothes, H 445

**weft**  woven fabric, L 3061

**weird**  fate, doom, H 160, ii. 119, 246, 327; L 2290, 3173

**weregild**  the price to be paid in compensation for the killing of a man, varying according to his rank, L ii. 177

**whin**  gorse, L ii. 195

**wieldy**  (capable of easily wielding body or weapon), vigorous, agile, H 1765

**wildered**  lost, H 188, 204, 1316, ii. 516; p. 146; bewildered, H 774; L 641 (see p. 323).

**winding**  (1) of the motion of wind or water (without any necessary suggestion of twisting), H 769, 1857. (2) (of trumpet) blowing, H 1832

**wist**  see **wot**.

**wold**  forested hills or uplands (see p. 88), H 1816, 1992, 1994; L 1742

**wolfham(e)**  wolfskin, L 3398; pp. 271–3, 283 (see p. 271).

**woof**  woven fabric, L 4149

**wot**  (present tense of verb *wit*), know, H 204, ii. 516; past tense **wist** knew, H 160, 200, 399, ii. 327; past participle **unwist** unknown, H 257

**wrack**  (1) ruin, disaster, destruction, H 27, 629, 2036, ii. 120; p. 142. (2) seaweed, H 1569

**wrights**  craftsmen, H 300, 1147, ii. 641, 671

# INDEX

This index is made on the same lines as those to *The Book of Lost Tales* Parts I and II, and like them it is intended to provide (with only a few exceptions) complete references to all entries, and includes occasional references to passages where the person or place is not actually named. The note on the submission of the *Lay of Leithian* and *The Silmarillion* in 1937 is not indexed.

*Arthad*   One of the twelve companions of Barahir on Dorthonion. 335, 349

*Arthurian legends*   160

*Aryador*   Name of Hithlum among Men. 29

*athelas*   Herb of healing. 269

*Aulë*   137, 139

*Balar, Isle and Bay of*   183

*Balrog(s)*   7, 36–7, 70, 97–100, 102, 142, 281, 288, 296, 301, 303

*Balthronding*   The bow of Beleg. 117, 127; later form *Belthronding* 26, 127

*Ban*   Father of Blodrin the traitor. 48–9, 52. See *Bor.*

*Bansil*   The White Tree of Valinor (Silpion, Telperion). 5, 73, 81–2, 195, 219. (Replaced by *Belthil.*)

*Baragund*   Nephew and companion of Barahir and father of Morwen. 335, 349

*Barahir*   Father of Beren (son of Bëor, 198, 334, 348). 25, 153, 161, 163–7, 170–1, 188, 190–1, 193, 198, 201, 213–14, 216, 220, 242, 245, 247, 249, 334–5, 337–43, 345, 348–9, 351, 360

*Battle of Sudden Flame*   83, 147, 171, 247, 284, 351; other references 55, 85, 221–2; described 212–13, 275

*Battle of Unnumbered Tears*   6, 11, 23–6, 59, 83–6, 92, 96, 111, 137, 146–7, 274, 310; *field of tears* 80, 85, (111). See *Nínin Udathriol/ Unothradin, Nirnaith Arnediad/Ornoth/Únoth.*

*Battle-under-Stars*   87

*Bauglir*   (1) Earlier name for Blodrin the traitor. 48–9, 52. (2) Name of Morgoth (replaced *Belcha, Belegor, Melegor*). 6–8, 10, 16, 21–2, 28, 41, 49, 52, 57, 59–61, 64–6, 84, 96, 98, 100, 116–17, 135, 168, 170, 182, 196, 211, 230, 282, 286–7

*Baynes, Pauline*   (Map of Middle-earth) 26

*Belaurien*   Rejected name for Beleriand. 160

*Belaurin*   Gnomish form of Palúrien. 160

*Belcha*   Name of Morgoth (replaced by *Belegor, Melegor, Bauglir*). 21–3, 52

*Beleg*   10–12, 16–17, 25–7, 30–51, 53–8, 60, 63–4, 76, 86, 89, 94, 110–12, 116–18, 127, 259, 311, 313–14; see especially 25–6, 127. In *The Children of Húrin* called *the Huntsman, the Hunter, the Bowman.* Túrin's elegy *The Bowman's Friendship* 64, 89, *Laer Cú Beleg*, the Song of the Great Bow, 89

*Belegor*   Name of Morgoth (replacing *Belcha*, replaced by *Melegor, Bauglir*). 21

*Belegost*   A city of the Dwarves. 44 (*black Belegost*), 306

*Belegund*   Nephew and companion of Barahir. 335, 349

*Beleriand*   83, 152, 155, 157–8, 160, 166, 168–9, 184–5, 195, 222, 226–7, 236, 243, 297, 304, 331, 333, 346. (Replaced *Broseliand*; for other rejected names see 160)

*Belthil* The White Tree of Valinor (Silpion. Telperion). 5, 81–2, 192, 195, 210. (Replaced *Bansil*.)

*Belthronding* See *Balthronding*.

*Bëor* Father of Barahir. 198, 334, 348; *Bëor's sons, Bëor's house* 187, 335, 348, 350–1

*Bëoring(s)* Men of the house of Bëor. 335, 348, 351

*Beowulf* 127

*Beren* 9, 12–13, 22, 25, 52, 61, 87–9, 104, 106–10, 112, 114, 120–2, 124–6, 136, 138; *passim* in *Lay of Leithian* and commentaries. Beren as Man or Elf 25, 124–5, 171; his second life 125–6. See *Ermabwed, Erchamion, Maglor* (1).

*Bilbo Baggins* 49, 159

*Bitter Hills* Name of the Iron Mountains in the *Lost Tales*. 29

*Bladorinand* Rejected name for Beleriand. 160

*Bladorwen* 'The wide earth, Mother Earth', name of Palúrien. 160

*Blasted Plain* Dor-na-Fauglith. 49, 55

*Blessed Realm* Aman. 334, 348, 358; *Blissful Realm(s)* 72, 93, 132

*Blodrin* The Elf who betrayed Túrin's band (earlier named Bauglir). 31–3, 40, 48–9, 52

*Blue Mountains* Ered Luin. 160, 313; not named, 83, 156, 332

*Boldog* Orc captain, leader of a raid into Doriath. 229, 235, 274, 288, 293, 310–13

*Bor* Father of Blodrin the traitor (briefly replaced *Ban*). 31–3, 40, 49, 52

*Bredhil the Blessed* See *Bridhil*.

*Bregolas* Brother of Barahir and father of Baragund and Belegund. 335, 343, 349

*Bregor* (In the later legends) father of Barahir and Bregolas. 25

*Bregu* (Old English)='Vala'. 127

*Brethil, Forest of* 50, 309–10

*Bridhil* Gnomish name of Varda; called *Bridhil the Blessed, Bridhil Queen of Stars*. 135, 139, 169–70, 219, 233; changed to *Bredhil* 133–5, 139. See *Timbridhil*; *Elbereth*.

*Brittany* 160

*Broceliande, Forest of* 160. See *Broseliand*.

*Bronweg* Gnomish form of Voronwë, companion of Tuor. 148

*Broseliand* Earlier name of Beleriand. 152, 157–60, 169, 194–5, 232, 243, 304, 312, 315, 322; at first spelt *Broceliand* 158–60, 169

*Bruithwir* Father of Fëanor in the *Lost Tales*. 137, 139

*Burning Briar* Name of the constellation of the Great Bear. 167, 170, 251, 345, 349

*Carcharoth* The Wolf of Angband. 107, 119, 125, 151, 208, 289–94, 304, 307–9, 313, 362. Earlier forms *Karkaras* 125, 208, 294; *Carcaras* 125, 208; *Carcharas* 208, 210, 258, 271, 292–3, 310; *Carcharos* 292, 294, 305, 309, 312; *Carcharolch* 119, 125, 208;

# 376    THE LAYS OF BELERIAND

*Gargaroth* 292. *Knife-fang* 292–4; *the Red Maw* 289, 292, 294
*Carpenter, Humphrey*   3, 315, 319, 363
*Celebrimbor   Son of Curufin.* 274
*Celeg Aithorn*   Mythological sword (lightning?) named in Beleg's 'whetting spell'. 45, 54
*Celegorm*   (1) Transiently used=Thingol. 158–9, 171. (2) Son of Fëanor, called 'the fair'. 65, 80, 84–6, 91, 135–6, 151, 159, 169, 171, 182, 195, 198, 211, 213, 216, 218–22, 229, 236–40, 244–9, 256, 260, 263–5, 270–4, 283, 310–13, 358–9 (see especially 84–6, 171, 220–1, 247).
*Chambers, R. W.*   143
*Chaucer, Geoffrey*   143–4
*Children of Húrin*   (poem in rhyming couplets) 130
*City of Stone*   (Gondobar), Gondolin. 145. *City of the Dwellers in Stone* (Gondothlimbar), Gondolin. 145
*City of the Gods, The*   (poem) 94
*Cleft of Eagles*   See *Cristhorn.*
*Cópas Alqalunten*   'Haven of the Swanships'. 90. See *Alqualondë, Swanhaven.*
*Côr*   21–2, 29, 73, 93, 98, 103, 118, 123, 132–3, 149, 219; *Kôr* 21–2, 24, 84, 93, 139–40, 149
*Corthûn*   7, 21, 29, 103. See *Tûn.*
*Cranthir*   Son of Fëanor, called 'the dark'. 65, 80, 86, 131, 135, 211; earlier form *Cranthor* 80, 86, 131
*Cristhorn*   'Eagles' Cleft' in the Encircling Mountains about Gondolin. 141–3; *Cleft of Eagles, gap of the Eagles*, 142–3
*Cuinlimfin*   Transient form replaced by Cuiviénen. 23, 29
*Cuiviénen*   18, 23, 347; *Waters of Awakening* 29, *Waking Water* 349. Original form *Koivië-Néni* 23
*Curufin*   Son of Fëanor, called 'the crafty'. 65, 80, 84–6, 91, 135, 151, 171, 211, 213, 216–18, 221, 223, 237, 239–42, 244–7, 260, 263–5, 270–4, 276, 303, 310–11, 313, 358–9; his horse 263–4, 269, 273, 275–6, 283–4; his knife (unnamed, later *Angrist*) 264, 272, 274, 303, 305–6, 309

*Daeron*   See *Dairon.*
*Dagmor*   Beren's sword. 344, 350
*Dagnir*   One of the twelve companions of Barahir on Dorthonion. 335, 349
*Dagor Bragollach*   83. See *Battle of Sudden Flame.*
*Daideloth*   Early name of Dor-na-Fauglith. 49
*Dailir*   Beleg's arrow that never failed to be found and unharmed. 42, 45, 53, 55
*Dairon*   Minstrel of Thingol. 104–5, 108–10, 119, 124, 156, 174, 176, 179, 181–2, 185–8, 190–1, 195, 197–8, 200–1, 203–6, 209, 270,